CHAPTER 1

Sunrise over Lagos is a beautiful sight. This morning is no different, as the first light of dawn gradually unfurls to pierce the deep blue sky with streaks of gold and burnt orange, and the Lagos Lagoon shimmers like a pool of molten glass. There, on a patch of the expansive banks of the lagoon, two figures carefully rummage through heaps of refuse dumped overnight from the more affluent estates on the Island of Lagos, looking for items of value to sell, wear, drink or eat. This is what they do – Bàbá àti Ọmọ, father and son, up before sunrise to scavenge for a life from the waste of others, and they are good at it too. Bàbá has done it for as long as he can remember, and Ọmọ has done it for most of his young fourteen years.

They navigate the mounds of waste like well-oiled machines, with eyes well accustomed to the dawn light darting around scanning for specific items that signal that a mound is worth digging through. Bàbá is suddenly captivated by something on a large pile and remains motionless as he stares. Ọmọ follows his father's stare and attempts to hurry towards the pile to begin digging, but Bàbá grabs him.

'Rara,' Bàbá says in Yoruba to stop his son. 'Dúró níbí,' he urges his son to wait.

Ọmọ nods, and Bàbá moves cautiously towards the pile. Each step brings the object into sharper focus, and with it, Bàbá's dread grows. As Bàbá approaches the heap of refuse, his worst fears are confirmed. The heap is deliberately arranged like an altar, with its centrepiece impossible to miss.

He stops, unwilling to get any closer. And even from a distance, it's clear this body belongs to a different Lagos – a Lagos of wealth, power, and untouchable privilege. Bàbá has seen dead bodies before, but this one is different. The young woman's face, unnervingly serene even in death, betrays no fear. Her skin is flawless, her features untouched by the scars of a hard life.

A chill creeps through him. Because people like her do not simply disappear. They are searched for and avenged by the select few Lagosians who wield immense power and harbour nothing but disdain for people like him. Bàbá knows the danger of being associated with such a corpse. No good will come of it for him or his family. He makes his decision quickly. This is not his burden to carry. He steps back, ready to leave it to the scavengers who will follow. But just as he turns to retreat, Ọmọ's startled scream shatters the stillness behind him. He'd seen it.

To my wonderful wife, son and daughter . . .
Everything I do is for you

A KILLING IN LAGOS

AMEN ALONGE

QUERCUS

First published in Great Britain in 2026 by Quercus
Part of John Murray Group

1

A CIP catalogue record for this book is available from the British Library

HB ISBN 978 1 52944 185 7
EBOOK ISBN 978 1 52944 186 4

Typeset in Swift by CC Book Production

Printed and bound in Great Britain by Clays Ltd, Elcograf S.p.A.

FSC www.fsc.org MIX Paper | Supporting responsible forestry FSC® C104740

Papers used by Quercus are from well-managed forests and other responsible sources.

Quercus
Carmelite House
50 Victoria Embankment
London EC4Y 0DZ

John Murray Group
Part of Hodder & Stoughton Limited
An Hachette UK company

The authorised representative in the EEA is Hachette Ireland,
8 Castlecourt Centre, Dublin 15, D15 XTP3, Ireland (email: info@hbgi.ie)

A KILLING IN LAGOS

Also by Amen Alonge

THE PRETTY BOY SERIES

A Good Day to Die

A Good Night to Kill

CHAPTER 2

In an upscale gym in central London, Remi Bankole, an athletically built black man in his early thirties, wearing a white gi with a brown belt, is in the second minute of a jiu-jitsu sparring contest with Vitor, the gym's jiu-jitsu instructor, an equally athletic man in his early forties also wearing a gi, though with a black belt. Neither has given an inch during the contest, as Remi and Vitor deftly counter each other's advances with lightning-fast transitions. However, Remi, Vitor, and the others in the class, who have a keen eye on the contest while also sparring with each other, know that at any moment, Vitor will outmanoeuvre Remi. Vitor always does. But each relentless second that ticks on with Remi displaying exceptional composure and scrambling impresses everyone.

Suddenly, amid a scramble, Vitor locks Remi's right arm between his legs and pulls Remi's wrist tightly as he thrusts his hips upward to hyperextend Remi's elbow. Remi should tap to end the contest before he damages his elbow. That's what everyone expects. Instead, Remi twists his arm and drives his legs along the mat until he spins out of the armbar. Remi then attempts to secure his superior position but feels Vitor's wiry arms latch around his ankle. Remi immediately taps Vitor's shoulder to submit, and Vitor lets go of Remi's ankle.

Vitor climbs to his knees and offers Remi a hand to help him up. Remi accepts the hand without hesitation, and Vitor pulls him up to his knees.

'Very smart,' Vitor says with a thick Brazilian accent. 'I wasn't expecting you to explode out of the armbar. Not your style. You're usually more patient and focus on fighting my grip.'

'And eventually lose,' Remi says with an elegant English accent.

Vitor smirks and shrugs. 'But what you did is dangerous,' he says with his calm teaching voice, and Remi nods to acknowledge. 'Next time, I break your arm.'

'Next time,' Remi says, respectfully accepting the challenge.

Vitor pats Remi on the shoulder and turns his attention to the rest of the class. Remi glances at the clock on the wall and walks to a corner of the large mat. It's nearly 7:30 p.m. Remi needs to check his work phone soon because he's sure he's received many emails, calls, and messages during the hour he's been in class. Still, he'll wait patiently for the few minutes left.

He sits in the corner watching the others spar, questioning why he came. He's the lead associate on a £3 billion acquisition nearing crunch time and had skipped jiu-jitsu for the past month to work on the deal. But he's missed it and feels in a much clearer headspace now than when he arrived.

As if aware of his wandering mind, Vitor ends the class a couple of minutes early. Remi gets to his feet and lines up to greet everyone with a hug and a bow, as is customary.

Remi hurries off the mat towards the changing room but hears a familiar voice call his name over the gym's music. He sighs under his breath and turns to see Peyton – late twenties, white gi, brown belt – sauntering towards him. They'd joined the class about a month apart four years ago, and while they got along fine, Peyton's competitive streak could be grating.

'Nice spar with Vitor,' Peyton says. 'You been watching YouTube videos . . . sneaking to other gyms these past few weeks?'

Remi forces a chuckle. 'Thanks. Just tried something different.' He nods towards the changing room. 'Let's walk. Need to log back on.'

'You working on something big?'

'Yep.'

'How much?' Peyton presses. He works in acquisition finance and always wants numbers.

'I can't right now. I'll tell you when we close.'

'Ballpark, come on.'

Remi laughs to himself, then glances at Peyton. Peyton is itching to tell him something – almost certainly a lie to boost his ego. 'I'll tell you when we close,' he repeats.

'You lawyers,' Peyton teases. 'Anyway, I've been sparring Vitor while you've been away. Softened him up for you.'

There it is. The lie. Normally, Remi would just ignore it, but this should be fun. 'Softened him up?'

'Yeah. I even tapped him a few times.'

Remi stays silent, just watching, until Peyton cracks.

'I'm just playing,' Peyton admits with a chuckle. 'Didn't tap him. I was close, though. Closer than you.'

'I don't doubt it,' Remi says, and bumps fists with Peyton. 'Spar next session?'

'Sure, mate.'

Remi turns around to his locker without waiting for Peyton to leave. He unlocks it, quickly grabs his work phone and scrolls through the emails as he pulls his trench coat over his gi. He takes his large gym/work bag and hurries out of the changing room as he types a quick response email to one of the two partners overseeing the deal.

Remi walks out of the gym into a light drizzle, still reading emails. He'd usually hop over to the underground station a couple minutes away and be back home in Fitzrovia in twenty minutes. But today, he needs to call Emily, a junior associate in the team, to work through the comments on the warranties they've just received from the seller's solicitors. He spots a black taxi approaching and raises a hand to stop it.

As the taxi sets off, Remi pulls his laptop from his bag and calls Emily. She answers after a ring.

'Hi, Emily,' Remi says, and logs on to his laptop.

'Hi, Remi,' Emily responds.

'Are you okay to run through the comments now?' he says, and opens an attachment in an email from Emily.

'Sure!' she responds, eager, as Remi expected.

'Thanks. I agree with you that most of their comments are acceptable, and I'll take instructions from the client on the points you flagged. But you'll need to push back with a hard line on a couple others.'

'Er, okay,' Emily responds.

Remi recognises the hesitation and understands that Emily is simply unsure how to approach the pushback. Which he was also expecting. No junior associate is entirely sure how hard to push back on a deal this size.

'Let's talk it through,' Remi says, and meticulously guides Emily through her response.

Ten minutes later, the taxi arrives outside Remi's flat in Fitzrovia. It's the middle floor of a Georgian house which has been converted into two flats and a penthouse, which is currently occupied by a Chelsea footballer. As Remi climbs out of the taxi, he hears an elderly voice call his name with the perfect Yoruba intonation and stops in his tracks.

Remi turns to the voice and recognises the elderly man who cautiously steps out from the back seat of a Mercedes sedan parked a few steps away. The elderly man is Uncle Tayo Olatunji. Uncle Tayo has no actual family relations with Remi, but he worked for Remi's grandfather, and then Remi's father after Remi's grandfather passed away, for over five decades before retiring to London, with Remi's father's blessing, to spend his last years with his family.

Remi's feet are seemingly stuck to the ground as he watches Uncle Tayo walk towards him with a grave expression. Remi pulls out his personal phone, which has been on silent the entire day as Remi focused on work, and there are several notifications of missed calls and messages. He turns back to Uncle Tayo, who is a step away, and he instinctively lowers himself to the floor to greet the elderly man in the traditional Yoruba manner.

Uncle Tayo attempts to bend down to stop Remi from prostrating, but Remi quickly pushes himself to his feet to stop Uncle Tayo from bending over.

'Ẹ káalẹ́, Uncle,' Remi greets, and bows his head.

'Káalẹ́, Remi,' Uncle Tayo responds, and gestures to the iPhone in his hand. 'Bàbá rẹ,' he says, and offers Remi the phone. 'Ó fẹ́ bá ẹ sọ̀rọ̀.'

Remi nods and accepts the phone. 'Dad,' Remi says into the phone in English.

'Remi,' Remi's dad calmly responds. 'I've been trying to reach you all day,' he says in English.

'I know. I'm sorry. I was . . .'

'No need to apologise, Remi. I understand.'

'Okay. Okay, Dad,' Remi says, anxious. 'Is everything okay?'

'No, Remi. Kike is dead.'

CHAPTER 3

Hours later, Remi peers through the window from his seat in economy, watching as the Virgin Atlantic flight from London Heathrow descends towards the Murtala Muhammed International Airport in Lagos. It's been almost a decade since he was in Lagos, and he scans to pick out anything that might evoke a touch of nostalgia. Something to anchor him. However, all he sees is a hazy sprawl of roads and buildings.

The plane taxis to a terminal to connect with a boarding bridge, and the passengers begin to empty out from the front of the plane. Being intensely aware of the long queues through customs, Remi bounces off his seat, grabs his small travel bag, and squeezes into the aisle, but as he approaches the front of the plane, a senior customs officer standing beside a couple of flight attendants spots him and waves with a keen smile.

'Good morning, Mr Bankole,' the officer says, and reaches out to shake Remi's hand.

'Good morning, sir,' Remi replies, with a level of respect the officer doesn't seem to be expecting. He shakes the officer's hand.

'Thank you . . . thank you, *sir*. Your father asked that I come and collect you and take you through to your people, who are waiting.'

My people, Remi thinks. He's not surprised by the special treatment; after all, this is how he always returned to Nigeria growing up, when he travelled with his father or when his father's private office organised his tickets. But he'd booked this flight at the last minute last night, so he wasn't expecting it. Plus, *people* . . . *waiting* . . . that's extra, even if his father, or whoever at his father's office that organised this, assumes he is distraught because of Kike's death. They should know better, as even if he is distraught, he wouldn't show it, not to anyone . . . and sometimes not even to himself. That's the *Bankole way*. He doesn't know how his father does it. But Remi just flows with the tide, keeping his head above water. Never dwelling. This time, though . . . he's not sure how long that'll work.

'Can I take your bag, *sir*?' the customs officer, who's at least a decade older than Remi, asks.

Remi glances at the officer's name badge, which reads 'Ikenna Obi'. 'It's okay, Mr Obi,' he says. 'It's not heavy. And please call me Remi.'

'No problem, Remi, *sir*,' Mr Obi says.

Remi fights back a smile. 'Just Remi, and I'll call you Ikenna. Is that okay?'

Mr Obi smiles. 'As you wish, *sir* . . . Remi,' he quickly corrects himself. 'Sorry, *s* – Remi. I'm very sorry, Remi.'

'It's okay, Ikenna. It happens to me all the time in London.'

Mr Obi hesitates, clearly missing the sarcasm, and the flight attendant nearest to them laughs. Mr Obi turns to her with a scowl . . . because she's of no station to laugh at or even with him.

But the flight attendant ignores his glare. Mr Obi turns back to Remi, and Remi gestures for Mr Obi to lead the way.

Remi steps on to the boarding bridge, and a wave of dry heat hits him full force. He thought he'd dressed appropriately for the weather in a silk-blend T-shirt and relaxed-fit linen trousers, but he's already sweating. Years of London weather have seemingly erased his tolerance for the heat, regardless of the countless Mediterranean holidays he's had. He was even in Bali for a colleague's wedding last year, which has a tropical climate like Lagos, but this heat feels different – it's harsh. But then, maybe it's not just the weather. Maybe it's the guilt for abandoning his sister, his family, Lagos.

'Can I have your ticket?' Mr Obi says. 'So that one of our boys can collect your bags straight from the plane and bring them to you.'

'I don't have any bags,' Remi says, and gestures to his travel bag. 'Just this.'

Mr Obi glances at it with surprise and then nods. He leads the way from the boarding bridge and heads in the opposite direction to the other passengers. Mr Obi and Remi walk through a secluded hallway reserved for customs officers and airport security, and doors open for them as they approach. All the officers they walk past greet Mr Obi with respect and glance at Remi with curiosity and deference. Mr Obi is clearly an important man at the airport, and all the officers know that the unknown young man Mr Obi is personally escorting is *somebody's son,* who will soon be that *somebody* when his father passes, so it'll be good for him to remember you fondly.

Mr Obi leads them into what looks like a VIP lounge, and Remi is glad to be in an air-conditioned room.

'Can I have your passport, so I can quickly stamp it?' Mr Obi asks, gesturing to a desk where another officer waits at attention.

'Thanks, Ikenna,' Remi says, and hands him his passport.

'Mummy's Boy!' an assertive voice calls from across the room, and Remi turns to it.

Remi recognises the man sitting comfortably on a pristine leather sofa that looks like it was brought out just for him. Chief Kayode Adeleke, in his early sixties, and a self-assured former senator and governor of Lagos state, is one of his dad's closest and oldest friends. The Chief's beaming smile and use of Remi's childhood nickname tell Remi that the Chief doesn't yet know of Kike's death. Especially because the Chief was even more fond of her than him because she was a founding member of the Three Ks (Kayode, Kike, and Kunle – his father). Remi puts on a smile and hurries over to the Chief.

'Good morning, Uncle,' Remi says. Like Uncle Tayo, the Chief has no familial relationship with Remi, but that's the respectful title of endearment for very close friends of your parents. Remi prostrates by the Chief's feet to greet him.

'Get up, get up, my boy,' the Chief says, and rubs Remi's head. 'At least London hasn't spoilt you.'

'Never, Uncle,' Remi says, as he stands. There is space on the sofa beside the Chief, but Remi waits for the Chief to give him permission to sit. He looks down at the Chief and spots a bald patch on the crown of his head in the midst of dyed jet-black hair. But other than that, he looks healthier than the last time Remi saw him, at a wedding in London about five years ago. Life away from the front line of politics has been good to the

Chief, although he himself would probably disagree – he craves the power.

'Good,' the Chief says, and gestures for Remi to sit beside him. 'And were you on the same flight? I didn't see you.'

'Yes, Uncle. Same flight.'

The Chief looks perplexed, and Remi knows he is wondering why Remi wasn't in Upper Class.

'Yes, Uncle. I was in economy.'

'Is everything okay?' the Chief asks, concerned. 'Have you lost your job or something?'

'No, not at all,' Remi responds with a smile. However, the Chief's disregard for the idea that Remi's father could have paid for the flight makes it clear that he knows about Remi's estrangement from his family.

'No? But are you not doing corporate law for one of those big London firms?'

'Yes, Uncle.'

'They pay well, abi. At least that's what I hear.'

'Yes, Uncle. They pay well. It was just an urgent flight. Economy is all they had.'

The Chief shakes his head, not believing Remi. 'My flight was also last-minute. I was in London for meetings. Only had one, had to postpone the rest. They will come over to Lagos. Me, I don't like all this *Zoom Zoom* calls.'

Remi smiles with a light shrug, understanding.

'So, how long are you going to stay in London?' the Chief asks. 'You've been working at this firm for how long?'

'Eight years, Uncle.'

'And you haven't made partner yet? Ahn ahn.'

'It's coming, Uncle.'

'It's coming? Nonsense. It's all about connections, Remi. I know your father taught you that. Here, in Lagos or Abuja, these law firms will tear themselves apart to make you partner . . . *yesterday*! The pay will not be the same, of course, but even London partner salary is nothing to you *Banks*.'

The Chief smiles and Remi can tell there is envy behind it. Remi could always tell the Chief envied his dad's successes, primarily because, on the face of it, they haven't stemmed from a political position or affiliation, so they aren't infused with the stench of corruption.

Remi wants to say he's remained in London because he wants to do his own thing, off his own name and hard work. But he knows the Chief, like his dad, will be insulted by that. Because both are sons of wealthy families who have built that wealth beyond their fathers' dreams. Just as his father wishes for him. Instead, Remi says, 'I know, Uncle. I just want to build a large enough client base so I can come back to start a firm of my own focused on bringing foreign investment to Nigeria.'

The answer impresses the Chief. Which is very different to Remi's dad's reaction to the same answer because Remi's dad knows it's mostly not true.

'You Banks are so ambitious,' the Chief says and turns to Dele, his private secretary, who's been patiently waiting to get the Chief's attention.

At the same time, Mr Obi approaches to offer Remi his passport.

'Thanks, Ikenna,' Remi says, and stands to accept it.

'It's okay, sir,' Mr Obi says, glancing at the Chief. Remi understands the Chief will frown upon Mr Obi's seeming familiarity with Remi if he calls Remi by his name. 'I will take you to your people now.'

'It's okay,' the Chief interjects, and takes his time to stand. 'My bags are ready. He will walk with me. Go back to your post.'

Mr Obi hesitates, which surprises Remi. But Dele, who is clearly not a private secretary but is more personal security, glares at Mr Obi.

'No problem, Chief,' Mr Obi says.

'Don't worry,' the Chief replies, in a voice steeped in condescension, and pulls out a wad of pound notes. 'I know you want something. Oya, take. And I'm sure his father will arrange something for you later.'

Mr Obi takes the money, but Remi can still sense a bit of unease and smiles to reassure him.

'Let's go,' the Chief says, and wraps an arm around Remi. Dele picks up the Chief's hand luggage and leads them towards the door. 'I know you've been in London for a long time,' the Chief says to Remi. 'But don't get too familiar with *these people*. They will take advantage.'

Remi disagrees, but he knows it's the prevailing sentiment of the affluent Nigerians – *his people*. 'I understand, Uncle,' he says.

Dele holds the door open for the Chief and Remi to step through, and Remi is again slapped in the face by the heat. They've stepped into a shaded in-between space at the back of the airport – a private exit hall not quite inside, not fully out – where the rich and powerful can slip away into their waiting vehicles, unseen.

'Does Yetunde know you're around?' the Chief asks, referring to one of his daughters, who was a year below Remi in boarding school.

Remi starts to respond but then notices Yinka across the hall, flanked by two sturdy young men. Once a trusted protégé of Shina – the family's formidable long-standing head of security – Yinka has since stepped up as his second-in-command. Yinka is visibly alarmed to see Remi with the Chief, which shocks Remi because the Chief and his dad are the closest of friends. He glances at the Chief, who is smiling again. But this time, there's a glint of smug satisfaction beneath it because he's also spotted Yinka's alarm and is enjoying it.

'No, Uncle. She doesn't,' Remi says, and follows the fixed stare of one of the sturdy young men flanking Yinka to four soldiers armed with rifles on the other side of the hall. The commonplace presence of guns, which was normal for Remi while growing up in Lagos, now unsettles him slightly.

'I'll let her know,' the Chief says, and leads Remi away from Yinka and towards the soldiers. 'She's planning Rose's wedding . . . you've met Rose, yes?'

Remi watches through the corner of his eye as Yinka briefly hesitates. Yinka's jaw tightens, and for a moment, he looks as though he might intervene. But then he falls into step behind them, keeping a respectful distance. Not so close as to appear disrespectful, eavesdropping, or openly suspicious. But close enough to signal that he is immovable. That he will be taking Remi home.

Remi takes all that in and doesn't react. 'No. I moved to London for university just before Rose and Aunty Nora moved to Lagos, and each time I've been back since, Rose and I have just missed each other,' he says.

Rose is another of the Chief's daughters, born to Nora, a different mother from Yetunde's. Nora, a former Lebanese diplomat who lived and worked in Dubai, kept Rose away from what she deemed the toxic environment in Lagos until Rose turned sixteen.

'Well, it's going to be the wedding of the year . . . you know Yetunde. I'm sure you're invited. She's having an exclusive pre-party at the Ikoyi house tonight. I'll tell her you're around.'

'Thanks, Uncle,' Remi says. He has no intention of going, and he knows that as soon as the news of Kike's death spreads, no one will be inviting him or expecting him to show up at any parties, exclusive or not.

'Remi,' Yinka calmly calls from behind.

Remi stops and carefully turns towards Yinka, and he's struck by Yinka's transformation. Yinka's no longer one of the *boys*; he carries himself with the confidence and authority of a man who's earned respect.

'I'm coming, Yinka. Just having a chat with Uncle.'

'What's the problem, Yinka?' the Chief says. 'You think I'm going to kidnap my nephew?'

'Not at all, Chief. I was not sure Remi recognised me.'

'And what is this *Remi* you're talking? It's Mr Bankole or sir.'

'Yes, Chief,' Yinka says, and turns to Remi. 'I'm sorry, sir.'

Remi nods and softly ducks under the Chief's arm to go shake Yinka's hand. 'Of course I remember you, Yinka. You used to travel with us to boarding school. Playing Fela all the way. I'm looking forward to some Fela on the ride home today.'

Yinka smiles. Good memories for him as well, it seems. Remi pats Yinka on the shoulder and walks back to the Chief.

'See you tonight, Uncle,' he says, and embraces him.

'Maybe . . . heading to Abuja now, but I'll try. It'll be good to see you and Kike. I'm sure she's invited. She has been the life of the Lagos high society since she's been back.'

The comment knocks the wind out of Remi, and he can't speak as he struggles to bury the thought of his sister exuding her vibrance everywhere, anywhere, all the time . . . but now no more. An image of her – laughing, commanding the room – flares so vividly it makes his eyes sting. Knowing he might crack, he quickly nods politely and walks back to Yinka.

'Let's go,' Remi says.

'Can I carry your bag, sir?' Yinka asks.

'No,' Remi snaps. 'And you call me Remi and nothing else.'

Yinka nods and leads him back towards the two sturdy young men, and as they approach, Remi notices the handguns holstered at their right hips. He watches the young men as Yinka quietly discusses the next moves in Yoruba. They are both wearing the latest Apple watches, and the handguns look too clean and state-of-the-art to be Nigerian military issue. They are either private security consultants or soldiers who work security for affluent families when needed.

Remi continues to scan the men, and although similar in age, physique, and their all-black outfits, it's clear one of them takes much more care of himself. He has a fresh haircut, trimmed beard, and a touch of the latest fashion with his relaxed cargo trousers and New Balance 327 trainers. Just then, the fresh young man briefly looks away from Yinka to lock eyes with Remi and nod reassuringly. Remi returns the gesture. The young man returns his focus to Yinka, who indicates for him and his colleague to take the lead. They walk out of the shaded exit hall into the half-empty staff car park, and Remi is suddenly gripped by the sight of the rising sun in the cloudless sky. This gives him a hit of the nostalgia he'd craved. He buries a smile and takes in the sky.

They approach two Toyota Land Cruisers with tinted windows, government plate numbers, and engines running. The fresh young man opens the back door of the second car for Remi to enter. Remi nods gratefully before he climbs in, and Yinka climbs into the car's front passenger seat. The two young men jump into the first car, and both cars instantly set off.

Remi is grateful that the car's air conditioning is on full blast and relaxes to soak in the cool air. But then he notices the windows – thicker than normal, darkly tinted, and with a slight lamination at the edges. They are bulletproof. He leans forward to see that Yinka is holding a powerful assault rifle, and there is another within easy reach of the stoic driver. The level of security troubles him, as the overwhelming mood is peril. He also fears that whatever has led to this mood could have something to do with Kike's death. Especially as he's yet to be told how or where she died.

'What's happening, Yinka?' Remi asks.

'What do you mean?'

'You know what I mean. What's all this?'

'The car? Sorry, Oga wanted us to pick you up in this car.' *Oga – boss.*

'Not the car, Yinka. All the security. The big guns.'

'This is what Oga wants.'

'Why?'

'I . . .' Yinka hesitates because he remembers Remi could always catch him in a lie, even as a teenager. 'Oga is worried and wants you to be safe.'

'From who . . . from what? And does it have anything to do with Kike?'

Yinka hesitates again. 'I think you should ask Oga that for yourself, Remi.'

Remi nods. 'Is he home?'

'No. Oga and Shina flew to Abuja this morning. But they will be back this evening.'

'This morning? It's 6 a.m.'

'Yes, 3 a.m. The private jet.'

'He has a private jet?'

'Yes. Oga has a personal one, and the company has two.'

Remi nods and sits back. There is so much to pick over. But clearly, his father is now even more successful than he was aware of. At the same time, he's not surprised that the extent of his father's success is not public knowledge, because his father, like his grandfather, preferred to operate in the shadows. However, to build wealth in Nigeria beyond Remi's imagination, his father would've had to make deals with several devils, all of whom are constantly battling to be the most devilish. His father enjoyed that fire – he thrived in it – but maybe it had finally burnt him, and Kike paid the price.

Suddenly, Remi remembers the Chief is also heading to Abuja straight from London, and wonders if he could be somehow involved in whatever led to Kike's death. The Chief was always a hungry devil, but he was the devil that was always there for them. The devil who taught him and Kike how to read, outmanoeuvre, and even dance with the others.

'And what was all that with the Chief?' Remi asks.

'Please, Remi. Speak to Oga about all this. Okay? I don't know what I'm supposed to say.'

Remi appreciates the honesty and nods, and Yinka connects his iPhone to the stereo to play 'Water No Get Enemy' by Fela Kuti before Remi asks more questions.

Yinka resumes scanning their surroundings for any hint of danger as they speed through the early morning traffic in Ikeja – the bustling capital city on the Mainland of Lagos that was once the jewel of Nigeria before wealth shifted to the Island, leaving the Mainland's infrastructure to crumble. Their convoy merges on to the Third Mainland Bridge – once the longest in Africa – now more a towering symbol of the divide between the Mainland's poor and the Island's elite. The bridge carries them across the Lagos Lagoon into Ikoyi, Nigeria's most affluent neighbourhood, where Remi and *his people* remain cloistered.

Remi stares out the window throughout the hour-long ride, searching for anything to brighten his mood. He finds nothing, though he's struck by how familiar it all feels. Massive billboards feature the musicians and footballers he recognises, selling beer or mobile plans. Street vendors and beggars eye the tinted windows with a mix of curiosity and caution. Lethargic police officers at checkpoints, wielding decades-old rifles often without bullets, suddenly snap to attention at the sight of the convoy's license plates to wave the cars through. This is Lagos, he thinks . . . and Lagos will never change.

CHAPTER 4

The convoy leaves the bustle of the main roads and drives through quieter residential Ikoyi streets to an imposing gate that leads to a secluded gated community. More armed guards, dressed in immaculately pressed uniforms, step forward to inspect the cars. Yinka lowers the tinted window and patiently watches the guards approach. Both guards recognise Yinka and immediately bow to greet him with deep respect before one of them speaks quietly into his earpiece.

'Welcome back, sir,' the guard nearest to Yinka says, and the imposing gates are slowly pulled open by two other armed guards on the other side.

'Thank you, Felix,' Yinka says to the guard. 'Are you boys all right? Any problems this morning?'

'No problem, sir,' Felix responds. 'Everything normal, sir.'

Yinka nods. 'Ṣe ẹ ti jẹun l'áárọ̀ yìí?' He seamlessly switches to Yoruba to ask if the guards have eaten.

Remi is impressed by the genuine care in Yinka's voice and leans forward slightly to watch Felix's reaction. He spots the slight hesitation in Felix's expression as he considers the best response.

The guards have all eaten but would greatly appreciate more food, especially the plentiful and high-quality food from the Bankole residence.

'Ẹ ṣé, sir. A ti jẹun,' Felix says, admitting they have eaten. 'But only a small amount of food,' he continues in Yoruba.

'It's okay,' Yinka says, as the conversation continues in Yoruba. 'There are six of you at the gate, right? And eight on patrol inside.'

'Yes, sir.'

'We'll send something from the house.'

'Thank you, sir.'

Yinka nods in acceptance, and Remi is further impressed by the calm authority Yinka's developed, and the fact that Felix ultimately didn't feel the need to lie to Yinka. Yinka smacks the car's roof to signal for the first car to drive through the gate, and they follow closely behind.

Beyond the gates, the estate feels like another world. Wide, tree-lined streets flanked by high walls that shield lavish residences from prying eyes. Each residence also has a fortified gate, elaborate enough to rival the estate's main gate, including uniformed personal armed security.

Eventually, the convoy approaches the grand gate leading to Remi's family home, and the gate slides open to reveal a sprawling compound much larger than Remi remembers. When Remi was last here, there was only the palatial mansion itself and the large staff quarters behind it. But as the line of vehicles glide past landscaped gardens, Remi realises that the compound has extended to include the neighbouring house, where the long-serving CEO of one of Nigeria's leading banks used to live with his family. That home has been demolished with no trace left behind – just its land, which is now theirs. The mansion has also been extensively renovated in a contemporary style, and two newly built houses flank it, echoing the mansion's modern opulence on a smaller scale. The walls surrounding the compound are also higher than before, crowned by electrified barbed wire and well-positioned security cameras.

The vehicles turn away from the driveway leading to the mansion's elegant front entrance and head towards one of the new houses. Remi shifts in his seat, surprised, as he expected to head straight to the mansion he once called home. Yinka notices Remi lean forward and quickly speaks before Remi can.

'Oga asked Mrs Ibeh to arrange one of the guest houses for you. And it is ready.'

Mrs Ifeoma Ibeh has worked for the Bankole family for over thirty years. She first joined the household in her early twenties as a housegirl, having moved to Lagos from Eastern Nigeria at fourteen to begin domestic work for other affluent families. A decade later, she rose to become head of household staff – a role she's held for over two decades. Mrs Ibeh is as proficient as she is formidable.

'But Oga says that if you still want your old room, you can have it. I just need to let Mrs Ibeh know, and they will get it ready for you very quickly.'

'No. It's okay,' Remi says. 'I'll stay in the guest house.'

Yinka nods, and it dawns on Remi that the changes here are beyond mere construction and renovation. Remi wonders what else has changed in his childhood home, which feels even more guarded than ever.

As the vehicles approach the front entrance to the guest house,

Remi spots Kehinde, a man of similar age that he grew up with and played alongside in the residence because Kehinde's father worked as the head gardener and lived in the staff quarters with his wife and three children. Kehinde stands confidently in front of the guest house's front door, watching the cars arrive, and Remi smiles as he reminisces about playing football with him and the other children of the house staff.

'Oga has not told the house staff about Kike,' Yinka says, pulling Remi out of reminiscing.

Remi turns to Yinka with a raised eyebrow, and Yinka waits for the car to park a few steps away from Kehinde before continuing. 'He's waiting to tell Madam first,' he says. 'But she's at prayer camp, and her phone is off.'

Madam is Zainab Bankole, Remi's mother.

'Prayer camp,' Remi says mostly to himself, unsurprised but angry. For at least the past two decades, his mother has been considerably more dedicated to her church than her family. 'When is my mother coming back?' he asks.

'We are not sure, Remi. This is a new church that Madam is helping to start – '

'She left her church?' Remi interrupts, surprised.

Yinka hesitates, surprised Remi doesn't know. 'Yes, Remi,' he confirms, deciding it's not his place to provide the necessary context Remi is missing. 'But we think it's for seven days, so Madam should be back tomorrow.'

Remi is infuriated by the thought of a seven-day prayer camp in the middle of nowhere with one's phone switched off. But he doesn't show it and moves on from the subject.

'I'm guessing my father wants me to keep my mouth and public displays of emotion in check until my mother returns.'

Yinka nods.

'Understood,' Remi says, and grabs his bag on the seat beside him. 'Thanks for picking me up.'

'It is no problem, Remi. And we'll be here if you want to go out.'

Remi pats Yinka's shoulder and wears a smile before he steps out of the car.

Remi takes the two steps to Kehinde with his arms outstretched for a hug. Kehinde is glad to see Remi but uneasy about the hug, as he knows that sort of over-familiarity is frowned upon by the older generation house staff, especially Mrs Ibeh.

'Kehinde,' Remi says, and embraces him. Kehinde hesitates for a moment, glancing around nervously, before he returns the embrace. 'How are you doing, buddy?'

'I'm doing very well, Oga Remi,' Kehinde says with a genuine smile.

'Hey,' Remi chides. 'Not you, too. You're not calling me Oga. Just Remi.'

'I . . .' Kehinde hesitates. 'I'm the head of guest house one's staff,' he says, and gestures to the house. 'I and my staff will be caring for you, so I must lead by example.'

'Fair,' Remi says, appreciating Kehinde's position. 'But when we are alone, you call me Remi.'

Kehinde smiles in acceptance, and Remi scans Kehinde's finely pressed, elegant kaftan.

'I like your style, buddy,' Remi says, and Kehinde chuckles before he offers to take Remi's bag. 'Nope,' Remi says, and gestures for Kehinde to lead into the three-storey house.

Kehinde laughs softly and takes them to the front door, which opens as they approach. Remi steps into the foyer, awed by the house's understated elegance.

'Good morning, Oga Remi,' two voices simultaneously greet from beside the sturdy door.

Remi turns to see a young man prostrating and a young woman on her knees. He's unsettled by the reverence but quickly buries the emotion with a smile.

'Good morning,' he says. 'Please stand up.'

They stand and quietly stare at Remi, and Remi instinctively reaches out to shake their hands. But both are frozen with indecision.

Kehinde deftly steps in. 'Ada,' he says, nodding towards the young woman. 'She's in charge of the food.' Then to the young man. 'Abimbola. He assists me and Ada, keeps the house in order, and takes care of your clothes.'

Ada and Abimbola smile with pride.

'Nice to meet you, Ada and Abimbola,' Remi says.

'There is an intercom in every room,' Kehinde says, and gestures to an intercom handset on the wall. 'The buttons to call each of us are marked on all the intercoms. And buttons for the main house and security – which I've been told to let you know will connect you straight to Yinka.'

'Thanks,' Remi says. 'Mrs Ibeh is as thorough as always. I hope she didn't make you guys work all night to prepare the house for me.'

The others smile uncomfortably for a fleeting moment before Kehinde breaks the awkward silence. 'Oga Remi, please leave your bag,' he says. 'Abimbola will take it to your room. I would like to take you on a tour of the house.'

'Sure,' Remi says, and hands Abimbola his bag. 'See you guys later, I'm sure.'

Abimbola and Ada graciously nod, and Kehinde leads Remi on a tour of the elegant and modern house.

'Ada is Mrs Ibeh's daughter,' Kehinde explains as soon as Ada and Abimbola cannot overhear their conversation.

'Oh, really?' Remi says, surprised. 'The awkward smiles make more sense now.'

Kehinde laughs softly.

'I didn't know Mrs Ibeh had a daughter. Thought Chidi was her only child.'

'She kept Ada with her parents in Onitsha until Ada graduated from culinary school a couple of years ago. Then Ada came to join the staff here. She cooks and bakes very well.'

'I look forward to trying her food. And please tell her and the other house staff not to greet me like that every time they see me. Once a day is more than enough.'

Kehinde visibly hesitates.

'I appreciate it's tradition,' Remi continues. 'But it can be relaxed, at least inside the house. You can blame it on me being in London for too long.'

Kehinde nods and then smirks.

'What?' Remi asks.

'When Madam Kike returned from London, she asked – no, she

demanded – that no one greet her like that or call her Madam Kike. She was very serious about it.'

'But you're calling her Madam Kike.'

'Not to her face, no,' Kehinde says, and he and Remi laugh. 'But we must call her Madam Kike when she's not around.'

'Must?'

'It is tradition, as you say. And Mrs Ibeh demands it. And I suggest you try not to be too *friendly* with Ada.'

'What do you mean by that?'

'Mrs Ibeh was not very happy with Madam Kike because Madam Kike, err . . .' Kehinde pauses to find the right words. 'Took Ada under her wing and started discussing ideas with her that Mrs Ibeh did not think were proper. Nothing *too controversial* . . .'

'Too controversial?'

'Female empowerment and the like, you understand. But Mrs Ibeh was not happy. Made it a big issue. She and Madam Kike argued . . . in front of the staff. But Madam Kike refused to stop. Madam had to step in.'

Remi wants to smile and cry because he can imagine his sister – with her righteous ferocity – trying to empower Ada and the other young women in the compound on her way to igniting a revolution, one household at a time.

'I'm guessing Ada was removed from Kike's house staff,' he says.

'No, Remi,' Kehinde corrects. 'Madam Kike did not have house staff. She stayed in the main house before she moved to a flat in Banana Island almost six months ago.'

The response sends a jolt through Remi, piquing his curiosity.

'Did the move have anything to do with her argument with Mrs Ibeh?' he asks, abandoning his usual subtlety.

'Oh no,' Kehinde says with confidence. 'This was a few months after. And Madam was not happy about it. But Oga gave permission.'

Kehinde's response further deepens Remi's curiosity because his father rarely goes against his mother's wishes, especially where he and Kike are concerned, and never so openly that the household staff would notice. He nods and follows Kehinde through the back garden to an outbuilding.

'We just finished setting this up before you arrived,' Kehinde says with pride, and opens the outbuilding's door to lead into a cool functional gym. He gestures to a worn punching bag in a corner of the room. 'Remember that? I can't lie . . . no one has touched it since you last used it.'

Remi laughs and walks over to carefully inspect the punching bag, lingering on each scuff, faded patch and frayed seam.

'No gloves yet,' Kehinde says. 'We couldn't find your old gloves, so I'm arranging for a new pair once the shops open today.'

'Thanks, buddy,' Remi says.

'You're welcome, Remi,' Kehinde says. 'Should I leave you to stay here, or do you want me to take you back to your room?'

'It's okay. I'll stay here for a bit. It seems to be the coolest spot in the house.'

'We know,' he says and chuckles – everyone knows Remi loves the air conditioner to be on full blast. 'The air conditioning in the house was on low till we started setting up early this morning, and the house takes a while to cool. But when it does, you'll like it very much.'

'Thanks. And no need to wait for me. I'll find my way to my room. If I get lost, I'll call you from one of the many intercoms.'

Kehinde laughs softly. 'Speak soon, Remi,' he says, and leaves the outbuilding, gently shutting the door behind him.

Remi slips off his shoes to feel the texture of the brand-new gym mat spread across every inch of the floor. He digs his toes into the soft yet sturdy surface, nodding at the premium quality, before lying on the mat and closing his eyes to sleep.

CHAPTER 5

A few hours later, Remi's phone loudly chimes and wakes him. He sits up and calmly scans the room as his brain takes a quick moment to recognise the unfamiliar surroundings. He pulls his phone from his pocket to confirm that the chime is the fifteen-minute reminder for the call with the other senior associates and partners in the deal team to properly hand over the work streams he was leading. He picks up his shoes as he climbs to his feet and strides out of the gym and back into the house, which is perfectly cool, as Kehinde promised.

He strides up the exquisite staircase into his large, artfully designed bedroom and heads straight to his bag on the carpet beside the bed. He picks out his laptop, headset and an unopened bottle of water he bought at Heathrow Duty-Free and settles at a reading desk beside the bed, slowly moving aside the Bible, the only item on the desk. He opens his laptop and immediately spots the Wi-Fi details on the intercom handset. Efficient as always, he says to himself before he notes the password and settles back at the desk. He logs on, takes a gulp of water, and readies himself for what he's sure will be a very long call.

As Remi expected, the call lasted almost three hours, with most of the first ten minutes spent on his colleagues sharing their condolences and reassuring him to take as much time as he needs to be with his family. He returns his laptop and headset to his bag and heads down to the kitchen for something to eat.

Remi walks into the state-of-the-art kitchen and startles Abimbola relaxing on a chair in the corner of the expansive room, engrossed as he watches a music video on his phone.

Abimbola immediately drops to the floor to prostrate. 'Ẹ káàsán, Oga Remi,' he says.

'Káàsán,' Remi responds. 'Please stand up. And do you mind if I call you Bola?'

Bola stands. 'Not at all, Oga Remi,' he says, and attempts to put his phone away.

'No need. Please continue. I'll just grab something from the fridge,' Remi says, and heads towards the fridge.

Bola's eyes widen in shock, reminding Remi that it is highly unusual for him to be in the kitchen at all, let alone serve himself. It would reflect poorly on Bola, the other house staff, and ultimately on Kehinde. Remi stops, allowing Bola to hurry ahead of him towards the fridge.

'What would you like, Oga Remi? Are you hungry?'

'Yes, I'm hungry. But I just want something cold to drink right now.'

Bola nods. 'Please, Oga Remi, wait in the dining room . . .' He hesitates and quickly corrects himself. 'Anywhere in the house, and I will bring your cold drink right away.'

'Thanks,' Remi says, and walks out of the kitchen.

Remi sits at the dining table in the dining room, which is the closest room to the kitchen. In under a minute, Bola walks in with a tray, carrying a single glass and a jug of ice-cold water infused with lemons, lime and mint. Remi softly nods to himself, impressed by how well briefed the kitchen staff are about what he enjoys.

'Thanks,' Remi says, watching Bola approach.

Bola places the tray on the table before responding. 'You are welcome, Oga Remi,' he says before filling the glass and carefully placing it in front of Remi. 'What would you like to eat?'

'Surprise me. I'm sure I'll enjoy it.'

'No problem, Oga Remi,' Bola says, confidently accepting the challenge. He picks a remote from a side table and switches on the large TV hung on the wall. 'What would you like to watch, Oga Remi?'

Remi turns to the TV and instantly recognises the young woman, Eki Abbey, leading a conversation with two much older men in a TV news studio. Eki was in the same year as Kike in their exclusive boarding school just outside Lagos, and he remembers that they were relatively close.

'You can leave this. Thank you.'

Bola nods, places the remote beside Remi and leaves.

Remi notes the channel and is mildly amused at the quasi-nepotism because the channel is owned by Derin Daniels, one of the most prominent media moguls in Nigeria and the father of Seun Daniels, who was also in the same year as Kike and Eki in boarding school and was close to them. Somewhat . . . because he remembers thinking Seun tried too hard to be Kike's friend.

Remi focuses on the conversation and is quickly drawn in by the deft way Eki steers the discussion with the two leading political pundits as they dissect the sudden influx of top figures from the president's political party into Abuja for a private meeting at the Aso Rock Presidential Villa. His father and the Chief's trips to Abuja this morning spring to his mind, and for a moment, he can't help but wonder if Kike's death and the hurried gathering are somehow connected. But he dismisses the thought as unlikely. The Chief is a prominent member of the president's party, but Remi is sure his father has no direct political affiliations – beyond strategically donating large sums to chosen politicians across various parties. The pundits eventually agree that the most probable reason for the gathering is to calm the simmering tensions within the party, sparked by the president's failing health and the looming power vacuum, and Remi concludes that his father's trip is likely just a coincidence.

While watching the hour-long conversation, peppered with throws to reporters on location at the Abuja airport and outside the Aso Rock Presidential Villa, Remi heard Ada enter the kitchen through the staff door to prepare his meal, occasionally directing Bola to assist her or fetch an item. Roughly halfway through the conversation, Bola entered the dining room and placed a plate of delicately presented ẹ̀fọ́ riro and spicy grilled whole tilapia in front of Remi, which smelt delicious and tasted even better than it smelt. As the conversation ended, Bola returned to replace the empty plate with a bowl of soapy water for Remi to wash his hands. Remi didn't need to wash his hands but didn't refuse the bowl of soapy water. The moment Bola leaves the dining room, Remi picks up the bowl and follows towards the kitchen, hoping to personally thank Ada and her team.

Remi casually enters the kitchen, and Ada and Bola turn to him with varying degrees of surprise. He stops a couple steps inside the door as a sign that he acknowledges the invisible barrier and presents the bowl, which Bola hurries to collect.

'Thank you both very much,' Remi says. 'The food was incredibly delicious. I'm looking forward to dinner.'

Ada fights back a smile, but not quick enough to go unnoticed. 'Thank you, Oga Remi,' she says with a distinct Igbo accent Remi hadn't recognised earlier.

Remi nods and heads out of the kitchen.

Remi walks through the house, unsure where to go or what to do. He just doesn't want to dwell on his thoughts, as he fears his mask of calm will dissolve. He walks through the hallway and spots the pair of new boxing gloves placed prominently at the foot of the steps. He smiles. He'll go back to the gym, but after the food has settled. He considers a stroll around the compound, but not in this heat; he'll wait till the sun goes down. He grabs the gloves and heads into the living room to relax on one of the exquisite couches and watch TV.

Half an hour later, Remi is just about paying attention to a repeat of a Champions League match played the night before when Mrs Ibeh steps into the living room and stops just inside the doorway. Remi spots her in the corner of his eye and turns to see her smiling at him. He stands and instinctively wants to reach out for a hug as he walks to her. However, her impeccably groomed presence, even acknowledging the smile, is too formal for a hug.

'Hello, Aunty,' he says with a smile as he approaches her.

'Hello, Mr Remi,' she says. 'Welcome back.'

Mrs Ibeh is fluent in Yoruba but has always spoken to Remi in English because he is most comfortable speaking English, and in the early days, it helped improve her English.

Remi considers asking her to call him *Remi* without the *Mr*, but he's sure that wouldn't go down too well. 'Thank you,' he says instead, and can't bring himself to say that it's good to be back. Because it's not . . . not under these circumstances.

She remains by the doorway, and Remi remembers that is his cue to invite her in to sit down. He gestures to the couches, and she nods before he leads them into the room. They sit on adjacent couches, not too close, but close enough so they can easily hear themselves speak. Out of respect, he lowers the volume of the TV anyway.

'Did you lose my number?' she asks. 'I know you are very busy in London, so I'm not expecting you to call to check up on your *aunty*. But you should've given me some notice of your arrival. We are still putting the final touches on the house to make sure everything is just right for you.'

'I understand. And thank you, but it's already perfect.'

'Thank you, but it is not,' she says, not leaving any room for debate.

He shrugs.

'How are you?' she asks, somewhat unexpectedly for Remi. 'I must say you look very healthy . . . strong . . . so I know you're taking care of yourself. But how is work? Last I heard, you were working all hours.'

Remi hesitates. It's strange, talking about work and house preparations, like everything is normal, like Kike isn't dead. But then, this must be what his dad expects of him. He fights back the pain and flows with the tide.

'I'm okay. Doing well . . . and work is work. I enjoy it.'

She nods. 'I should repeat what I know your mother has told you several times . . . that you should come back to Lagos, and you won't have to work that hard. But I know. You're like your father. You will find the work to fill the hours.'

Remi chuckles.

'What about finding a wife? I was hoping you'd be arriving with a guest.'

'It'll come,' he says, and smiles.

'Please, stop wasting time, oh.'

'I'm not, I promise.'

'So there is somebody?'

Remi hesitates. 'Not exactly.'

'So you are wasting time.'

'I've got time . . . I'm very healthy, as you said.'

She tuts in disapproval. 'I bu onye amamihe karịrị akarị, mana ọ naghị enyere onwe gị aka,' she says in Igbo language, meaning he's too smart for his own good.

'Whatever that means, I disagree,' he says, and laughs as she rolls her eyes. 'How are you? I met Ada, she's a fantastic cook.'

'Thank you,' she says, filled with clear pride. 'She worked very hard to learn, and I am very proud of her.'

Remi fights back a smile. 'And how are you?'

'Oh, I'm doing well. The house is getting bigger and bigger every day, with more staff and more things to manage and plan. But as you said, I enjoy it.'

'Good. That's all about work, though. How is *life*?' he asks, intentionally overstepping etiquette for a reaction.

She hesitates, considering a response, and Remi recognises that he's hit a nerve. 'Thank you for your concern, Remi. I work for your family, and your *father* and *mother* treat me very well. You should not need to concern yourself with my *life*.'

He nods, quietly pondering her words. The message is subtle but pointed. And it's hard to miss the implication that, in her view, Kike hadn't treated her well and had been overly concerned with the staff's lives. He remains quiet, allowing the pregnant silence to linger and carefully watching her.

As he'd hoped, she continues speaking. 'I understand that abroad, in the West, people feel that some of our traditions here in Nigeria should be left in the past,' she says, her tone measured but firm. 'I agree that some should be. But until everyone agrees and these traditions are put aside for *better* ways, only a select few have the luxury to choose which traditions to follow, or to break away from the ones that no longer serve them. The rest of us don't have that freedom. If we try to pick and choose, the system will crush us. Just like that.' She snaps her fingers. 'And no one will do anything about it. Not even these people in the West that talk and talk about our traditions. They will just keep talking.'

She pauses, waiting for Remi to react. But he remains silent, allowing her to say everything on her mind, especially when it comes to Kike.

'I'm saying all this, my dear Remi,' she continues, her voice softening slightly, 'to kindly ask that you respect our traditions – your family's, mine, the traditions of this house – while you are here.'

'This is about Kike, isn't it?' he asks.

She considers denying or deflecting, but hesitates, remembering Remi's supposed – and, in her view, unnatural – ability to detect lies. She never witnessed it herself, likely because she'd never lied in front of him, but stories of his talent spread through the household when he was still a teenager. For a time, the compound was captivated. The more religious among them were fearful, suspecting something supernatural. Madam dismissed it too, until an incident at Remi's boarding school prompted her to pull him out and take him to a prayer camp behind Oga's back. Three days later, they returned. Madam declared Remi had been delivered and warned everyone never to speak of it again. Most believed the ability disappeared after that. But now and then, someone still whispers a different story.

She decides to address the issue head-on. 'Yes. It is about Kike,' she says with a measured tone, mindful that, although he and Kike have fallen out and not spoken for years, he was once fiercely protective of her. 'Kike showed a lack of respect for many of our traditions, for me, and for *your mother*.' Her tone sharpened at the mention of his mother, injected with a dose of moral indignation because she knows that, although he hasn't shown much affection for his mother recently, he once adored her – even after the traumatic *deliverance* – and will never disrespect her.

'Is that why Kike moved out?'

'No. Not at all,' she says, and shakes her head. 'I made the mistake of trying to push back. You see, my Ada admired your sister, looked up to her, and your sister was filling her head with . . .' She pauses, reconsidering her choice of words. 'Your sister was encouraging unrealistic expectations for Ada and the other young women in my staff. Expectations that would be dangerous for them here in Nigeria.' She slips into pidgin, her voice laced with emotions. '*Na hope go kill person pass bullet.*' She switches back to English. 'I tried to challenge your sister. I should have known better, but I forgot – your sister never backs down from a challenge. Anyway, your mother would've never let your sister move out because of the lack of respect. In fact, your mother is still angry about it. It is not right for a young woman to leave her father's house before marriage. But your father permitted it.'

'Why?'

'I don't know,' she says, pausing to consider the question she has ruminated on since Kike moved out. 'I don't know. But your father – and I know you will understand that this is not intended to disrespect him at all – still has some of the *West* in him. He spent too long there, just like you and your sister. And this is clear to the few who truly know your father, and anyone in his household paying attention.'

'Hmm,' Remi mutters, simply to encourage Mrs Ibeh to keep talking.

'Oh yes. Let us put to one side that he permitted his only daughter to leave his house before marriage. But he was in no rush for her to return home from London in the first place. He's still in no rush for you, his firstborn and only son, to return home. He did not hesitate to say to me when I asked that you will come back when you are ready. Yes, I asked. Because we all missed you.'

She chuckles, and Remi forces a smile. He knows his dad allowing them to return to Nigeria when they were *ready* has little to do with his father's supposed Western traits and more to do with his father ensuring that his children do not go through the same trauma he quietly suffered for years.

'Your father is in no rush for either of you to get married. Has refused to even talk to Kike about any of the very good matches your mother has organised since Kike returned home. Your father does not go to church or pray . . .'

'Christianity is a *Nigerian* tradition?' he softly challenges.

She smirks. 'Remi, Remi, the careful one. That is why I came to speak to you early. Because your sister . . .' She gestures with a strong fist. 'Alágìdí. You will see her coming from far away, and you can prepare, but the power of her agídí will still cause you plenty trouble. You! Iwa tutu. We will not see or hear anything until you have finished us. And you will be greeting us every day, oh.'

He smiles.

'You know what I mean, Remi,' she says. 'We Nigerians are a very religious people. Your father has no religion – that is for people in the West. And these all-expenses-paid five-star holidays your father arranges for the senior household staff every year? It is not good for them. Nigerians . . . it is not *traditional* or healthy to live beyond our means. It kills the hustle. All of my staff worked very hard to get a position here – we pay more than double what other houses pay. But once they become senior staff, the hustle disappears. None of them are ready to take over from me. Talk less, push me aside.'

Remi shrugs. 'Dad probably thinks it's the least a man that owns a place like this – and has a private jet – should do for the people that live and work where he and his family call home.'

She sits back in his chair, considering his words. 'Okay, Remi,' she says after a few quiet moments, then stands up. 'Thank you for taking the time to talk to me.'

He stands as well. 'Thank you for coming to check on me.'

She nods and heads towards the door.

'I will respect our traditions,' he says just before she steps out of the room.

She pauses and turns back to him. 'I know you will, Remi,' she says warmly, and steps out.

Remi waits until Mrs Ibeh's footsteps fade away, then draws in a deep breath and exhales slowly, releasing the anger that had threatened to erupt while she spoke of Kike as though Kike were still alive. He isn't angry at Mrs Ibeh – she's said or done nothing wrong. He's angry with himself, his father and his mother for having to pretend that nothing is amiss, that his younger sister isn't dead.

He didn't have to rush on to the next available flight to Lagos; his father had expressly told him not to. But the compulsion to return immediately was overwhelming. Why, though? He was already too late to be there for Kike. He'd failed her. It wasn't to support his mother, either; he hasn't been there for her in years, and she certainly wouldn't seek him out for solace. She believes he's been poisoned by the *Bankole way* of coldness in the face of anything and everything. She's not wrong. And it's definitely not for his father – the very embodiment of the *Bankole way* – though, to his father's credit, he's endured enough tragedy to warrant such detachment. Kike's death is just one more.

So why am I here? The question echoes in his mind, and he can feel the answer fighting to break through. But it is buried beneath too much emotion and too many thoughts. He needs a distraction, something to keep him from being crushed by it all. He snatches the boxing gloves and heads for the outbuilding gym.

Inside, he strides straight to the battered punching bag, strips down to his underwear – he hadn't packed any gym gear – and pulls on the gloves. For nearly two hours, he pummels the bag with punches, kicks, elbows, and knees until his muscles burn and his mind finally quiets. Exhausted, he collapses on to the mat and drifts into sleep.

CHAPTER 6

The intercom in the gym rings, waking Remi. He climbs to his feet and carefully stretches his neck before striding to pick up the intercom handset.

'Hello, it's Remi,' he says politely.

'Káalẹ́, Remi,' Mrs Ibeh responds.

The greeting triggers Remi to look out of a window to see that evening has settled over Lagos, and he's surprised he slept so long. 'E káalẹ́, Aunty.'

'Oga would like you to come and have dinner with him in the main house.'

'He's back?'

'Yes, Remi. He arrived a couple of hours ago. He asked us to leave you to rest.'

'Okay,' Remi says with understanding. 'I'll be there in fifteen minutes. Just need to take a quick shower.'

'I'll let Oga and the kitchen staff know. Would you like to drive the golf cart yourself? Or do you want me to arrange for one of the boys to drive it?'

'Golf cart?'

'Yes. There are two in front of the guest house for guests to move around the compound.'

'Do we have a golf course in here?' he asks with a hint of sarcasm.

'No, Remi,' she responds, ignoring the sarcasm.

He shakes his head, mildly amused, but it dawns on him that he might consider using a golf cart to get around the compound during the day to avoid the heat.

'I'll walk,' he says.

Remi is showered, dressed and out of the guest house in twelve minutes. He sets off at a brisk pace towards the main house a distance away, and quickly realises that even at his pace, walking the scenic footpaths wouldn't get him to there in under three minutes. He plots a straight route across the gardens that'll get him there in good time, but that's through the immaculate lawns. No, he decides. He takes off his sandals, picks them up and jogs the footpath.

He arrives at the lavish front entrance in just over a minute and stops to catch his breath. He dusts the soles of his feet, puts on his sandals and walks calmly towards the door, which is pulled open from the inside as if the person behind the door watched him approach.

'E káalẹ̀, Oga Remi,' the young man that opened the door greets as he prostrates.

'Káalẹ̀,' Remi responds with a nod. He waits for the young man to stand up and shut the door. 'Where's my father?'

'Oga is in the dining room. He's expecting you.'

'Thanks,' Remi says, and heads towards the kitchen. But he stops abruptly, remembering that the house has been extensively renovated.

'The dining room's location has not changed, Oga,' the young man says.

Remi fights back a smile. 'Mrs Ibeh told you to be ready for that, didn't she?' he asks, and the young man nods. 'Thank you.' He heads through the ground-floor hallway decorated with beautiful Nigerian-inspired paintings – half of which he recognises from the family's collection – to the dining room.

Remi steps into the dining room to find his father, Kunle Bankole, at the head of the table, framed by a large family portrait commissioned when Remi was twenty-five. Kunle is dressed in an elegant black kaftan made of the finest silk and hardly seems to have aged since that painting, looking at least a decade younger than his actual years – thanks to being meticulous about his health as a result of another family tragedy. He is studiously working on an iPad but immediately sets it aside when he notices Remi. Remi walks to his father and prostrates by his feet.

'E káalẹ́, Dad,' Remi says.

'Evening, Remi,' Kunle responds, and gestures to the chair beside him. 'Please sit.'

Remi sits, and both silently acknowledge that this is not a *good* evening.

'It's good to see you,' Kunle warmly says.

Remi hesitates, surprised about how deep and genuine the words felt. 'It's good to see you too, Dad.'

Kunle nods. 'We'll need to be strong for your mother,' he says, quickly returning to his calm, almost cold tone.

Remi nods. 'Do you know when she'll be back?'

'No. But soon, I'm sure. And I appreciate that this *pretence* is a lot to ask of you. But I know you understand why it is necessary.'

'I do,' Remi says, and pauses for a moment before asking, 'Who knows?'

'You, me, a handful of others that need to know . . . and a few more that did not. But that was my fault. I thought *this* . . .'

'Kike's death?' Remi interrupts, not with malice, but for clarity.

'Yes. I thought it was connected to something I'm working on. But it isn't. I'm certain of that now.'

Remi notes that his father doesn't seem able to mention Kike's death. 'That's why you went to Abuja this morning?'

'Yes.'

'And the reason for the extra security?'

'Yes. But that's no longer necessary. Shina is debriefing them now, and they will be sent home with our gratitude.'

Remi nods, and as though sensing the quiet moment between him and his father, a young man rolls a service trolley full of food and drinks into the dining room, trailed closely by a young woman. They set down identical plates – a modest portion of amala surrounded by a generous serving of ewedu soup and grilled chicken thighs. The presentation is delicate, but the aroma remains as rich and traditional as ever. The young man and woman then present small trays, each holding a warm, damp hand towel, which Remi and Kunle use to wipe their hands. The servers then quietly withdraw, leaving Remi and Kunle to tuck into their dinner with their hands – the *traditional* way.

Later, after they've finished eating, Remi is waiting for his dad to break the silence with more information about Kike's death.

But his dad doesn't speak and focuses on reading the notifications on his phone.

'Why did you think what you are working on was connected to Kike's death?'

Kunle looks up at Remi and slowly sets his phone on the table. He weighs his words carefully – he doesn't want Remi knowing too much about the work. He's sure how his son would react: first, Remi will object, then he will do everything he can to support his father through it, just like Kike. And while the work may not have caused her death, it doesn't make it any less dangerous.

Kunle opens his mouth to speak, ready to lie, but hesitates. Remi's eyes are locked on to him, studying – watching for the truth. Kunle had wondered why his son rushed back so suddenly. Now, he understands.

Remi came back for answers.

'Because of who we are,' Kunle says with a measured tone. 'Only a small amount of people will have the temerity to hurt us this deeply . . . and so publicly.'

'Publicly?'

Kunle nods. 'I'll talk about that when your mother returns. I'd rather not do it twice.'

Remi nods. 'Where is she?'

Kunle takes a deep breath, as if steeling himself to visualise his daughter's lifeless body. 'At a private forensic pathology clinic in Lekki. They are excellent and will treat her with respect. I've used them before.'

'For an autopsy?'

'Yes.'

'What happened, Dad?'

Kunle takes another deep breath. 'I don't know, Remi. The pathologist will let me know soon enough.'

'Okay,' Remi says with understanding, but his eyes remain locked on his father, studying him. Kunle is slightly uncomfortable under the gaze and subtly shifts in his seat, which Remi notices. Remi softens his stare. 'Sorry about that, Dad,' he says.

'It's okay, Remi,' Kunle calmly responds. 'I need you to do me a favour.'

'Sure, Dad,' Remi says.

'Yetunde sent someone earlier with your invite for Rose's pre-wedding party tonight. I'd like you to go.'

Remi leans back against his chair, intrigued. 'Why? I'd rather not. And I got the vibe when I ran into the Chief at the airport that you and him are not exactly on good terms right now.'

Kunle nods. 'We are going through a rough patch.'

'It's more than that,' Remi says, unequivocal.

Kunle suppresses a smile, amused that Remi doesn't realise his gaze has once again locked on to him. 'It is,' Kunle admits. 'But going will be good for you.'

Remi is struck by the apparent sincerity of his father's words. 'You think going to a party today will be good for me.'

'Yes. It will be good for you,' Kunle repeats with certainty, knowing it is the truth, but not for the reason Remi assumes. It will be good because 95 percent of the small amount of Lagosian families with the temerity to hurt the Bankoles so deeply – so *publicly* – will be represented at the party. There is no better place for Remi to continue his pursuit for the answers he . . . *they* seek.

'I don't have anything to wear,' Remi says. 'I didn't pack for a party.'

Kunle considers a solution, but Remi beats him to it before he can respond. 'Do you have more of these kaftans, though?' Remi says, gesturing at his dad's kaftan. 'They are beautiful.'

'Thank you,' Kunle responds with a smile. 'And yes, I have quite a few more. You know me.'

'Black one?'

'Yes. But the fit is more *relaxed* . . . I know you young people prefer slim.'

'First, Nigeria is too hot for slim fit. And fashion has come back around to your style . . . it's all relaxed fit now.'

Kunle chuckles. 'Ẹ̀ṣò aṣọ ìgbà kan tún padà wá,' he says in Yoruba, and then says in English, 'and for you . . . fashion is a wheel that keeps turning.'

'Oh, come on, Dad,' Remi jovially protests. 'I understood the Yoruba.'

'Really? Who are you speaking Yoruba with in London?'

'No one. But that doesn't mean I'll forget. We could've had this entire conversation in Yoruba.'

Kunle raises an eyebrow, doubtful. 'Ó dáa. Jẹ́ ká rí,' he says, and continues speaking in Yoruba. 'A black kaftan and other necessities will be delivered to the guest house in fifteen minutes.'

'Ẹ ṣé, Dad.'

Kunle nods and stands up, and Remi stands up as well. 'Shina has also arranged for one of the security officers who escorted you from the airport to be your personal security while you are in Lagos. He'll be with you at all times when you're outside this house,' Kunle says and continues before Remi can object. 'I know you don't like a crowd, so he will also be your driver. I met him last night, and I think you will like him.'

Remi isn't exactly pleased, but he acknowledges that it is better than the convoy of security officers he had earlier. 'I understand,' he says in Yoruba, and continues in Yoruba. 'Thank you, Dad.'

'I'm going to my office; I have work to do,' Kunle says, and turns to leave. But he pauses and turns back to Remi. He places a hand on Remi's shoulder. 'It is very good to see you, son,' he says.

The warmth in Kunle's words almost overwhelms Remi, but he buries the emotions. 'It's very good to see you too, Dad.'

Kunle nods, then leaves the room, heading to his home office. Remi lingers for a few moments before making his way back to the guest house.

CHAPTER 7

Remi approaches the front door of the guest house with a purposeful stride and hesitates when he realises he doesn't have a key. But the door is gently pulled open from the inside. Remi steps through the door, and Bola, who'd opened the door, greets him in Yoruba. Remi nods graciously and waits for Bola to stand up before he returns the greeting.

'Would you like the kaftan ironed, Oga Remi?' Bola asks, and gently shuts the door.

Remi doesn't respond for a brief moment as he considers if he even needs keys in this compound, where every front door is opened for him as if there is a proximity sensor embedded in his neck.

'How did you know I was approaching the door?' Remi asks, and smiles. 'Happened at the main house as well. It's very smooth.'

Bola smiles back, filled with pride. 'I was told,' he says, and gestures to an iPhone in his hand – a newer version than Remi's. 'When you left the main house and when you were getting closer to this door.'

'Hmm. Told by who?'

'Security, Oga Remi.'

'This is not just for me, right?'

'No, sir. Your family and any guests.'

Remi nods. 'I'm going out in a bit. Not sure when I'll be back, but it'll be late. I don't want you staying up just to open the door for me.'

'Don't worry, Oga Remi. I will be sleeping. But somebody will be here to open the door.'

Fair enough, Remi thinks. 'Does the kaftan *need* ironing?' he asks, knowing his dad has every clothing item steamed before being hung in his walk-in closet, which is larger than most new-build living rooms in London.

'No, Oga Remi. But we are not sure if you would like us to put pleats in the trousers. Oga doesn't like that, but we know it is the fashion.'

Remi fights back a smile. 'It is the fashion, I suppose. But I'm okay.'

'Okay, Oga Remi. I will bring it up to your bedroom.'

'Thanks,' Remi says, and walks towards the staircase. He stops and looks back over his shoulder to Bola. 'O mọ pé o lè bá mi sọ̀rọ̀ ní Yorùbá, abi?' he says, letting Bola know that he can speak to him in Yoruba.

'Bẹ́ẹ̀ ni, Oga Remi. A mọ̀. Mrs Ibeh sọ fún wa pé ká bá yín sọ̀rọ̀ ní English.'

Fair enough again, Remi thinks. He understands where Mrs Ibeh is coming from. 'No problem,' he says in English and walks up the stairs.

Remi walks down the staircase five minutes later, dressed in his dad's incredibly silky and light kaftan, which fits perfectly – a little short, but ankle length is *the fashion*, as Bola would say. Remi intends to ask for more of these kaftans to wear during the day because they're perfect for the Lagos sun. Yinka waits patiently by the door, holding a large brown envelope and an iPhone.

'E káalẹ̀, Remi,' Yinka says.

'Rara, Yinka. Please drop the "E",' Remi says, asking Yinka not to use the formal respectful honorific to refer to him. He reaches out for a fist bump. 'Káalẹ̀.'

Yinka meets the fist bump, then hands over the iPhone. 'It has a Nigerian SIM, and we have put all our numbers inside. Including Oga and Madam's.'

Remi nods, noting the phone is the same model as Bola's.

'The code is 1-1-1-1-1-1. The phone number is saved under your name.'

Remi unlocks the phone and scrolls through the contacts. 'I see it,' he confirms.

'Please change the code when you can.'

'I'll do it now,' Remi says, never one to procrastinate. He quickly switches the code to 1-4-0-7-2-1 – a date he'll never forget. The last time he saw his sister.

Yinka hands over the brown envelope, filled to the brim, and a sleek card holder with one bank card. 'From Oga,' he says.

Remi opens the envelope and is unsurprised, although slightly annoyed, by the number of 1,000-naira notes inside.

'How much is this?'

'Three million,' Yinka says. 'There is no limit on the card.'

'No limit?'

Yinka shrugs. 'That is what I was told. PIN is your year of birth.'

Remi wants to refuse the money because he doesn't need or want it. But not today. This is how his father shows love. 'Okay,' he says.

'Are you ready?'

'For the party?'

'Yes.'

'What time did it start?'

'The guests are expected to arrive from seven.'

Remi glances at the new phone for the time – it's 8:40 p.m. In his estimation, he'll get there roughly two hours *late* – the perfect time to arrive at a Nigerian party. However, Yetunde usually kicks off her events with eye-catching, social-media-friendly experiences designed to encourage early arrivals. Remi prefers to avoid those as well.

'I'm ready,' he says.

'Okay. Rasaq is waiting outside. Oga said he's spoken to you about him already. He's one of the two security officers you met at the airport today. He's excellent at what he does . . .'

'Which is?'

'Personal security. Rasaq was a decorated captain in the Nigerian army. He's been running his own personal security business for almost two years now. Very highly recommended. He can be like a ghost if you want him to be. But he also has a friendly approach. This is why Shina chose him for your personal security.'

'Because I like the friendly approach?'

'Oga believes so,' Yinka says, ending that line of questioning. He pauses, then adds, 'Shina asked me to greet you for him. He would've come himself, but he's . . . *making enquiries in his own way*. Trying to make sense of things. And to make sure you, Oga and Madam are safe.'

Remi nods. 'Please greet him for me.'

'Of course, Remi.'

Remi gestures towards the door. 'Okay. Let's meet Rasaq,' he says, already certain from the description which of the two security officers Rasaq is.

Yinka leads Remi out of the guest house, and Rasaq stands alert by the back door of a sleek black Bentley Continental. Remi is surprised by the choice of car but doesn't show it. He understands the optics, especially for such a short drive between two highly secure estates, and walks towards Rasaq. Instinctively, Rasaq attempts to prostrate, but Remi quickly raises a hand to stop him just as his shoulder dips.

'Please, none of that, Rasaq,' Remi says, and reaches for a handshake. 'And call me Remi. Otherwise, I'll have to call you Captain.'

Rasaq shakes Remi's hand firmly. 'Okay, Remi,' he says with a deep but friendly voice before glancing over Remi's shoulder to check that Yinka is comfortable with the informality. Yinka subtly dips his head, and Rasaq continues. 'Nice to meet you again. And I'm not a captain anymore.'

Remi had noticed the quick interaction between Rasaq and Yinka but doesn't acknowledge it. 'Nice to meet you as well,' he says. 'I know you're no longer a captain. Yinka's given me a quick briefing on you. And I'm sure you've been well briefed on me. I appreciate how thorough Yinka and the rest of the team here are, but some of their information might be a few years out of date.

So, do you have any questions, or is there anything you need from me to make your life easier?'

Rasaq glances over Remi's shoulder to check with Yinka again, but this time, Remi interjects before Yinka can react.

'Okay, no more of that,' Remi says, and turns to Yinka. 'Thanks, Yinka. Do you have anything more for us?'

'No, Remi. I just want to make sure you have everything you need.'

'I do. Wait – my dad mentioned an invitation.'

'I gave it to Rasaq.'

'Great,' Remi says. 'Just making sure we have it. Knowing Yetunde, we might need it to get through their gate.' He turns back to Yinka. 'We're all set, then.'

Yinka forces a smile, and for the first time, Remi notices the anxiety Yinka has been working hard to hide. Remi recalls that from the moment Yinka was hired, he was directly responsible for Remi and Kike's security. Now, Kike is dead, and he's handing over Remi's safety to someone else. No matter how excellent and well recommended Rasaq may be, this must be incredibly hard for Yinka.

Remi faces Yinka. 'I'll be all right,' he says reassuringly, and extends his arms for a hug. 'And come on.'

Yinka hesitates.

'Don't make me command you, oh,' Remi teases.

Yinka can't help but smile at the gentle humour, and the two share a warm embrace.

Rasaq watches them, genuinely surprised by Remi's good-hearted nature. He's worked for families far less affluent than the

Bankoles, and the adult children of those families, especially those educated overseas, either didn't acknowledge the staff or treated them like second-class citizens. And those were the *polite* ones.

'All right,' Remi says, and gestures for Yinka to leave. 'Jo, lọ.'

Remi watches Yinka walk back towards the main house for a few seconds before returning to Rasaq.

'So, any questions or instructions for me?' Remi asks.

'When we are outside,' Rasaq continues, his deep voice taking on a more serious tone, 'I will give you as much space as you require and not talk much. But when I do, you must listen and do what I say. Immediately. Do not question me or do your own thing. You can question me afterwards. Or even fire me. But you must first listen.'

Fair enough, Remi thinks, and nods. He's impressed by Rasaq's natural authority.

'And you are my priority. Not your friends or anyone else you ask me to protect. You first, others only when I decide you are safe.'

Again, fair enough, he thinks, and nods.

'Do you have any questions or instructions for me?'

'No,' Remi responds unequivocally.

Rasaq is surprised by the response, as he'd usually get a long list of instructions at this point, but Remi clearly has none. Rasaq nods and opens the back door.

'I'm sitting in the front,' Remi says, and opens the passenger door for himself. 'You focus on keeping me safe. I'll open doors myself. It might be the only chance I get.'

Remi laughs softly to himself as he shuts the door. Rasaq is puzzled by the laughter for a fleeting moment as he hurries around to step into the driver's seat.

Rasaq shuts the door and glances at Remi as he puts his seat belt on, ready to ask Remi to do the same. But to Rasaq's surprise, Remi is already strapped in. Rasaq notes that it must be a Western habit, as all his foreign clients who are briefly in Nigeria for business, politics, or *pleasure* wear their seat belts without him having to ask. He'll see how long Remi lasts when he remembers that wearing seat belts is far from the norm in Lagos.

Rasaq switches on the car's engine, which purrs to life with a satisfying rumble. He fights back a surge of delight at the chance to drive such a car. He's no stranger to luxury cars, as his foreign and local clients routinely rent similar cars for special nights out, however, on the rare occasion that he was inside the vehicle, he was in the passenger seat, brandishing an automatic rifle solely for the client's posturing – an essential accessory for his client's Instagram or TikTok videos. More often than not, he was in one of his company's security cars, either leading or trailing the luxury vehicle.

Rasaq switches on the air conditioning to full blast and picks the sleek black invitation card from the dashboard. It has Remi's name in gold on one side and an address on the other. He enters the address into the car's satnav, but Remi interrupts him.

'Where is it?'

Rasaq reads the address, and Remi nods – it's exactly where he expected the party to be. A lavish, bordering on garish, mansion ostensibly owned by a relative of the Chief's first wife. But in reality, it is owned by the Chief and used primarily for hosting parties or events. Remi knows the Chief doesn't live there but isn't sure which of the Chief's three wives (and their children) might. Or it could just be the Chief's adult offspring that live there now. The

Chief has seven kids from the three mothers – six daughters and one son, the latter being the youngest and currently in boarding school in the UK. Despite their mothers' constant and sometimes bitter battle for positioning, all the Chief's children get along admirably, led mainly by Yetunde, the oldest.

'I know it,' Remi says. 'It's fairly close. I'll direct you.'

Rasaq knows the neighbourhood where the party is relatively well. It's another exclusive estate in Ikoyi, with opulent mansions overlooking the Lagos Lagoon. It is not as secluded as the estate where the Bankoles reside but it is larger and certainly more extravagant. That estate wears its opulence as a badge of honour. Rasaq was simply putting in the address to get a direct route to the party, as there are several routes to get to the same location in that estate. But he doesn't point this out and graciously accepts Remi's offer to direct them.

'Thank you, Remi,' he says.

Rasaq drives through the compound towards the large gate, and it smoothly opens for them as they approach, which amuses Remi. Rasaq is puzzled by Remi's amusement but doesn't react and focuses on scanning the street ahead.

Remi assumes Rasaq is waiting for him to give directions and is about to speak when he notices the left indicator flashing – the correct direction. In hindsight, he surmises that Rasaq is well acquainted with the estate and was simply indulging him. After all, the estate is one of the most popular in Lagos, with more than a few people with dubious pasts, questionable ongoing activities and even murkier intentions – a client base tailor-made for Rasaq's particular set of skills.

Remi sits back and quietly watches Rasaq navigate out of his estate towards the party, making the correct decision at each turn, and his thoughts soon drift to the party. He'd avoided these sorts of parties for many years, even before everything broke between him and Kike, because they reminded him of the person he was desperate to forget – the seemingly entitled, self-absorbed and swaggering Remi of yesteryear. A lot of that persona was put on because he felt that was expected of him by his peers. But he wore it so convincingly that it became his identity. He hopes that his old friends and acquaintances no longer expect that version of him, but he knows otherwise because none of them have changed. He will have to play the part . . . for tonight only. It's the version of him they've embraced . . . even celebrated. And the one that'll let him move among them freely, without his real purpose being noticed.

He reaches into his pocket for his UK phone with his Apple Music account, but realises he's left it in his bedroom.

'Can you connect your phone to the car for some music?' Remi says, and takes the opportunity to put the brown envelope full of cash in the glove compartment. 'This phone is new, and I haven't connected my Apple Music.'

Rasaq glances at Remi, clearly hesitant.

'And I want to listen to your playlist,' Remi says. 'It'll tell me a lot about you.'

'No problem,' Rasaq says, excitedly accepting the challenge. 'Let me park first.'

Rasaq stops at the side of the road, connects his iPhone to the car's stereo, and scrolls to his Spotify account.

'No cheating,' Remi teases. 'Just put your favourite playlist on shuffle.'

'No cheating, lai lai,' Rasaq responds, picks a song, and continues driving.

Remi instantly recognises the song – 'Ask About Me' by Mohbad.

'Okay, okay, Rasaq,' he says, bumping along to the beat. 'Great start.'

'Oh, you know it?'

'Ahn ahn. Ọmọ Lagos ni mi now. And Afrobeats is played everywhere in London. In the gym, restaurants, shops, arenas . . . everywhere. And this song is on my playlist, too.'

'Good . . . good,' Rasaq says, proud.

'You been to London?'

'No, but soon, Lord willing.'

Remi nods. 'Travel much, though?' he asks.

'Yes. Just the past three years after I left the army. Mostly for work. I have travelled around Africa, the US, Canada, Dubai, and China. UK visa is tough.'

Remi nods again. 'China? How was that?'

'I don't know. Straight from airport to hotel and back to airport. Less than twelve hours. It was for work.'

'Must've been a fun twelve hours, though.'

'I'm not hoping for *fun* while working. Especially not in China.'

'True.'

The car approaches the gate leading to the estate where the party house is located, and Remi sits up, ready to speak to the security officers. But as soon as they spot the car, they open the gate for the car to drive through.

'Kí ló ń ṣẹlẹ̀,' Remi questions, amused by another gate opening for him without delay.

'Yinka called ahead for them to expect us,' Rasaq says, correctly reading the source of Remi's amusement.

'I'm sure he did,' Remi says, and notices that Rasaq is driving slowly and with less assurance. 'Want me to direct you now?'

'Yes, please.'

'I was waiting for that,' Remi says, half smiling, and directs Rasaq to the party's location.

Three minutes later, Remi bumps along to 'Holy Ghost' by Omah Lay as the car approaches the black and gold gate leading to the party. Several luxury cars are parked along the street leading to the mansion, and half a dozen heavily armed soldiers stand guard in front of the gate. Remi expects Rasaq to park outside beside the other cars. However, like clockwork, the soldiers step aside, and the gate is pulled open from the inside.

Rasaq scans the soldiers as he drives slowly past them into the opulent residence, and then another heavily armed soldier leads the car on foot as it crawls towards a makeshift car park with three other luxury cars.

'I know these boys,' Rasaq says.

'The soldiers?'

'Yes. They are 81st Division, like me. Same battalion but different company. I know their captain.'

Remi can sense the camaraderie and pride in Rasaq's voice. 'You miss being a soldier?'

'No,' he says, and laughs softly. 'But I miss being a captain. I miss leading my boys.'

'No girls then, eh?' Remi teases.

Rasaq laughs. 'Not in the 81st Division.'

Rasaq carefully parks in the space the soldier directs, and a young man waiting by the space attempts to open Remi's door, but Remi beats him to it and steps out of the car.

'Welcome, sir,' the young man says. 'Please follow me, sir.'

Remi nods.

Rasaq considers following Remi to the house's front door, but he knows that will be overkill. 'I'll wait in the car, Remi,' he says.

Remi looks over his shoulder at Rasaq. He's ticked off with himself because he hadn't considered what Rasaq would be doing while he was at the party. Rasaq wasn't just a driver to be left in the car, waiting for Oga to come out. Remi turns back to the young man.

'Can you arrange for some food for him?'

The young man hesitates. 'I'm not sure they will let me bring him food, sir,' he says.

'No problem,' Remi says. 'Don't worry.' He leans back into the car to open the glove compartment and pulls out a thick wad of 1,000-naira notes. He hands the wad of notes to Rasaq. 'Get some food for yourself and your 81st Division boys.'

Rasaq's eyes light up at the number of notes. 'Thank you, Remi. But this is . . .'

'Rara,' Remi interrupts. 'Have a good night. I'll be out in a couple of hours.'

'Thank you, Remi,' Rasaq repeats. 'I'll be around. But my number is in your phone if you need me before then.'

Remi nods and gestures for the young man to lead him to the party.

The grand front door of the mansion swings open as they approach, releasing a burst of Afrobeats from inside the house. Remi pauses at the threshold and takes a moment to compose himself before he wears the persona of the Remi he used to be and swaggers through the door.

CHAPTER 8

Remi is led through the darkly lit mansion's ground floor to a large manicured garden the size of a football field, which has been converted into an immersive celebration of luxury. There is a grand marquee with elegant tables set for casual dining and a photo booth in the corner, a chic cocktail lounge, and a dance floor, all surrounding a state-of-the-art stage framed by tastefully arranged plush seating for an intimate performance.

The young man passes Remi to a young hostess, who thankfully simply greets Remi with a slight bow, which Remi returns, before leading him through the illuminated pathway towards the heart of the party.

'Where would you like to go, sir?' the hostess asks with a slight French accent, and stops at an intersection leading to the different curated areas. 'Tems should be on stage in the next two minutes, so I'll suggest the stage. I will arrange for your drink of choice to be delivered to you.'

Remi scans the party. The stage area and dance floor are empty, with the guests socialising in the grand marquee and the cocktail lounge. To his surprise, he recognises almost all of the roughly fifty guests.

'I'd like to blend in for now, so the lounge.'

'Okay, sir,' the hostess says, and leads Remi to the lounge.

Michael Balogun, known as Balo to his mates, an old friend of Remi from boarding school who moved to the UK for university at the same time as Remi and is now married to one of Yetunde's closest friends, spots Remi the moment he steps into the lounge.

'Remz!' Balo exclaims and jumps off his comfortable chair. 'Is that you, *fam*?' he adds in a playful, exaggerated London accent as he strides towards Remi.

Remi is both amused and unexpectedly delighted to see Balo. He's also aware that all the eyes in the lounge have turned to him with varying degrees of surprise and intrigue, which Remi attributes to his sudden exit from the social scene four years ago. In the past, Remi would have maintained a cool composure, and suppressed most of his delight at seeing Balo. Now he cracks a genuine smile and struts to meet his friend halfway. They embrace, and Remi makes eye contact with a young woman he knows only socially, and she awkwardly smiles before looking away. Instinctively, he scans the room, searching for any expressions that hint at something beyond the expected surprise.

He only manages to scan about a quarter of the room before Balo pulls away from the embrace, and none of the reactions appear out of the ordinary.

'It's good to see you, Remz,' Balo says. 'But where have you been?'

'It's good to see you too, Balo,' Remi says, and subtly raises his voice so it carries across the lounge. 'I just got out. It was . . . *tough*.'

'Tough? What are you talking about? What . . . where did you get out from?'

'Prison,' Remi calmly says, scanning over Balo's other shoulder – again, nothing out of the ordinary. Just the piqued attention of those overhearing the conversation.

'Ehn,' Balo exclaims, shocked, and then whispers, 'what happened?'

Remi shrugs and exaggeratedly looks away from Balo as if embarrassed. But instead, he uses the opportunity to observe the remainder of the faces in the room – again, just the expected reactions.

'It's okay . . . it's okay,' Balo says with genuine concern. 'I don't need to . . .'

Balo's concern stabs at Remi, and he instantly ends the charade. 'Calm down, brother. I'm teasing.'

Balo shoves Remi, and they laugh.

'I can't believe you fell for that,' Remi says.

'Abeg shut up! We have not seen your brake light in three years. Your phone number stopped working. You left Instagram. Prison sounds very plausible if you think about it.'

'Fair. Just been focusing on work.'

'Ehen?' Balo questions with a raised eyebrow. 'C'mon, stop that nonsense. Is it only you that is working?'

Remi returns the raised eyebrow with a knowing smirk – a silent nod to their ongoing joke that Balo, despite being the managing director of his father's massively successful construction company, does no actual work.

'Get out, jọ,' Balo says, and they laugh. 'I'm working hard enough.'

'That's a lie,' a male voice interjects from a table behind Remi.

Remi and Balo turn to the voice, and Remi has to fight back the urge to burst into laughter. Seun Daniels – Derin Daniels's only child, heir to Derin's media empire, and one of Kike's old schoolmates – sits on a throne-like chair wearing an incredibly ostentatious outfit, highlighted by a deep purple high-collared blazer with golden buttons and intricate embroidery, complemented by a silk scarf delicately tied around his neck, large-framed sunglasses, and a fedora hat. Remi recalls that Seun was always flamboyant, even back in boarding school, but this outfit borders on parody. Yet, fashion is in the eye of the beholder, and Seun is wearing the outfit with unbridled confidence. Good for him, Remi thinks.

'This stupid fool,' Balo says with a casual familiarity that surprises Remi because Balo only had disdain for Seun in boarding school. But then Remi remembers that Balo's wife – Yetunde's friend – is Seun's first cousin, so they must've developed a fond relationship over the years. 'Shut your mouth,' Balo continues. 'What are you doing apart from *scouting talent* for one of your father's TV programmes.'

'Oh, behave, you idiot,' Seun says with equal familiarity. 'I'm an executive producer. And it's hard work finding the right talent.'

Remi gives only half his attention to the playful banter between Seun and Balo because his gaze is drawn to Eki, the news host he'd watched earlier that day. Eki is seated at the same table as Seun, engrossed in conversation with two young women Remi recognises from the social scene. Observing Eki in person, Remi notes that she's a far more impressive sight than her on-screen presence ever conveyed.

'Oh. I'm sure it's *hard*,' Balo says.

'Get your mind out the gutter, you neanderthal,' Seun retorts. 'I've got an eye for talent.' He gestures at Eki. 'I scouted Eki.'

Eki turns away from her conversation with Seun when she hears her name.

Balo rolls his eyes. 'Oh yes, you scouted your on-and-off girlfriend to work for your father. You had to look very far for that talent, I'm sure,' he says, and then turns to Eki. 'No disrespect,' he says to her, with a tone dripping with disrespect.

'Plenty disrespect, actually,' Seun quips. 'And this is coming from a man who is the managing director of his father's company and doesn't do one thing.'

Balo laughs. 'And what? We are not hiding that. That is straight nepotism. My father built the company. I'm his first son. Na like that it dey happen. But this wuru wuru one you are doing . . . me, I don't know.'

Remi can sense that Eki is hurt by Balo's words and insinuations. However, she bites her tongue and calmly turns back to her conversation.

'Be quiet,' Seun chides. 'And where is my cousin? Locked at home, abi? To clean and take care of your baby?'

'Your cousin hasn't lifted her finger to clean a day in her life!'

Seun and Balo laugh, and the hostess approaches Remi with a tray carrying one glass of gin and tonic.

'Gin and tonic,' she says, and offers Remi the glass, which he graciously accepts. 'Yetunde says that's your drink of choice.'

Remi nods.

'Yetunde is busy at the moment,' the hostess continues. 'But she says she'll come find you after Tems's performance, so you *must not* run off.'

Remi smiles – recalling how, ever since he and Yetunde were teenagers, their fathers had subtly tried to manoeuvre them into marriage. They'd even dated for about six months before Remi realised that a romantic relationship between them simply wouldn't work. Although Yetunde had agreed then, most of their friends and family believe she still carries a torch for him.

'I can't promise anything,' he says.

'Well, Remi, she's ordered security not to let you leave until she's seen you.'

'Touché.'

'Oui.'

'And that's where my French ends.'

The hostess laughs, then turns to the group to kindly ask everyone to follow her to the stage area, as Tems's performance is due to start once the guests are gathered around the stage.

As promised, Tems makes a dramatic entrance on to the stage just as all the guests settle around it, opening with a breathtaking performance of 'Me & You' – one of Remi's favourite songs. Remi is evidently far from alone in his appreciation of the song because the crowd erupts in excitement, dancing and singing along.

During Tems's performance, several old friends approach Remi and, like those in the cocktail lounge, express surprise and delight at seeing him. Remi tries to read for any underlying or suppressed reactions, but there is nothing.

Tems's performance draws to a spectacular close with 'Love Me JeJe', yet most of the guests linger around the stage as though waiting for an encore. Remi continues to socialise, engaging with as many people as possible, including Rose and her fiancé, hoping to spot a reaction that's out of the ordinary. But to no avail.

Ten minutes after Tems's performance, Yetunde, looking stunning, approaches Remi with a joyous smile. Remi smiles back, happy to see her looking so happy, and they embrace affectionately.

'How are you?' Yetunde asks, and leads Remi towards the near-empty cocktail lounge, with her assistant diligently following a few steps behind.

Remi can tell from Yetunde's demeanour that she doesn't know of Kike's death yet. Although she and Kike aren't as close as they once were as young kids – having drifted apart as their paths diverged, culminating in frequent clashes over their opposing views on patriarchy, with Kike staunchly against it – Yetunde still sees Kike as family. She would undoubtedly be affected by Kike's sudden, unexpected loss.

'I'm okay,' Remi says. 'How are you?'

'Good. Exhausted with all the planning . . .' She gestures at the party. 'But good. You know I love it.'

'I know,' Remi says, and smiles.

Yetunde and Remi sit across from each other in a quiet corner of the cocktail lounge.

'Sparkling water,' she says to her assistant, and turns to Remi. 'Another gin and tonic?'

Remi is surprised that Yetunde ordered sparkling water, but he doesn't show it. He turns to address Yetunde's assistant directly. 'Hey,' he greets, and she bows her head to return his greeting. 'I'll have the same.'

The assistant nods and heads to the bar.

'You've had your two-drink maximum, abi?' Yetunde asks, referring to Remi's policy of only having a maximum of two alcoholic drinks per occasion.

Remi nods, though he's barely had one.

'Same,' Yetunde says. 'I adopted your two-drink rule.'

Remi cracks an embarrassed smile. Her relentless social drinking was one of the many excuses he used to end their relationship. It was easier than telling her the truth – that she saw their marriage as inevitable, and he didn't.

'It's not about you,' Yetunde says, reading his embarrassment. 'I have a lot of things to focus on at my events, so I like to keep a clear head.'

'Fair.' He gestures at the party and mimics Future's voice. '*Sensational.*'

She laughs. 'Thank you. I love organising events, so I'll happily do it just for myself. But it's even better when everyone is having a great time.'

The assistant returns and places the glasses of ice-cold sparkling water in front of them before walking away to wait by the bar.

'They are,' Remi says before sipping from his glass of sparkling water. 'And Rose is over the moon.'

'Oh, you met her? Beautiful, right?'

'Yeah, sure.'

Yetunde chuckles. 'When we didn't work out, my dad tried to set you up with Rose. He thought maybe you preferred a lighter skin tone, straighter hair.'

'Wow,' Remi exclaims, with a wry smile.

'Oh yes. It could be true. I'm the last Nigerian you've dated.'

'How you do you know that?'

'It's a very small circle.'

Remi is tempted to ask which exact circle she means. However, he's sure she's referring to the exclusive circle of daughters of the Nigerian elite – a circle that, in truth, includes all his previous girlfriends before Yetunde. He shrugs.

'But no one could find you,' she continues. 'And my dad tried. Rose was keen, too.'

Remi hesitates before asking, 'And you were okay with this?'

The question amuses Yetunde, and she rolls her eyes. 'I know you love yourself. But I'm fine.'

'It's not that. I couldn't do it.'

'Yeah, yeah,' she says dismissively.

'Well, she looks happy with her fiancé.'

She smirks. 'That's your problem, isn't it? *Happiness* has little to do with it, Remi.'

Remi would love to debate the point, but not today. He nods.

Yetunde's assistant signals her from the bar, and she nods. 'I've got to go handle something,' she says, and leans over to kiss him softly on his cheek. 'It was lovely to see you.'

'It was lovely to see you too.'

'Are you going to be around for my birthday party?'

'Yes,' Remi lies, not remembering when her birthday is. 'I'll be there.'

'It's going to be incredible. In the meantime, we should have lunch or dinner soon. What's your number?'

'We should,' he says, and pulls out his phone for them to exchange numbers.

She stands, and he immediately stands as well. She's amused by the courteous gesture and kisses him on his cheek again before leaving the lounge with her assistant. Remi watches her walk away and is struck by the fact that she never mentioned Kike. He doesn't think it's because Yetunde has anything to do with Kike's death. It's more a clear indication that she's aware of his fallout with Kike. He flinches and wonders how many more people at the party know about the fallout, which might explain why they haven't brought Kike up to him.

He sighs and considers leaving, as his social battery is spent. However, he spots Eki alone at the cocktail bar, appearing somewhat ostracised – a sight that doesn't surprise Remi. Although Eki is from a wealthy family, they're not part of the elite of Lagos society like most others in the party. She's outside of the *very small circle* Yetunde referenced. Plus, her celebrity status, which would be an advantage in most other circumstances, is a disadvantage at an event like this. Because most of the guests will go out of their way to make her aware that – despite her being a celebrity – they believe her to be of much less status than them, they will diminish and trivialise her achievements, just like Balo did.

Remi walks to Eki, and she straightens up and wears the confident smile that he recognises from boarding school.

'I saw you on TV today,' Remi says. 'On a news programme discussing the Abuja thing. You were impressive.'

Eki is surprised by the compliment and doesn't bother to hide it. 'Thank you, Remi,' she says, visibly relaxing.

'You're welcome. The conversation was really engaging. How long have you been doing that?'

'I've been on TV for seven years. The lead news and current affairs host for the past two. Before that, I was mostly doing entertainment. Hosting reality shows and all that. Was fun. But I prefer news and current affairs.'

Remi nods. 'Looks like you found your calling.'

Eki smiles with appreciation. 'You're the last person I would've expected to give me a compliment. I don't think you said more than one word to me at a time in school. You used to act too cool for all of us. And I was one of Kike's closest friends. She used to abuse us for being your fangirls.'

Remi laughs softly and shrugs. 'I was pretentious.'

'We all were, Remi. Most of our friends still are. But you made it look good, and we all loved you for it.'

'Oh. Wow,' Remi says with genuine surprise.

'Please, stop. Don't act like you didn't know. You're still carrying yourself like everyone loves you.' She nods towards the guests. 'And I'm sure you've noticed they still do.'

'They missed me, that's all.'

She exaggeratedly rolls her eyes, and they laugh before smiling at each other.

'You enjoying the party?' she asks.

'Yeah,' he says without an ounce of enthusiasm.

'All right, Remi,' she says, amused by his lack of enthusiasm. 'Better not let Yetunde catch that attitude.'

'It's not that. It's an awesome party. It's just not the right time.' He shrugs. 'How about you? Are you enjoying the party?'

'Well, no.'

'That's direct.'

'Yes. I don't think Yetunde or Rose will care about my opinion of the party. I wasn't invited. Seun dragged me here as his plus-one at the last minute.'

Remi nods with understanding.

'I'm enjoying this conversation, though,' she adds.

'Thanks. Me too.'

They quietly stare at each other, smiling.

'Hello, Remi,' a female voice greets Remi from behind him.

Remi looks over his shoulder to Ngozi Chukwu, another of Kike's close friends from boarding school.

'Hey, Goz,' Remi says, and positions himself so he, Eki and Ngozi can easily see each other.

To Remi's surprise, the greeting between Ngozi and Eki is nothing more than a frosty smile.

'When did you get back from London?' Ngozi asks. 'I spoke to Kike a couple of days ago, and she didn't say you were around.'

'Got in today.'

'Oh. Okay. And where's Kike? She said she'll be here tonight.'

Remi notes that Ngozi is the first one to ask about Kike's whereabouts, but before he can respond, Seun joins them. 'Probably trying to avoid some of the people she's done her investigative reports on,' he nonchalantly interjects.

'Kike would never run from anyone,' Eki retorts with bite.

'I know, I know,' Seun says, and raises his hands in surrender. 'I was just—'

'What investigative reports?' Remi interrupts.

The other three turn to Remi, surprised he doesn't know.

'Are you living under a rock in London or something?' Seun teases.

'*What reports*?' Remi quietly but fiercely demands.

'Kike has an investigative programme on YouTube where she exposes corruption, mainly,' Ngozi responds. 'She's done four episodes now.'

Remi nods, puzzled as to why his father had not mentioned this.

'They are excellent,' Ngozi adds. 'She takes her time with each one – they are very well researched – and she aggressively challenges people with evidence when they try to lie during the interviews.'

'She interviews the people she investigates?' Remi asks.

'Yes,' Ngozi responds with pride. 'That's the highlight of each episode. And everyone watches. Each episode has about 500,000 views.'

'More than most of Eki's shows,' Seun quips.

'It's making real change,' Ngozi continues, ignoring Seun.

'I don't know about that,' Seun says. 'Well, more change than any of Eki's shows, that's for sure.'

Seun laughs, and Eki walks away.

'Ahn ahn, come on,' Seun says with a smirk, and follows after Eki.

'What's the name of the show?' Remi asks Ngozi, not paying any attention to Eki and Seun.

'*Spotlight Nigeria.*'

Remi falls silent, pondering whether Kike's *investigative programme* could be tied to her sudden death, and Ngozi watches him patiently. In truth, it isn't much of a consideration because Remi knows it's absolutely possible. After all, she wouldn't be the hundredth person in Nigeria to be killed for exposing or even just attempting to expose corruption. However, she just might be the first daughter of the elite to meet such a fate . . . not that many children of the elite are striving to expose corruption in the first place.

Remi gestures to the crowd and asks, 'Who here has she—'

'Remz!' an angry voice growls, interrupting Remi.

CHAPTER 9

Remi casually turns to the voice and doesn't recognise the burly man with a full beard. But he recognises the burning rage in the burly man's eyes.

'You good?' Remi asks.

'You don't remember me, do you?' the burly man slurs – he's tipsy.

Remi doesn't respond.

'You don't remember slapping me about, abi?' the burly man asks again, stepping closer to Remi and Ngozi.

A memory flashes into Remi's mind – one he'd rather forget, but it confirms the burly man and the source of his rage. Bode Aluko. He was in Kike's year in boarding school and was a notorious bully. Back then, Remi wouldn't have cared – he was two years above, and Bode wasn't on his radar. Not until Bode started harassing Kike, trying to pressure her into being his girlfriend.

Kike, far more emotionally intelligent and sharp, publicly humiliated him. Remi can't recall how she did, just the aftermath. How Bode raged, insulted her, then beat up the boy who stepped in to defend her.

That night, Remi visited Bode's dorm to remind him and the entire school why no one dared to mess with Kike. Bode left the school soon after. And Remi appreciates how that night might remain a traumatic experience for Bode, because the memory haunts Remi, serving as a troubled reminder of how far he'd go to protect his sister.

Remi steps forward to stand between the grown bully and Ngozi, who's frozen with fear.

'I remember you,' Remi calmly says. 'Bode, right?'

Bode cackles. 'You still think you're fresh, abi?' he asks. 'I will smash your head.'

Remi nods. He doesn't want this. Not today. 'I understand why you are angry. It's not something I'm going to apologise for. But I know I went too far.'

Bode cackles again. 'Coward!' he shouts, getting the attention of many more guests. 'Now that I'm a grown man, you don't want any trouble, abi?'

Grown man is a stretch, Remi wants to say. However, he doesn't want to inflame the situation. 'Okay. How do you want to handle this as a *grown man*?'

'I will smash your head with my grown-man fists!' Bode barks, taking Remi's words as a challenge.

Remi sighs and considers another approach to defuse the situation, but Bode approaches him with menace.

Remi shoves Bode back. Firm, controlled. Just enough to keep distance between them. 'I can't let you get close,' he says calmly.

'You can't do anything to stop me!' Bode takes off his expensive gold watch, tosses it to the floor, and raises his arms in a poor fighting stance.

'You're drunk. You're going to hurt yourself in front of all these people.'

'You too dey talk!'

Bode launches a wild punch, but Remi is already moving. He grabs Bode's collar mid swing and uses Bode's momentum to throw Bode over his hip. Bode crashes to the floor, winded, and Remi drops his weight on to Bode's chest. Remi pins Bode and drives his forearm into Bode's throat, choking him. Remi watches the rage in Bode's eyes give way to panic . . . then releases the choke just before the burly man passes out – struck by the quiet truth that he trained to compete, not to hurt.

Remi allows Bode to catch his breath. 'Apologise,' Remi demands.

Bode hesitates, looking around to gauge the number of spectators.

Remi leans in, tightening the choke again. 'Don't worry,' Remi says. 'We have an audience, and a few are even recording. So only God knows how many of their followers will watch me put you to sleep like a grown baby. Apologise, now.'

Bode nods, and Remi releases the choke. 'Sorry,' Bode croaks.

Remi could push. Make Bode grovel. But he doesn't. He stands up and takes a few steps away, and a few guests get in the middle of them as Bode struggles to stand up.

Remi notices Yetunde approach with two huge guards. 'It's okay,' he says aloud to no one in particular, but for Yetunde's attention. 'Bode has apologised. We're okay.'

Just then, Bode bends over and vomits, sparking laughter from several guests. Remi sees the rage return to Bode's eyes and braces himself for the inevitable. Sure enough, Bode charges at him, ploughing through the guests between them like a battering ram. Remi deftly sidesteps, grabs Bode's arm, and uses Bode's momentum to hurl him to the floor. Bode crashes face first, and Remi swiftly drops a knee on to Bode's back and twists Bode's arm into a tight wristlock. Bode screams.

Remi notices Yetunde casually direct the guards to escort Bode out of the party, and he keeps Bode's arm twisted until the guards bend over to pick Bode up.

'Don't touch me!' Bode yells at the guards, and struggles to break free from their tight grasp. 'Are you mad? Do you know who I am?'

'Be quiet, Bode,' Yetunde says. 'You're leaving. On your feet or they carry you out. Which one?'

Bode snarls and turns to Rose's fiancé, who nods, struggling to hide his embarrassment. Just like that, the fight leaves Bode.

'I need to find my watch,' he says.

One of the guests who picked up the watch earlier walks over to hand it to Bode, and then Bode is led out of the party.

'Okay, everyone. That part of the night's entertainment is over,' Yetunde says, and gestures to Remi. 'Let's all put our hands together for Remi. Such a wonderful performance.'

The mood lightens as most guests clap, and although Remi is uncomfortable with all the attention, he forces a smile.

Yetunde watches the guests disperse before she approaches Remi, and Remi braces himself for her deserved anger.

'I can't leave you alone for five minutes without you trying to steal all the attention,' Yetunde quips.

Remi is surprised by Yetunde's genuine composure. 'You're not angry?'

'Oh no, you've only made the party more memorable. And nobody got hurt.'

'Fair enough. I apologise, though. I tried to defuse the situation. But . . .'

'Don't worry. Nobody likes Bode anyway.'

'Then why invite him?'

'You don't remember Rose's fiancé's name.'

Remi shrugs.

'Tola Aluko. Bode is his first cousin.'

'Oh. Should I apologise to Tola?'

Yetunde raises a questioning eyebrow. 'Why? Even Tola knows Bode is an idiot. And anyway, what's Tola going to do? He's punching way above his weight with this *arrangement*. And his mother *needs* my father – and yours.'

Remi notes Yetunde's cold designation of the upcoming marriage as an arrangement, but he's more focused on the *need*. 'Why does his mother need their help?'

She shakes her head. 'You're really keeping out of the loop in London, aren't you? She's a senator and intends to run for governor of Ogun State in the next election. But the current governor, who will be running for re-election, has good backing.'

Remi understands why the senator needs the Chief's political clout, but questions why she needs his father, as Kunle Bankole is not the only man with extremely deep pockets in Lagos.

'Tola is a very sharp one as well, so he'll probably come and apologise to you soon,' Yetunde adds.

'He'll have to do it some other time. I'm going to bed.'

'Oh, I don't think you'll be leaving anytime soon,' she says, subtly gesturing to the guests. 'They all want to hang with you after that performance.'

Remi looks towards the guests and notices a few eyes glancing his way. He sighs, which amuses her.

'I'll leave you to it,' she says. 'You never know. You might be done in an hour.' She chuckles and kisses him on the cheek. 'I'll see you soon, yes? Answer your phone when I call.'

'I will.'

CHAPTER 10

Hours before the altercation between Remi and Bode

Rasaq watches Remi walk away towards the party, studying him carefully. Shina had warned him that Remi wouldn't show any outward signs of distress, but Rasaq is struck by how composed Remi appears just a day after his sister's sudden death, which only a handful of people know about. Rasaq is one of them, quietly entrusted with the news earlier that morning. He is no stranger to stoicism, but Remi and Kunle's complete lack of any visible reaction goes beyond mere restraint. Yet, according to Yinka, they seemed entirely *normal*.

However, in the brief time Rasaq had spent around Kunle, it was apparent to him that the man was quietly scheming. He recognised the signs – subtle but unmistakable – traits he had seen in a handful of standout senior army officers who always operated several steps ahead of everyone else.

Remi, however, was different. He didn't appear to be plotting anything; he simply seemed to be taking everything in stride, including attending this party – something Rasaq knew he was reluctant to do. Shina had all but confirmed as much during their briefing. It was also clear, without being said outright, that neither he nor Yinka thought it was the best idea under the circumstances. But Kunle wanted Remi there, and Shina was confident that Remi wouldn't be in any danger at the party.

A thought flickers through Rasaq's mind – what if Remi was simply better at hiding his machinations than anyone he'd ever encountered? Burying it all beneath his effortless charm and easy politeness. Rasaq's eyes drop to the thick wad of 1,000-naira notes Remi had handed him. Judging by the weight, it amounts to over 400,000 naira – nearly five times his monthly salary as a captain. Under different circumstances, such a casual display of wealth would quietly irritate him. But it doesn't. Because it feels sincere. Besides, Remi treated him with respect. And in Rasaq's opinion, that had little to do with Remi's years living and working in the less traditional West, because Rasaq had dealt with plenty of Western clients just as entitled and disdainful towards Nigerians of lower status.

'Private,' Rasaq calls to the armed slender soldier who had directed the car to the parking space.

The soldier is heading back towards the gate, but Rasaq's commanding tone stops him in his tracks. The soldier turns to Rasaq and instinctively recognises Rasaq's air of authority.

'Yes, sir,' the soldier responds. He considers saluting but doesn't.

'How una dey?'

The soldier hesitates. 'You be officer?'

'Not anymore. I don retire. I was captain in the 4th Mechanised Battalion.'

The soldier dips his head with respect. 'We are okay, sir.'

'How many una dey? My Oga talk say make I buy suya and coke for everybody.'

The soldier's eyes light up. 'Twelve, sir.'

Rasaq nods and walks quickly to catch up with the soldier, and they head towards the gate.

'All of una from the same company?' Rasaq asks.

'Yes, sir. Na our colonel send us here.'

'Colonel Shittu?'

'Yes, sir. Na him be that.'

Rasaq isn't surprised, as Colonel Shittu is a political animal, probably utilising his soldiers as free security to curry favour with the Nigerian elite.

'But this post better pass the other posts wey the colonel they give. We no dey get wahala for here. Everything quiet.'

'Una dey here every day?'

'No, sir. Only when they do party,' the soldier says, and sniggers. 'They dey do party plenty for here.'

Rasaq and the soldier approach the other soldiers standing guard inside the gate, and the soldier quickly introduces Rasaq as a former captain of the 4th Mechanised Battalion who will be buying them suya, instantly eliciting respectful greetings. Rasaq reciprocates the greetings and takes their soft drink order before he and the slender soldier step out of the gate and go through the same process with the soldiers guarding outside.

Rasaq scans the luxury cars parked along the mansion's high walls, counting the drivers and a few personal security officers, all keeping to themselves. He'll change that. He pulls out his phone and orders enough suya and soft drinks from Ikoyi Club for everyone.

The suya arrived roughly thirty minutes later, and once Rasaq announced that the suya and drinks were for everyone, the atmosphere became convivial as the men socialised and happily filled their bellies. The merriment only quietened twice – once when the men tried to catch a glimpse of Tems as she departed the party in a G-Wagon that was parked inside the gate, and again when Bode Aluko was ushered through the gates by two guards. Bode screamed for his driver as he launched a rage-fuelled tirade towards the guards, who didn't respond. The guards just watched to ensure Bode left in his car before returning to the mansion.

A few minutes after that, the slender soldier approaches Rasaq. 'It's your boss that caused that guy to turn mental,' he says in broken English.

'My boss? How?' Rasaq questions, surprised.

'Your boss beat the guy. Did some MMA moves on him. Two times!'

MMA moves, Rasaq ponders. That Remi is full of surprises, he notes. But then Rasaq recalls that Bode didn't appear injured; his clothes were dirty and rumpled, but he had no visible bruises. Rasaq fights back a smile as he supposes that getting beat up is different in these affluent circles.

'Who is he?' he asks, trying to gauge the possible fallout from the *beating*.

'Bode Aluko.'

Rasaq immediately recollects the last name, as Shina had given him a short briefing ahead of the party on Tola Aluko and his mother, Senator Tope Aluko. Shina hadn't mentioned that the senator has a son called Bode, and Rasaq knows Shina wouldn't miss out information like that.

'Is he related to Tola Aluko?'

'Yes. His cousin.'

Rasaq racks his mind for other well-known Alukos, but none come to mind. 'Are his parents also politicians?'

As Rasaq expected, the slender soldier shrugs.

Rasaq moves on. 'Are those big boys that escorted Bode with you guys?' he asks.

'Ah, no! We don't have permission to touch the guests, oh. The Madam brings them from Cameroon for the parties. Different guys every time, and they only speak small English.'

Rasaq appreciates the thinking behind that. It ensures the guards are not apprehensive about handling anyone and that things remain confidential.

'Thanks for letting me know,' he says.

They bump fists, and Rasaq returns to socialising with the others.

Several minutes later, Bode's car returns with two other vehicles filled with armed men. The cars screech to a halt in the middle of the road, and Bode jumps out of his car to lead the armed men – who are not wearing uniforms but are handling their weapons with training – towards the gate. The soldiers outside the gate are on edge and about to react, but Rasaq instinctively gestures for them to remain calm. They listen.

Bode bangs and kicks the gate, demanding it be opened. But nothing happens. He turns to the youngest soldier standing outside the gate.

'Open it, now!' he demands.

The young soldier hesitates. 'Madam talk say the gate don close for tonight.'

Bode strides to the young soldier and slaps him across the face. The soldier stumbles backwards and then keeps his eyes down, not wishing to show anger or insubordination.

'Open the gate!' Bode screams at the young soldier.

'Madam talk say the gate don close for tonight,' the young soldier repeats while keeping his eyes fixed to the floor.

Bode slaps the soldier a few more times and then kicks him to the ground. He reaches over to continue slapping him, but Rasaq has seen enough and steps in.

'The gates are locked, Mr Bode,' Rasaq says with his commanding tone, which perks the ears of the armed men around Bode. He calmly walks past Bode to help the young soldier back to his feet. 'It is the Madam's orders. Nothing can be done without her permission.'

Bode considers striking Rasaq, but something in Rasaq's demeanour tells him it's a terrible idea. 'Go get those boys that touched me. Bring them out now!'

'I can't do that, Mr Bode.'

'What do . . .'

'They work for the Madam personally. I will have to ask her permission.'

'Nonsense! Tell those baboons I want them out here now!'

Rasaq doesn't react and calmly watches Bode.

'Are you deaf?' one of Bode's men shouts.

Rasaq switches his attention to the man for just a second, which is enough for the man to recognise that he overstepped. Rasaq returns to calmly watching Bode.

'Are you trying me?' Bode demands.

'Not at all, sir. I'm just waiting for you to tell me to go and ask Madam for permission,' Rasaq smoothly responds.

Bode snarls, trying to hide his hesitation. He knows involving Yetunde is another terrible idea. But he's already gone too far. And she will be just as annoyed when she finds out he brought armed men to her gate.

'Yes!' he snaps. 'And ask her boyfriend to come out too. If he's a real man, he'll fight me fair and square right here.'

It quickly dawns on Rasaq that Remi is the *boyfriend,* and he dials his menace up a notch. Given the general lack of awareness surrounding Kunle Bankole's immense wealth and influence – Rasaq only caught a glimpse of the extent of both after he was hired to guard Remi – Rasaq focuses on the widely known dangerous ramifications of disrespecting Chief Kayode Adeleke. He turns to the men around Bode.

'Do you know whose house this is?' he asks.

The men exchange uneasy glances, then look towards Bode. They don't answer . . . they can't answer because they don't know. Bode didn't tell them.

'He didn't tell you, abi?'

'Don't talk to my guys. Talk to me!' Bode demands.

Rasaq ignores Bode and continues addressing the men. 'I'm not surprised,' he says. 'This is Chief Kayode Adeleke's house.' He pauses for effect, looking at each man in turn to confirm they recognise the name. 'Our esteemed former governor and senator.

And the *Madam* is his daughter, Yetunde Adeleke. I'm sure you see her in the newspapers all the time.'

'You better shut up, or I will slap you!' Bode growls. 'Go and bring me those baboons!'

Rasaq ignores him, watching regret, fear and simmering anger towards Bode slowly infest the men. Then, he pounces. 'After all this commotion tonight, Mr Bode's mother, father, grandfather, grandmother, uncle, aunty . . . everybody that cares for him . . . will beg and beg the Chief to forgive him. It will take time, but soon enough, he will be forgiven. The Madam will never invite him to any of these parties again, but Mr Bode will survive that.' He switches to Yoruba to properly deliver the menace in his next words. 'Wọ́n máa sọ̀ yín dànù.'

The meaning – that they will be discarded like trash – resonates heavily with each man.

'You should leave now,' Rasaq adds with finality.

'This idiot!' Bode says. 'You don't tell my guys what to do.'

One of the men behind Bode speaks up. 'Sir, we need to go and check with the senator first before we continue this.'

'What!' Bode snaps, and spins around to the men, ready to lambast them. But he quickly notices their resolve. He shakes his head and marches back to his car, still parked in the middle of the road. He steps into the back seat, slams the door shut, and the car drives off.

The men left behind are embarrassed and apologetic.

'Sir,' the man who spoke up earlier says to Rasaq. 'Please don't report us. We are from Ogun State. We didn't know.'

The comment confirms Rasaq's thoughts that they are Senator Aluko's personal security team.

Rasaq turns to check if the young soldier is okay with not reporting the incident, and the young soldier nods. Rasaq turns back to the men.

'Don't worry. Leave now. No harm, no foul.' A few of the men are perplexed by the idiom, so Rasaq adds in broken English, 'No wahala.'

The men hurry to their vehicles and drive off.

The convivial atmosphere never quite returns as most of the drivers and personal security men return to their cars. But Rasaq remains with the soldiers outside the gate, trying to lighten their mood with small talk as he'd done many times as a captain.

A few minutes later, the side gate is opened from the inside, and the soldier who opened the gate informs Rasaq that Remi is on his way out of the party. Rasaq wishes the soldiers an uneventful rest of the night and hurries through the side gate straight to the Bentley.

Rasaq slips into the driver's seat just before Remi emerges from the mansion and strides towards the car. Rasaq observes him carefully, scanning for any distress or lingering agitation from the confrontation with Bode. But aside from a hint of fatigue, Remi's composure remains unaffected.

Remi spots Rasaq in the driver's seat and smiles politely before opening the passenger door and sliding into the car.

'I hope you weren't waiting in the car all night,' Remi says, concerned.

'No, I spent some time with the boys,' Rasaq says, gesturing at the soldiers. He then remembers the substantial balance of the cash Remi handed him – the suya and coke cost just under 100,000 naira. He pulls the remaining money from his pocket.

'Ẹ ṣé. Everyone was grateful.'

Remi acknowledges the gratitude with a gracious nod and briefly lets his gaze linger on the cash. He looks back up at Rasaq and doesn't make a move to collect the money. Rasaq picks up on the unspoken cue and returns the cash to his pocket. Even in that interaction, Rasaq is impressed by how subtly Remi exerts his position.

Rasaq steers the car smoothly out of the parking spot and towards the gate, which slides open as they approach. He glances at Remi, half expecting some amusement at yet another door opening for him without effort. But Remi is distant, lost in thought, his expression unreadable.

Rasaq gives Remi space and focuses on the road as he drives back to the Bankole residence.

Several minutes pass before Remi breaks the silence.

'Have you ever watched *Spotlight Nigeria*?'

Rasaq hadn't watched it, but he'd heard plenty about it, particularly the episode on Malaki, the legendary Nigerian musician. He'd heard that it exposed the self-appointed *King of Surulere* – one of the most deprived and densely populated areas in Lagos – as a drug trafficker, shattering Malaki's carefully crafted reputation as the boy from the slums who used his talent and grind to create a successful business empire that provided opportunities for others like him to succeed. Rasaq intended to watch it, but programmes like that never made it to the top of his queue in his limited spare time.

'No, I haven't,' Rasaq says. 'But I've heard about it. Heard very good things.'

'From your friends?'

'I have not really been keeping up with friends lately. But I see mentions of the programmes on the group chats. Sharing video clips and memes. Especially from the Malaki episode.'

'Malaki?' Remi questions, more to himself, struggling to piece together his sister's strategy and motives.

'Supposedly, Malaki is a major drug pusher.'

'Hmm.'

That information provides valuable context for Remi but doesn't clarify why Kike would specifically target Malaki. He, and surely Kike, knows that Malaki isn't the only major player in Lagos's drug trade. Some of their friends' parents are just as established in the drug trade but have the advantage of hiding behind legitimate businesses, family names or political affiliations.

Rasaq studies Remi, surprised by his apparent lack of judgement. The revelation about Malaki shocked many, including Rasaq, given the musician's success and carefully cultivated image. Social media had erupted in outrage for months after the episode.

'It doesn't bother you that Malaki is a drug pusher?' he asks.

'No,' Remi responds casually. 'If it's not Malaki, it'll be someone else. There is a huge demand and a lot of money involved.'

Rasaq nods, although not in complete agreement. He understands the limitless demand and vast sums of money involved. However, despite not being as religious as he was growing up, he remains adamant that selling and using illegal drugs is *haram.*

'Does it bother you?' Remi asks, picking up on Rasaq's unease with the topic.

Rasaq is momentarily caught off guard by the question. He hadn't expected Remi to care about his opinion. However, he'd rather not divulge his genuine opinion because he doesn't want Remi to look at him like a judgemental fanatic. He glances at Remi to check his level of interest, and it is immediately apparent that Remi is observing him. Yinka had advised Rasaq never to lie to Remi. He hadn't explained why, and Rasaq had assumed it was simply to build trust quickly. But now, he realises it's more than that.

'It is haram,' Rasaq says, telling the truth.

Remi nods softly as if to say, *fair enough*. 'Are you devout?' he asks.

Rasaq is glad Remi asked. 'Not so much anymore. Less and less as I grew up.'

'But haram is haram, abi?' Remi asks, smiling.

'Yes,' Rasaq says, returning the smile. 'Haram is haram.'

Remi returns to his thoughts, and the car is quiet for the rest of the journey to the Bankole residence. As before, the gate opens as they approach the residence, and Rasaq guides the car to the front of Remi's guest house.

'See you tomorrow,' Remi says, and puts his fist up for a bump.

'See you tomorrow,' Rasaq repeats, and bumps Remi's fist with his. 'When would you like me to be ready?'

'I don't know. I don't have any plans. But I imagine my dad will have some for me. So you'll probably know before me.'

'Can I request something?'

Remi is intrigued. 'Sure.'

'Can we use another car?'

'Absolutely!' Remi says, amused. 'I was going to suggest it, but it seemed like you were enjoying driving this car.'

Once again, Rasaq is surprised – not just by Remi's choice of the word *suggest*, but by the fact that Remi would have let him continue driving the Bentley simply because he was enjoying it. He isn't used to clients who *suggest* rather than *instruct*, let alone ones who consider his enjoyment over their own preferences.

'Oh, I enjoy it. It's a fantastic car. But it draws too much attention. And it is not as safe as others.'

Remi nods. 'Pick whatever car you want. As long as the air conditioner is fully functioning.'

'Of course!'

'Have a good night.'

'You too, Remi.'

Remi steps out of the car. He walks towards the entrance of the guest house, and the door opens as he approaches.

CHAPTER 11

A knock on the bedroom door wakes Remi, and he instantly sits up in bed. He takes a moment to gather himself as he scans his bedroom in the guest house. The lights are switched on, and his laptop is beside him on the large bed, plugged into a nearby wall socket with its screen up. The sight reminds him that he'd drifted off, exhausted, as he waited for the laptop to charge enough to switch on and watch the *Spotlight Nigeria* episodes.

He'd fallen asleep in just his underwear, as is usual for him, so he grabs the kaftan trousers from last night, neatly set on the floor, and slips them on before responding to the knock.

'You can open the door,' he says.

Bola gently opens the door but remains just outside the bedroom. 'Good morning, Oga Remi,' he says, and prostrates.

'Morning, Bola,' Remi returns the greeting. 'Everything okay?'

'Yes, sir. Can I enter?'

Remi nods, and Bola walks in carrying a simple black short-sleeved kaftan.

'Oga is coming to pick you up in ten minutes,' Bola says, and gestures at the simple kaftan. 'He offered this for you to wear in case you don't have any casual *trad*.'

Remi knows his dad is well aware that he doesn't have any trad, making the simple kaftan more a subtle instruction than an offer. This piques Remi's curiosity about where they could be going. However, he knows Bola wouldn't have an idea, so he doesn't bother asking.

'No problem,' Remi says, and slides his hands into his trouser pockets for his phone, but it's not there – it's on the bed, just out of reach. 'What time is it?'

Bola carefully hangs the kaftan by a large mirror before responding. 'Just after 5 o'clock.'

Remi nods in thanks, the early hour only deepening his curiosity. He also understands why he doesn't feel rested, as he must've had at most three hours of sleep.

'Do you want any food or drink to take with you?'

Remi shrugs. 'I'm fine, thank you.'

'Okay, sir,' Bola says, and bows. He withdraws from the room and shuts the door.

Remi hurries to the bathroom to brush his teeth and wash his face before putting on the simple kaftan, which is made from the same luxurious material as his dad's other kaftans. He grabs his phone and heads down the stairs.

Bola is waiting by the front door, watching Remi approach.

'They've just arrived, sir,' he says before opening the door.

Remi pats him on the shoulder to thank him and steps out into the early morning darkness with hints of daylight seeping through. The two armoured Toyota Land Cruisers with tinted windows that picked him up from the airport are parked in the driveway, and one of the residence's security guards immediately opens the back seat of the second vehicle.

'Good morning, sir,' the security guard says, and gestures to the open door. 'Right this way, sir.'

'Thank you,' Remi says, and heads towards the car.

He steps into the back seat beside his father, who is wearing an identical kaftan in dark grey. 'Ẹ káàárọ̀, Dad,' Remi says as the security guard shuts the door behind him.

Kunle looks away from his iPad at Remi as the Land Cruisers set off. 'Káàárọ̀, Remi,' he says, and smiles softly before continuing in Yoruba. 'The kaftan fits you better than it does me.'

'Of course, Oga,' a tired, gruff voice says in Yoruba from the front passenger seat. 'Remi is the upgraded version.'

Kunle laughs softly, and Remi, recognising the gruff voice, turns to Shina. Approaching his late sixties, Shina looks as though he's aged a decade since Remi last saw him, though Remi is sure it's because of Kike's death. He looks drawn but also wired, as if he's been walking a tightrope for days but is incredibly determined to reach the other end.

Shina served Remi's grandfather before Kunle and has been the family's head of security for as long as Remi can remember. He was there for the past tragedies that shaped the *Bankole way*, standing guard as grief calcified into stoicism. Now, though Shina tries to follow his Oga's lead and put on a brave face, going so far as to attempt humour, Remi can see him fraying at the seams as the emotions threaten to break through.

'Ẹ káàárọ̀, Uncle Shina,' Remi greets.

'Káàárọ̀, my dear Remi,' Shina responds warmly. 'It's good to see you. You look very well.'

'Thank you, Uncle.'

Shina forces a smile and turns back to the road, as if to hide something he doesn't want Remi or Kunle to see.

Remi glances at Kunle, who gives a subtle nod – he's noticed it too.

'I'm sure you want to know where we are heading,' Kunle says, and gestures to his iPad. 'Give me a few minutes, and I'll fill you in.'

Remi nods, and Kunle returns to studiously working on his iPad. For a moment, Remi considers peeking at the screen to check what has his dad so focused at 5 a.m. But Remi knows his dad is a workaholic and has probably taken on more workload to keep his mind occupied. Instead, Remi shifts his attention to the quiet streets beyond the tinted, reinforced window.

The convoy glides out of the estate, picking up speed as they cruise through Ikoyi's main roads, bathed in the soft glow of streetlights. Remi watches the joggers – men and women of varying ages – moving unhurriedly. Running has never been his thing, so he admires their discipline, regardless of the near-perfect early morning weather. But more than that, he notes what their presence, especially the many solo runners, signifies – Ikoyi is a safe place . . . most of the time.

The vehicles swing on to Third Mainland Bridge and pick up even more speed as they weave through the light morning traffic. The bridge is busier, though most of the congestion is on the opposite side, with commuters making their daily journey from the more affordable Mainland to their jobs on the more prosperous Island.

Remi is captivated by the orange hues of the sun rising over the lagoon and its reflection dancing across the rippling water. He's at peace, but for only a brief moment.

'Remi,' Kunle calls, pulling Remi out of his peaceful moment. He waits for Remi to turn to him before continuing in Yoruba. 'I heard you had an eventful night.'

'It was nothing serious, Dad.'

'Not according to Senator Aluko. She's been trying to reach me for hours to apologise. But I hear you handled yourself very well at the party, and Rasaq took care of things outside.'

'Outside?' Remi repeats. 'What happened outside?'

'Rasaq didn't tell you,' Kunle calmly remarks. 'He didn't tell us either.' Kunle pauses, considering, and Remi can't tell if Kunle is angered by Rasaq not letting them know. 'Senator Aluko's nephew, the one you handled, went to the senator's house to bring her official security officers to . . .' He veers off track, his tone injected with a hint of irritation. 'I don't even know what that young man intended to do, but he must not have been thinking clearly or at all.' His tone returns to its usual calm, and he gets back on track. '. . . *cause trouble* at the party. Rasaq defused the situation outside the gate just before it boiled over. He then promised the senator's officers that he would not report the incident. He's a good operator, as advertised. And a man of his word. I like him. But Shina's right – he should have told us, especially now. So it's up to you.'

'What's up to me?' Remi asks.

'If we let him go.'

'Oh. Sounds like it wasn't that serious.'

'That Aluko boy brought young, eager soldiers with guns to confront other young, eager soldiers with guns in the middle of Banana Island,' Shina passionately interjects. 'That is a very serious matter, my dear Remi. These are things your personal security must inform us of so we can all ensure you remain safe.'

'I completely understand, Uncle,' Remi says with deference, and pauses for a beat as if weighing the options – but he isn't. 'I'd like to give him another chance. But please, Uncle, have a word with him to remind him of his duties and our expectations.'

Shina nods, seemingly appeased. 'No problem, Remi. I will get Yinka to handle it.'

Kunle watches the exchange with quiet admiration. He had known from the start that Remi wouldn't let Rasaq go, but he's impressed by how deftly Remi navigated Shina's strong objections.

'How was the party?' he asks Remi.

'It was good. Other than the incident with Bode. But everyone seemed to enjoy that . . . especially Yetunde.'

Kunle nods. 'Anyone ask of your sister?'

With that question, regardless of how casually Kunle asked it, Remi's suspicion of why Kunle had asked him to go to the party is confirmed. 'One person . . . Ngozi Chukwu.'

'Hmm.'

'I think most of the guests knew that Kike and I weren't on the best of terms . . . so they didn't bring her up.'

'Or maybe some of them *know*,' Shina interjects. 'So didn't bring her up or avoided you.'

'I don't think so,' Kunle responds. 'If any of them knew, I'd expect they'd want to bring your sister up around you. See how you react. Especially considering your sudden arrival from London. They would be unable to resist.'

Remi nods in agreement.

'That's why I wanted you to go, Remi,' Kunle confirms.

'I understand,' Remi says.

'How was the interaction with Ngozi?'

'This Chukwu is the former president of Paramount Bank, abi?' Shina cuts in.

'Yes,' Kunle confirms, turning to Shina. 'That's Ngozi's father. I'm sure you've met Ngozi . . . she has been at the house many times.'

Kunle turns back to Remi, and Remi reads the unspoken cue to answer Kunle's question.

'It was ultimately interrupted by Bode. But she approached me when I was speaking to Eki Abbey . . .'

'The television personality?'

Remi is slightly irritated by the repeated interruptions, but if Kunle is, he doesn't show any signs. Kunle just stares at Remi, waiting for him to continue.

'Yes, she is,' Remi responds. 'She and Ngozi were classmates with Kike in secondary school.' He waits for Shina to acknowledge the response before continuing. 'Ngozi asked where Kike was and mentioned that Kike told her she'd be at the party. But before I could answer, Seun Daniels inserted himself into the conversation with an unfunny joke that Kike was probably avoiding the subjects of *Spotlight Nigeria*.'

Remi deliberately stresses *Spotlight Nigeria*, hoping to trigger a reaction from Kunle. But before his father can even respond, Shina interjects again.

'Seun Daniels . . . that's the gay one, abi?' Shina remarks.

'He's not gay,' Remi responds, his irritation flashing in his tone. He quickly tamps it down and continues. 'Camp? Yes. But he's straight.'

'Camp?' Shina repeats with contempt. 'Which one is that now?'

'Don't worry, Uncle Shina,' Remi says, not wanting to go further down that rabbit hole. 'But Seun is straight.'

'That's not what the society papers and magazines are implying,' Shina says.

'Probably his father's competitors pushing those implications,' Kunle adds.

'Must be,' Shina agrees. 'But Seun is not helping matters. Not at all. He's always present in the society pages . . . at this event or the other . . . posing for pictures in ridiculous clothes. Even in his father's magazines.'

Something about that strikes Kunle as unusual. He knows Seun's mother is a ruthless operator who wouldn't allow such rumours to persist unchecked. Plus, the Danielses have the power and connections to crush any editor or magazine in Nigeria that dared to print such implications . . . no matter how subtle. Kunle considers it for a moment longer before dismissing the thought. Ultimately, it's of no importance to him.

The vehicles suddenly veer off the bridge at the next exit, and Remi turns to look out the window, trying to find his bearings. He doesn't remember ever taking this exit.

'We're going to Ebuto Ero police station,' Kunle says. 'That's where the investigation is based, and Shina has set up a meeting with the head of the station and the officer in charge of the investigation.'

There are so many questions swirling in Remi's head, but even through them, he notes again that his father still can't bring himself to mention Kike's death.

'Why is the investigation based there?' he asks, immediately answering his question with another question. 'Did Kike die around there?'

Kunle doesn't respond, calmly staring at Remi, and Shina steps in. 'We do not know where Kike died, my dear Remi.'

'But . . .' Remi begins to say.

'But her body was found around there,' Shina interrupts.

The comment unsettles Remi, and he fights back the mental image of his sister's lifeless body being discovered by a stranger in some desolate place. He glances at Kunle, and there isn't a crack to his father's composed demeanour, which unexpectedly strengthens him.

Remi turns back to Shina. 'Are we expecting an update on the investigation?' he asks.

'Not sure,' Shina admits. 'We have been pushing for one, but nothing concrete has been shared so far. So I arranged this meeting to ginger them. I gave them six hours' notice, so I'm sure they will have something for us. Otherwise . . .' Shina trails off, letting the silence speak for itself and leaving the repercussions to Remi's imagination.

Remi nods, and the car falls silent. He turns to watch the street, wondering how close he is to the place where Kike's body was found.

CHAPTER 12

A few minutes later, the vehicles carefully navigate several large muddy potholes to park in a secluded area behind the run-down police station. Shina makes a call on his mobile phone and puts it to his ear.

'A ti dé,' Shina says, and pauses briefly to listen to the person speaking on the other end before continuing in Yoruba. 'Yes, I'm with my Oga and his son.' Pauses to listen. 'We are parked at the back.' Pause. 'No problem, we will wait. Two minutes.'

Shina ends the call and turns to Kunle and Remi. 'The head of the station – Chief Superintendent Akomolafe – will come himself to take us inside.'

Two minutes later, a small gate is pulled open, and Chief Superintendent Akomolafe, a slightly overweight man in his late forties dressed in his police uniform, hurries through the gate, followed by two junior police officers. Chief Akomolafe is anxious and doesn't look like he's slept since Shina called to arrange this meeting. He spots the vehicles and straightens up before heading towards them.

'Let's step out,' Kunle says. 'Shina, tell Yinka and the others in the second car to stay inside. Chief Akomolafe looks nervous enough already.'

Kunle, Remi, and Shina exit the car, and Shina quickly signals to the second vehicle before stepping towards the approaching chief superintendent.

Shina and Chief Akomolafe exchange a firm handshake, and Remi notes the measured familiarity between them.

Shina then introduces Chief Akomolafe to Kunle, followed by Remi. Chief Akomolafe dips his head slightly as he greets each of them with a firm handshake.

'Please follow me,' Chief Akomolafe says. 'Senior Inspector Moshood – the most experienced investigative officer in my command – is leading the investigation. He is a very thorough man. He will join us in my office for the meeting. But first, I want to show you the work my other officers have been doing.'

Shina shoots a quick glance at Kunle, who nods almost imperceptibly. 'Okay,' Shina says, and gestures for Chief Akomolafe to lead.

Chief Akomolafe turns and commands the two junior officers to walk ahead of him. They immediately heed, and he follows, with Shina, Kunle and Remi a few steps behind.

One of the officers keeps the back gate open for the others to walk through, and Chief Akomolafe commands the officer to shut the gate and wait there for further instructions.

Chief Akomolafe marches through the station compound to a side entrance, and the other junior officer quickly unlocks it for the chief and the others to step into a tight corridor. The moment Remi steps through the door, he is almost overwhelmed by the stifling heat and the stench – a mix of stale sweat, body odour and the building's decay.

The door shuts behind Remi, and a wave of voices crashes over him. Loud, harrowing pleas interspersed with equally loud and aggressive commands are coming from behind the door at the end of the corridor. The door opens as they approach, and Remi can pick out individual voices in the sea of distress, which causes him to flinch and almost pull back. But he catches himself and walks through the door into the dark holding area of the police station, with four large cells. Three of the cells are overcrowded with men, mostly in their late teens to mid twenties, who have now switched the focus of their cries for mercy to the new group that just entered with Chief Akomolafe, immediately appreciating that this is where the authority lies. Three officers are working over another man in his late thirties in the last cell, intentionally in plain sight of the others. Remi quickly scans the men, trying not to make eye contact, and he can tell that each has already had at least one round in the 'interrogation' cell.

'These are all the area boys that are causing trouble for us around here,' Chief Akomolafe says with pride, and gestures to the man being worked over. 'This agbàyà is the ring leader.'

Shina nods. Kunle and Remi do not react, although Remi struggles to hide his fury at the treatment of the men.

'My officers rounded them up last night, and we have just started questioning them.'

'We don't know anything!' someone cries from a cell, and a baton cracks against the bars before one of the officers orders the men to shut up.

'Any useful information?' Shina asks Chief Akomolafe.

'Not yet,' Chief Akomolafe says. 'As I said, we just started. One of them must know something.'

Shina gestures to the ring leader, who is in a flood of tears, his spirit broken. 'He wants to speak,' he says.

'Oya now!' the officer nearest to the ring leader commands, kicking him.

The ring leader recoils and then tries again to muster words, but he's incoherent. The officer slaps him across the face and commands him to speak *properly*.

'We are done here,' Kunle says in Yoruba with his usual composure. 'Let's go speak to your senior inspector.'

Chief Akomolafe is stung by Kunle's cold response to his efforts, especially in front of his officers, whom he'd driven hard for the past six hours to round up and interrogate the area boys, hoping to impress. However, he knows better than to show his annoyance to Kunle or, even worse, Shina, whose reputation as the sharp, unflinching edge to the Bankoles' otherwise poised image precedes him.

'Yes, sir,' Chief Akomolafe says to Kunle before turning to his officers. 'Continue. Get me answers kíà kíà!'

Chief Akomolafe leads Shina, Kunle, and Remi out of the holding area, and the area boys' frantic pleas crescendo to an almost deafening level as they watch their best chance for mercy and an early release depart.

Chief Akomolafe leads them through the police station, past tired officers who straighten at the sound of his approach. He slows down considerably as he climbs the stairs, his own exhaustion and lack of fitness combining to ensure that every step is deliberate.

At the top, Chief Akomolafe shoves the door leading to his office with exaggerated force, startling his secretary awake.

She shoots up to her feet, then drops to her knees when she sees the others walk in behind Chief Akomolafe.

'Ẹ káàárọ̀,' she greets, trying to hide her alarm. She had not been informed, so she had not prepared the office for such lofty guests – there weren't even enough chairs.

Kunle, Remi and Shina nod to acknowledge the secretary's greeting, but Chief Akomolafe doesn't.

'Is Moshood inside?' Chief Akomolafe asks, walking to the inner door into his office.

'Yes, sir,' the secretary confirms.

Chief Akomolafe opens the door to his office and scowls at the chairs – there is only one available for the guests. 'What nonsense is this?' he barks, turning to his secretary. 'Oya, bring your chair and go and get another one.'

The secretary picks up her chair, but as she hurries past Remi, he gently stops her.

'I will take this one inside,' Remi says. 'Go get the other one.'

'No. It's okay, sir,' she says, near frantic, and glances at the others following Chief Akomolafe into the office. 'I will be quick, sir.'

Remi steps aside, and the secretary rushes into the office. He walks in after her.

Inside the office, Senior Inspector Moshood, a tall and wiry man in his late forties, had been pacing restlessly beside Chief

Akomolafe's desk, too anxious to sit as he waited for the meeting with Chief Akomolafe and Shina. Moshood is running on fumes, having barely closed his eyes since being assigned the case. Chief Akomolafe had passionately made the stakes painfully clear – the investigation concerned the Bankoles, with their vast wealth and far-reaching influence, all of which was unknown to Moshood. Chief Akomolafe was clear . . . failure was not an option.

To stay alert, Moshood had downed a large mug of strong coffee laced with four heaped spoons of sugar before entering the office. It had jolted his system awake and sharpened his focus for the meeting.

Moshood now heard the outer room door open, quickly sat down, and tried to settle himself to appear composed. He noticed the footsteps in the outer room were more than expected but wasn't worried because he assumed some officers escorted Shina and Chief Akomolafe – they would be waiting outside as was customary. However, once Chief Akomolafe opened the door and Moshood caught a glimpse of Kunle Bankole over Chief Akomolafe's shoulder, all the composure Moshood had managed to muster dissolved.

Chief Akomolafe walks around to his side of the desk, greeting Moshood with a heavy pat on the back, ostensibly to show support but more to break Moshood out of his daze, as Moshood hadn't even stood up to greet their visitors. Moshood reads the cue and leaps off his chair with a sudden caffeine-fuelled burst of energy, which causes Shina to glare at him with deathly menace. Moshood forces a smile in apology and instinctively prostrates to greet the guests, which is out of place for a man of his age and office. Kunle is used to this kind of reverence, and Shina has witnessed it more times than he can count. They wait for Moshood to stand up before greeting him with a respectful nod.

Remi is less familiar with such displays and is further struck by how close Moshood is to being overwhelmed by their presence.

'Ẹ kááàrọ̀, Senior Inspector,' he says with warmth and respect, hoping to calm Moshood and remind him of his hard-earned station.

Moshood smiles graciously, then turns back to the desk as Chief Akomolafe gestures for the guests to sit at the three chairs squeezed opposite his desk. Kunle and Shina sit, and Moshood steps aside for Remi to take the last chair, but Remi shakes his head.

'Please sit, Senior Inspector,' Remi says, gesturing to the empty chair. 'I'll wait for the one that is coming.'

Moshood nods and returns to the desk to take the seat mere inches beside Shina, trying not to be unsettled by Shina's barely contained presence.

'Senior Inspector Moshood,' Chief Akomolafe says, and gestures to the files on his desk in front of Moshood. 'Please update us on the investigation.'

'Yes, sir.'

Moshood quickly rearranges the files, bringing the file at the bottom to the top. He had planned to go through each line of enquiry, starting with the least promising and ending on a high note with the most promising, which his officers are actively pursuing. But Moshood doesn't think he has enough saliva or nerve to go through all of them, and he's certain Kunle will only be interested in the most promising.

Moshood clears his throat to begin speaking, but the secretary rushes in with the last chair, and he waits. The secretary places the chair beside Remi, and Remi softly thanks her before sitting. She hurries out, and Moshood clears his throat again.

'We were able to reduce the time frame for when the body was placed at the location to a one-hour window between 4 and 5 a.m. on Wednesday morning,' Moshood says. 'And . . .'

'How?' Shina interrupts. 'How did you do that?'

Moshood hesitates and glances at Kunle and Remi, unsure how vivid he should be. 'We confirmed the time the . . . pile of garbage the body was placed on was dumped at the site and the time the body was found.'

Remi is stunned by the revelation. Until now, he hadn't known any details of Kike's death, or where her body was found. He shifts in his seat, but that is the extent of his response.

Shina nods for Moshood to continue.

'There is only one route to that location by car, and we found a good-quality security camera with a good view of one of the streets on the route. Nine cars used that street during the window. We have located eight of those cars and interviewed the drivers. None are involved – we examined their alibis and the vehicles. However, one of the drivers is a potential witness because he saw the ninth car driving out of the dump site with its headlights off. We have a partial plate number from the camera. And I have put that and the car's description as a priority search for all police in Lagos and Ogun State.'

Moshood stops speaking and stares at the men in the room, hoping for a reaction. Chief Akomolafe seems pleased, although he just might be putting on a brave face. Kunle and Remi have no reaction. But Shina appears furious.

'Is that it?' Shina demands.

'We are also asking those area boys about the car,' Chief Akomolafe adds. 'At least one of them will have seen or know the car.'

'What car is it?'

Moshood hesitates because he'd hoped that question was not asked. 'White Toyota Camry,' he says, knowing that Shina would immediately recognise that as the most popular car in Lagos.

Shina shakes his head, his fury threatening to boil over. 'Did your witness see the driver or a passenger?'

'No. It was too dark.'

'What is this?' Shina growls and briefly glares at Chief Akomolafe before returning his glare to Moshood. 'What about your other files?'

'These lines of enquiry are not as developed.'

Shina laughs uncontrollably, but there is no humour to it. Just burning rage.

Moshood is consumed with fear and glances at Chief Akomolafe for help, but no help is forthcoming.

'What about the man that found the body?' Chief Akomolafe asks Moshood. 'I told you to allow me and my boys to *question* him and his son. I will get something from them.'

'I released them,' Moshood says, showing his backbone for the first time. 'I confirmed their statements. I spoke to the Danfo driver who dropped them off myself, and we saw them on the camera walking to the site. They were not involved, and the boy was getting badly sick in our custody.'

'No. No. No. You must bring them back for me to question personally. It was – '

'Gbé ẹnu rẹ ṣónù!' Shina cuts off Chief Akomolafe, commanding him to shut up. 'This is a shambles. I will be sure to let Umar know of this,' he says, referring to the recently appointed Inspector General of the Nigerian Police – the most senior police officer – by first name.

Chief Akomolafe and Moshood are stricken with fear by the reference to their ultimate boss.

Moshood recovers first and looks to Chief Akomolafe, hoping he'll say something to assuage Shina's fury. But he quickly sees that Chief Akomolafe has yet to muster the nerve to speak, so he does.

'Just give us a couple more days,' Moshood pleads. 'We will locate the car.'

'Come on, Moshood!' Shina chides. 'The car is probably in the lagoon. Or it's crushed or torn to pieces in some scrapyard. But let's say you find the car in one piece. What next, ehn? You think whoever is responsible for this would have used their own car, abi? Or maybe their mother's car? What, Moshood? What?'

Shina shakes his head with anger, and as he does, his eyes lock with Kunle's enough for him to read Kunle's subtle gesture that it's time to leave.

'We are going,' Shina says, and stands. 'You will hear from Umar personally very soon.'

Shina patiently waits for Kunle and Remi to stand up and then leads them out of the office.

CHAPTER 13

Shina leads Kunle and Remi back towards the vehicles parked behind the police station. Shina is still visibly furious and wants to lash out at the incompetence of Chief Akomolafe and Moshood, but he knows Kunle will not take kindly to that public display of fury, and so is holding back until they are inside the car. He'd tried to hurry Kunle and Remi out of the station and back to the car by walking at a brisker pace than usual, but Kunle and Remi maintained their usual calm pace, and he had to slow down.

Yinka and another security officer step out of the passenger seats of the second vehicle and walk briskly to open the back doors of the first vehicle for Kunle and Remi to step in. Yinka, recognising Shina's anger, was careful to stay out of his way and give him enough space to swing the front passenger-side door open.

As soon as Yinka and the other officer close the car's doors, Kunle signals the driver to remain parked, then breaks the silence.

'What do you think?' he asks, turning to face Remi, ensuring that Shina gets the clear message to wait and hopefully calm down before speaking.

'About what exactly, Dad?'

Kunle nods, appreciating that his question was broad. 'Do you think their investigation will be fruitful?'

'No, Dad. Inspector Moshood seems to be doing as much as he can and will continue to do so. But I don't think his investigation will be fruitful.'

'I agree,' Kunle adds, and turns to Shina. 'We already know where you stand.'

'Yes, Oga,' Shina passionately responds, the tap bursting open. 'Absolute non – '

Kunle raises a hand to stop Shina. 'You will give it a few minutes –' *to calm down* is left unspoken – 'then you will call Chief Akomolafe and arrange for those men in the cells to be released. You will then arrange to show our gratitude to Chief Akomolafe and Inspector Moshood. Good amounts. Much more for the inspector, and you make sure they both know that.'

'Yes, Oga,' Shina obediently responds, grasping from Kunle's tone that this is not a point for discussion. 'You want them to stop their investigation?'

'No. Leave them to do their jobs. But make sure they report any important information to you first.'

Shina nods, silently acknowledging and accepting Kunle's instructions.

Kunle turns to Remi. 'I'm very sorry you had to hear some of those details like that,' he says, completely heartfelt. 'I was hoping your mother would've returned by now. But things are moving quickly, and I did not want to leave you out of this meeting. I knew it would be important to you. Plus, selfishly, I wanted you there for your insights.'

Remi unconsciously raises an eyebrow in response to his father's last comment, and his father catches the reaction before Remi drops the eyebrow.

'You know what I mean,' Kunle says with a hint of reprimand.

'Yes, Dad. I do,' Remi says, and pauses for a beat before continuing. 'Thank you for bringing me. It was important to me to be there. I would also like to know all the . . .' Remi pauses again, knowing his dad also wants him to know all the details.

'I understand, Remi. You've been patient, and I know you will continue to be patient if I ask. But considering what you have already heard, it's best I tell you now what we know. Honestly, Remi, I expected to know much more by now, but . . .' Kunle sighs, gathering himself. 'She was found at the garbage dump by the lagoon at 6 a.m. She was not killed there, but her body was placed there. The pathologist said it was blunt force trauma to the back of her head. A single powerful strike with something small but very hard . . .'

Kunle pauses, noticing the strain in Remi's eyes. 'Breathe, Remi,' he says gently, placing a hand on Remi's knee.

Only then does Remi realise he's been holding his breath, battling to stay composed. He exhales slowly, then glances at Shina, who is silent, staring straight ahead with tears sliding down his weathered face. Remi turns back to his father, his expression now a careful mask of calm.

'Should I continue?' Kunle asks.

Remi nods.

'She died instantly. The pathologist places the time of death just after midnight, early Wednesday morning. There were some marks on her body, inflicted after death.'

Remi's eyes flare, and Kunle raises a hand to steady him.

'She was strangled. Then some bruising from being moved.' He pauses. 'She was found naked, placed on the largest heap of refuse at the site . . . after being washed. But there are no signs of sexual assault.'

Remi focuses on keeping his breaths steady, then nods.

'We will find them,' Shina declares. 'And we will deal with them. *Thoroughly.*'

Kunle nods. 'We will.'

'We will,' Remi echoes, like a mantra.

Silence settles over the car.

After a moment, Remi asks, 'Do you know when Mum will be back?'

Kunle tries to hide it, but Remi detects a flash of anger directed at his mother for her absence. 'I don't know, Remi. Her phone is still off. But this is her typical pattern of behaviour during prayer camp. And we know she is safe. Nike is the head of your mother's personal affairs. She's there at the camp with a few of her staff. Shina has spoken to her a few times already.'

Shina is Nike's father, so Kunle turns to him to fill in any relevant information from the conversations with his daughter.

'Yes, Madam is safe,' Shina says. 'Nike is sure of that. But Nike hasn't been able to speak to her. She has passed some messages. But we are not . . . You know Nike and your sister were very close, so we are not telling Nike the true reason why we want your mother to return home, because Nike will not . . .' He pauses, struggling with his emotions. 'Will not handle the news . . .'

Shina pauses again to wipe his teary eyes, and Remi fights to hold back his emotions as he watches. But then Kunle unexpectedly leans forward to place a gentle hand on Shina's shoulder, reassuring Shina and Remi.

'If Nike knows, it will be very difficult for her not to tell your mother. I want to tell her the news myself.'

Remi nods, understanding. 'What about the messages being passed to her?'

Kunle turns to check if Shina is okay with responding, and Shina seizes the cue.

'Yes,' Shina confirms. 'The messages are that there is a very urgent matter your father wants to discuss in person. And every six hours or so, Nike sends another message about the matter becoming more urgent.'

'And we are sure she is getting these messages?'

'Yes. Nike is sure.'

Remi is surprised and visibly angry that his mother is ignoring such messages.

'I made a mistake with the first message,' Kunle adds, noticing Remi's anger. 'I tried to introduce more urgency . . . said I needed to speak to her in person before travelling. She saw through that.'

Remi nods, sensing that his father doesn't want him angry with his mother during this trying time for the family.

'Why can't Nike approach her directly?' he asks Shina.

Shina uncharacteristically hesitates, then glances at Kunle to check how to respond. Kunle dips his head to the side ever so slightly, and he can tell that Shina got the signal. Kunle is also aware that Remi picked up on the subtle interaction, so Remi will easily spot that Shina isn't telling the entire truth – which was the intention.

'Madam is part of the church's inner circle,' Shina says. 'So she is secluded from the other churchgoers during the camp.'

'There is VIP in prayer camp now?'

Shina chuckles, but Kunle doesn't react, so he quickly cuts off his laughter. 'Something like that,' he says.

As Kunle expected, Remi knows Shina's response is not close to the truth, but as close to the truth as he will get during this conversation.

Shina's iPhone notifies him of a WhatsApp message from Yinka, and he doesn't need to open the message because he gets the gist from the preview on his screen.

'Rasaq has arrived,' he says.

Remi is unsure what to make of Rasaq's arrival, but before he can speak, Kunle steps in.

'Rasaq will take you back home,' Kunle says. 'I have a few things to handle today, and I'm sure you have your plans. I'll be home tonight, or earlier if Nike confirms your mother is on her way back. As I said, I want to tell your mother personally, so I will be back home before her. I'm sure you'll want to be there as well, so I'll make sure you know your mother is on her way as soon as I do, wherever you are.'

'Okay, Dad,' Remi says with a gentle nod. He reaches for the door handle but stops and focuses on his father. 'Have you watched *Spotlight Nigeria*?'

'Yes,' Kunle responds, immediate and final.

The speed and finality of the response, coupled with its stillness, tells Remi there is more to it. Much more. But Remi knows this is not the right time or place to press.

Almost on cue, as if attuned to the shift, Shina winds down and signals to someone nearby, and a moment later, Remi's door opens.

Remi briefly notes another door being opened for him, but he buries his mild amusement. 'See you tonight –' *and we'll finish this conversation then* is left unspoken – he says to his dad, who nods. He turns to Shina. 'See you soon, Uncle.'

Shina nods, and Remi steps out of the car.

CHAPTER 14

Remi sits quietly in the passenger seat of another armoured black Toyota Land Cruiser, the rising sun casting a warm amber glow over the Third Mainland Bridge as Rasaq drives them back home. Remi and Rasaq are the only ones in the car, and beyond the friendly greeting when Remi stepped out of the car with his father to see Rasaq holding the door open for him, they haven't spoken to each other. This is because Remi is deep in thought about what he'd just experienced in the police station and the conversation with his father and Shina afterwards, but Rasaq misreads Remi's distance as Remi being unhappy about Rasaq not letting him know about the incident with Bode outside the gates the night before.

Eventually, Rasaq decides it's best to address the elephant in the room. 'I am sorry for not telling you about Bode last night,' he says. 'It will not happen again.'

'Oh,' Remi says, turning to Rasaq. 'You did the right thing . . . at least with me. But Shina and Yinka like to know all the details, so it's best you debrief them on everything. Especially now.'

'Yes, sir.'

Remi raises an eyebrow, and it takes Rasaq a moment to spot it because he is focusing on the road.

'Sorry. Yes, Remi,' Rasaq corrects.

Remi nods with a soft smile. 'And I understand you wanting to keep your word to Senator Aluko's soldiers. Let me know next time, and I'll sort it.'

'Okay,' Rasaq says, and repeats, 'okay.'

It's clear to Remi that Rasaq is carefully considering his next words. 'Just say it,' he says.

'Those men were fired by the senator and arrested this morning.'

Remi is shocked, but only briefly, as he knows Shina is cutthroat. 'I'll talk to Shina.'

'It wasn't Shina. It was Chief Adeleke.'

'That is not good for them,' Remi says, knowing the Chief will not miss the opportunity to use them as a reminder of why he is so feared.

'Very bad,' Rasaq says, the resignation in his voice making it clear that he knows the men's fates are sealed.

The car falls silent as Remi weighs how involved he wants to get in the men's fates. Under normal circumstances, it wouldn't take much. He'd simply ask Shina or Yinka to liaise with their counterparts in the Chief's household to arrange the release. However, considering the tensions between the Chief and Kunle, he knows it's not a favour Shina or Yinka would be eager to request.

'You are staying at the house, abi?' Remi asks, as he'd noticed that, unlike him, Rasaq had freshened up since last night.

'Yes, Remi,' Rasaq confirms. 'Very nice quarters. Better than many hotels I've stayed at with my clients.'

'Good. Mrs Ibeh would be very proud to hear that.'

'Ah. Yes. Mrs Ibeh,' Rasaq says, and nods slowly.

'You've met her then,' Remi says, amused.

'Yes. She gave me a long talk about respecting the house rules. And she was more intimidating than a lot of my senior officers in the army.'

Remi smiles with a hint of admiration. 'She gives that talk to everyone. Including me. And I could say that she's actually a softie when you get to know her . . . but that would be a big lie.'

Rasaq laughs, then lets the moment settle. The car eases back into silence for the rest of the drive as he gives Remi the space to drift back into his thoughts.

A few minutes later, Rasaq parks in front of the guest house.

'Yinka said my phone number is already programmed in your phone. Under "Personal Security". So please call me directly when you are ready to go out.'

Remi nods and takes a moment to confirm the phone number in his address book. 'You have mine as well, abi?' he asks as he changes the name associated with the phone number from 'Personal Security' to 'Rasaq'.

'Yes.'

'What name is it under?'

Rasaq hesitates, unsure why Remi has asked that. 'RB,' he answers.

Remi nods, glad it wasn't something overly reverential or silly like a secret service code name.

'I changed it to that,' Rasaq says. 'It was Ìran Keji first.'

Remi raises an eyebrow. 'The heir?'

Rasaq nods. 'That's also what they call you on the group chat I was added to.'

'What?'

'I'm joking,' Rasaq says, amused. 'It was always RB.'

Remi chuckles.

'And they call you Oga Remi in the group chat. At least, that's what they've called you so far.'

Remi nods and turns to the front door of the guest house. 'You think if I jump out of the car now and run to the door, I'll get to it before someone can open it from the inside?'

'Absolutely not,' Rasaq responds and chuckles.

'I'm very fast, oh.'

'I don't doubt it. But they've already been alerted that you have arrived, and someone is waiting there for you.'

'Fair enough,' Remi says with a nod. 'I don't intend to be heading out today, but I'll call you if that changes.'

'Okay.'

Remi reaches out for a fist bump, and Rasaq doesn't hesitate to respond.

Remi steps out of the car and takes a couple of calm steps towards the door before suddenly exploding into a run. But just before Remi reaches the door, it opens.

Remi slows down and jogs through the open door with a sheepish smile. He stops and turns to Bola, holding the door open with a restrained smile.

'Welcome back, Oga Remi.'

CHAPTER 15

A few hours later, Remi leans back from his laptop as the credits for the final episode of *Spotlight Nigeria* scroll across the screen. He's alone in the elegant library of the guest house but still maintains his outward composure even as pride and anger churn quietly within him.

Pride, because each of the four episodes was the culmination of Kike's meticulous investigation, fearless tenacity, and astonishing cunning. Each exposé subject had been masterfully convinced, or outmanoeuvred, into sitting for a final, explosive interview. It helped that Kike never appeared on screen and each episode had a different sham branding. The ruse was perfect as each subject sat smugly in the hot seat, only to be blindsided as Kike's voice cut through with one incriminating question after another.

But what followed was always the same. The shock on the subject's face morphed quickly into something else – rage, or something close to it. Fear, vengeance, calculation – the instinctive response of the cornered. Not the performative anger of public denial but the kind of raw emotion that could fester and easily lead to something far worse in a country like Nigeria.

And that's why Remi is angry. Angry at her brilliance. Angry at her recklessness. Angry that no one, not even their father, had been able to convince her just how dangerous it all was. And maybe, most of all, angry at himself for not finding a way back to her before it was too late.

Remi leans back towards his laptop to cancel the unrelated video queued to autoplay, which returns him to the *Spotlight Nigeria* homepage. He focuses on the thumbnails for each episode, which are professional shots of each subject taken just before the final interviews. Each looks composed – not necessarily smiling, but confident. Remi works his mind again to find a connection between them. Still, he can't see one or understand why Kike would go after them specifically. There had to be more to her choices than the righteous indignation so clear in her voice.

The first episode featured Stephen Okolie, a tycoon and founder/CEO of one of Nigeria's leading chemical companies. Kike had gone after him for illegally dumping toxic waste into the Osun River. She sliced through the polished lines he'd repeated in other interviews, backing her accusations with data, leaked memos, and even drone footage that left him nowhere to hide. By the time Kike wrapped the interview, Stephen's confident expression in the thumbnail had collapsed into a tight-lipped grimace of disbelief and seething contempt.

Next was Pastor Biodun Ayomide, founder and general overseer of the influential House of Grace Ministries – the same church Zainab – Remi's mother – had attended for decades. Pastor Biodun appeared composed in the thumbnail – shoulders squared, expression serene, the picture of moral authority. Kike's voice was clinical and unyielding as she accused him of embezzling church funds to bankroll a life of opulence: a new G-Wagon among his fleet of luxury vehicles, a waterfront mansion in Lekki, and two properties in central London. Pastor Biodun was stunned by the accusation but tried to reassert control, claiming he was blessed by God and the opulence was all a manifestation of divine favour. Then Kike struck with specific allegations of inappropriate relationships with female congregants. Her tone remained steady, but Remi recognised the weight behind her words. A weight that hinted at something deeper, something personal. Pastor Biodun was blindsided and tried to deny the accusations with the high-octane passion and charisma that he'd used to build his large flock, but it had no effect on Kike, and the pattern of behaviour clear in the statements, texts, phone records, and even pictures she presented was overwhelming. By the end, Pastor Biodun's mouth was drawn tight, and his gaze was fixed off camera as if grappling not just with the ambush but with who had delivered it.

Malaki, the legendary musician and self-proclaimed King of Surulere, came next. In the thumbnail, he looked relaxed, reclining in a low chair with a mischievous glint in his eyes, jewellery catching the light. He began the interview in full performer mode, revelling in his rise from the streets to success, still being a man of the people, and his efforts to uplift the local boys 'hustling' in his neighbourhood. But when Kike coolly accused him of using those boys to traffic drugs through his logistics companies, the glint vanished. She laid out the evidence – shipment records, anonymous testimonies, even hidden camera footage from one of the drop-offs. Malaki barely spoke after that. There was an initial flash of anger, but more at himself for letting his guard down and trusting one of these *ajebutters*. However, his eyes didn't burn with outrage like the others; they narrowed with calculation, as if he was less concerned about the allegations than with figuring out who had betrayed him. There was no panic, and perhaps most telling, he didn't even bother to deny it.

Abe Nosa was last. Younger than the others, barely in his mid thirties and a member of the House of Representatives, Abe had attended the same boarding school as Remi, a couple of years ahead. However, they'd rarely interacted at the time. They'd become friendly acquaintances later through mutual friends and as part of a group that played high-stakes poker regularly, first in London during university, then back in Lagos after most of the others returned.

In the thumbnail, Abe looked every bit the polished politician with his tailored suit, confident smirk, and the posture of someone used to steering conversations to his advantage.

But Kike didn't give him the chance. She was sharper now, as she'd become more refined with each episode. Her voice cut with precision as she accused him of using constituency funds to bankroll shell companies – companies that, according to bank records, paid kickbacks to a long list of unnamed associates. Abe tried to laugh it off, dismissing it as political sabotage, but Kike pressed on with land registry documents, leaked emails, WhatsApp chats, and even voice notes. His smirk faltered. He kept glancing off camera, no longer in control. He looked like he wanted to get up and leave, but something held him in his seat.

By the end, he wasn't raging like Stephen or shaken like Pastor

Biodun. He looked cornered. And in his eyes, Remi saw what unsettled him most – not just fear of political ruin, but the dangerous pride of someone who wouldn't go down without a fight.

Remi sits back again, quietly assessing them all, the soft hum of the air conditioning the only sound in the room. They all had the rage and the motive. But only Stephen, Pastor Biodun and Abe have the means and connections to dare such a thing so publicly . . . and to cover their tracks. Malaki, no matter how successful he might be today, doesn't have those trusted connections in the uppermost echelon of Nigerian society. No one would protect him. He'd instead be their fall guy, and they would throw him into the fire to burn brightly the moment they felt the heat from the Bankoles. Plus, the very people Malaki claimed to uplift would likely hand him over to the Bankoles in exchange for favours . . . or even kill him themselves to demonstrate their unending loyalty . . . to money.

Remi sits up straighter, the fatigue from barely three hours of sleep and the emotionally draining hours spent at the desk suddenly overtaken by a fresh surge of resolve. He will do what he's always done – ask the right questions, then carefully observe for the truth and the lies.

It started when Remi was a child. Not with any great revelation, but in quiet moments, such as catching classmates in playground fibs, sensing when adults made promises they never intended to keep, or spotting his older cousin exaggerating a story for effect. What tipped him off wasn't just the words, but everything around them: the too-quick denial, the forced laughter, the glance that didn't quite land, the twitch of a mouth trying too hard to hold its shape.

Over time, as his instincts kept proving right . . . when friends joked about Remi having a sixth sense . . . he'd started to pay closer attention. He read books about body language, lie detection, and how people reveal more than they intend. Studied high-stakes interviews of politicians, CEOs and criminal suspects, even scripted ones, to spot the cracks in performances and the tells behind polished answers. He learned to spot micro expressions, mismatched emotions, changes in blink rate and posture shifts. The way hands betray nerves even when voices don't.

He practised obsessively as a young teenager until the incident in boarding school that seemingly convinced the teachers that he was possessed by some sort of evil spirit. His mum was called in, which was the last straw for her because she also feared that he was possessed. What followed – the deliverance, overseen by Pastor Biodun – was initially traumatic. But he fought past it with his father and Kike's support. Then simply added it as another pillar to consider – no one, especially pious adults, likes being called out on a foundational lie, no matter how subtly or tactfully it is done.

Since then, he's practised quietly. Tested himself in legal meetings, deal negotiations, poker games, conversations with friends and acquaintances . . . keeping mental notes, and then confirming facts later. More often than not, his instincts were right.

But this would be different. His instincts had never been tested against something like this. Grief, rage, fear, guilt . . . these weren't boardroom posturings, poker bluffs or harmless fibs. This was life and death. Kike's life. And perhaps the truth of her death. The police couldn't – or wouldn't – get close to men like Stephen, Pastor Biodun or Abe. Too powerful, too protected, too far beyond the reach of real accountability. But Remi could. Because of who he is. He could get them in a room. Ask the right questions. Watch them answer.

He isn't certain it will work. But he believes it will. He has to. And if it does . . . maybe, just maybe, he'll learn the truth.

CHAPTER 16

Remi skips up the stairs towards his bedroom with purpose. He'd barely begun to consider how to approach Stephen, Pastor Biodun and Abe when a quick, natural, and hopefully disarming way to approach Abe struck him – poker. Remi knew the poker group he was once an active member of before everyone besides him moved back to Lagos played every Saturday night, each taking their turn to host.

At the time, Abe had been one step away from a poker addict. That step was a keen awareness of the limits of his ability to tangle with the seemingly bottomless wealth of some of the other regulars, as these were no-limit, real money cash games – where every chip on the table represented actual pound sterling, and the only limit was the size of your stack and your risk appetite or ego. For the uninitiated, in this game, a person could win or lose their entire stack in a single hand.

So skill and luck were essential in the games, but almost more important for some was the amount of chips they bought at the start of the game to ensure they had the largest stack – or at least large enough to bully the smaller stacks – and the amount of cash they had in reserve to keep buying back in each time they ran out of chips. It could be an extremely expensive night, and it almost always was, but Abe had always known when to stop buying back in. He almost always returned the following week, though, with the same enthusiasm, regardless of how good or bad the previous game was. And from the chatter on the group chat, before Remi exited the group, Abe continued that regularity in Lagos. And then Remi also realises: today is Saturday – game night.

Remi is hurrying to his London personal phone charging in his bedroom, hoping that one of his friends from the poker group has tried to reach out to him. Not for the game tonight, but more to check in, because Remi knows the incident with Bode last night would've announced his return to the circle with a loud bang. People would be talking, and most of them would love to talk to him about it.

He strides into the bedroom and heads straight to pick up the phone from the bedside table. As he expected, there are several messages and even a few missed calls. He unlocks the phone and heads straight to WhatsApp and doesn't have to scroll through the messages for long before he spots one from Lade, the exact friend from the poker group he was hoping would reach out. The message simply reads: *Bro you are in Gidi and didn't even tell me?*

Gidi is a slang term for Lagos, and Remi knows that will be the sentiment of most of the other messages.

Remi messages back: *Brother, haven't been back for long. Was going to reach out, but haven't settled down yet.*

Remz! Settling down, abi? Not what I heard, oh, Lade replies, taking the bait.

Whatever you heard. Not true.

Stop it! I've heard what happened last night from lots of people.

What happened last night?

At Rose's pre-wedding party?

Yeah I was there briefly. What happened?

As Remi expects, Lade calls the instant he reads Remi's last message.

'You good, brother?' Remi casually answers.

'Shut up, you idiot!' Lade chides in jest, and they laugh. 'Why are you trying to deny it? There are many videos, oh.'

'I was just playing. Bit bored is all.'

'Ahn ahn, don't insult us now. It's Gidi . . . how can you be bored?'

'I know. I know. But everyone's talking about this party or that club. That's not me anymore, brother.'

'Look at your sweet mouth,' Lade chides again. 'Lagos parties are not good enough for you again, abi? Unless it's to go there and beat somebody.'

Remi laughs softly. 'I didn't beat—'

'Shut up,' Lade cuts in. 'I said there are videos!'

Remi laughs again. 'I don't even do parties that much in London.'

'Really?' Lade asks, feigning concern. 'Ah. That's very sad,' he says softly, and his voice suddenly rises again. 'Come on, behave yourself!'

'I'm serious. I'm on that relaxed vibe right now. Chilled things only.'

'Okay. Come for poker tonight, then.'

'It still happens every week?'

'Wait . . . did you actually remove yourself from the group chat? I thought you just stopped responding! Ahn ahn! This your fresh guy thing is too much, oh, Remi!'

'No. It's not that,' Remi calmly protests. 'There was just no point—'

'You would've known there was a game tonight,' Lade cuts in with more than a hint of indignation. 'There is the point, no?'

Touché, Remi thinks, then gives it a beat before he coolly says, 'Fair enough, Lade.'

From someone as typically subtle as Remi, his tone and the deliberate use of Lade's name are flashing neon signs for Lade to watch his tone. And Lade reads it loud and clear.

'It'll be good for you to come, though,' Lade says excitedly. 'There are a few new regulars that I need you to come and pattern up.'

'Pattern up, eh?' Remi teases.

Lade chuckles. 'Come and teach them some manners, abeg.'

'What about the old guys?' Remi asks, as if uninterested in playing with these new guys.

'Oh, most are still around. It's the biggest game in Gidi,' Lade says, and lists a few older players before mentioning the name Remi wants to hear. 'Abe . . . you know that one will always be there.'

The confirmation sends a jolt of electricity through Remi, but he doesn't react as Lade continues to mention other old players who remain regulars.

'That's a lot of players,' Remi says when Lade completes his list.

'Are you not listening? I said it's the biggest game in town. Two tables – a main one with eight players and an overflow table with six players max. We are not even rotating hosts anymore. We have a permanent, *very* private spot. Food, drink, everything sorted every week. We fund all of it from a cut of the money on the table each week. We even had to open a bank account because we had too much money in reserve. Remi, I'm telling you, it's a big game.'

'Impressive. Things are progressing.'

'Yes, oh!'

'But it's 2025, and still no female players?'

'Abeg, leave that one,' Lade says, amused. 'Your sister played with us a bit, though.'

'Sorry?' Remi remarks, failing to hide his surprise.

'Yes. Kike was a regular for about three or four months. Fam, your sister is savage! With her playing style and her mouth!'

Remi forgets to respond as he tries to put the pieces together. Kike enjoyed poker and was good at it, but she had no time for the closed circles of the uber-rich or any hyper-masculine space where ego passed for strategy. But like him, he is pretty sure that she was there for Abe.

'You there, Remi?' Lade asks.

'Yeah, sorry,' Remi says. 'Was distracted by a work email.'

'Why am I not surprised you are still working in Lagos!'

Remi forces a note of amusement into his voice. 'Can you WhatsApp me the address? And any secret hand signals or passwords I need to get in?'

Lade laughs. 'No problem! And message me your plate number so the security let you through the gate with no wahala.'

'Sure.'

'What time will you get there?'

'What time does the game start?'

'Eight . . . nine. But people get there from about seven to chill . . . catch up . . . get the drinks in . . . some weed . . . some food.'

'Hmm,' Remi mutters with a distinct lack of interest.

'You don't care about any of that, do you?'

'Not really,' Remi admits. 'And I'm also not interested in talking about last night.'

'Ah. That one might be impossible. Everyone has seen the video. Even me, I want to talk about it.'

Remi forces a chuckle, as he really doesn't want to dwell on last night's altercation. He feels he took out some of his festering pain on Bode.

'I'll be there for the game around eight,' he says, fully intending to arrive by 10 p.m. at the earliest, hoping that Abe will be there by then.

'All right. See you then.'

'In a bit,' Remi says, and ends the call.

Remi sits on the edge of the bed, quietly contemplating the night ahead, running through every possible reaction Abe might have to his presence – from aggression to evasion to indifference. Whatever the response, one thing is certain – he'll get Abe alone, talking, answering the right questions.

His thoughts are interrupted by the chime of a WhatsApp message from Lade with an address in Eko Atlantic, the newly developed, ultra-modern enclave on the edge of Victoria Island, famed for its gleaming high-rise towers and luxury real estate. Remi barely reacts but subconsciously notes that Lade wasn't exaggerating. This really is the biggest game in town if a decent cut of the money on the table could buy, or even rent, a permanent place in Eko Atlantic.

He calls Rasaq on his Lagos phone.

CHAPTER 17

A few hours later, the Land Cruiser edges out of Remi's serene neighbourhood into the Saturday night current, merging into the steady stream of cars already heading towards the Island's nightlife. It's just after ten, but the Island's roads are wide awake, with drivers weaving through traffic and horns blaring over loud music from open car windows. The Island's nightlife is just beginning.

Remi, wearing another of his dad's smooth, casual kaftans, sits in the front passenger seat, watching the blur of streetlights and taillights. His thoughts circle the night ahead. Not the poker game. Abe, the questions he'll need to ask and the truths he's determined to uncover.

Rasaq, sharp as ever, senses the mood and gives Remi space. He focuses on the drive, his eyes constantly scanning the road and the mirrors, noting each car behind them and every figure loitering at the edges. His alertness never dips, not even on a seemingly routine drive like this. For a while, the only sounds in the car are the soft whir of the air conditioning and the occasional click of the indicator.

Traffic begins to thin as they cross into Victoria Island, and Remi exhales. He knows he needs to ease out of the tense state of preparation he's been in for the past few hours before walking into the poker game. Slowly, he lets his thoughts settle and, for a few moments, slips into the rhythm of the night, allowing the vibrance to carry him forward.

He notices Rasaq check on him out of the corner of his eye and turns to address him. 'Sorry about the silence,' he says. 'Please put some music on.'

Rasaq nods and connects his phone to the stereo, eyes still on the road. He'd spent part of the day curating a playlist for this exact moment, anticipating the request. But now, sensing the quiet tension in the car, he isn't sure what fits. He taps shuffle and lets fate decide.

The sultry voice of Caron Wheeler singing 'Back to Life' floats through the speakers, and Rasaq instantly recognises the song as Burna Boy's 'Update', which heavily samples the classic. He glances at Remi, who is already vibing with the song, even before Burna's voice kicks in. But it's a muted reaction. Nothing like the energy Remi had during the drive to Rose's pre-wedding party. Back then, he'd been lost in the music. Now, there's a distance.

Rasaq opens his mouth to speak but hesitates, unsure if he should ask the question at the tip of his tongue. He glances again at Remi, and something in Remi's eyes convinces him to go with it.

'You all right, Remi?' he asks with a steady tone that conveys concern with a light touch.

Remi reads the concern and appreciates it. 'Just . . .' he says, and gestures at his head. 'In my head. I get like that sometimes.'

'Okay,' Rasaq says, and nods. 'Let me know if there is anything I can handle for you tonight.'

Remi smiles softly. 'Thanks, Rasaq. I appreciate that.'

Rasaq nods, and both return to quietly enjoying the music.

Soon, they reach the gates of Eko Atlantic, and the private security guards wave them through without pause. The plate number evidently cleared in advance. Inside, the air shifts. Quieter. More controlled. They pass sleek residential towers rising into the night with glass façades catching reflections of the city behind them. Most windows are dark, but the few lit ones offer glimpses of the opulence inside – art-lined walls, high ceilings and the soft flicker of large screens or chandeliers. Somewhat unusually, interspersed among the finished towers are others still in progress. The scaffolding, cranes and half-lit shells of future towers serve as reminders that the glittering city is still under construction.

'This is all new to me,' Remi says. 'You seem to know your way around, though.'

'Yes,' Rasaq confirms. 'I've had a couple of clients who stayed here while they were in Lagos.'

Remi nods. 'I can see the appeal. And you seem to have a lot of fun clients. But then, you are not hoping for fun in your line of work.'

Rasaq is impressed that Remi remembered his earlier words almost verbatim. It makes it clear that Remi listens, not simply making small talk. 'Correct. But these two clients that stayed here – didn't know each other, sha – were *too much fun* and were outside every day and night while they were in town looking for more *fun*.'

'Sounds ominous.'

'Sorry? I don't understand ominous.'

'Troubling. For you and the clients.'

Rasaq laughs softly. 'It was close. But I took care of them. I always take care of my clients,' Rasaq says, not boasting, but more to reassure Remi.

'I don't doubt it.'

Rasaq glows a little at the quiet confidence in Remi's tone. 'Thank you,' he says, and nods ahead. 'We're here.'

Rasaq pulls into one of the taller buildings with penthouses that promise views of the city's skyline and guides the car into the underground parking. He glides past the kind of cars Remi expects and parks in a spot with a clean line of sight across the car park.

Remi doesn't move at first. Then, with a breath, he cracks a confident smile and reaches for the door handle. But just before opening the door, he turns back to Rasaq.

'I might need your help tonight,' he says.

The private lift opens directly into the penthouse, and Remi coolly steps out. He pauses a moment just inside the threshold to take in the penthouse and immediately notes the cool air and the appealing scent, which is a minimal mix of oud and citrus. The expansive space is immaculate, with a large open-plan layout stretching from the entrance to the windows. Floor-to-ceiling windows line the far side, revealing the city's buzzing patchwork of lights, towers and traffic on one side and the endless dark shimmer of the Atlantic on the other.

On one end of the expansive space is a sleek bar with a staff member preparing a drink and another waiting to serve a tray of already prepared drinks. Both are in black attire. Just beyond the bar, a chef moves quietly in the state-of-the-art kitchen, preparing small plates of food in full view of everyone.

Two oval-shaped professional poker tables dominate the centre of the room. The smaller one with just six spots is empty. The main table is almost full, with seven players, one empty spot and an expressionless dealer in black attire. The seven players also seem well into the game as the banter and laughter flow while the dealer expertly shuffles ahead of another hand. Remi scans the players and quickly realises that Abe is not among them. He fights back the disappointment boiling inside him and holds on to the fact that Abe always liked to show up late – when the others were too tired, too drunk or too high, making them easier prey. He thought he'd factored that in, showing up three hours late. Guess not.

He walks towards the table, his steps muted by the Afrobeats playing not too loudly through the speakers distributed around the penthouse, and subconsciously registers the dynamics of the game. Noting who's relaxed, who's trying to appear relaxed, who's already calculating how far their current stack can take them, and who's more focused on their drink and the banter, simply here for a good night. The latter was the predominant state of mind during the games in London, but Remi can see that the game has taken on a harder, more serious edge since.

Remi approaches the table, close enough to assess the number of chips in front of each person, and notes the uneven stacks as the winners and losers of the night are already taking shape. He heads towards Lade, not the open spot at the table, and Lade is the first to notice him.

'Remz,' Lade calls, warm with recognition and just a touch of performance for the crowd. He stands.

'Lade,' Remi says, warm but without the performance, and he and Lade hug. 'Good to see you, brother.'

'Likewise, fam,' Lade says.

'Thanks for the invite,' Remi says, and turns as he notices the three other old players standing up. 'No, please, I'll come round. You guys are playing.'

They all nod and return to their seats.

Remi graciously pats Lade on the shoulder. 'We'll catch up in a bit.'

Lade nods and switches his attention to the serving staff, and Remi circles the table, greeting everyone. Remi shakes each person's hand, and with the old players, he leans in for a quick, familiar half hug. With the new players, he first introduces himself personally and then waits for them to introduce themselves before leaning in for essentially a shoulder tap.

One of the new players, a well-built mixed-race man in his mid thirties, who Remi had noticed staring at him intently since the moment they all became aware of him, smirks as Remi approaches.

'A hugger, yeah?' he teases, with a fading London accent.

'It's not by force,' Remi says with an easy smile.

'It's calm,' he retorts, trying to match Remi's effortless cool but missing the mark – not by much, to be fair.

Remi shakes his hand and introduces himself. 'Remi.'

'I know who you are,' he retorts.

'Abeg, behave, Yellow,' Lade interjects. 'I'm sure everyone knows who he is. It's just polite.'

Yellow shrugs with that smirk of his.

'And I don't know who you are,' Remi adds, calm but deliberate.

Yellow's smirk fades. 'Patrick,' he says.

Remi and Patrick tap shoulders.

'Is that seat taken?' Remi asks, gesturing to the empty spot at the table.

The table almost responds in unison, confirming it is not.

Remi sits at the empty spot and offers the dealer a fist bump. The dealer hesitates briefly, surprised, before bumping Remi's fist. In the next moment, the serving staff member appears beside Remi with a drink. He doesn't want one but appreciates that it's exactly what he'd have ordered – gin and tonic. So he accepts it.

'Thank you,' Remi says to the serving staff, then graciously raises the glass to Lade, who he's sure ordered it.

Lade raises his glass in return.

'How much would you like to buy in, sir?' the serving staff asks, and hands him a small card with several ways of transferring funds instantly to a UK account for the game.

Remi turns to the table. 'What's the average buy-in?' he asks.

'That's a different approach to your sister,' Patrick immediately remarks, as if he's been waiting to reference Kike. 'She'd be asking for the biggest stack and then double that for her buy-in.'

Remi nods in quiet acknowledgement and turns to the others. 'The average?' he asks again.

'A grand,' one of the others answers. 'Sterling.'

Remi nods and pulls out his London phone to make the transfer.

As Remi waits for his chips, he notices the eclectic collection of pre-rolled designer weed with unique markings denoting the particular strain on a rolling table just to the side. He then notices that most of the table is smoking a roll of weed, but the whiff in the air is minimal. Some of that has to do with the ventilation and scent being constantly filtered into the penthouse. However, much of it has to do with the quality of the weed – even this close, the smell barely lingers.

'That's quite a collection of weed,' Remi says, gesturing to the rolling table.

'Oh yeah,' Lade responds. 'Good ones too. All thanks to Yellow with the connect. Although the options have been slacking lately.'

'Don't smoke it if you don't like it,' Patrick retorts, with clear annoyance.

'Calm down, Yellow. I like these ones too. Just you had some funky options before. One tasted like champagne . . . another one tasted like lemon and strawberry ice cream. Fam . . . beautiful stuff.'

'And what's this one?'

'Good too. Tastes a bit like vanilla cake.'

'The strain is called *Wedding Cake*,' Patrick adds.

'Want to try it?' Lade asks.

'No. I'm good,' Remi says.

'You want something else?' Patrick asks. 'There are a couple here that taste like fruit candy. And, of course, the OG strain.'

'Thanks, mate. But I'm good.'

'Different from your sister there again,' Patrick says with a knowing smile. 'She was a big fan of the Zkittlez strain – the fruit candy one. And a rare Biscotti strain I never shared with those greedy boys. She is a connoisseur.'

The table falls silent, waiting for Remi to respond.

Remi isn't scandalised by Patrick highlighting his sister's habits. He always knew of them and wasn't entirely bothered because she kept it under control and got the best money could buy – a connoisseur, as Patrick put it. No one on the table would be shocked by it either if she played poker with them for as long as Lade said she did. But what infuriated Remi was Patrick's inference that he and Kike had an intimate relationship beyond the game. Remi isn't surprised by that – the moment he saw Patrick, he recognised that Patrick looks very much like her ex-boyfriend; he was her type – but Remi firmly believed in keeping things private, and he knew Kike believed in that, too. So he was overcome with the urge to drive his fist through Patrick's nose or, even worse, get Shina to handle him how Shina knows best. But that urge died when Patrick casually referred to Kike in the present tense when he said, 'She *is* a connoisseur'. That saved Patrick's nose ... and probably his knee, and livelihood – whatever that is.

Remi smiles softly, which surprises everyone, especially Patrick. 'You like the sound of your own voice, don't you, Patrick?' he asks.

Patrick chuckles and then attempts to speak, but Remi calmly raises a hand, and he instinctively stops, as if in a trance.

'That's enough from you for a bit, don't you think, Patrick?' Remi says.

The table erupts into laughter, and Patrick is forced to laugh along, though the sting of being put in his place burns behind his eyes. And Remi can clearly see it.

Remi's chips are soon placed in front of him, and he joins the game and the casual banter across the table. For the first hour, while glancing periodically towards the lift for signs of Abe, he mostly observes – the game, the conversations and each player – to confirm his instincts about the familiar players and build his reads on the new ones. Still, he's up roughly £400.

On the next hand, Remi is dealt pocket tens (diamonds and spades), and he raises the big blind substantially pre-flop. All the players except Patrick fold, leaving only Remi and Patrick in for the flop. The dealer neatly sets out the three cards – nine of hearts, three of hearts and nine of clubs. Ordinarily, the pair of nines would give Remi pause, but he'd watched Patrick closely as the flop landed, and his read is that the pair of nines didn't improve the chances of Patrick having the winning hand any more than they did his. But then Patrick tosses in £190, an arbitrary mix of chips delivered with a snap Remi instantly reads as theatre, designed solely to get him to fold. Remi calls, and Patrick smirks – another tell that it was a bluff.

The dealer places the turn on the table – eight of hearts. The immediacy of Patrick's even larger £400 bet tells Remi that Patrick didn't care what the turn was. He'd prepared that bet prior. Remi takes his time to count his chips as if considering his options. All the while, he keeps an eye on Patrick, who is trying to act nonchalant but is just properly assessing the community cards for the first time. It's clear to Remi that Patrick has nothing, at least nothing better than his pair of tens. But it's also clear that Patrick has just spotted a chance at glory – a flush (five cards of the same suit). There are currently three hearts on the table. One more will make it four, giving Patrick the opportunity for a flush even if he's only holding one heart card. Remi is sure Patrick has just one heart, and knows the chances of another heart on the river are slim. He also already knows Patrick's move on the river – Patrick will go all in, heart or not – so Remi calls.

The dealer places the river on the table – queen of hearts. As Remi expects, without hesitation, Patrick goes all in and smirks. Remi knows Patrick has the winning hand – the flush. Regardless of that, the hand wouldn't necessarily have been over if Patrick hadn't gone all in. Remi could've presented as having a higher flush and induced Patrick to fold. But that's too late. Patrick made the right play by going all in. Remi offers a small congratulatory nod to Patrick and folds.

Patrick grins and theatrically turns over one of his cards – four of spades. The table reacts, most impressed at his supposed bluff.

Remi knows it wasn't a bluff, but is happy to let the others, especially Patrick, think he believes it is. It'll come in handy later. But Patrick just can't help himself.

'Lade,' Patrick says, gesturing at Remi. 'I thought you said your guy can read a bluff easy.' He shakes his head. 'Jokes!'

Lade shrugs, amused.

'Oya, Yellow man, show us the second card then, abi?' the player beside Patrick asks.

'No. That's not how it works,' Patrick says, and gestures at Remi. 'It's not free.'

Remi pushes the rest of his chips into the middle of the table. 'I'll give you the rest of my chips . . . if that card you're hiding is not a heart.'

'No. It's too late,' Patrick says, trying to exude confidence. 'I'm not betting anything. Hand is over.'

Patrick's reaction does the opposite of what he intended – it reveals his weakness and piques the curiosity of the others at the table.

'Big man, show the card, abi,' a player across the table pokes at Patrick. 'I'd do it if it was me. Free money.'

'Shut up. That's why you're losing,' Patrick retorts.

Remi smiles and gambles. 'I'll make it sweeter for you, then. You can take those chips if that card you're hiding is not a four of hearts.'

Everyone's attention is drawn to Patrick and the card. And Patrick caves. He grabs the deck of cards from the dealer and shoves both his cards randomly into the stack.

The table erupts into laughter and derision at Patrick's expense, and as before, Patrick joins the wave of laughter. But his humiliation is clear to Remi.

'This seems like the perfect time to talk about you embarrassing people,' one of the other familiar players says, and Patrick again struggles to hide his annoyance but bites his tongue. 'What happened with Bode?'

Remi had been expecting this question, and he appreciates the patience it took for them to wait over an hour to bring it up. 'He just hadn't gotten over something that happened in boarding school.'

'What? You bullied him?' one of the new players asks, with a hint of mockery at the idea that a person could still be affected by bullying years later.

'No. Not that. He was a couple of years below me . . . in Kike's year. And *he* was the bully. But then he overstepped with Kike. And

I overstepped with him. To be fair to him, I overreacted. Probably was a traumatic experience. He hadn't seen me since. And he's a big boy now, so he thought . . . you know . . . why not get his own back.'

'We are talking about fifteen, sixteen years later,' Lade says, surprised. 'He held on to it for that long?'

'Yeah,' Remi says, and nods. 'I really did overreact.' A thought strikes him, and he immediately voices it. 'Do you know if he confronted Kike?'

Patrick laughs. 'Bode wouldn't have tried that,' he says. 'You, you're a fresh guy. I've seen the video, and no doubt, you can handle yourself. You could've broken Bode's arm. But you didn't. Kike is a savage. She would've broken it. Then she'd go for his knees or his throat. Bode knows that. Everyone does.'

There is quiet agreement across the table, and then Remi nods at Patrick in appreciation of the unexpected tribute.

Just then, Remi spots Abe and a new player walking towards the table from the lift with a pep in their step. Remi experiences a rush of adrenaline, but his outwardly composed demeanour doesn't change.

'Àwọn boys,' Abe says with his usual confidence as he approaches the table. 'Have I missed any fireworks or we're just getting started?'

'Speaking of Kike's savagery,' one of the new players murmurs, loudly enough for the table but not for Abe to hear, gesturing towards Abe.

A few on the table laugh, but Remi doesn't. He calmly watches Abe, waiting to read Abe's body language the moment Abe notices him.

'What?' Abe says, trying to understand the reason for the amusement. He heads straight to one of the old players and greets him with a handshake. He scans the table, mostly looking at the chip stacks for anyone about close to losing all their chips. 'I guess IK and I will set up on the other . . .'

Abe locks eyes with Remi, and his confidence dissolves, replaced with fear. Abe forces a smile at Remi, and Remi cracks a smile back.

'Actually, I'll just come back,' Abe continues, maintaining his visible confidence but already retreating.

'Ahn ahn,' the old player Abe just shook hands with says. 'Chill with àwọn boys, drink, fá igbo.'

'That will come. And I don't want to be drunk and high even before I start playing with you boys. I know you all want my money. But you'll have to work for it. Anyway, it's just someone to check on quickly on the next street, you understand.' He smiles suggestively. 'I should be back in an hour or so, fully gingered, you know.'

'Aren't you just coming from there?' IK asks Abe as Abe walks past him towards the lift. 'That place will finish you.'

'Never!' Abe says with a flourish, and fades away back into the lift.

Remi is sure that the place on the next street is a high-end brothel, but he's equally sure that Abe isn't going back there and isn't coming back here tonight. But he doesn't panic and calmly stays engaged in the hand he's currently playing until it's over. It takes almost five minutes, and it's a relatively big hand, which he wins.

'I'm going to sit out for a bit,' Remi says before standing. 'I'll be right back.'

The players all gesture their understanding, and Remi walks away towards the lift.

Abe hurries through the underground parking towards his Range Rover Sport, anxiously trying to reach someone. He's called twice, but no answer, which is unusual. This person always answered, no matter the hour. And the person called at odd hours too.

He frantically types a message – *Uncle. Call me back. Or call Remi. Abeg!* – as he nears his car, not bothering to look up as he pushes the button on his key fob to unlock the doors. But just before he presses send, he hears his driver-side door swing open and nearly jumps out of his skin.

Rasaq holds the car door open for Abe with the perfect blend of respect and menace. 'Good evening, Mr Nosa,' Rasaq says, polite but unyielding. 'My Oga, Mr Bankole, would like to have a chat with you. And has asked that you kindly wait for him.'

Abe freezes. His fight-or-flight instinct flashing an error message.

'Please,' Rasaq calmly says, gesturing for Abe to enter his car. 'Mr Bankole will be down shortly. He's just finishing a hand.'

Abe tries to surreptitiously scan the car park for any witnesses, but he can't see anyone else besides Rasaq. He relents and swaggers into the car.

'Thank you, Mr Nosa,' Rasaq says, and shuts the door gently.

Abe waves Rasaq off, trying to project nonchalance, and Rasaq retreats a couple of paces to a spot with a full view of Abe and the car – and, importantly, where Abe can see and feel him watching.

Abe strongly considers driving off. But there's nowhere in Lagos the Bankoles can't reach him if they want to. And as a politician, a public figure, disappearing isn't an option. More than anything, he'd rather take whatever's coming here in private than risk going viral like Bode.

Abe's eyes stay fixed on the door leading to the penthouse's private lift, becoming more anxious with every passing moment. He remembers the unsent text, but instead of sending it, he calls instead. No answer, which further increases his panic level. Just as he hits send, he spots Remi calmly walking towards the car. Abe glances over his shoulder for Rasaq, but Rasaq is not there and is nowhere to be seen.

It all gets too much for Abe, and the moment Remi slides into the front passenger seat, he unravels.

'I listened to Shina. I did, I swear!' Abe says, almost pleading. 'I stayed away from the game until I was sure Kike wasn't coming anymore. I even checked with Shina first before I started coming back. He said it was okay.'

Abe stares expectantly at Remi, but Remi doesn't react.

'And I have stopped all that nonsense. No, yes, there is one left. Only one. It's complicated . . . lots of moving parts. But I am close. I have it under control.'

Remi has no idea what Abe is talking about, but he doesn't show it. He doesn't show anything as he still doesn't react.

'Oh, yes. I'm sorry for raising my voice at Kike . . .'

Remi raises an eyebrow.

'Sorry . . . I mean for threatening her,' Abe corrects, misreading Remi's raised eyebrow. 'But Kike punched my eye before I even finished shouting. Then Yinka manhandled me there and then. The next day, Shina slapped me in my house in front of my wife and threatened my life. Now you are here.' His voice rises as his frustration boils over, and he smacks the steering wheel with a closed fist. 'What else now, ehn? What else do you Bankoles want? It was a mistake. A big mistake. I was just angry. She ambushed me. I thought everything was over for me. I lashed out.'

Abe slumps back, eyes closed, trying to contain his emotions, sweat dripping down his head.

Remi quietly studies Abe, noting the desperation, the fear, and the amount of nervous sweat pouring out of him. It's apparent to Remi, even without asking the questions he so carefully prepared, that Abe was not involved in Kike's death. Remi can see that it would be difficult to put the Bankoles as the wounded party regarding whatever had happened with Abe. The Bankoles seem to have already taken more than their pound of flesh.

But more importantly for Remi – not that he expected different – is that he's now certain that Kike had all the resources of the Bankole machine at her disposal for *Spotlight Nigeria*.

'So, brother,' Remi finally speaks, surprising Abe with the lightness of his tone. 'You really should switch the air conditioning on.'

CHAPTER 18

Remi sits at the dining table in the guest house, breakfast finished, eyes on the news playing on the large television hung on the wall. Fuel shortages, the devaluing naira, a political scandal brewing in the East, a fresh government anti-corruption drive . . . all familiar. But this channel – owned by Derin Daniels, the same one Eki works for – had also been giving disproportionate airtime to speculation about the sudden gathering of the top figures in the president's party in Abuja. Remi notices this, but he ultimately doesn't pay much attention to it. His mind is elsewhere, still locked on the events of the night before.

After confronting Abe, Remi had returned to the poker game, slipping easily back into the rhythm of cards and conversation. Outwardly composed, even winning a few more hands. But ever since that confrontation, just like now, his mind had been elsewhere, struggling to shake the creeping sense of futility that had taken hold.

He leans back in his chair, unconsciously drumming his fingers against the table. His self-appointed mission to meet each subject of *Spotlight Nigeria*, ask the right questions, and observe for the truth had seemed precise enough. But it was starting to feel naïve.

If Abe, as connected and arrogant as he was, and despite being a long-term acquaintance, had crumbled so easily under the mere threat of a private conversation, what chance was there that the others wouldn't either crumble or be so on edge that Remi would read nothing but fear?

And it would have been clear to Stephen, Pastor Biodun, Malaki and Abe almost immediately after the interviews – and certainly after the exposés aired, because Remi was sure they would've tried everything to stop it – that Kike hadn't acted alone. That she had moved under the full protection and influence of her father, Kunle Bankole. Whatever rage they felt, whatever vengeance they might have dreamed of, would have withered quickly. His father's influence wasn't just substantial; it was terrifyingly unquantifiable, because it operated quietly, in the shadows, only revealing itself to destroy or overwhelm.

Pushing further, forcing confrontations, would only corner already wounded animals. Worse, it might provoke consequences Remi couldn't predict or control. And Remi, for all his instincts, knew when to stop. When to fold a losing hand.

Still, the question gnawed at him. If not them . . . then who? Who had the reach and the reckless boldness to move against the Bankoles so drastically and so openly?

Maybe his father knew. Maybe that was where the real answers lay. He had protected her, perhaps even encouraged her. He might know more about her enemies, maybe even his, than he had let on. Their next conversation would have to be more direct. About *Spotlight Nigeria*. About why Kunle sent him to Rose's pre-wedding party. And about everything else Kunle hadn't yet said.

A sharp knock interrupts his thoughts.

Kehinde steps inside, composed as always but with a glint of urgency in his eyes.

'Ẹ káàrọ̀, Remi,' he says. 'Madam is on her way back. Oga says she should be home within thirty minutes. He's asked if you could join him in the main house to welcome her together.'

Remi stands, quick but calm, sliding his chair back with a quiet scrape against the polished floor. Everything else will have to wait. His mother is coming home.

A few minutes later, Remi walks through the main house's front door and is guided towards the living room. He enters the elegant waiting lounge/anteroom just outside the living room, adorned with more beautiful Nigerian-inspired artwork, and immediately locks eyes with Shina, who's speaking on the phone.

'Dúró,' Shina says into the phone. 'Mo fẹ́ kí Remi.'

'Ẹ káàrọ̀, Uncle Shina,' Remi says with a slight bow, and reaches out for a hug, remembering that Shina was one of the few house staff who was comfortable, even happy, with an affectionate embrace.

'Káàrọ̀, my dear Remi,' Shina says, and they hug briefly. 'Oga is waiting for you inside,' he continues in Yoruba, gesturing towards the closed living room door. 'And Madam is –' he shakes his hand to signal *roughly* – 'twenty minutes away. I will make sure Nike brings her straight to you and Oga.'

Remi nods, thankful for the information, and walks into the living room.

The living room is exactly as he left it, and yet, somehow, very different – its structure has been subtly reworked, and the furnishings, artwork, and electronics have been upgraded. Only the family portraits remain untouched. Kunle sits exactly where he always used to, watching the business news, though now on a newer, sleeker sofa with discreet slots built into the armrests for his gadgets and remote controls.

Kunle turns to Remi, and the focus in his dad's gaze is like Remi is the only thing in the world that matters at that moment. Kunle rarely expressed his affections, but his love for Remi and Kike was always evident in his eyes . . . and his actions.

Remi approaches Kunle and prostrates by his feet. 'Ẹ káàrọ̀, Dad,' he greets.

'Káàrọ̀, Remi,' Kunle says.

Remi sits on the sofa closest to his dad and is surprised by how comfortable it feels.

'What do you think of what your mum's done with the house?' Kunle asks in Yoruba.

'It's lovely,' Remi responds. 'Were the art pieces her choice, too?'

Kunle cracks a soft smile. 'Not your mum's style, is it?'

Remi nods, scanning the artwork. 'Nothing about Jesus.'

'Kike worked with the art consultant I used for the new office in VI, but she only wanted emerging Nigerian artists. It was tough for the consultant, but Kike threw herself into it and loved every second. She even started an art foundation in our name to support emerging artists – the Bankole Foundation for the Arts. It's doing very well.'

Remi nods, and they are silent as they both picture Kike joyfully choosing each piece of art and try not to think of her not being able to do that anymore . . . or them not witnessing that joy ever again.

'How was your night?' Kunle asks, and the tone of the question makes it clear he already knows about last night's events.

'Rasaq told Shina . . . Yinka?'

Kunle shakes his head. 'Rasaq is loyal and discreet. That's what we were told before we hired him and what I've seen so far. He will not say anything about your movements to Shina or Yinka unless he thinks it's necessary. Shina called Abe back this morning, and Abe told him about last night. I don't know how long you intend to stay in Lagos, but knowing you, I told Shina that you wouldn't care if Abe showed up to the games while you were around. So Abe doesn't need to stay away. But I think he will.'

Remi nods. 'I don't intend to go back to that game anyway.'

Kunle shrugs and focuses on something on the large TV screen.

Remi knows this will be the perfect time to subtly transition to asking Kunle about *Spotlight Nigeria*. But his mother is ten minutes away. Not enough time to have that conversation. He settles into the sofa, eyes focused on the business news without taking any of it in.

The distant sound of car doors shutting outside draws Remi's attention from the television, and he stiffens in his seat. Kunle also hears the distant sound over the low television and immediately stands, switches off the TV, and faces the door, his expression composed but solemn.

Remi rises too, a knot tightening in his chest.

He knows what's coming and thought he was ready for it. But he isn't.

Remi listens to his mother's brisk but confident footsteps approach . . . her exchange of polite greeting with Shina in the reception lounge, and then the living room door swings open.

Zainab Bankole enters the living room with the easy grace of a woman utterly at home in her wealth and status. She's in her mid fifties, though she looks closer to forty, as she has taken careful, loving care of herself over the years. There's an effortless glamour to her – the fine cut of her silk kaftan, the understated gold Cartier watch, the subtle scent of oud that drifts with her – nothing ostentatious, but far less muted than Kunle or Remi's restrained style.

Her face lights up with pure, uninhibited joy the moment she sees Remi. 'Remi!' she exclaims, hurrying towards him, arms outstretched.

But halfway across the room, she slows, feeling the weight in the room. Something in the way Kunle stands, something in the shadow behind Remi's eyes. The light in her face flickers.

'Where is Kike?' she asks, her voice already pulling taut with instinctive dread.

Kunle steps forward, careful, steady. He places a hand gently on her arm, guiding her further into the room. His voice, when it comes, is steady but heartbreakingly soft.

'Zainab,' he says quietly. 'Our daughter . . . she passed. It happened on Wednesday.'

At first, Zainab doesn't move. Doesn't speak.

The words seem to hover in the air, suspended, disbelieved.

'No!' she gasps. 'No, no, no . . .'

Then, as if reality crashes in all at once, her knees buckle, and she grips the arm of a nearby chair for support as a raw, wrenching sob tears loose from her. Her elegant posture collapsing under the weight of the news.

Remi's chest tightens painfully at the sight.

Every instinct urges him forward, to cross the space and catch her, anchor her somehow.

But something about the way Zainab folds into herself, the rawness of her pain, warns him that his comfort would be unwelcome, at least in this first explosion of grief.

Still, he steps forward, hesitant but ready to offer what he can.

At that moment, the living room door bursts open, and Nike, his mother's security, bursts into the room, tears streaming down her face, having just heard the news from Shina in the reception lounge.

She rushes straight to Zainab without hesitation, wrapping her in a fierce, trembling embrace. Zainab clings to Nike like a lifeline, her wracking sobs seeming to shake the walls.

Remi steps back, giving them space, feeling helpless in a way he has never felt. He glances sideways at his father, standing very still, his sorrow in his eyes only. He follows his father's eyes across the room, through the half-open door to the reception lounge to Shina, and spots the small, almost imperceptible nod exchanged between his father and Shina. Both knew this moment would come and knew Zainab would need someone to grieve with . . . and neither Kunle nor Remi would be near enough for that. Zainab needed Nike.

The sound of Zainab's howling, broken sobs roll through the house like thunder, and Remi lets the inescapable and suffocating sorrow settle over him.

CHAPTER 19

Nearly a week has passed, but Zainab's wrenching sobs still echo in Remi's head as the day of the funeral arrives.

The Bankole estate has been transformed. Elegant white tents stretch over the manicured grounds, the sides tied back to let the humid Lagos air drift through. The muted scent of the carefully prepared flowers hangs in the air, and quiet climate control units hum from discreet corners, gently circulating cooled air to temper the heat. Nothing is gaudy, but it is obvious to anyone who steps on to the property that no expense has been spared. Every seat, every flower arrangement, every uniformed attendant speaks of quiet, calculated wealth.

Kike's closed casket rests on a simple raised platform in a tent in the centre of the gathering, a bouquet of her favourite white flowers set gently atop it. The flowers were chosen by Zainab, who, despite how strained things had become, still knew exactly what her daughter would have wanted aesthetically. Remi sits a few steps away from the casket. Beside him, his mother sobs, and his father remains composed and silent. Neither Remi nor Kunle have shed a tear, and they do not look on the verge of it.

Most of the guests in the surrounding tents are dressed in black, and while the outfits vary, a quiet cohesion runs through the crowd. Even the traditional wear is subdued. Everyone understands what's expected. No flamboyance. Not today. It wouldn't be in keeping with the Bankoles. It wouldn't be what Kike wanted.

Kike's friends are easy to spot. Among them, Eki clutches a folded tissue in one hand, twisting it unconsciously in her lap. Ngozi stares ahead, blinking rapidly with heavy eyes. Seun Daniels, ever himself, wears oversized gold-framed sunglasses, his posture upright and stoic, almost like he's posing for a picture. But there are no cameras in sight.

Kunle's world is present in full: tycoons, diplomats, judges, CEOs, and politicians, including the Chief himself, flanked by Yetunde, his other children, and their mothers. The President of Nigeria is also present, sat in the front row of a tent and surrounded by other senior politicians. Their faces are carefully schooled, but their low murmurs suggest the calculations beneath their presence.

Zainab's family is here, too, in the same tent with Remi, his parents and the casket. His and Kike's favourite aunt, Aishat, sits next to Zainab, her older sister, with a steady hand resting lightly on Zainab's trembling hands to offer support when grief threatens to overwhelm. Their two brothers are farther back, wearing their military dress uniforms. Their faces are impassive, unreadable. Their long-held and vociferous objections to Zainab and Aishat's conversion from Islam to Christianity are quiet today. Even they, as proud as they are, would not cross this moment.

In the same tent, tension simmers quietly between Zainab and Nike, who sits a row behind Zainab and beside her father, Shina.

The silence between them is sharp, filled with things unsaid. Zainab had expected Pastor Biodun to preside over the funeral prayer, and it was Nike's job to arrange it. Nike tried everything to make it happen. But the pastor refused – out of spite. Zainab knows this, but the pain of the pastor's absence sharpened the edges of her grief, and Nike is bearing the brunt of it. Remi watches their dynamic slowly shift and feels anger towards the pastor stir in him. Even the dead are not beyond the pastor's cruelty.

When the time for the prayer arrives, Aishat rises to deliver it. Her voice is clear and strong, part Yoruba, part English. Behind her, a choir hums a slow, mournful harmony. Elders from both sides of the family bow their heads, whispering a dua for the deceased or traditional Yoruba mourning prayers. Although Kike was not traditional or religious, she would've appreciated the blend of cultures, traditions, and religions.

After the prayer, Mrs Ibeh rises to announce that the ceremony will draw to a close and that the burial will be held privately.

The final hymn begins, and some guests step forward to pass by the casket, offering whispered prayers, a touch to the wood or a lingering glance. Remi stands motionless as the mourners stream past. Kunle bows his head, hands clasped in front of him. Zainab grieves loudly, her body bent with sorrow, Aishat doing her best to hold her sister up. Remi glances at his mum and is forever marked by her devastation – it's an image he knows he will never forget.

The ceremony ends, and the guests drift towards their waiting cars, slow and solemn beneath the beating sun. Remi moves among them like a man underwater, offering brief words of gratitude and nodding when needed. He goes through the motions, but somewhere beneath his buried grief, the questions surrounding his sister's death remain sharp and waiting – and he won't leave Lagos, his family, without answers.

CHAPTER 20

The dull thud of fists against leather echoes through the gym, each strike sharp, deliberate and unrelenting. Remi is alone, stripped to his boxer briefs, sweat-soaked fabric clinging to his body. He's been at it for hours, long enough for the burn in his muscles to fade into something quieter. His fists hammer the heavy bag in a steady rhythm. But there is no catharsis in the motion. Only control. Containment.

It isn't rage that fuels him. Not entirely. It's the quiet ache of helplessness, knowing that whatever truths still lie ahead, none of them will bring Kike back. And beneath that ache, a deeper, buried emotion lurks – the feeling that he abandoned her. That he failed her.

The door creaks open behind him. He doesn't stop punching but softens the rhythm – less force and more control. He already knows who it is.

Bola stands in the doorway with one hand on the door and the other behind his back, as if stepping into a sacred space. He doesn't speak right away. And when he does, it's with gentle formality.

'Ẹ káàrọ̀, Oga Remi,' he greets.

Remi stops and pulls off the gloves, his chest rising and falling with each breath. 'Káàrọ̀, Bola,' he says.

Bola takes a step inside. 'Oga asked if you would join him in the main house for breakfast. Madam is back and . . .' He hesitates, then straightens. 'He would like you to come.'

Remi nods slowly. He'd heard the distant sound of his mum's car pulling in just after midnight as he was struggling to sleep. She'd left with Aishat immediately after the funeral. No one had said where to, and he hadn't asked.

'I'll be there in fifteen,' he says.

Bola bows slightly but doesn't turn to leave. Remi studies him for a moment, and it's clear Bola is still finding his footing, unsure whether to offer a sympathetic word or gesture, some combination of both, or just to leave.

Remi saves him the trouble. 'I'm okay, Bola. Just struggling to sleep. How are you?'

'I'm okay, Oga Remi,' Bola replies quickly as if his feelings aren't supposed to matter.

Remi reads this but doesn't press. He appreciates the effort Bola and the other house staff have made to maintain a sense of calm since the news broke.

'I'll go shower now. And I'll walk over to the main house.'

'Okay, Oga Remi,' Bola says with a nod. He retreats and closes the door quietly behind him.

Fifteen minutes later, Remi walks the path to the main house, freshly showered and dressed in one of his father's understated kaftans. The sun is up, and the day is already warming. The grounds are spotless. There is not a single trace of the funeral left behind.

Tents, flowers, chairs – all gone, as if the estate has quietly swept the grief aside overnight.

As usual, the front door to the main house opens automatically as Remi approaches. He steps through into the cool reception vestibule, and the young man holding the door open gently closes it behind him before prostrating to greet Remi. Remi nods softly and walks through to the main hallway of the house.

He immediately spots Nike, dressed in a soft blue wrapper and blouse, standing just beneath the sweeping staircase ahead, her posture tight with expectation.

She glances backwards at his approaching footsteps, and her expression shifts between surprise, sorrow, and relief.

'Ẹ káàrọ̀, Remi,' she says quietly.

'Káàrọ̀, Nike.'

They stand a few paces apart, the silence between them tender but weighted, especially by the anxiety in her eyes.

'Are you following your mother to church?' she asks, eyes dropping briefly to his elegant kaftan, a flicker of hope in her voice.

'No. Just here for breakfast with her and Dad,' he says, running a hand along the smooth fabric. 'I didn't bring many clothes, so I'm wearing Dad's.'

She nods, and the hope fades from her face.

'And today's Saturday, right?' he says with a soft smile. 'There's church today, too?'

'There's church every day,' she says without a hint of amusement.

'Are you okay?' Remi asks.

Nike is momentarily taken aback by the gentleness of the question. She recovers quickly with a response that sounds rehearsed, something Mrs Ibeh might have advised. 'Yes, I'm okay,' she says without conviction. 'How . . .'

'Are you okay?' Remi repeats, cutting in gently. 'Seriously.'

'It's not about me . . .'

'Nike,' he says, calm but firm. 'We're all feeling Kike's loss in our own way. But I'm asking you. Beyond that . . . are you okay?'

She clasps her hands together. 'Madam . . . she's barely speaking to me. I've tried. I am trying. But she doesn't want me near her.'

Remi nods, understanding. 'As I said . . . we're all handling the loss in our own way. Give her time. It might be a while, but be patient.'

Nike nods, then blinks fast, suddenly having to fight back tears. 'I just want to be here for her. I . . .'

Remi steps forward and rests a gentle hand on her arm, cutting her off. 'You're trying. That's what matters.'

A voice carries faintly from upstairs. It's Zainab's, clear but muffled with impatience. Nike instinctively turns towards the sound, then looks back at Remi.

'I should go see if she needs my help,' she says softly.

Remi nods. 'Of course.'

She lingers momentarily, then turns and ascends the stairs, her footsteps light but purposeful.

Remi watches Nike disappear up the stairs before turning towards the dining room. He walks down the hallway, scanning each piece of art as he passes, newly attuned to their significance. He now knows each one was curated by Kike. The house is quiet, the staff moving like whispers, doors opening and closing with studied care.

The dining room door is open, and Remi steps inside.

Kunle is already seated at the head of the table. No iPad. No phone. An artful teapot and three cups sit in front of him, untouched. His posture is straight and composed, but Remi recognises the quiet calculation in his eyes. Kunle turns to him and offers a pleasant smile that Remi wasn't expecting.

Remi approaches and prostrates. 'Ẹ káàrọ̀, Dad,' he greets.

'Káàrọ̀, Remi,' Kunle replies, extending a hand to help him up. 'Sit.'

Remi takes the seat beside him.

'These kaftans look like they were made for you,' Kunle says with a glint in his eye. 'I should give you my entire wardrobe.'

Remi smiles. 'I'll be taking a few back with me.'

Kunle nods, and after a beat of silence, he asks, 'And when will you be going back?'

Remi tries to read his father's tone, searching for emotion behind the question, but finds none. It seems Kunle is asking only for information.

'Not sure, Dad. The partners told me to take my time.'

Kunle nods again. 'I'm sure they know your value.'

They lapse into silence, but it is not uncomfortable. Not between them. Over the years, they have learned that sometimes silence says more than anything else, especially at times like this

One of the staff quietly brings in a tray of breakfast things: boiled yam, scrambled eggs, homemade sausages, akara, and a small basket of fresh bread. The server sets it down without a word and bows. Kunle and Remi return the gesture, and the server withdraws.

Neither of them reaches for the food, and after a while, Kunle speaks again.

'Your mother will be down shortly. She'll have breakfast with us before going to church.'

Remi nods. 'I saw Nike . . . she's waiting for Mum.'

Kunle exhales but offers no further comment. But Remi senses that his father has thoughts about the deterioration of Zainab and Nike's relationship, thoughts he will never voice. Especially not now.

Kunle pours tea into two cups, offers one to Remi, and they sip in silence.

A low murmur filters through the door. It's Zainab's voice. Steady. Dismissive.

'There's no need for you to follow me,' she says in Yoruba.

Nike's softer reply is harder to hear, but the tone is unmistakable. Pleading.

Another pause. Then Zainab again. Firmer. 'I said no, Nike. That's final.'

The hallway falls quiet. Remi and Kunle don't react. They sip their tea as if they've heard nothing at all.

Moments later, the door opens, and Zainab strides in. She's dressed in an elegant flowing dress with a large clutch bag tucked under one arm. Her face is composed, her make-up flawless, but the faint redness around her eyes betrays the night she's had. Her steps are measured, and she doesn't look at Kunle.

'Káàrọ̀,' she says, addressing no one in particular. Her eyes move past Kunle and settle on Remi, and affection, dulled by pain and restraint, flickers in her expression.

'Ẹ káàrọ̀, Mummy,' Remi says, rising to greet her.

She crosses the room and kisses his cheek. 'Káàrọ̀, my dear.' She does not sit. Her posture remains poised but resolute. 'I'm going to church,' she says. 'To pray. Alone.'

Kunle nods once. 'We'll see you when you return.'

Zainab says nothing. She glances at Remi again, her expression softening just slightly, then turns and walks out.

Her footsteps retreat into the silence once more.

Kunle reaches for the eggs. 'Oya,' he says. 'Let's eat.'

CHAPTER 21

Soon after breakfast, Remi makes his way to the staff quarters. The path from the main house, between the manicured low hedges and flowering shrubs, is familiar. But as he approaches the exit of the footpath, he immediately sees that the staff quarters have also been extensively renovated, highlighted by a newly built three-storey block of studio flats. He's proud that some of the care and detail embodied in the main house is present here.

Remi steps off the path and approaches one of the renovated one-bedroom bungalows nestled in the middle of other larger bungalows. He knocks gently on the front door, and it opens a moment later to reveal Ada, Mrs Ibeh's daughter. She looks surprised to see him.

'Good morning, Oga Remi.'

Remi shakes his head and gestures towards the main and guest houses. 'There, Oga Remi is fine. But here . . . it's just Remi.'

She nods again. 'Good morning, Remi.'

'Morning, Ada. I was told this was Nike's place. Is she in?'

'Yes. This is her place. She's inside, but she's . . .' She hesitates, trying to find the right words.

'I know,' he says, understanding. 'Please let her know I'd like to talk to her. She can take her time. I'll wait here.'

'Are you sure you don't want to come inside?'

'I'm sure.'

Ada nods and gently shuts the door. Remi turns around to scan the rest of the staff quarters, noting the unique signs of habitation around each residence.

The door soon opens, and Remi turns to see Ada presenting him with a glass of ice-cold water.

He accepts it with a smile. 'Daalụ,' he says, thanking her in her native Igbo language.

She bows her head. 'You're welcome, Remi. Nike will be out soon.'

He nods, and Ada gently closes the door.

He enjoys every drop of the cold water before the door opens again, and Nike steps out, trying to appear confident though it's clear she's been crying.

'I was hoping we could talk,' Remi says gently, and hands her his empty cup.

'Okay,' she says, accepting the cup. 'Want to come inside?'

'Let's head to the gallery, if that's okay with you. I hear it's impressive, and I haven't been. Plus, you helped Kike collect the artwork, so you can talk me through them.'

'It is very impressive, but it was more Ada that helped with the artwork. I mostly helped with organising the party to celebrate the opening.'

'I heard that was wonderful,' he says, pausing for a beat to stress his next words. 'My dad just told me.'

The comment and the memory of the party clearly lift her spirits. 'I will do my best to talk you through the art collection,' she says, glancing over her shoulder to Ada inside the house. 'And if there's anything I don't know, Ada can help you later – she's there almost every day.'

'I look forward to that,' he says, loud enough for Ada to hear inside.

Nike places the cup just inside the threshold before shutting the door, and they both head back towards the rear of the main house, where a stunning glass-walled outbuilding, more than twice the size of the guest house's outbuilding gym, serves as the Bankoles' private gallery.

Remi and Nike walk in comfortable silence through the maze-like manicured low hedges towards the gallery. As they approach, the quiet elegance of the outbuilding becomes more apparent, with understated stonework and sleek glass that invite in the light and the view of the surrounding grounds without demanding attention.

The automatic doors slide open with a gentle hush, and Nike leads Remi inside. He pauses at the entrance, momentarily taken aback by the space itself – open, airy, and cleverly designed to feel both expansive and intimate.

Daylight spills in from full-height windows and a skylight that runs the length of the ceiling, and the artworks are spaced with intention, each one given room to breathe.

Most of the pieces are African-inspired, predominantly Nigerian – a mix of bold canvases, mixed-media sculptures, and intricately beaded textiles. Some are clearly modern, others deeply traditional. Each piece feels chosen with deliberate care, evoking a balance of boldness and poise.

Remi moves slowly from one piece to the next, pausing now and then, his hands clasped behind his back. He doesn't speak, and Nike seems to instinctively understand not to fill the silence.

'This one came from an artist in Yaba,' she offers quietly at one point, gesturing to a vivid abstract painting. 'Ada said Kike bought it on the spot.'

Remi nods, observing the painting.

Further along, Nike says, 'Kike fought for this sculpture. The consultant didn't think it fit the theme of the gallery, but Kike insisted. I remember her saying it reminded her of something your grandfather once said.'

'What was that?' Remi asks gently, still facing the piece.

Nike frowns slightly, searching her memory. 'I can't remember exactly. Something about stubborn beauty. Ada might know.'

Remi smiles faintly. 'Don't worry. I know. It was about our grandmother. She died before we were born, but he always used to tell us stories.'

They walk on to the far end of the gallery, where a wide, low bench sits beneath a wall-sized canvas of the Lagos Lagoon at dawn.

They sit, and for a few seconds, neither of them speaks. Then Remi says, calm and measured, 'Now let's talk about Pastor Biodun.'

Nike instantly tightens up, and Remi can sense her apprehension.

'I know he's been your pastor for decades, and you and Mum even followed him to this new church. But you have no loyalty to him . . . especially not after yesterday.'

Something in his words eases her tension, though Remi is not sure what. Nothing he said should have come as a revelation.

She nods, as if asking him to lead the conversation.

'Did he know how much Mum wanted him to preside over the funeral?'

'Of course,' she says, the bitterness clear in her voice. 'He even tried to use it to ask for more investment in the church. More gifts for himself personally.'

'More *investment* . . . *gifts* . . . what exactly are we talking about?'

She hesitates, considering how much to say. Then, she decides not to hold back.

'He was forced out of House of Grace after the *Spotlight Nigeria* episode, and since then, Madam has been funding everything about this new church. One hundred percent. And we're not talking small funds. I've been keeping records – you never know when someone will ask. So far? Over a billion naira.

'He and his people call it "investment", but Madam won't ask for anything back. They know that. And this . . . funding . . . didn't start after *Spotlight Nigeria*. Madam was already paying for all sorts of things at House of Grace.'

Remi nods, outwardly calm but seething inside.

'Gifts?' she continues, with a bitter laugh. 'That one has been happening since before I even started going to House of Grace. So I don't even remember what I've forgotten. But today? His fleet of cars – G-Wagon, S-Class, Range Rover, Tesla. Gifts from Madam.

'His flat in Ikoyi? His wife kicked him out after *Spotlight Nigeria*. Madam bought that flat. He's back home now, oh, but he's keeping the flat. Still a gift, abi?' She waves a hand dismissively. 'Watches? Plenty. Suits? Plenty. Shoes? You don't want to know.'

Each detail hits like a punch, but Remi keeps his expression steady, letting her speak.

'Now this last one . . . this one was too much. Madam told me to arrange for him to oversee the funeral service. She asked him directly. And he said yes, of course. But then his people said he'd be in Ilorin before the service, so he'd need a helicopter to make it back in time. Madam agreed. Told me to organise it sharp-sharp. I arranged it.

'Then they said he had another engagement that night . . . and the next day . . . and the day after that. So they wanted the helicopter and pilot on standby. For a month.

'I kept quiet. Last last . . . I'd just cancel it after the service. But then . . . the pastor himself called me. Said God told him he needed to spread the word internationally. That he needed 300,000 dollars to lock in a prime-time slot on TBN. For two years. Madam said yes. We transferred the money.

'Then yesterday morning . . . helicopter arrives. Pilot calls me – Pastor won't come out. I call the pastor. He said God told him in a dream that he would die if he entered the helicopter. Okay. I arranged for a police escort through traffic. Pastor said no. Too dangerous.

'After that, he stopped answering my calls. I called his people. They said he was talking to God and could not be disturbed.'

She shakes her head, breathless. Not just from the rant but from the months of silent exhaustion behind it.

'Does my dad know about all these investments and gifts?'

'I don't know,' she says, glancing away.

Remi notes the lie but doesn't push. The lie itself is an answer.

'He doesn't approve these payments? These are large sums.'

She blinks, slightly thrown by the question. 'Madam approves it,' she says at last, her tone edged with faint annoyance at Remi even questioning the Madam's authority.

Remi nods slowly. 'My mum went to pray in that new church, right?'

'Yes.'

'And I'm sure you've told her about what happened yesterday?'

'I have. But somehow, it's still my fault. She's not even angry with Pastor Biodun. Just with me. Says I didn't do enough. That I ruined the funeral service for her.'

The weight of it suddenly hits her. She buckles, silent tears falling as the emotions overwhelm her.

Remi lets her cry. Then, after a moment, he places a calm hand on her shoulder.

'What's the address of this new church?'

CHAPTER 22

The next morning, Rasaq pulls into the church's car park, and Remi, sat in the passenger seat and dressed in another of his dad's kaftans, observes the unexpectedly large church compound. It's a few minutes before 9:30 a.m. – when Remi was advised the Sunday service would begin – but the car park is already busy with cars lined up in neat rows and uniformed attendants guiding the new arrivals towards the remaining spots. The church building itself is newly constructed and impressive, with a sleek blend of contemporary and traditional Nigerian aesthetics. The building is a monument to Pastor Biodun's vision and apparent prosperity, and it's clear that no expense has been spared.

Remi spots his mother's car – a black Mercedes S-Class – parked in the reserved section near the church's grand entrance. A few cars down, he notices the unmistakable presence of Pastor Biodun's G-Wagon, parked right in front of the church's entrance. It's unmistakable because of the personalised plate number – 'The Chosen 1'. Remi shakes his head, slightly annoyed but also amused by the hubris.

Rasaq finds a spot close to the back of the car park, with a good view of the whole compound and the church's entrance.

'It looks nice,' he remarks, nodding towards the church as he switches off the engine.

Remi nods. 'I'm sure it's even better inside,' he says. 'Want to come in?'

Rasaq shakes his head lightly. 'I'll wait here. Yinka confirmed that inside the church is safe.'

'Safe? Shina has people inside watching my mum?'

'Yes. But your mother doesn't know. She doesn't want any security at church.'

Remi nods, biting back a remark about his mother believing Jesus himself will protect her in the church. 'I'm going to stay for a bit after the service is over, so you can go relax somewhere and come back in a couple of hours.'

'It's okay, Remi. I'll wait.'

'All right. In a bit,' Remi says, and steps out of the car.

Remi pauses for a moment just outside the car, adjusting his kaftan and scanning the church entrance. He hopes he won't be recognised in there, especially by friends, as he doesn't want their condolences. He appreciates the sentiment but also feels them observing his reactions, judging or waiting for a crack in his composure.

He heads towards the entrance and hears the faint sounds of a live band warming up the churchgoers with songs of praise. He steps through the doors and is immediately met by a large screen showing the relatively young musicians on the stage, jamming away on several instruments to contemporary gospel music and enjoying every moment of it. Remi can't help but admit that their joy is infectious.

He steps into a vast theatre-like hall with high ceilings, tiered seating, and modern furnishings. Several large screens are distributed across the tiers, and the church's logo – a stylised flame – is everywhere, seemingly on every item. The stage itself is the grandest of all, with gleaming marble steps leading up to a lectern fit for the Pope.

Remi takes a seat towards the middle, and as he'd hoped, he blends into the crowd. He spots his mother up front in a slightly raised section marked as the VIP area, alongside other high-society Lagosians he recognises, including one of Nigeria's most famous ex-professional footballers. Zainab is standing, clapping softly as she sings and vibes with the live band. Remi is quickly struck by the frequency of people approaching her to whisper their condolences. Some walked all the way to the front just for that. She acknowledges a few with a quick word and hug, but most with a gracious nod.

The band leaves the stage at exactly 9:30 a.m., and everyone returns to their seat. It doesn't take long for the service to begin, with another energetic worship session led by the choir and a small orchestra. Like the band, the choir and orchestra are exemplary, their voices and music rising and falling in unison as they lead the church in singing and dancing to more traditional Nigerian church music. Remi watches the crowd and can't help but feel the warmth in the room.

The first offering round soon follows, and Remi notes how seamlessly the giving is incorporated into the service as a cheerful usher dances through the aisles in his section with a collection basket. Remi is prepared for this and drops a good amount of the cash he'd pulled out earlier from the brown envelope in the car's glove compartment – the same envelope he'd noticed had been moved from the Bentley and quietly replenished since Rose's party. However, there are three more rounds of offering – one specifically for the building fund, another for missions and outreach, and the last for a local children's home. Each time, it is accompanied by a well-practised appeal from one of the senior workers in the church and video packages on the screen. Remi drops some money the second time but stops after that.

The sermon is just before the final offering round. Pastor Biodun steps up with a commanding yet approachable air. He's dressed in a sharp double-breasted striped suit with shoes and a tie to match the debonair aura. He's a confident orator, weaving personal anecdotes with scripture in a way that makes the sermon feel intimate. There's no denying his skill as he moves seamlessly from empathy to exhortation, bringing the congregation from quiet reflection to rousing agreement with just a few well-placed words.

Remi notices his mum being captivated by the sermon early on, and after that, he's more focused on watching her reactions than the sermon. Her devotion is evident with every response, even more so when the pastor unsubtly veers close to Kike's situation with references to sudden loss and unexpected trials. For Remi, those moments – especially the fact that the pastor never actually mentions Kike's name – reinforce why he is here.

The service ends, and the band resumes, softer this time, providing a backdrop for prayers and personal reflections. The congregation slowly disperses into smaller groups, some lingering to chat, others filing out. Zainab doesn't move. She remains seated as more people approach – some to offer condolences, others to engage in light conversation, perhaps hoping to be noticed . . . to be remembered by *Madam Zainab*.

Remi waits until the initial crowd around her thins before making his way to the VIP section. She spots him as he approaches, and her face is flooded with a mix of emotions. Remi instantly recognises the surprise and joy, but there is one more emotion in the mix that Remi doesn't quite come to grips with before she buries it. It seems like anxiety, maybe even fear, but he quickly brushes that off because he knows his mum is not afraid of him.

'Remi,' Zainab says, and reaches out for a hug.

He hugs his mum and unexpectedly sinks into her embrace. She feels it as well and holds him tightly for a long, quiet moment before they release each other.

'You came?' she says, and adds, 'Here.'

Remi senses that emotion again for a fleeting moment when she adds the *here*.

'Yes,' Remi says. 'I was here for the entire service.'

'Ah. Why didn't you let me know? I would have arranged for you to come and sit with me.'

'It's fine,' he says, gesturing to a few sections behind. 'I wasn't too far. I was able to see the stage very clearly . . . and there are screens everywhere.'

'Did you enjoy the sermon?'

Remi nods, which isn't that much of a lie. 'And I saw you were enjoying it as well.'

The emotion flashes across Zainab's face again. 'Ah, you could see me?'

'Yes.'

At that moment, one of the last remaining VIP members of the church approaches to offer condolences, which Zainab and Remi graciously accept before engaging in small talk about the sermon for another five minutes before the VIP member leaves them.

'I still have some things to do here,' Zainab says. 'So let me walk you outside.'

'Err . . .' Remi says, stopping her in her tracks, before softly adding, 'I didn't just come for the service.'

'Oh,' she says, her expression shifting to one of wary expectation.

'What's happened to Kike . . . to us . . . has made me question my faith. Or . . . well, my lack of faith. And it's left me hoping Kike is in a better place.'

The first half of that was a lie, and Remi feels more guilt at telling it to his mother than he expected. But . . . this is why he's here.

'I understand, Remi,' Zainab says, her tone softening. 'Would you like to talk to one of the junior pastors . . . or a church elder?'

Remi is slightly surprised she didn't immediately suggest Pastor Biodun, but he keeps his expression neutral. 'I'd like to speak to the pastor,' he says calmly.

She nods, thoughtful. 'That might be difficult because his Sundays are very busy. You will have to wait a long time.'

Remi shrugs. 'I expected to wait.'

She nods and reaches out to gently squeeze his hands. 'I will let them know. Wait here, and someone will come and get you when Biodun is available.'

Remi notes her use of the pastor's first name without his title, and he must've reacted to it in some way because Zainab immediately realises that she did it. She covers it with a smile and walks away through a side door leading to the church's inner sanctum.

Remi sits in the exact same chair his mother did and waits quietly and patiently. He is alone . . . except for the two occasions when an usher comes to ask if he wants any refreshments. Two and a half hours pass before a sharply dressed young man approaches.

'Mr Remi,' the young man says without any sign of deference. 'The pastor will see you now.'

'Thanks,' Remi says, and stands.

He follows the young man through the same door his mother had gone through two and a half hours earlier.

The young man leads Remi down a long hallway, past many closed doors, some of which are seemingly occupied based on the muffled voices leaking through. At the end of the hall, they reach a door that looks more like the entrance to a presidential suite than a pastor's office – dark wood, gold fixtures, a statement piece. The young man knocks once, waits for a beat, and then opens the door, gesturing for Remi to enter without making eye contact. Remi nods anyway before stepping inside.

The office is a shrine to Christianity and the pastor's ego. Framed photos of him shaking hands with celebrities, politicians, dignitaries, and even Pope Francis line the walls, interspersed with religious iconography: Jesus at the Last Supper, the Crucifixion, and biblical quotes in ornate calligraphy. The room smells faintly of leather and expensive cologne.

The pastor finally looks up as if tired of waiting for Remi to act like the typical spoilt rich kid who would waltz across the Persian rug to sit in one of the plush leather chairs without invitation.

'Blessings, Remi,' the pastor says, his voice dripping with patronising warmth. 'Good to finally meet you. Come and sit. I have another engagement in ten minutes, but I'm squeezing you in now as a favour to your mother.'

Remi nods, crosses the room and sits. 'Good afternoon, Pastor. Thanks for taking the time.'

The pastor barely acknowledges the gratitude, maintaining his air of superiority. He leans back, staring expectantly at Remi. But Remi just calmly returns his stare without an ounce of hurry, spotting the G-Wagon's keys hanging prominently on an exquisite angel figurine on the desk.

The pastor breaks the silence. 'So, I gather you are having a crisis of faith in the Lord Jesus Christ,' he says, his tone confident.

'Not exactly,' Remi responds. 'But that's what I told my mother.'

The pastor's eyebrows knit briefly, revealing a crack in his composure.

'It's more that I can't stop thinking about how much I want vengeance on the person who killed Kike,' Remi continues, voice steady. 'Not just an eye for an eye. Both their eyes. And anyone else who saw, who knew, who kept quiet or helped them. I want them all. But even then . . . it won't be enough. That's why I'm here.'

Remi leans back, his eyes never leaving the pastor. 'You understand I couldn't say any of that to my mother. She wouldn't know how to counsel me. She'd be disappointed that I'm harbouring so much hatred.'

The pastor shifts, trying to settle back into his authority. 'You want us to pray over it?'

Remi shrugs. 'More a conversation about how you suggest I work through the hatred . . . how I can come to forgive them all. But sure, I would appreciate a prayer as well.'

The pastor nods, as things are back in his wheelhouse, but before he speaks, Remi cuts in.

'But first, I need to be sure you're a better person than me . . . at least when it comes to forgiveness.'

A flash of anger darts across the pastor's face. 'What do you mean by that, Remi?'

'Why didn't you officiate Kike's funeral? My mum wanted you to.'

The pastor straightens. 'I was busy.'

'But you'd agreed. And there was a helicopter waiting for you.'

The pastor pauses, clearly irritated. 'I had a vision. God told me not to enter that helicopter.'

'And the police convoy too?' Remi asks, as if genuinely curious.

The pastor's mouth tightens. 'Listen, Remi, your sister ruined my life. She destroyed my marriage. Got me cast out of the church I built from a garage in Mushin. Almost destroyed my reputation. I – '

'So it wasn't the actual philandering with the female members that led to that?' Remi cuts in as if driven by polite curiosity. 'Not the use of the church funds to bankroll your *indulgences*?'

The pastor's eyes flare, but he says nothing.

'You're not still denying those, are you?' Remi asks. 'John, chapter 8, verse 32 . . . the truth will set you free.' Remi pauses for a beat. 'You should be grateful to Kike. Holding those lies for that long can't have been good for your soul. She set you free. And now –' Remi gestures around the room – 'look what you've built.'

The pastor's rage simmers, but Remi senses it's not purely anger . . . it's helplessness from knowing he didn't dare lash out. His entire world – his image, his power – is underpinned by Zainab Bankole's patronage.

'You're no better than me,' Remi says with a seemingly understanding tone. 'That's fine. But I'll seek advice elsewhere. Thank you for your time.'

Remi rises and heads for the door.

'Such spoilt children!' the pastor snaps. 'You and your sister!'

Remi stops, then walks back to the desk with deliberate calm. 'What did you say?' he asks.

'Your father! He spoilt you and your sister! Dumping you in London where you forgot all your home training. How dare you come into my office—'

'Our office, Pastor,' Remi cuts in. 'My father's money paid for it. This new beautiful church. The clothes on your back. The cars in your garage. Your flat in Ikoyi. All of it. My father's money. You're the one he has spoilt. So don't speak about how he chose to raise us. Because all those things will get cut off like that.' He snaps a finger, and the effect is like a gunshot in the quiet room.

'Just so you know how serious I am,' Remi says, and reaches for the G-Wagon's keys. 'I'm taking this back. Someone will drop off the plates when we get around to it.'

The pastor stares, dumbstruck, and Remi nods and walks out of the office without looking back.

Remi strides out of the church, spotting the Land Cruiser parked right at the entrance, where Rasaq had moved it once the car park started to clear. He walks to the driver's side, and Rasaq lowers the window.

'You'll be driving that back,' Remi says, holding out the G-Wagon's keys. 'I'll follow you in this.'

Rasaq hesitates for a moment, processing what could've happened inside the church for Remi to be coming out with the pastor's G-Wagon keys. Then he cracks a smile, impressed by Remi's calm ruthlessness. Rasaq had heard some details about the pastor's actions on the day of the funeral. Many of the household staff were very angry with the pastor because they all loved Kike and respected Nike, especially the younger ones. Now it makes sense to him why Remi suddenly wanted to attend church . . . and this church specifically. To deal with the pastor.

'No problem,' he says, accepting the keys. 'I'll drive that one. But we'll leave this one here, and I'll message Yinka to send someone for it.'

Remi nods, and Rasaq hops out, places the Land Cruiser's keys on the front tyre, and walks to the G-Wagon while texting Yinka.

They settle into it, and Rasaq switches on the air conditioning before navigating smoothly out of the car park. Remi leans back, eyes forward, feeling the weight of his earlier anger start to dissipate . . . replaced by a quiet satisfaction.

CHAPTER 23

A few hours after the service, Remi sits in the living room watching a premier league football match on the television, though he isn't engrossed in it. He hadn't thought much about the pastor since leaving the church. To him, that situation was done and dusted. There would be some ramifications, as he imagines his mother would be displeased . . . maybe even angry. But she would understand why it had to be done. She might've even wanted it done to put the pastor in his place for abandoning his promise at Kike's funeral service, but without dirtying her hands or carrying the guilt of knowing it was going to happen.

There is a soft knock on the living room door before footsteps enter the room. Remi turns to see Kehinde waiting just inside the door, and, for a moment, he notices the quiet spark of pride in Kehinde's eyes before it is buried.

'Afternoon, Remi,' Kehinde says.

'Afternoon, Kehinde,' Remi responds.

'Madam and Oga have requested your presence.'

'*Requested my presence?*' Remi repeats with a raised eyebrow. 'Those words exactly?'

Kehinde nods. 'That's what Mrs Ibeh just said on the intercom.'

Remi shrugs and stands, and although he is in his early thirties, this feeling of being summoned to see his parents still sends a gentle chill through him, and he can feel the goosebumps.

'My mum's evidently back from church,' he remarks as he walks towards Kehinde.

'Yes,' Kehinde responds, and then adds with clear deliberation, 'less than five minutes before the intercom call from Mrs Ibeh.'

Remi nods, thankful for the information, and Kehinde leads him out of the living room towards the front door.

Kehinde opens the door for Remi, but as Remi walks through, he places a soft hand on Remi's shoulder. Remi stops and turns to him.

'Thank you,' Kehinde says after a brief moment of hesitation. 'And that is from many more than just me . . . including Nike.'

Remi pats Kehinde's shoulder in appreciation and turns to walk out of the guest house.

A few minutes later, Remi walks past the G-Wagon, parked in the driveway of the main house as he'd requested, and heads towards the front door. As always, the door opens as he approaches, and after the usual greeting, the young man at the door lets him know that his parents are expecting him in the living room.

Remi steps into the waiting lounge just outside the living room, and Mrs Ibeh steps in from the living room. They exchange greetings, and it's clear from Mrs Ibeh's stiff manner that she's disappointed in his actions, which isn't surprising to Remi. He can also sense reproach at the tip of her tongue, but she thinks better of it after weighing the moment.

Remi steps through the door and immediately notices that his father isn't in his usual seat; he's on the seat anyone walking through the door would immediately notice. Kunle locks eyes with Remi and makes a subtle hand gesture Remi recognises from years before when his mother was consumed with righteous fury – back then it was about Remi openly saying that he didn't believe in God, while pinpointing the logical fallacies behind religion, specifically Christianity. The gesture demands that Remi not say a word and just take everything his mother says with seeming contrition. Remi acknowledges with a subtle nod before turning to his mother across the room, and he's immediately struck by the rage in her bearing. His stomach tightens at the unfamiliar sight, because her fury appears sharper, colder, and much more personal than he anticipated.

Remi is also perplexed by the distance between his parents and quickly considers who to approach to greet first. He decides on his mother, as he's sure that is what his dad would want. He advances towards her, but she unleashes before his second step.

'What nonsense was that, eh, Remi?' Zainab demands in Yoruba, her voice razor-sharp. When she's angry, she reverts to Yoruba, and each word is laced with venom. 'What nonsense!'

Remi is taken aback by the instant vitriol. There is usually some preamble about expecting better from him, and the decibel never reaches this level. He doesn't speak but maintains a contrite demeanour while keeping eye contact with her. In his experience, that usually dampens the outburst . . . but not today.

'Who do you think you are? Ehn? Doing what you did to a man of God? I raised you better than that. But you've lost all your home training in London, abi?'

The almost identical phrasing to what the pastor used in making the same accusation raises the hairs on his neck. He wants to point it out subtly, question the pastor's version of events, but he glances at his dad, and his dad's composed gesture reinforces the request to not engage and appear contrite. So Remi does.

'And you lied to me!' she continues, her voice faltering for just a moment before regaining its sharpness. 'Used me to get a meeting with Pastor Biodun . . . only to pull that rubbish!'

Remi is dumbfounded by the selective outrage because this is the same Pastor Biodun who couldn't bring himself to oversee Kike's funeral service out of vengeance. But again, he doesn't respond.

'The same thing Kike did for her nonsense YouTube video. But why should I be surprised? You probably taught her that one, too. Same as you taught her to be a non-believer.'

The accusation lands like a punch to the gut, winding him. For a moment, he can't breathe . . . can't process how she could believe that. Especially because he knows his mum is very aware that no one was going to influence Kike to do what she didn't want to do. Still, he doesn't react.

'Carried her to London. Taught her to drink, smoke Indian hemp and to party . . . party . . . party every day. Socialite, abi? No concern for God. Now look?'

Remi's heard enough and doesn't turn to his father before speaking. If he did, he'd see Kunle gesturing to remain stoic.

'I don't know what's going on, Mum,' he gently says. 'But you really can't be this angry because I had a word with your pastor . . . frank, yes, but in private . . . after he bailed on—'

'Remi,' Kunle says, calm but firm, stopping Remi.

Remi turns to Kunle and apologises for speaking out with a slight bow. Zainab notices the interaction and is further enraged.

'You took her from me. Both of you. I told your father to bring you both back after university. Or at least bring her back. Stop her living in the same building as you. But no. He said you'd be a good influence. Just because you got that big job in London. That's the only influence your father cares about, sha. The ones that bring more money . . . connections. And just like I feared, you turned my Kike into something else. She came back hating tradition. Religion. All the *patriarchy nonsense. Hierarchy nonsense.* Women's rights. Just trying to fight everything. And then, on top of all that, when she got too much for you, you went and slapped her and sent her back to us in broken pieces.'

Remi is hurt by his mother's words and overcome with indignation. He opens his mouth to object, but Kunle beats him to it.

'Zainab,' Kunle says sternly.

'Abeg, don't Zainab me,' she retorts. 'I'm not one of your children or the people you are moving around like ayo seeds. You don't shut me up with a word. I am Zainab Aderonke, the first daughter of the greatest Olubadan of Ibadanland. I was somebody before you, and I will be somebody after you.' She glares at Kunle, then Remi. 'You are both the same. And I tried, oh. I tried to show you the way of God. Instead of the money and power your father worships. But no. That one is too sweet for your blood. You Bankoles are cursed with it.'

'Remi,' Kunle calls, and Remi turns to his father, his eyes heavy from fighting back tears. Kunle acknowledges Remi's emotions with a slight nod before gently saying, 'Please leave us.'

Remi nods and blinks once to bury his heavy eyes and emotions. He turns to his mum, and she rolls her eyes, recognising his pain and dismissing it.

'Have a good day, Mum,' Remi says, and leaves the living room.

CHAPTER 24

14 July 2021, 2 a.m.

The piercing ring of Remi's phone jolts him awake. Disoriented, he fumbles on the bedside table to grab the phone and squints against the screen's harsh light. It's Kike.

He instantly snaps out of sleep and picks up. 'Kike?' he says, calm, hiding his anxiety.

Her voice is low, almost a whisper, but something about the way she says his name sets every nerve on edge.

'Remi,' she says. 'He's threatening me.'

Adrenaline shoots through Remi, and he is on his feet in an instant. 'I'm coming,' he says, already moving, adrenaline cutting through his sleepiness.

He ends the call, grabs his keys, and runs out of his penthouse flat. He doesn't bother with the elevator as Kike's flat is just a floor down in the renovated Chelsea townhouse. He takes the stairs two at a time, his heart pounding louder with each step, and concern and fury knotting in his chest.

When he reaches Kike's door, his pulse is hammering so hard

he can feel it at his fingertips. He slides his spare key into the lock, pushes the door open, and immediately hears loud, angry voices further inside. He doesn't stop to listen or think; he sprints towards the noise.

He bursts into the living room, and Kike and Miles are arguing by the coffee table in the middle of the room. Miles's back is to him, blocking his view of Kike's face. But then, a pool of blood on the cream rug between them catches his eye. A switch flicks in Remi's mind, and he crosses the room in an instant. Miles hears him approach and glances over his shoulder, eyes widening in fear, but before he can react, Remi drives a fist into his jaw.

Miles's head snaps back, and he collapses to the floor, his head clipping the edge of the coffee table before he lands in an awkward heap. Remi stands over him, chest heaving, his pulse roaring in his ears. He has a clear view of Kike for the first time and can see that she isn't bleeding. She doesn't even appear roughed up as she looks down at Miles's body indifferently.

She glances at Remi and shrugs, and he wants to challenge her reaction. But he doesn't. Instead, he follows her gaze to Miles, who isn't moving as blood trickles from the corner of his mouth. Panic sets in like ice spreading through his veins.

'Oh God,' Remi mutters, dropping to his knees by Miles's head.

He presses two fingers to Miles's neck to check for a pulse, but he can't feel anything beyond the loud beating of his own chest. Remi pulls his hand away, taking a few deep breaths. Kike's eyes flick to him for a moment before returning to stare at Miles like he's a stain on her rug rather than a bleeding, unconscious human being.

Remi places his fingers back against Miles's neck and finally feels a faint pulse. Relief washes over him. He turns to Kike, hoping to share that relief, but she remains indifferent.

'Kike!' Remi snaps. She turns to him with an annoyed expression. 'What happened?' he demands.

She shrugs. 'He got what he deserved,' she says.

Remi swallows hard, his throat dry. 'What do you mean? Did he hit you?'

She doesn't respond, her cold focus on Miles, who is slowly regaining consciousness.

'Kike,' Remi presses. 'Look at me.'

She turns to him with a defiant stare, which he recognises for what it is . . . her shield.

'He didn't touch you, did he?' Remi says, his calm slowly returning.

She shrugs again. 'I never said he did. I hit him. Because he tried to steal from me.'

'So that's his blood?' Remi asks, gesturing at the bloodstained rug.

Miles groans, his eyes half-open but unfocused.

'Yes . . .' Miles mumbles, trying to move. 'Mine . . . my blood.'

Remi's mind races. 'Why?' he asks Kike.

'He's a thief,' Kike says, like it's obvious.

Miles tries to stand, but his hand can't carry his weight, so he gently lowers himself back to the floor. Remi then carefully helps him sit up against the couch.

Miles glares at Kike. 'You're crazy,' he says, weak but full of venom, and turns to Remi. 'She's crazy. I didn't take anything.'

Kike scoffs. 'He's lying.'

Remi looks at her, his instincts kicking in. He can see it in her eyes . . . her face . . . her nonchalant bearing. She's not telling the truth. 'Kike,' he says. 'Just tell me what really happened?'

She narrows her eyes at Remi, then rolls them dismissively. 'Whatever. You can believe him if you want.'

'It's not him, Kike. I'm looking at you, and I don't believe you.'

'Oh shut up, Remi,' she says. 'You don't get to do your *thing* with me. Not. At. All.'

Miles clutches his head. 'She went off because I took some cash,' he says. 'Just enough to go pick up some weed for both of us. We'd smoked all of it. But then she freaked out and started hitting me.'

Kike smirks. 'I know how much the weed costs, Miles,' she says. 'And you've been taking more money than it cost for a while. Too long, but I let it go. This time was too much.'

Miles glares at her. 'Pause on that! I'd never do that.'

Kike scoffs. 'I called the dealer, you idiot!'

That pulls the rug from underneath Miles's feet and ends his attempts at denial. But he still shakes his head, more out of performance than conviction.

'Uhum,' Kike mutters, and turns to address Remi. 'I asked him to return it . . . politely . . . you would've been proud. But he tried me. Tried to gaslight and intimidate me into backing down. So I hit him in his throat with my palm . . . like you taught me . . . then I burst his lip with a straight punch . . . like you taught me.'

'I was down in seconds,' Remi says. 'Why didn't you just wait?'

'Oh. That was after I burst his lip. He didn't learn. So I called you to come down and resolve it with words like you're so good at before I actually hurt him. But . . .' She shrugs, gesturing at Miles.

Remi feels a tightness in his chest; he is fighting the urge to yell. He and Kike both know what she just said was a plausible version of events . . . one she'd crafted before making the call. If she genuinely wanted him to resolve things calmly, she would have been clear. Instead, she gave just enough detail to get his blood boiling while staying vague. Regardless of her intent, he knows he overreacted to the blood on the rug. So he bites his tongue.

'Kike, it's just money,' he says, trying to ease the tension.

'It's *just money* to us, Remi,' she counters, and fixes Miles with a cold stare. 'Not to him. That's what matters.'

Miles wipes blood from his mouth, wincing in pain. 'I need an ambulance. My head is banging, and I can't keep my eyes open.'

Kike chuckles, and Remi's pulse quickens despite his best efforts to stay calm.

'It's okay, Miles,' Remi says. 'Let's give it a bit. Let's see if you'll get better.' He turns to Kike. 'Can you get some ice?'

'Don't have any ice.'

'Frozen peas . . . vegetables. Anything, Kike.'

'None of those, Remi,' she responds, unbothered.

'Oh, it's like that?' Miles says, and forcefully declares with an intensity and alertness that reveal he isn't as hurt as he's portraying. 'I'm calling the police!'

Kike chuckles again.

'No need for that,' Remi says, appearing calm but feeling far from it. He glances at Kike, disturbed by how unaffected she is by the possible consequences for them.

'Mate, what are you guys trying to do?' Miles asks with a renewed sense of purpose. 'Keep me here against my will?'

'No,' Kike says. 'I'm happy to call you an Uber right now.'

'Let's just relax,' Remi says, trying hard to de-escalate. 'Take a few minutes. See if your head starts to feel better.'

'No, mate,' Miles says, and turns to Kike. 'Where's my phone?' I'll call myself.'

'Don't ask me. What do I care about your phone,' she retorts. 'Find it yourself.'

'Kike,' Remi gently says, and gestures for her to calm down.

She sighs, annoyed, but appears to visibly calm down. Remi takes a deep breath before returning his attention to Miles.

'You're scared, aren't you, Remi?' Miles asks, his voice sharp – the pretence of pain forgotten or abandoned. 'You know what this is. You're one of those fancy lawyers, aren't you? This is straight GBH, mate. For both of you. But—'

'But what?' Kike cuts in with a smirk. 'You'll drop it for a price, right, Miles?'

Remi is angered by Kike's assertion, but Miles's lips curl into a bitter smile, confirming she is spot on.

'You guys are like . . . filthy rich . . . billionaires and all that . . . right?' Miles posits. 'Her friends are always talking about it. So, I'm not asking for too much . . .'

'How much?' Remi cuts in, fists instinctively clenched in anger. Anger that he'd underestimated Miles . . . that his sister would date such a money-hungry leech.

'Just enough to go to a private hospital that won't ask—'

'Miles,' Remi interrupts, calm but firm. 'Just the number.'

'Ten thousand.'

Remi is surprised and relieved by the low number but doesn't show it. However, before he can feign deliberation in a way that'll ensure Miles feels he's getting the better end of the bargain, Kike laughs derisively.

'What?' Miles challenges, turning to Kike. 'You spent more than that in Harrods earlier.'

'Okay. And?' Kike says.

Miles is about to engage Kike, but Remi steps in. 'Miles, I imagine Kike spent that on her credit card,' he says. 'No one has ten thousand in cash lying around.'

'You can transfer it, then. I'll give you my bank details.'

Remi is struck by Miles's greed, eagerness, and, most of all, criminal ineptitude in wanting the blackmail funds transferred into a personal account, leaving an indelible trace.

'You're so stupid,' Kike chides. 'Just . . . I can't believe I haven't seen how stupid you were till now.'

'Shut up!' Miles barks.

'And ten?' she continues. 'Sure. Why not? We're *filthy rich billionaires*, no? Actually, why not twenty . . . fifty . . .'

Remi turns to Kike and tries to lock eyes with her to stop her from escalating without using words. But she ignores him, and he's suddenly overcome with how much he'd failed her. Their father had bought the penthouse flat and this flat for them both so they could live next to each other, and so Remi could look out for Kike, like he'd promised he would. But Remi was never around, spending all day at work, and never wanted to be overbearing whenever he was around, allowing her room to find herself . . . her path. He decides in that moment to be around more, even if that meant moving to another firm with a better work–life balance.

'Okay,' Miles says, provoked. 'Fifty. I want fifty thousand!'

'What about a hundred?' she pokes.

'Yes. Well . . .'

'Stop!' Remi commands with a strong, booming voice out of nowhere. 'Stop. Let's get serious, okay?'

'Serious?' Kike repeats, and approaches to stand beside Remi. 'Sure. He's not getting anything. He's a stray. You don't feed strays. You throw them out.'

Remi shoots her a glare, infuriated by her cavalier goading. 'Kike, be quiet.'

Miles shakes his head slowly. 'I'm serious. I want a hundred.'

'That's ridiculous,' Remi says. 'And you know it. Get serious . . . fast!'

Remi's tone shakes Miles and forces him to reconsider. But Miles seems lost in the opportunity and unable to come up with a revised number.

'We'll settle back at ten,' Remi concludes.

Before Miles can respond, Kike sneers at Miles. 'You're pathetic. A thief and a low-class rent boy.'

Remi's patience snaps. His hand moves before his brain catches up, connecting with Kike's face. The slap rings out, freezing the room.

Kike stumbles back, one hand pressed to her cheek, eyes wide with shock.

Regret floods Remi like a tidal wave. 'Kike . . . .' he starts.

She doesn't look back. She grabs her bag and storms out, the door slamming behind her.

Remi looks down at his trembling hands, his chest aching with guilt.

Miles smirks. 'She de – '

'Get out,' Remi says, calm but firm.

'What about . . .'

Remi glares at Miles, and the intensity of the glare causes Miles to instinctively recoil.

Miles stands, quickly scans the living room for his phone and spots it on the kitchen counter. He grabs it and hurries out of the flat.

Remi watches the door, heart heavy. He knows he's crossed a line and there is no going back.

What he doesn't know, though, is that this is the last time he and his sister will be in the same room.

CHAPTER 25

Present day, 2 a.m.

A knock on the bedroom door wakes Remi from a light, restless sleep. He switches on the bedside lamp before sitting up. Before acknowledging the knock, he checks the time on his phone, sure that he's only been in bed for three hours at most – and he's right: it's 2:16 a.m.

He gets out of bed. 'Mo n bọ,' he says, letting whoever is behind the door know that he heard the knock and is on his way.

He opens the door and sees Kunle, dressed for golf and holding up an almost identical outfit, right down to the shoes. 'I thought you might be struggling to sleep,' Kunle says in Yoruba, offering Remi the golf attire. 'I thought a visit to the driving range would do us well.'

Remi bows his head before he takes the golf attire. 'Thanks, Dad. I was struggling,' he says, gesturing at the outfit. 'It's 2 a.m., though.'

'Wealth comes with certain privileges,' Kunle says with a soft smile. 'And we own the place. Although I suspect not even the senior employees know that.'

Remi nods, unsurprised. 'I'll be ready in five minutes.'

'Okay. I've parked outside in your driveway, so I'll wait in the car.'

'You've parked . . . you're driving?'

'Ahn ahn. Don't be so shocked. I like to drive . . . especially around this time of the morning.'

'You do this a lot?'

Kunle nods. 'Over a decade now. I struggle to switch off sometimes, and the drive helps . . . sometimes.'

'You drive alone?'

'Well . . . I'm driving alone. But Shina and a couple of others always follow in another car. As we speak, Shina, Yinka, and Rasaq are waiting outside.'

'Alone-ish,' Remi remarks in English.

'Alone-ish,' Kunle confirms in English.

A few minutes later, Remi, dressed in the golf attire, walks down the guest house stairs.

Outside, he spots a black Mercedes-AMG S-Class and a black Land Cruiser, both with tinted windows. He salutes the Land Cruiser, imagining Shina, Yinka, and Rasaq returning the salute, before heading straight for the Mercedes, knowing it's the car his dad is driving.

The Mercedes falls into a comfortable silence as Kunle guides the car out of the gate and through the estate. Remi watches the quiet streets, noting that the only other cars they pass are patrolling security vehicles with guards armed to the teeth.

At the estate exit, the guards open the gate as the Mercedes approaches, but Kunle still stops.

He leans out of the window. 'Olaitan,' he calls. One of the officers hurries over and prostrates by the window.

'Thank you so much, Oga,' Olaitan says in Yoruba. 'My wife and I are so grateful for what you have done and the things you sent for the babies. May God continue to bless you, Oga.'

'God bless you too, Olaitan,' Kunle says graciously. 'But what are you doing here? It's just been two days since your wife gave birth to the twins.'

Olaitan hesitates. 'Yes, Oga . . . but . . . it's my shift.'

Kunle nods, understanding that Olaitan won't get paid if he doesn't work. 'I understand,' Kunle says. 'Finish your shift today, but I will talk to Dennis in the morning to give you a break for three weeks . . . fully paid.'

'Thank you, Oga,' Olaitan says, prostrating again. 'God bless you, Oga.'

Kunle nods again, taking in the effusive thanks with ease. 'Take care of your wife and twins, okay?'

'Okay, Oga.'

Kunle drives through the gates on to the Ikoyi main roads, and the car returns to silence. Remi quietly observed the interaction, unsurprised, and knows that Kunle doesn't want to dwell on it.

'Do you still golf?' Kunle asks, as if confirming his desire to move on.

'No. Golf is just not for me.'

'You prefer the martial arts, abi?'

Remi nods. 'How much do you golf?'

'As much as I can.'

'Which is once a month?'

Kunle chuckles. 'Maybe twice.'

Remi laughs, and the car returns to a peaceful quiet for the rest of the ride to the driving range.

They approach the large gates, and a young security officer immediately begins pulling them open when he spots Kunle's Mercedes. Kunle drives through and parks right by the entrance. The Land Cruiser, however, stops by the gate as Shina, sitting in the back seat, runs through several questions with the nervous young security officer to ensure everything is as instructed and the premises are empty, apart from the single employee who will be setting things up for Kunle and Remi.

The employee hurries out of the building as soon as Kunle switches off the engine and zealously guides Kunle and Remi to a private booth on the second floor, already prepared for them.

Kunle goes first, driving the golf balls with practised ease. And Remi can't help but notice how effortlessly Kunle moves with minimal warm-up, as if early morning golf is the most natural thing in the world.

'How are you feeling?' Kunle asks as he prepares for a swing. 'I know it was very intense with your mother.'

'It hurt, Dad,' Remi says. 'What she said about Kike and me. It really hurt. And I won't deny that I slapped her. I hate that I did, and I will regret it forever. But that's not how it happened. And I certainly didn't want her to leave.'

'I know, Remi. Your mum knows, too. Kike was honest about it. She didn't go into detail, but she made it clear she behaved very badly that day, and she certainly regretted it.'

'Oh,' Remi says, surprised.

'You should know better, Remi. Kike would never lie about you. The truth was bad enough.'

Remi nods, his shoulders relaxing. 'I just . . . I don't know why I did it. I wish I could take it back. Every day. Even more now.'

'You were wrong to hit your sister,' Kunle says, stepping away from the tee box and gesturing for Remi to take his turn. 'You know that, and I know you regret it. That's yours to carry – but no more than that.' He pauses, letting the silence settle. 'There's enough regret to go around, even for your mother. That's partly why she's so angry with you . . . and me. She had that same type of conversation with me a few days ago. Actually, even worse. Blamed me for everything.'

He pauses to watch Remi line up a swing and nods in mild satisfaction at Remi's drive.

'Some of those things you've already touched on.'

'*Spotlight Nigeria*?'

Kunle nods. 'That was Kike's idea. Governor Adelaja was at the house complaining about his ongoing battle with Okolie Chemicals, trying to stop them from dumping toxic waste. They stopped them dumping in the lagoon, but they moved to dumping it close to residential areas. Kike was infuriated, and she read the room correctly . . . the governor had come to ask for my help without actually asking for it. His hands were tied politically because Stephen Okolie was very well connected. The governor was hoping I could do something about it.'

'Why you?'

Kunle pauses, waiting for Remi to complete his swing. 'I suppose it's time you were fully aware of my . . . *efforts*.'

Remi glances at Kunle with a raised eyebrow.

'*Influence* would be a better word, but –' he frowns slightly – 'it sounds rather . . . Machiavellian.'

Remi nods, understanding.

Kunle continues, his tone thoughtful. 'About fifteen years ago, I decided to test how much influence my money could buy if used in a targeted way. Before that, I stayed away from politics. Considering what happened with your grandfather. But I kept getting asked to make donations to campaigns. I would give to some. Not give to others . . . simply because I didn't like how they approached me or what they stood for. There was no method to it. I picked one politician the Chief said was the future – Adekoye Aina of Ondo State. I gave when Aina asked, and continued to give and give without asking for anything in return . . . I even gave to other politicians at Aina's behest. He must've thought I had more money than sense.

'Over time, as Aina rose to prominence . . . from senator, to governor, to breaking away to start his own political party . . . and then running for president and winning two years ago . . . alongside wins for many of his allies in his new political party . . . my influence grew beyond anything I anticipated. Beyond what I am truly comfortable with. Àgò kì í gbà láti báni wáyé,' he says and then casually translates, 'there's no going back now.'

Remi steps away from the tee box, and Kunle steps in for his turn.

'So you're the reason why all the heavyweights from the president's party suddenly had to be in Abuja.'

'Yes. I showed my hand too strongly there. But I was . . . I was lost when I heard about Kike. I thought it had to be one of them . . . the *heavyweights*. I demanded they all come from wherever they were to account for themselves.' He shakes his head. 'I will have to pay for that.'

'What do you mean?'

'They were all happy when they thought I was just the quiet man with the bottomless pockets.' He pauses to take a swing. 'But I bore my teeth a little too much. And with the president's ailing health, they are all trying to position themselves as the inevitable next man in line. One . . . more than that, actually . . . sees me as a threat. You see, I wasn't just making friends with those men. While their open political allegiances prevented them, I took the opportunity to make the right friends across the political spectrum.'

'Do you intend to run?'

'Absolutely not,' Kunle says firmly. 'But I am exposed . . . and I must find a way to carefully return to the shadows.'

'How's that going?'

'Deliberately. But the Abuja gathering was too much of a power play to just ignore. Especially as the president supported it. He really liked Kike . . . and, like me, suspected a few of the *heavyweights*.'

Remi instinctively takes a deep breath.

'I know,' Kunle says, catching the reaction. 'It's a lot to take in.'

'Is the Chief one of those who sees you as a threat?' Remi asks.

Kunle shakes his head slowly. 'No. The Chief knows I have no desire to run. That issue is different . . . but related.' He drives a golf ball into the darkness and takes a moment to track its flight. 'The Chief tried to jump the line during the presidential primaries. It was already decided that Aina would be their party's candidate, but the Chief tried to pull a fast one to snatch the candidacy at the last minute. And in his plan to overthrow Aina, my loyalty was a foregone conclusion. It ended up being a closely run affair. But I stuck to my word and backed Aina. It ended up being the deciding vote.

'Chief wasn't exiled from the party – it is a young party, so they still need his political clout – but he's been pushed right to the back of the line. I have forgiven him for putting me in that situation. But he has not forgiven me.'

Kunle shrugs before driving another golf ball far into the darkness.

'Any more questions about that?' Kunle asks. 'Or should I return to Okolie Chemicals and the birth of *Spotlight Nigeria*?'

Remi shakes his head. 'No more questions.'

'It doesn't have to be questions, then. Tell me what you are thinking.'

'I'm surprised you've taken this course of action,' Remi says. 'It's not something I would've advised. But I trust you, and I'm here for you.'

Kunle unconsciously taps the golf club on the mat, a crack of pride clear on his face. He nods, then takes a final swing before stepping out of the tee box for Remi to step in.

Kunle quietly watches Remi line up his next swing before continuing. 'Kike came to me with an honestly brilliant idea to deal with the Okolie issue,' he says. 'Okolie loved the limelight . . . loved the sound of his own voice. But he was selective about his public appearances. He only did interviews with friendly press who would push him on the toxic dumping issue just enough to give him the chance to deny everything and promise to investigate.

'Kike had the idea all planned out before she came to me. She had already gathered the necessary evidence from the governor's office.

I thought it was a risky move. But then . . . we take risks. I would've let you do it, so I wasn't going to stop her. Plus, I had never seen her that driven. I said yes and wanted it to be a success . . . for her. I provided the funds, gave her complete autonomy to execute her plan, and gave her access to all the top minds in our employ. The finished product . . . what you have seen . . . was incredible. It sent shock waves through Okolie Chemicals and other chemical companies beyond Lagos. It also secured the governor's loyalty.'

'I'm not surprised,' Remi says with a touch of pride.

'Oh, but this is Nigeria. These things have a way of being ignored and then buried. That's what Okolie was expecting.'

'But not when you're involved.'

Kunle shrugs. 'I understand how things work here. Normally, I would've made an arrangement with Okolie. But it was Kike's work. I wasn't going to cut her off at the knees. I let her decide. She said ordinarily she would've removed it, considering the impact it had already made . . . but in her investigations, she found out that Okolie was a bully . . . and especially *wicked* to his female staff. That was it for her.'

Remi fights back a smile, imagining Kike's determination when she learned the truth. He takes his final swing of the round and steps out of the tee box.

'You're getting better,' Kunle says, and steps into the tee box.

'Thanks. I'm trying to copy you.'

Kunle chuckles and takes another easy swing. He doesn't speak as he focuses on placing the next ball on the tee.

'Your sister and I did not speak or mention *Spotlight Nigeria* for months, and I started to get sad because I missed that spark I saw in her. But . . .' He smiles at a memory. 'Your sister played it very well. I was starting to have problems with Abe Nosa. Spurred on by the unexpected success of being involved with President Aina from the ground, I decided to invest in a few other young politicians. Abe Nosa was one of them. The plan was to provide the necessary funding for their campaigns and lifestyle – to insulate them from the seemingly inevitable corruption.' He half smiles. 'I know how that must sound to you. It's how it sounded to your sister – idealism wearing a silk agbada.' He pauses, just for a beat. 'Specific to Abe, I arranged for his Doyin, his wife . . . you know her as well, right?'

'Yes, Doyin and I went to the same law school in London.'

'Yes. I remember her saying that. I arranged for her to be general counsel at one of the foreign investment funds here in Lagos that we work closely with. Put her on the sterling-equivalent salary for similar roles in London.'

'That's a lot.'

'Intentionally so. Enough to keep them living a life of luxury. Abe was elected as a member of the House last year, and it didn't take him long to start embezzling. We reminded him of our arrangement several times . . . Doyin even took it upon herself to remind him. But one night, Doyin came to us with bruises, crying . . . that Abe was going off the rails. Shina wanted to go over to their house and beat the sense into Abe. But I had another idea. I approached Kike . . . and she was expecting me. She was ready with her own plans. She offered to use *Spotlight Nigeria* to help me with any of my issues . . . provided that she was given complete autonomy to choose her own *targets*.

'*One for you, one for me* . . . is how she put it.' He smiles at the memory. 'I agreed. Immediately. Because that spark was back. She started her work on Abe . . . joining that poker game to get friendly with him. But she had already been working on her next episode. On Pastor Biodun Ayomide.' He hesitates before driving a golf ball. 'I wouldn't have advised that had I known.'

'Why?'

Kunle glances at Remi as if to confirm the sincerity of the question. 'You have a gift for reading people. But your mum and sister always knew how to dampen or work around it. Most of that was on you. You always gave them the benefit of the doubt, whereas you wouldn't do it with others. But that was to be expected. But they also knew the best way to affect your instinct was to get you emotional. Just like your mother did earlier.'

'Mum's outburst was to stop me reading something?'

'Not just that. She was furious. But she was . . . Okay, let me first give some context that I could only give your sister when it was too late. Your mum and I were an arrangement by your grandparents. To make a long story short, the Bankoles had immense wealth but not much prestige, and the Aderonkes had generations of prestige but waning wealth. But your mother was . . . is . . . stunning, and I was . . . charming . . . so it worked . . . for a few years . . . We had you and Kike . . . Life was good. But then we gradually became just friends who lived together and raised our children. Slowly, I started drifting, focusing more on work. Then I had an affair. She found out and took it very badly. There was no talk of divorce, but things were essentially over between us romantically. She found someone soon after . . . Pastor Biodun Ayomide . . . and they've been . . . having an affair since.'

'Wow,' Remi says, stunned by the revelation. 'How long?'

'Over fifteen years . . . since she started going to his church.'

'But he's married and has had three kids with his wife since,' Remi says with more than a hint of scorn.

Kunle shrugs.

Remi is infuriated and struggles to understand how his dad can speak about the affair so calmly. 'That's—'

'She loves him, Remi,' Kunle cuts in. 'But I understand your anger. I was furious when I found out. Remember when I went to New York for business for three months?'

Remi nods.

'Yes,' Kunle says, trying to brush aside the memory. 'But I realised it wasn't my heart that was broken. It was my pride. I'd been unfaithful first, and the truth is, our hearts were never truly in our marriage. So, I learned to live with it. I focused on you and Kike. In time, I hope you will learn to live with it, too.'

'I don't know, Dad. But I guess her outburst makes sense now,' he says before something snaps into focus. 'Did Kike know this before targeting the pastor?'

'It is why she targeted the pastor. Kike picked up on it very early on. Zainab was missing too many of Kike's teenage milestones because she was always in church or at some church activity. You remember when Zainab forgot to show up for Kike's under-17s tennis final?'

Remi nods.

'That was it for Kike. From that day, she held tightly to that anger until it found an outlet in *Spotlight Nigeria*. I asked Kike to take the video down, but she was not having it. She was riled that the pastor was sleeping with many young women in the church. And in Kike's view . . . in your mother's face, because he really wasn't hiding it. She hoped that revelation . . . the testimonies of the young women . . . would force your mother to question her love for the pastor. It did not.'

'Does Mum know this is why Kike targeted the pastor?'

'Deep down, yes. Although she claims I convinced Kike to do it to discredit the pastor.'

'She didn't confront Kike?'

Kunle raises an eyebrow. 'How do you think that would have gone? And your mother knew Kike was waiting for it. She confronted me instead.'

'So they never cleared the air?'

Kunle shakes his head, solemn.

Remi takes a deep breath, anger, disappointment, and sorrow swirling.

Kunle focuses on the next few drives, leaving Remi to process his thoughts.

'I'll apologise to Mum in the morning,' Remi says.

'She's left the house.'

'Left? When is she going to be back?'

'I don't know. And her phone is off. But she'll be back.'

Remi wants to ask where she is, but he knows the answer. He rides the wave of his anger to refocus his mind. 'Malaki was one of Kike's targets, right?'

Kunle is surprised by the sudden pivot and waits for a beat to respond to ensure Remi wants to move on. 'Yes.'

'So the next target would've been yours, then?'

'No. It had become more organic. I think Kike was working on something . . . she had that look in her eye . . . but I don't know who her target was. I've asked our investigators, but she hadn't engaged them.'

'Do you know if anyone else will know?'

Kunle shakes his head. 'I've asked everyone. No one does. We have checked her car's GPS, and nothing is out of the ordinary. Just visiting old friends from school and the usual going out.'

Remi feels a surge of frustration. He'd been waiting to have this conversation with his father about *Spotlight Nigeria*, but despite exposing hidden aspects of their family dynamics, it hasn't brought him any closer to the answers he desperately seeks about Kike's death.

'I don't know what to do next, Dad.'

'I understand, Remi. But I do.'

Remi is surprised and intrigued by his dad's assurance.

'I want you to go back to London. As soon as possible. The ground is about to get shaky around me. I can already feel the tremors. I will feel much better knowing you're safe in London. Came back in a month, maybe two. By then, things will've calmed down, your mother will be back home, and we should have more leads on Kike . . . if we don't already know the answers by then.'

'Are you sure I can't help?'

'I'm sure you can. By being safe in London.'

'Okay. But please call me the moment you need me.'

Kunle nods. 'I will,' he says, and gestures to the empty tee box. 'Oya. It's been your turn for the past five minutes.'

CHAPTER 26

Remi wakes up to the hum of the air conditioning in the otherwise silent guest house. He glances at the sunlight seeping around the edges of the curtains, confirming the sun has risen and it's a good time to get up. He rolls over to check his phone – it's 10:30 a.m., and there is a message from Kunle at 7.30 a.m. It reads: *I hope you got some rest. I have left the house for some meetings but will return before your flight tomorrow. Call me if you need anything.*

Remi sits up, stretches, and takes a deep breath. His thoughts are still heavy after the conversation with Kunle at the driving range, but the weight is lessening because his mind is slowly coming to terms with putting aside his self-appointed duty to find Kike's killer . . . if only until he returns. Deep in his mind, a voice is fighting back with muffled screams that this postponement of his duty is the first step to abandoning the duty. But he ignores it because he's already agreed to leave Lagos, and Kunle has already arranged the return flight for tomorrow morning.

Kunle made the call as they walked back to the Mercedes at around 4 a.m. after finishing at the driving range. Remi wasn't entirely surprised that someone was available to answer his dad's call at that time, but he was certainly surprised by the immediate execution of the request as he received the flight details in a text to his Lagos phone five minutes later. It was a vivid reminder that the Bankole machine was not only powerful and well oiled but never slept – seemingly just like Kunle, as he mustn't have slept before leaving the house for *meetings* this morning.

Despite everything that has happened, Remi decides to make the best of his last day in Lagos. He calls Rasaq and arranges to go out for suya at his favourite spot as soon as it opens at noon. Remi visits the spot at least once on every trip to Lagos. It's a personal ritual that reminds him of childhood, and the suya is fantastic. To pass the time, Remi heads down to the gym.

It's approaching noon, and Rasaq and Remi are in the Land Cruiser weaving through the bustling streets towards the suya spot, vibing to Rasaq's Afrobeats playlist currently playing 'MMS' by Asake and Wizkid.

Remi notices Rasaq glance at him, and it dawns on him that he's been silent since the initial greeting before getting into the car. Rasaq might be unsure of his state of mind considering the events of the past few hours, regardless of them vibing along to the music.

'You've been to this suya spot before?' Remi asks.

'Oh yes! It's the best one . . . on the Island.'

'On the Island?' Remi questions, amused.

'Yes,' Rasaq confirms. 'There are a few better ones on the Mainland.'

'A few? Stop it!'

'Seriously. If you weren't leaving tomorrow morning, I'd have taken you there.'

Remi quickly realises from the remark that Rasaq's glances might not have solely been about his state of mind. Remi was leaving tomorrow and hadn't even mentioned it to Rasaq.

'I'll be back in a month. So, I'll be holding you to that,' Remi says. 'But we can try one of them tonight. Grab some takeaway from my spot and do a blind comparison with your Mainland spot.'

'Okay then,' Rasaq says excitedly. 'And no excuses about this one not being warm, oh.'

'Abeg, stop,' Remi says, laughing. 'But as a lawyer, I must add that will not be an excuse . . . it will be a mitigating factor.'

Rasaq laughs.

'How was it in the car with Shina and Yinka this morning?' Remi asks.

'Oh,' Rasaq says, and smiles. 'It was good. A bit quiet at first, but then Shina started telling lots of stories. There were even a few that Yinka hadn't heard before.'

Remi nods. 'Yeah. He's been with the family for almost fifty years. He worked for my grandfather.'

'Yes. There were some stories about when he just started working for your grandfather.'

'Oh, I haven't heard any of those. Any fun?'

'Yes.'

Remi glances at Rasaq, expecting him to tell one of the stories, but it's clear Rasaq won't be doing that. 'You're not going to tell me, abi?'

Rasaq smirks. 'It's not my story to tell.'

Remi nods. 'Fair enough.'

'How was the early morning golf?'

Remi shrugs. 'Golf was okay . . . I'm not very good,' he says. 'But the conversation was enlightening.'

Rasaq nods, and another of Remi's favourite Afrobeats songs, 'Rush' by Ayra Starr, comes on.

'Your playlist is perfect,' Remi says. 'Remember to share it with me before I leave, abeg.'

Rasaq nods with pride. 'You like Amapiano?'

'Sure,' Remi says with a keen nod.

Rasaq picks up his phone and quickly switches to his curated Amapiano playlist. A song called 'Nawe Dali (feat Mthunzi)' by Wanitwa Mos, Nkosazana Daughter and JL SA plays, and although Remi has never heard it before, he immediately vibes to it.

'This is good,' Remi says.

'Oh yes.' Rasaq nods.

They enjoy the song without speaking for the rest of the ride to the suya spot.

Rasaq pulls up to the stall, surrounded by parked cars and bustling with life. He guides the Land Cruiser past a few people leaning against their cars, eating directly from the old newspapers wrapped around the suya spread across their bonnets.

Rasaq parks, and although Remi believes it's safe, he waits for Rasaq to complete his scan of their surroundings. Rasaq nods to confirm all is clear, and then he and Remi hop out.

Remi and Rasaq are immediately hit with the unmistakable, delicious aroma of grilled meat mixed with pepper and onions which fills the air. Remi grins before heading towards the chaos that surrounds the hut-like stall. Rasaq follows a step behind.

Remi approaches the stall and scans over people's heads for anyone he recognises on the other side of the counter, but he doesn't recognise any of the faces . . . even those further inside working the charcoal grills. No problem, he thinks, and steps behind one of the people currently ordering.

Remi is soon at the front, but louder voices from around him constantly get the attention of the salespeople at the counter.

Remi sighs and prepares to get loud, but Rasaq's voice, speaking Hausa, booms from behind him. The salespeople are immediately drawn to Rasaq, and each apologises with either words or gestures before the salesperson closest to Remi abandons the order they are currently taking to attend to Remi.

Remi places his order and pays in cash, leaving a considerable tip. He turns to Rasaq. 'Thanks for that,' he says. 'They were just ignoring me.'

Rasaq laughs. 'You were too calm for them. They were just waiting for you to join the madness.'

'I was close,' Remi says, amused. 'Didn't know you spoke Hausa.'

'I do. Igbo, too, and some Edo. Learned from my fellow soldiers.'

'You should be lined up to run this country one day,' Remi says spontaneously. 'You are the best of us.'

Rasaq is honoured by the remark. 'Thank you very much, Remi.'

Remi notes the gratitude in Rasaq's voice and glances at him, realising the weight of his spontaneous remark. 'You're welcome,' he says, choosing not to downplay or lessen the moment.

They quietly wait about five minutes before their order arrives, then stroll back to the car.

'Let's eat in the car with the AC,' Remi says. 'Out here is way too hot for me.'

Rasaq agrees with a nod and unlocks the car so they can hop in. He switches on the engine, and the air conditioning automatically restarts. Remi hands him one of the carefully wrapped steaming suya portions and an ice-cold water bottle. Remi unfurls his portion of suya, leaving one extra in the bag as agreed, and they enjoy the suya and ice-cold water while listening to more Amapiano.

Once finished, Rasaq collects the empty newspaper wrappers and bottles of water and hops out of the car to place them in a nearby bin. As Rasaq returns, Remi's eyes wander to the giant billboard on the opposite side of the road. It catches his attention not because of its size but because of the Okolie Chemicals logo and the bold text – *Mourning the Tragic Loss of Our Founder and CEO, Stephen Okolie.* An image of Stephen Okolie is beside the text, but it wasn't immediately recognisable because the details had begun to fade, due to neglect.

Remi's stomach drops. He hadn't heard anything about Stephen's death, and his father hadn't mentioned it either. He tries to make sense of that – was it guilt? Coldness? Or did Kunle genuinely not know?

Remi pulls out his phone and searches Stephen Okolie's name as Rasaq slides back into the driver's seat. The top result is an article from over a year ago with the headline: *Stephen Okolie, Founder and CEO of Okolie Chemicals, Dies by Suicide.* Remi clicks in and skims through the article, his mind racing. The article details how Stephen jumped from his tenth-floor office window a week after the *Spotlight Nigeria* episode exposed him as the primary driver of his company's toxic dumping practices. Remi clicks out of that article and skims through the following three results, which all detail the suicide, making a point to reference the *Spotlight Nigeria* episode as the instigating factor. Although one, a more business-focused outlet, referenced in passing that this was a few hours before the Okolie Chemicals board were to meet to force Stephen to step down as CEO.

Remi's thoughts are suddenly pulled to Stephen's tall and broad-shouldered twin sons, whose reputation as school bullies was known to him even though he was in a different boarding school. Outside of school, he and the twins moved in somewhat similar circles because they were the same age, but he never interacted with them for two reasons. First, Remi was stuck-up and thought them crass. But far more critical, he was uncomfortable with their temper and violent streak, especially when drunk. A memory from over a decade ago of a particularly violent incident in the VIP section of a Sean Paul concert flashes into his mind. Both twins savagely attacked a young man, slightly older than them, who'd started dating an ex-girlfriend of one of the twins. They were also violent with the ex-girlfriend when she tried to stop them, and seemingly weren't going to stop until the military police accompanying one of Remi's friends were instructed to intervene. He remembers how remorseless they were and how heavily they leaned on their father's name and influence to stop them from being detained.

Violent, short-tempered, and ruthless. They wouldn't handle their father's suicide well, and they would blame Kike.

Rasaq notices Remi's silence. 'You good, Remi?'

Remi gestures at the billboard. 'Did you know about that?'

Rasaq had noticed it, so he only glances at it for Remi's benefit. 'Yes. It was all over the news when it happened.'

Remi nods slowly, his mind sharpening with sudden resolve. He knows it's impulsive, but seeing the billboard has stirred something inside him that will not be stilled until he sees it through. 'There's something I need to do right now,' he says. 'And I'll need your help.'

'Of course. Tell me what you need.'

'Let's head to the Oniru Estate,' Remi says. 'I need to pay the Okolies a visit.'

Rasaq nods and guides the car out on to the road.

The Land Cruiser's government plate number lets them through the gates of the upscale estate on Victoria Island, and Rasaq's natural command convinces the soldiers operating the gate to provide them precise directions to the Okolie mansion, which Remi knew was in this estate. Rasaq follows the directions, but as soon as they make their final turn, the Okolie mansion is unmistakable, even in the distance, as it is the only dilapidated property in the area. They approach, and the once-grand gate with what looks like a family crest is rusted. The windows visible over the large gate and high walls are dirty, and the building's paint is peeling. But what is most stark is the large 'For Sale' sign bolted to the gate.

Rasaq parks just outside the gate and performs his usual scan of their surroundings before they both step out. They walk to the entrance, and Remi peers through the gap between the gate, hanging at an odd angle, and the wall. The garden is overgrown, and a once-impressive fountain is cracked and dry. It looks deserted, but Remi knocks on the gate anyway.

There is no response, so he tries again, harder. But still nothing.

A gleaming BMW slows to a stop behind them, and a middle-aged man leans out of the window. 'They owe you money, too?' the man asks, half joking.

Remi turns to the man and forces a polite chuckle. 'Not quite,' he says. 'Just looking for the twins.'

The man's expression hardens. 'You're not a friend, obviously. One of them died in a car accident on Third Mainland Bridge around five years ago.'

Remi is surprised by this but doesn't show it.

'The other one still sleeps in the house,' the middle-aged man says. 'But you will not find him inside there during the day. He'll be in the beer parlour just opposite the estate. He's always there. It is a sad case.'

Remi nods in thanks, and the man drives off without another word.

Rasaq gives Remi a sidelong glance. 'Beer parlour?'

'Beer parlour,' Remi confirms, and they head back towards the Land Cruiser.

A few minutes later, Remi and Rasaq step into the makeshift bar, a dim, open-sided space wedged between a mechanic's workshop and a row of makeshift stalls. The roof is a patchwork of rusted corrugated-iron sheets, and the air inside is thick with heat and the smell of stale beer and sweat. Plastic chairs and tables, branded with faded Star and Guinness logos, are scattered around, and a small, flickering TV mounted on the wall murmurs a football match recap, barely audible over the conversations in the room.

Near the back, half hidden in shadows, a lone figure sits hunched over a table with his fingers loosely curled around a near-empty bottle of Gulder resting in front of him. No one pays any attention to the man; he's just part of the scenery now. Remi is sure the man is the surviving twin.

Remi walks over, Rasaq following a step behind, and for a moment, Remi doesn't recognise the twin. The once-imposing figure is now gaunt and hollow-eyed. His clothes are creased and stained, and a stale stench of alcohol oozes from him. Remi is close enough to see the dandruff in the twin's unkempt afro, but the twin is unaware of Remi.

'Okolie,' Remi calls, calm but firm enough to get the twin's attention.

The twin grunts in return and slowly turns his head to Remi, eyes barely focusing.

'Do you know who I am?' Remi asks.

The twin forces himself to focus on Remi, but there is no recognition for a moment before he suddenly grins. 'Remz . . .' he mutters. 'Freshest guy.'

Remi nods. 'That's me.'

'Come . . . come . . . have a drink with me,' he slurs.

Remi shakes his head.

The twin scoffs, and you can see the flash of temper in his eyes. 'You still think you're too good for us, abi?' He takes a final swig from the bottle in his hand, then shakes it as if surprised it's empty. He grunts, annoyed. 'At least buy me another one! Why else are you here?'

Remi doesn't respond.

The twin turns to the man behind the bar. 'Oya! Mugu, bring another one, and have two more on ice for me,' he says, and gestures at Remi. 'My guy will take care of it and clear my tab. He's a very . . . very rich man. Not like we used to be, oh. This one, their money is different.'

The bartender stares at Remi with hope, and Remi nods slowly. The bartender excitedly reaches for a Gulder from the fridge.

'Not now,' Remi says sternly. 'And I'm only paying for that one and his tab.'

'Ahn ahn,' the twin grumbles. 'Don't be selfish.'

Remi ignores the grumble. 'Just heard about your dad and came to pay my respects.'

The twin shrugs. 'Respects?' He sniggers. 'Forget that one,' he says dismissively. 'He was a coward.'

Remi flinches at the remark. He glances at Rasaq, and he can see in Rasaq's bearing that he's come to the same conclusion. The man in front of them is a shell of his former self, physically and mentally. There's no way he could have been involved in Kike's death.

Remi watches as the twin returns to his stupor and feels a wave of sadness, not just for the man but for the unintended consequences of Kike and Kunle's actions. A whole family, once wealthy and powerful, now reduced to this.

Remi turns to Rasaq. 'I'm done here. Let's pay this guy's tab and go.'

Rasaq nods and follows Remi towards the bar.

As Remi approaches, the bartender readies himself for an argument about the amount of the tab, but Remi places a thick wad of 1,000-naira notes on the table, shutting him up.

Remi turns without saying a word and follows Rasaq out of the beer parlour, heading back to the Land Cruiser.

CHAPTER 27

Remi's mind spins as the Land Cruiser heads away from Oniru Estate. He can't shake the feeling that in pursuing answers about Kike's death, he's mired in much more than her death; in the ripples of the choices she made chasing the truth. He wonders how many lives her pursuit affected and how many more would unravel if he kept digging. Yet, he can't ignore the uneasy feeling that continues to stir inside him because there is one more piece to the puzzle – Malaki.

Remi pulls out his London phone and scrolls through the flood of unread WhatsApp messages offering condolences from the last few days, until he finds one from Balo.

Balo began displaying his talent for rapping and producing beats in boarding school. He then pursued music seriously through university in London and even more ambitiously back in Nigeria, using his father's wealth and connections to launch his own record label.

But the audience suddenly shifted away from his heavily east-coast-influenced hip-hop sound, which came with a pronounced American accent. More authentic Nigerian sounds were now in vogue, and the artists Balo had once dismissed as razz or uncool – those using thick 'local' accents and mannerisms – were leading the new wave. Many came from the same privileged background as Balo and attended the same kinds of expensive schools but had rebranded themselves as *area boys* – cultivating a gritty, streetwise image that masked their elite upbringing.

Initially irritated, Balo quickly adapted, signing a string of these faux-authentic artists alongside a few genuinely authentic artists. Some of those real-deal artists had ties to Malaki, who'd been pioneering the sound long before it was trendy. That connection led to a cordial working relationship between Balo and Malaki until Balo grew tired of running the label and sold it off for a cushy role at his father's thriving construction company.

Still, Balo never stopped bragging about his ties to Malaki and other big-name artists. So now, Remi decides to put that claim to the test.

Remi calls Balo. The phone rings for nearly thirty seconds with no answer. Frustrated, Remi hangs up and begins typing a message asking Balo to call him back, but before he finishes, Balo calls. Remi lets it ring once, then picks up.

'Remz,' Balo says. 'How you dey?'

'I dey,' Remi replies, his voice calm, as if a switch had flipped.

The calmness of the response doesn't surprise Balo, and he presses on. 'You sure, Remz? I'm here for you, you know.'

Remi hears the genuine care in Balo's voice and softens. 'Thanks, brother. That means a lot.'

'No worries, bro. You'd do the same.'

'I would?' Remi says with a flicker of playfulness.

'You already have. You don't remember?'

Remi hesitates, not wanting to drag Balo back into those memories. But Balo goes there himself.

'Is it not you that came to drag me by my dreads when I was talking all that . . .' He trails off, embarrassed. '. . . that giving-up-on-life rubbish.'

The memory is vivid now.

It was about ten years ago. Balo had flown back to London early to surprise his girlfriend for New Year's, cutting short his usual Christmas stay in Lagos, only to find her in their living room midway through loud, frantic sex with one of her classmates. Balo spiralled, talking about being done.

Remi didn't hesitate. He took a cab across town, stormed into Balo's place, dragged him out by his dreads. Balo stayed with him until the end of the academic year when he graduated and returned to Nigeria.

'You wouldn't have done it,' Remi says.

'I don't know, bro,' Balo says.

Stephen Okolie's fate flashes in Remi's mind. 'You're here now, brother,' he says gently.

'Oh yes,' Balo says, then adds with excitement, 'living my best life!'

'*Oh yes*,' Remi says, mimicking Balo perfectly.

They laugh briefly.

'Anyways, Remz. You called. You don't call,' Balo says, and adds with a solid Caribbean accent, 'so, wagwan bredrin?'

'Need a favour.'

'You don't ask for favours either. So this must be serious.'

Remi nods to himself. 'I need you to link me with Malaki today.'

'Malaki? Today?' Balo questions, and pauses for a beat. 'You want to talk to him?'

'Yes. In person.'

'I don't know, bro. I don't know,' Balo rambles. 'Not sure about that, bro.'

Remi doesn't respond, leaving Balo to struggle with his conscience alone.

'Remz?' Balo calls.

'I'm here.'

'First things first, bro. I don't know what you're thinking . . . but Malaki would never be involved with what happened to your sister. I know he was vexed after the *Spotlight Nigeria* episode, but nothing directed at your sister. The man knows levels dey. And your family's level is a different kind of level. Even if he didn't know before, Malaki would have done his research and wouldn't want that kind of wahala.'

'I understand,' Remi says with disarming calm. 'But I just need to talk to him.'

'Talk? That's all?'

'That's all.'

'No Bode nonsense?'

'Bode tried me. I was just defending myself.'

'Right,' Balo says, full of sarcasm. 'But just talk, yeah?'

'Yes. Just talk.'

'Okay. Okay. I don't have a connect to him anymore—'

'So why are you stressing—' Remi cuts in, failing to hide his frustration.

'No direct connection,' Balo cuts back in quickly. 'But I can get you to see him . . . today sef. I just need to make a call to Seun Daniels.'

'Why him?'

'Seun is running these unplugged-type sessions for DBN Plus. Stripped back, intimate gigs. It's doing very well, becoming the spot for breakout artists. There's a session for Suru Boi, one of Malaki's artists, tonight. Seun invited me a few weeks ago, but it's on the Mainland, so a no for me. Not that I was at the top of Seun's list, oh. He was struggling to get his usual crowd because it is filming on the Mainland. Even if it's full now, I'm sure he'll be happy you are interested. That one was always trying to feel among with your sister.'

Remi has never heard about Suru Boi, but then he hasn't exactly been scouring Apple Music for hidden gems. 'You're sure Malaki will be there?'

'He will. It's on the Mainland cos of him; he doesn't like us Island people. And he's living through his artists now that he's not making music. But I will confirm with Seun. Let me call you back.'

'Thanks, brother,' Remi says with feeling, and then adds, 'and two backstage passes, yeah?'

'You and who?' Balo asks, curious.

'Just ask. Me plus one.'

'Okay, oh. In a bit.'

'In a bit.'

Remi ends the call and turns to Rasaq, who's been silent for the entire ride, focusing on the road ahead with frequent glances to check on Remi.

'You know Suru Boi?' Remi asks.

'Yes,' Rasaq answers. 'One of Malaki's artists. Alté vibes – mixing Afrobeats and reggae.'

'Any good?'

Rasaq shrugs. 'He's *okay*.'

'Okay?' Remi repeats, surprised that a relatively unknown *okay* artist is the focus of a televised intimate gig.

'Yes. Been around for a few years, but hasn't really blown. No hits really, but has been featured on a few popular songs.'

Remi nods, subconsciously noting that Suru Boi isn't exactly a candidate for breakout artist.

The car returns to silence for a few minutes before Balo calls back. Remi picks up after one ring.

'Brother,' Remi says, answering the call.

'Remz,' Balo says, and continues. 'I spoke to Seun, and he's arranged the VIP backstage passes. He won't be there, so they'll leave it for you at the door . . .'

'He's not going to be there?' Remi questions. 'Thought he's running it.'

'That's what he – and every magazine – says. But who knows? His father owns the magazines sef, so they will write whatever Seun wants. But then . . . I don't think Seun has ever touched the Mainland except on his way to the airport.'

'Fair enough,' Remi says, and adds, 'thanks a lot, brother.'

'Wait first, oh.'

'What now?' Remi asks, calm but with bite.

'Relax, Remz. Seun wants to talk to you first.'

'Why?'

'C'mon, Remz. He was there at Rose's party . . .'

'Exactly,' Remi cuts in. 'He was there. You were there. You both saw Bode was the aggressor. And I actually held back.'

'That was you holding back?' Balo questions, half joking.

Remi doesn't respond.

'Relax, Remz. It's just a quick call to put him at ease.'

'I'm not doing that,' Remi says with cold finality, but then adds to soften the tone, 'I've given *you* my word. That's enough.'

'I agree,' Balo says, then chuckles. 'And I told him this was going to happen. But he was pushing, sha. Almost like he just wanted to talk to you.'

Balo pauses for a beat so that Remi can acknowledge the comment, but Remi doesn't respond.

'The VIP tickets will be there for you at the entrance.'

'Thanks, brother.'

'And if you're going to beat Malaki, abeg record it,' Balo says, and ends the call before Remi can respond.

Remi shakes his head, slightly irritated but mostly amused, and returns his phone to his pocket.

'Where are we headed?' Rasaq asks.

'Home, now. Tonight, Mainland.'

CHAPTER 28

The drive from Ikoyi to the Mainland at night feels like slipping into another rhythm of Lagos. Remi can sense the shift even with the windows up and the AC humming. On the Island, the streets are quieter, a little too well behaved, as even the chaos wears cologne. But the city sharpens again as he and Rasaq cross the Third Mainland Bridge in the Land Cruiser.

Pockets of light spill from storefronts and roadside stalls, making up for the scattered street lamps. Hawkers move between cars with the ease of instinct, with trays of soft drinks, pure water, and snacks balanced on their heads. Danfos swerve and honk like the road belongs to them. It's messier and louder, and the roads are far less forgiving, but there's a rawness here that isn't trying to impress.

Remi doesn't say much during the ride as Rasaq's Amapiano playlist softly fills the silence. He's calmly observing the streets as they move through the city. But in his mind, he's running through the approach with Malaki. What to say, when to say it, what to hold back, and his bearing. Each imagined version of the approach and conversation plays out a little differently, but in none does he get the answers he's looking for. That optimism has seemingly faded. Still, he keeps turning it over, adjusting for tone, timing, and the unpredictability of Malaki's reaction.

They arrive at the studio just after 10:30 p.m., tucked behind a nondescript gate on a relatively quiet stretch of Allen Avenue, as if trying to keep its exclusivity under wraps. But the security presence says otherwise tonight, with armed guards in branded tactical gear and handheld radios clipped to their vests surrounding the building. Rasaq pulls up to the gate and lowers his window to give Remi's name to a flamboyantly dressed young woman checking off guest names on a tablet. She confirms Remi's name and waves for the guards to open the gate for the Land Cruiser to enter.

Inside, the car park is a showroom of Lagos wealth, including a Ferrari that looks like it's never touched a pothole. Rasaq guides the Land Cruiser into a bay near the back, between two luxury SUVs with tinted windows. He parks, kills the engine, and scans their surroundings out of habit before nodding to confirm it's all clear.

'All right,' Remi says, pocketing his phone. 'Let's go meet Malaki.'

Remi and Rasaq approach the entrance, and a young man in a black DBN Plus vest with red-dyed hair, sitting apart from three armed men guarding the door as if not wanting to be confused as having the same status as them, looks up.

'You guys are so late,' the young man says, clearly irritated as he stands to approach.

Remi fixes the young man with a cold stare, demanding without words if the young man knows who he is talking to.

The young man quickly buries his irritation and checks his

tablet for guest names. He looks up to Remi and Rasaq. 'Remi Bankole, plus one?' he asks with a practised, courteous smile.

Remi nods.

The young man hands over two laminated VIP backstage passes attached to soft lanyards. 'Up the stairs to the main studio,' he says, motioning politely. 'VIP section just in front of the stage. Door to the backstage area is to the left of the stage.'

Remi nods, and he and Rasaq walk into the building.

The corridor is softly lit and tastefully curated with portraits of past performers and the programme's minimal branding. There's money behind this, and taste, too. They reach the doors of the main studio, having not heard a sound through the soundproofed walls and doors, and Rasaq subtly gestures for Remi to step behind him, which Remi does. Rasaq pushes open the door, and Suru Boi's performance envelops them.

The studio is smaller than Remi expected but just right for the event. The stage setting oozes an intimate and stylish living room vibe. Even with all the production in and around the stage, the intimacy of sitting around it on cushioned sofas or armchairs is unaffected. There can't be more than thirty people in the room, and most, male and female, look similar with dyed, stylised hair, thrifted-looking bold outfits, and sunglasses indoors. Alté, but expensively so.

Suru Boi is on stage mid song. He's lanky, with dyed blond tips, wearing a silk shirt unbuttoned to the chest and loose, flared trousers. His voice is good, he has the vibe and energy down, but the music doesn't quite land for Remi. But then Remi isn't really paying attention to the music. He's scanning the small crowd for Malaki, but doesn't see him.

Remi spots the door leading backstage, and the large man, who doesn't look like a DBN Plus employee or part of their security team, who stands guard beside it.

Remi leans towards Rasaq. 'Let's head backstage.'

Rasaq nods and leads around the room, behind the audience, to the door. The large man scowls and steps in front of the door, but Remi and Rasaq calmly flash their passes. The man offers a cursory glance at the passes but then focuses on their faces before nodding. He steps aside and opens the door for them to step through.

The backstage area is surprisingly calm. There are three doors in the tight hallway. The two clearly marked as production and leading to the stage are closed, but the last door is unmarked and ajar. Remi and Rasaq lock eyes and agree without words that the door leads to Suru Boi's backstage area. Rasaq leads the way.

Rasaq and Remi step into the darkly lit room, and a strong, unique voice cuts through before Remi's eyes adjust to the darkness.

'You finally arrived,' Malaki says from across the room.

Remi turns to Malaki, reclining on a low sofa on the other side of the room, an almost identical posture to his interview with Kike.

Malaki is dressed in all black. Black cargo trousers, a black T-shirt, black leather boots – not Alté at all. The only colour is the faint glint from a silver chain with diamonds and ivory beads and a diamond-studded bracelet. He's not smiling, but he doesn't appear hostile either.

'I've been waiting,' he says.

Remi had prepared for Malaki's poised manner but not for Malaki to be waiting for him. Very well, he thinks.

'Then let's talk,' he says, stepping forward confidently.

'Please,' Malaki says, and gestures to the sofa across from him.

Remi nods and steps towards the sofa. Rasaq follows a step behind, clocking the other men in the room behind Malaki.

Remi sits and spots a more eclectic array of pre-rolled designer weed on the table between them than at the Eko Atlantic poker game.

Malaki spots Remi's eyes scanning the weed. 'It's all there for you, Remi,' he says. 'Pick any one you want and enjoy.'

'I'm good, thank you.'

Malaki is mildly surprised. He gestures at Rasaq, standing a step behind Remi. 'What about your *boy*? Is it okay for him to have some?'

'He's not my *boy*,' Remi responds, calm but firm. 'His name is Rasaq. He does what he wants, so you can ask him yourself.'

Malaki cracks an instinctive smile, which he quickly buries. He turns to Rasaq. 'Rasaq, you want some weed?'

Rasaq shakes his head. 'Not for me,' he says, then adds, 'thank you.'

Malaki nods and turns back to Remi. 'Your parents did well for you and your sister,' he says.

Remi is surprised by the comment but doesn't react.

Malaki gestures to himself and Rasaq. 'You see us,' he says with a touch of admiration. 'You treat us the same as you treat your rich Island people. It's what convinced me to do the interview with your sister. Regardless of her intentions, she never treated me like some area boy with dirty money like the rest of your people do.'

Remi nods; he wasn't expecting that compliment either. 'Thanks.'

'Doesn't mean I'm going to let you play me like your sister did,' he says, adding in Yoruba, 'Ẹni tí ejò bá gbé lẹ́ẹ̀kan, kì í ṣeré pẹ̀lú òkété mọ́.'

Remi appreciates the sentiment – one bitten, twice shy. 'No play here,' Remi says. 'I'll be straight.'

'That's good,' Malaki says. 'And this my domain, and there are no cameras. So I, too, will be straight.'

Remi nods. 'Did you have anything to do with my sister's death?'

Malaki leans away, and Remi notes that he seems genuinely offended by the question.

'You see, Remi . . . yes, I sell weed. I am the biggest plug on the Mainland. I'm not trying Island anymore. And yes . . . I have to do some rough things to people. I can't avoid that one.' His tone shifts, infused with indignation. 'That doesn't mean I go around killing people. For what . . . ehn? On top of an interview that has actually helped me. No, Remi. I am insulted by the question. But –' he pauses, his tone shifting back to its original poise – 'I understand.'

Remi doesn't react as he calmly watches Malaki, who remains unflinching. His instincts are that Malaki is telling the truth and that his emotions are genuine. But he wants to glance behind to check if Rasaq is getting the same vibe from Malaki. If so, this is the end of the pursuit for answers. Remi decides to push further.

'How did the interview help you?' Remi asks.

Malaki smirks. 'You don't believe me, abi?'

Remi shrugs. 'The interview didn't help the others. And that's putting it kindly.'

Malaki nods exaggeratedly as if it's something he's considered. 'I know. But you see, the others were lying and cheating those around them. Your fellow Islanders and them, you know. But my people. They all know who I am . . . what I do. It was not a revelation to them. What that interview did for me with your people was –' he shifts to the lyrical tone of his music – 'cut the grass, make we see di snakes.'

Remi understands but still doesn't react. 'Why did she target you?' he asks.

Malaki lets out a short, bitter laugh. 'Yesss . . .' he says, stressing the 's', and instinctively smacks the table a couple of times, showing a flash of anger for the first time. 'She was lied to. Specifically – and I don't know if you know him – Patrick lied to her.'

Remi's eyebrows curl at the revelation, and Malaki spots it.

'Ah. You know Patrick,' Malaki says, smirking. 'Patrick is the weed connect for you rich Island people. He didn't like that I was stepping into his territory. Smart boy, sha. He knew he couldn't fight me directly. So he tried to get your sister to destroy me with that interview. He lied that I was using young to sell. Said I was responsible for some of the horror stories on the news.' His tone shifts again, the humour disappearing as he asserts, 'It was not me. Yeah? I need you to know that. Malaki would never do that.'

Remi nods, but he's more consumed with Patrick's possible involvement. 'Did my sister know Patrick lied?'

'Oh yesss,' Malaki says, his smirk returning. 'A little too late for me, but I dropped some hints after the interview, and she chased it up. She came back to apologise.'

'She did?'

'Yesss. We enjoyed some weed together, and she brought a gift.'

'A gift?'

Malaki nods, now grinning. He gestures at the table of designer pre-rolled weed. 'You think sey I dey sell all this rich person designer weed before? No. Your sister gave me the details of Patrick's supply.'

Remi is shocked but doesn't show it. 'Does Patrick know this?'

'Oh yesss,' Malaki says. 'She told him after slapping him a few times. I heard about the slaps. I wasn't there, of course. But . . . I don't like the boy and would love you to slap him up more. But he was not involved in anything to do with your sister. He's a cunning one, not a violent person. Even with me, he used your sister. Levels dey. And that boy doesn't have the connection to anyone with the *liver* to come after you people. And from what I've heard of you Bankoles, nobody does have that liver. But something happened, abi?'

'Something happened,' Remi repeats.

'Yesss,' Malaki says, and shrugs. 'And me and Patrick came to an arrangement that was . . . *mutually beneficial.* I stay away from the Island in exchange for exclusive supply of some very popular designer strains. The ones that are popular enough for you Island people to send your drivers to come and pick up from the Mainland.'

'One that tasted like champagne and another that tasted like strawberry and lemon ice cream,' Remi says, recollecting Lade's complaint about the funky options Patrick no longer had.

'Yesss,' Malaki says. 'I see you are a customer. I can give you some to take away.'

'I'm good, thanks again.'

'No . . .'

The door bursts open, and Suru Boi and three similarly Alté-dressed young men from Suru Boi's posse charge into the room.

'Wetin una want again!' Suru Boi barks at Remi, as he and the other young men advance towards him and Rasaq. 'Leave our Malaki alone!'

Remi spins off the sofa instantly to see that Rasaq has made a human barrier in front of him.

Malaki had initially cracked an amused smile at the commotion, believing Suru Boi was posturing. But he spots another of Suru Boi's posse waiting by the door, recording, and his tone changes.

'Oya, stop it!' he shouts, but Rasaq's booming voice drowns him out.

'Stop, now!' Rasaq commands.

Rasaq's tone scares Suru Boi, but, aware of the camera recording behind them, he simply falls back behind the other three in his posse as they approach Rasaq.

Rasaq has a gun on his waistband, but he's also spotted the young man recording and doesn't want things escalating that drastically on camera, especially with Remi just behind him. But he is ready and won't hesitate if someone else draws a weapon. The first of the posse gets within his range, and Rasaq drives his heel into the young man's knee mid step. The young man's knee hyperextends, and he buckles to the floor. Rasaq doesn't hesitate once the violence starts; he advances to the next closest member of the posse and meets him with a clean, sharp punch to the centre of his chest. The young man stumbles back, breath catching like his lungs have seized, and his eyes widen as he fights for air.

The third man in the posse dives towards Rasaq's hips the

moment after the punch, and Rasaq is driven backwards past Remi towards the table. Rasaq tries to untangle the third young man and toss him off quickly, but from the young man's grip, it's clear he is a wrestler and that Rasaq has to tread carefully if he doesn't want to be driven over the table.

Suru Boi has a clear path to Remi, and Remi calmly puts a hand out to stop him. Suru Boi knows better than to physically engage Remi, but he is caught in the moment and barrels forward.

Remi suddenly shifts his weight, steps off the centre line, and lets Suru Boi's momentum pass him. At the same time, he loops his right arm tightly around Suru Boi's neck, trapping one of Suru Boi's arms inside the hold. It looks almost like a sideways hug, but there's nothing friendly about it.

Remi tightens the hold, pulling Suru Boi in close, and his bicep presses into one side of Suru Boi's neck as Suru Boi's own shoulder crushes the other side. Remi adjusts his stance, feet planted, posture upright, no wasted movement.

Suru Boi flails for a second, stunned by how fast it all turned, then drops to his knees. Not from choice but because the world is starting to go dark. Remi doesn't release the pressure, feeling the fight seep from Suru Boi. But then Rasaq's voice cuts through.

'Remi,' Rasaq calls. 'We're all clear.'

Remi snaps out of his intense focus and drops Suru Boi to the floor.

Remi scans the room to see that Suru Boi and his posse are all down, unconscious or in severe pain, and Rasaq is now holding down one of the other men who were behind Malaki when he and Remi initially stepped into the room. Remi turns to Malaki, and there is rage in Malaki's eyes, but he can sense that neither Malaki nor the other man, now standing close to Malaki as if protecting him from Rasaq, will try to attack them.

'I thought we were getting on, Malaki,' Remi says. 'I don't know what all that was about.'

Malaki doesn't respond, but Remi notices Malaki's glance over his shoulder. Remi follows Malaki's eyes, turning to see the Alté-dressed young man recording. Remi wonders how long he's been recording and why he didn't abandon it to come help once he saw things were going badly for friends. But then, their sense of loyalty is none of his business.

'Let's go,' Remi says to Rasaq, calm as usual.

Rasaq nods, lets go of the man, and walks towards Remi, scanning everyone, ready for the slightest hint of aggression. There is none. So Rasaq turns around and leads Remi out the door, past the young man, still recording.

CHAPTER 29

Rasaq leads Remi out of the studio at a steady pace. He hadn't expected trouble inside, but his eyes are sharp now, sweeping for any sign of it outside. The guards at the entrance look just as bored as before, and the DBN Plus rep with the red-dyed hair is nowhere to be seen. Rasaq ignores the guards as he strides past, but Remi gives them a polite nod, which they all earnestly return.

At the Land Cruiser, Rasaq waits for Remi to slide in and buckle up before getting behind the wheel. He starts the engine, buckles in and pulls away, his eyes still scanning for any trouble.

As they approach the gate, Rasaq's grip on the wheel tightens. He's ready to ram through it if needed. But when he glances at Remi, he sees only calm and certainty that the gate will open. And it does, without hesitation. The guards see them coming and step aside to swing it open.

The Land Cruiser glides back into the night, rejoining the restless rhythm of Allen Avenue, and Rasaq finally relaxes into his seat. He glances at Remi, who still appears calm – composed, even – but is clearly lost in thought as his fingers tap absently against the armrest, the neon signs blurring past the window casting their brief glow on to his face. Rasaq leaves him to it.

Remi turns over the conversation with Malaki, playing it back in his mind. His instincts tell him Malaki was telling the truth, even the part about Patrick. Still, part of him considers having a word with Patrick in person. But the idea doesn't land with much force. Because the unease that had gripped him all day since seeing Stephen Okolie's face on that faded billboard has finally stilled. In its place is a quiet acceptance that the hunt for answers, for now, will have to be left to Kunle and the Bankole machine. He decides to leave Shina to deal with Patrick, which would be worse for Patrick, but that might be what Patrick deserves.

And just like that, Remi stops drumming his fingers.

'I don't think Balo is going to be very happy,' Remi quips, turning to Rasaq.

Rasaq laughs. 'Not at all.'

'Unless he sees that recording. But I don't think that will see the light of day.'

'Oh, it will!'

'I don't think so. It'll be damaging for Suru Boi's *street rep*. Malaki knows that. He'll make sure that video goes nowhere.'

'I don't know, Remi. Some of these guys are more loyal to social media likes than their day ones. Didn't you see the guy didn't stop recording even after all his guys were down? Viral content loading.'

Remi nods. 'That was mad. But Malaki seemed surprised and vexed about them bursting in, so he'll probably want to bury any trace of all that.'

'Hmm. I'm not sure Malaki didn't know it was going to happen. He smiled when they burst in.'

'Oh. I missed that.'

'Yes. You had already jumped up to face Suru Boi and the others, but I was making sure the guys standing behind Malaki were not going to join from behind us. That's when I saw it. It was quick. He covered it fast.'

That forces Remi to turn over the events at the studio again. But his instinct remains that Malaki wasn't lying and was surprised by Suru Boi's actions, especially because of his genuinely fraught demand for Suru Boi to stop. Maybe Malaki had changed his mind.

'I saw you had one of Malaki's guys down. What happened?'

'That last one trying to wrestle me was his brother.'

'How do you know that?'

'He said it when I was holding him down. I don't know if he was talking to me or Malaki. But he kept repeating it as if that's why he couldn't stop himself getting involved.'

That lines up with Remi's reading of events, but he sees no need to point that out, as Rasaq's clear-eyed, independent perspective is just as valuable – maybe even more so, given the nature of his job.

'Thanks for handling that with minimal . . . *violence*,' Remi says.

Rasaq wants to say that assessing and applying the right level of force is a core part of his job, but he's learned that Remi doesn't see it that way. And most of his other clients would've wanted him to do far more damage.

'No problem, Remi,' Rasaq says.

'I mean it,' Remi continues. 'I know you have a gun on your hip, and it might've been easier to pull it out just to get those idiots to back off.'

Rasaq nods. 'I only pull it out if I intend to shoot. I will never put you in that position. Unless it's the last resort.'

'I get it,' Remi says with a gracious nod.

'And you handled yourself very well,' Rasaq says. 'You were up and ready so fast. No hesitation. And where did you learn that hold?'

Remi smiles. 'I'm a blue belt in jiu-jitsu . . . used to compete in boxing and Muay Thai for a long time . . . still train in both every week, and I trained Krav Maga for about two years before that.'

'No wonder,' Rasaq says, impressed, then adds, 'Why all that training?'

Remi shrugs. 'I enjoy combat sports. Never expected to, but once I started training, I loved it. As for Krav Maga, I just felt it was important to know how to defend myself.'

'Okay,' Rasaq says, and pauses, considering if he should ask the follow-up question on his mind. He does. 'Why was it important?'

'Just a feeling,' Remi says – he's pondered that question himself and hasn't yet come up with a logical answer. But something he can't identify drove him to learn to take care of himself in every situation.

Rasaq nods, appreciating that is all he will get from Remi on that topic.

The car returns to a comfortable silence, and Remi watches the streets, noting how people still move with purpose at nearly midnight. The city is too stubborn to sleep.

After a few minutes, Remi turns to Rasaq. 'Let's check out one of your suya spots.'

Rasaq glances at Remi, eyes lighting up. 'Now?'

Remi nods. 'Why not? Let's see if your Mainland favourites actually match up.'

'Oya now,' Rasaq says, excited.

They swing off the main road, and Rasaq drives through side streets for about fifteen minutes until they reach a wide clearing that barely looks like a car park. A handful of cars are scattered around, engines idling, men and women leaning against bonnets, tearing into newspaper-wrapped suya with bare fingers.

Remi spots the modest stall through the thick smoke surrounding it. There is no branding or polish – just the open flames, the wire mesh grills, and an old speaker to the side blaring a Fuji classic. But the smell is heavenly – spice, fire, grilled beef and fat and onions.

Rasaq parks near the edge and kills the engine. 'Wait here,' he says, and hops out before Remi can argue.

Remi watches from the car as Rasaq moves with the ease of a regular. A couple of men hail him, nods exchanged, and backs clapped. One man calls him 'Captain', and Remi watches as Rasaq laughs, orders and gestures animatedly.

A few minutes later, Rasaq returns with two tightly wrapped bundles. They eat in the car, windows rolled halfway down to let the air in. The suya is blisteringly hot, oily, and bold, the spice kicking harder than Remi expects.

'Okay . . . okay,' Remi says between mouthfuls. 'I'm not saying it's better than my Island spot, but . . .'

'But it's better,' Rasaq finishes, grinning.

Remi shakes his head. 'I'll say it's . . . about equal.'

They laugh and return to enjoying the suya in silence.

Minutes later, they are back on the road, their bellies full and the tingling from the heavy spice mellowing. They drift through the nightscape towards the Island, the city growing quieter around them.

The car rounds a bend, and a burst of vibrant drums seeps through the windows. Remi turns towards the sound to see the New Afrika Shrine – an open-air music venue and cultural hub with deep ties to Fela Kuti's legacy.

Remi is captivated by the faint sounds of the energetic performance of 'Shakara (Oloje)', a Fela classic, from inside the venue that's spilling out into the street.

'Wait,' he says.

Rasaq brakes gently. 'The Shrine?' he asks.

'Yeah,' Remi says. 'I've always wanted to check it out. And don't worry, I'll sleep on the flight.'

'Oya!'

Rasaq parks the Land Cruiser on a roadside close to the Shrine because the Shrine compound has no parking space. They approach the Shrine's entrance. There are no guards, just the vibrant rhythms of another Fela classic calling them in. They enter, and the space is hot, packed and electric – the sweat-soaked live band on the stage completely in control of the crowd.

Remi and Rasaq blend in, and no one notices them because no one cares. For a moment, Remi and Rasaq are not who they were before they walked in, but two friends swaying to the beat, letting the music cut through the residue of everything else.

A couple of hours later, they slip out of the Shrine and back into the early morning drive to the Island. It's around 3 a.m., and the city is much quieter; the roads mostly deserted.

They are in the middle of a conversation about the London music scene, grime in particular, when the Land Cruiser nears the police checkpoint that every car must pass on the only plausible route out of Ikeja towards the Island at this hour. The barrier doesn't lift as they approach, even when they get close enough for the police officers to recognise the government plate number. Remi doesn't pay much attention, putting it down to their tiredness at this time in the early morning.

Rasaq stops the car a few metres from the barrier and scans the three armed officers waiting in front of it as a fourth officer approaches the vehicle.

The fourth officer unexpectedly veers to the front passenger side and knocks on the window, and Remi reaches to lower the window.

'No,' Rasaq gently says to Remi, and lowers his window. He leans out. 'Come this side!'

'I dey here,' the fourth officer responds. 'Abeg, wind the window.'

'Abeg, make you no disturb my Oga. Come this side,' he says, then adds with his commanding voice, 'Oya!'

The fourth officer hesitates, glancing at the other officers waiting at the barrier.

'Oya, now! Don't waste our time,' Rasaq says.

The fourth officer begrudgingly walks around to the driver's side, and Rasaq raises the window just below his eye level before the officer arrives.

'Wetin you want?' Rasaq asks. 'You no see plate number?'

The fourth officer doesn't respond and looks past Rasaq to check the passenger. He deliberately glances at the other officers waiting by the barrier before responding.

'Wetin you think say I want?'

Rasaq notices two of the officers waiting at the barrier casually making their way towards the vehicle.

'What station are you from?' he asks the officer by his window.

'How does that concern you?'

Rasaq notes that the two other officers have positioned themselves around the car – one in front, the other by the passenger side. He glances back to the barrier, and the last officer has positioned himself in line with the driver's seat. Each of those officers already has their weapons half raised, ready to shoot.

The hairs at the back of Rasaq's neck stand as his awareness sharpens. He quickly checks on Remi, and Remi appears calm as usual, but his eyes are fixed on the officers.

'I dey look your badge number,' Rasaq says to the officer by his window, carefully pulling out his phone. 'But the station number for there no be Lagos.'

'Wetin you dey talk?' the fourth officer chides. 'Badge number no dey show station.'

Rasaq nods. 'At least you be real officer,' he says, and gestures to the other officers. 'But your friends. Mi ò ro bẹ́ẹ̀. Their rifles . . . not police issue. And too fresh.'

The analysis stuns the officer, and he turns to the others as if trying to communicate without words.

Rasaq seizes the opportunity and takes a picture of the officer's face and badge number before tossing the phone into the footwell and gripping the steering wheel tightly. He glances to confirm Remi's seat belt is secure. It is.

'Head down,' he whispers, and Remi immediately drops his head at once.

The officer by his window turns back to Rasaq, his confidence gone, replaced with fear and guilt. Suddenly, he turns and runs off.

Rasaq doesn't hesitate; he slams down on the accelerator just before the officer in front of the car opens fire. The Land Cruiser drives over the officer as bullets impact the windows from the officer at the barrier and the other officer positioned by the passenger side. The windows hold up, and Rasaq makes a point to steer the Land Cruiser directly into the officer at the barrier, who dives at the last moment, but doesn't get away from the vehicle's path. There is a crunch as the Land Cruiser speeds over the officer, and another almost immediately as it bursts through the barrier.

CHAPTER 30

The Land Cruiser tears down the quiet streets at breakneck speed. Rasaq stays sharp, scanning the surroundings and stealing repeated glances at Remi, who sits silently in the passenger seat. But it's not Remi's usual calm – it's blank. Hollow.

Rasaq swings on to a relatively busier road a few minutes away from the ambush and pulls into a patch of secluded darkness. He puts the car in park, then turns gently to Remi.

'Remi,' he calls.

No response. Still blank.

'Remi,' he says again, softly.

Still nothing.

Rasaq reaches over and places a hand on Remi's shoulder. The touch gets Remi's attention, and he turns slowly to Rasaq, calm but silent.

'Are you okay?' Rasaq asks.

Remi nods once. Then his eyes drift, scanning the bulletproof windows, which are intact but spiderwebbed with bullet impact marks. He lingers on each mark as if reimagining the impact of every shot, one by one. He nods again.

'Take me home,' he says, calm. 'Please.'

Roughly an hour later, the Land Cruiser glides through Remi's serene neighbourhood with its headlights off, hoping to go unnoticed as Shina instructed. Kunle wants to keep the ambush under wraps – no noise, no headlines.

The Bankole residence's gates are already open as the vehicle approaches, so Rasaq swings in smoothly without braking and heads straight to the main house's driveway. He guides the car past three identical Land Cruisers lined up at the edge of the driveway and parks right in front of the main house, where Kunle waits, flanked by Shina and Yinka.

Kunle immediately reaches for the front passenger door and pulls it open to check on Remi.

'Are you okay?' he asks, scanning Remi for physical injuries. He doesn't spot any.

Remi slowly turns to his dad. 'I'm okay,' he says. But he doesn't move, not even to unbuckle his seat belt.

Kunle senses that although Remi isn't physically injured, he's deeply traumatised by the ambush. So Kunle doesn't hurry his son and patiently waits for him to make that first move to step out of the vehicle.

A timeless moment later, Remi unbuckles his seat belt.

'I'm just tired,' he says. 'I don't think I'm going to make the flight. Need to sleep.'

'No problem, Remi,' Kunle says and offers Remi a hand to help him out of the car.

Remi smiles softly at the offered hand. 'Thank you, Dad. But I'm okay. Seriously.'

Kunle nods before stepping aside for Remi to climb out of the vehicle.

'Please stay here until you are fully rested,' Kunle says, gesturing at the main house. 'They've prepared your old room.'

'Thank you, Dad.'

Remi and Kunle walk towards Rasaq, Shina, and Yinka, who are huddled together a few feet from the main house's front door, discussing their next moves.

As soon as Rasaq had parked, Shina had eagerly beckoned him over. He'd hesitated, not wanting to leave Remi alone in the car, but Kunle had quickly approached to open the passenger-side door and check on Remi, so Rasaq had hopped out, knowing he was in the safest hands.

'Excellent work, Rasaq,' Shina had said as Rasaq approached them, and patted him on the shoulder.

'Agreed,' Yinka said, nodding, and slapped Rasaq's back.

Rasaq dipped his head slightly to acknowledge their respect.

Shina glanced at Remi in the car. 'How is he now?'

Rasaq shook his head. 'Still the same, sir,' he said.

They all turned to watch the quiet exchange between Kunle and Remi, and a flicker of rage crossed Shina and Yinka's faces – rage that's been simmering since Rasaq called an hour ago to brief them on the ambush and Remi's movements on the Mainland leading up to it. Shina's jaw tightened, and he smacked his thigh without realising it. Beside him, Yinka's nostrils flared, his breath quickening.

'Don't worry,' Shina said, turning back to Rasaq. 'We've briefed Oga; he will personally make sure our Remi is taken care of.'

Rasaq nodded, grateful for the update.

'The picture you sent of the officer has been invaluable,' Yinka said. 'We apprehended him at his home in Surulere before he could abscond with his wife and three children.'

'Surulere?' Rasaq said, pointing out the apparent connection with Malaki.

'Uhun,' Yinka said, confirming that they are aware of the connection.

'He's being spoken to right now,' Shina added. 'I will be updated shortly. As for the others . . . not officers, as you suspected. Our people have already recognised the two dead bodies at the scene. Soldiers from Cotonu, including the last one that has escaped . . . for now. The three of them have been hired guns in Lagos for a few years. Frequently engaged by Ma-la-ki.' He stressed each syllable like gunshots. 'We have been aware of them since assisting Kike with her *Spotlight Nigeria* episode on Malaki. Our last information was that he'd fallen out with them over their callousness. But I imagine that madness is what he needed for this ambush . . . and . . .' He left the rest of that sentence for their imagination.

The men fall silent, considering the information and its seemingly inevitable conclusion.

'Our people are waiting at the usual spots and the Benin border for the last Cotonu soldier. He will not escape,' Shina continued. 'We already have people surrounding Malaki's house in Surulere. They have confirmed he is inside. I will stay here with Oga and Remi.' He focused on Rasaq. 'I would like you to accompany Yinka right now to deal with Malaki. I know this is not what he hired you for, so you don't have to go. Yinka is a big boy. He will handle it. But . . .'

'I will go, sir.'

Shina smiled, and Yinka patted Rasaq on the back.

Before Shina could continue, Remi stepped out of the car, and he doesn't speak as all three men turn to watch Remi and Kunle approach.

'I'm all right,' Remi says, and forces a soft smile.

The smile doesn't calm their rage. It deepens it, and Remi notices that immediately. He also sees that they are charged up and ready for action.

'No more deaths,' Remi unexpectedly says.

Shina and Yinka are surprised by the request, but Rasaq isn't. He understands. Yinka glances at Shina for a response, and Shina nods at Remi. But it's a half-empty gesture that's just enough to acknowledge but not enough to mean it.

Remi reads the emptiness of the nod and turns to his dad. 'No more deaths, please.'

'I understand, Remi,' Kunle acknowledges without promising.

Remi turns to Rasaq. 'Are you going with them?'

'Yes. I'm going with Yinka.'

'No more deaths, yes?' he asks Rasaq directly. 'I'm asking you . . . as a friend. No more.'

Everyone's eyes are on Rasaq, but only Remi's matter to him. He nods.

'I want to hear it, Rasaq,' Remi says.

Rasaq hesitates for a brief moment before he spots Kunle's subtle nod. 'No more deaths,' he confirms.

'Thank you,' Remi says, and continues towards the main house's front door.

Kunle and Shina exchange a look that Rasaq doesn't recognise before Kunle follows Remi. The door opens as Kunle and Remi approach. They step through, and it shuts gently behind them.

'Oya,' Shina says to Rasaq and Yinka. 'Ẹ lọ! I will call you when I hear back from our people talking to the officer.'

Yinka nods and heads towards the first of the Land Cruisers lined up at the edge of the driveway.

Rasaq hesitates, wanting clarity on the response to Remi's request, but Shina has already turned to his phone. Rasaq follows Yinka into the vehicle, hoping there will be no more deaths but expecting more.

CHAPTER 31

They ride in silence. Rasaq sits in the back seat of the lead Land Cruiser beside Yinka. Neither has spoken since their driver pulled out of the Bankole compound. The convoy moves in tight formation, three identical black SUVs, headlights off, gliding like shadowed phantoms through Ikoyi's sleeping streets.

They cross Third Mainland Bridge as the first hints of light crack the sky – that strange, uncanny Lagos hour when the city hasn't fully let go of the night, but dawn is already in motion. The lagoon glimmers with just enough light to remind you it could drown you if it wanted to.

Yinka's phone vibrates. Once. Twice. Then he answers.

He listens. The call ends. He leans over. 'The officer confessed,' he says. 'The Cotonu soldiers hired him. Said it was to set up one of Malaki's rivals. Didn't know it was a Bankole.'

Rasaq's jaw doesn't clench. His hands don't move. But something in him adjusts – a tightness that settles deeper into his chest.

The rest of the drive passes in stillness. No further words. Just the rhythm of tyres on tarmac, the quiet hum of four engines moving as one.

They arrive in Surulere just as the sky turns slate blue.

The neighbourhood is already stirring. It's not fully awake yet, but the air has changed. The vehicles park in the shadows beside a pile of tyres next to shuttered shops, a street away from Malaki's compound.

Senior Inspector Moshood is already waiting, flanked by two junior officers. Moshood is in plainclothes but still looks like the veteran policeman that he is. He nods once. No handshake. Shina has briefed him personally – official arrest and process, to the extent it can be done. Despite Shina's frustration with the investigation, he and Kunle rate Moshood. He's one of the few they trust to do the job properly, when the system lets him. But first, unofficial entry. Moshood will wait back – this part is off the books.

Yinka gives the signal. Two teams, four each. One with him and the other with Rasaq. There are no words, just hand signs and glances.

They move fast and quietly, approaching the compound from two angles: Yinka's team flanks left, and Rasaq's slides right.

The compound is a fortress. High walls. Tall gates. Barbed wire. But they've come prepared; Rasaq's team scale the rear wall like shadows and drop into the garden soundlessly. The house looms. Big. Lavish. Tinted windows. The kind of wealth that doesn't come with invoices.

They advance. Quiet movement. No noise. Then it happens – a shout from a neighbour. It's just one at first. But enough. Then, a cacophony of screams shatters the silence.

Movement in the house. Lights flickering on. Noises of alarm.

Yinka's voice crackles through the comms, ordering the switch to a loud entry but confirming Malaki is to be taken alive.

Rasaq doesn't hesitate. He leads his team forward, drawing his sidearm as they surge through a side entrance. The door gives way with one kick. He leads them through the corridors like they already know where they are heading. But he's just looking for the stairs – the main bedroom is always upstairs.

He hears a voice and movement around the corner, and commands, with his booming voice, 'Everybody, drop to the ground!' Then he repeats the command in Yoruba.

Most people obey. Staff. Extended family. Sleepy-eyed, terrified, barefoot.

Gunfire bursts from a room to Rasaq's left and whizzes past him. He drops to one knee and returns fire in a single clean motion before even seeing the shooter. The shooter, a large young man, crumples backwards and collapses.

A volley of shots breaks out on the other side of the compound – Yinka's team. Rasaq doesn't flinch. He directs one of his team to cover the hallway, and the other two sweep forward with him.

When Rasaq reaches the staircase, the house has fallen silent again. He moves fast but methodically up the stairs, his team behind him.

He advances through the first floor and meets Yinka and the others from Yinka's team outside a pair of massive gold-trimmed double doors.

Yinka looks grim. Blood on his sleeve. Not his.

'He's inside,' Yinka confirms.

Rasaq kicks the door down, and Yinka is first through with his gun raised. But the garishly opulent bedroom is quiet. Too quiet.

They quickly spot Malaki sprawled across a king-sized bed. Shirtless. Barefoot. A faint layer of sweat glistens on his skin. His mouth twitches as though trying to speak. His pupils flutter. His lips move. But no words come.

Rasaq looks at the bedside table, and there is an empty syringe, crushed pill foil, and a near-empty glass of whiskey for courage.

Overdose. But not clean, as there's still a fight in Malaki.

Malaki's eyes snap into sudden focus, locking on to Rasaq with something that almost looks like a plea.

Rasaq turns to Yinka, waiting on the call that will decide what comes next. Yinka snarls with frustration and pulls out his phone. One call. Shina.

The order comes back in seconds. Kunle wants Malaki alive.

Rasaq and Yinka lift Malaki carefully. Rasaq takes his legs; Yinka has the arms. Malaki is heavy. Deadweight, but not yet dead. His breath is shallow, chest rising and falling in quick bursts.

They carry Malaki out of the bedroom through the first-floor corridor, down the stairs and out the front door. Their teams are leading the way with guns raised.

They burst out of the front door towards the gates, and Rasaq hears it first. Then the others. They all look up to the drones. At least four. Buzzing overhead like mosquitoes. Lights blinking red in the sky. Watching.

Rasaq looks to Yinka, checking to see if he knows anything about them. Yinka shakes his head. But there is no time to dwell on it. They race through the gates and around the corner back to the Land Cruisers and place Malaki in the back seat of the first vehicle.

Rasaq slides into the driver's seat with someone from his team. Yinka stays behind to coordinate the rest and deal with Moshood, who's approaching the vehicles with concern.

Rasaq speeds off, and the car tears through Surulere like a bullet. There is no need for sirens – just caution and the car horn.

Rasaq repeatedly checks on Malaki through the rear-view mirror, and Malaki is slipping deeper into the space between living and dying.

By the time they reach the hospital gates, Malaki is gone. Rasaq knows this because of the stillness in the back seat. But he parks the car a few steps from the hospital's emergency entrance and leans over to check Malaki for a pulse. There is none.

He sits in silence, watching the sky finally bloom into morning. He has no tears for Malaki. No prayers, either. Just the quiet recognition of another casualty of Lagos.

CHAPTER 32

A gentle touch wakes Remi, and he opens his eyes to find Kunle standing over him, wearing a faint, affectionate smile.

Remi smiles back and sits up slowly. It takes him a moment to register where he is – his childhood bedroom. Except it doesn't quite feel like it. The space looks different, curated almost like a guest room. He remembers Kunle guiding him here, lying down, and surrendering to sleep. But not the room itself. Now, though, he sees it all clearly.

He turns back to Kunle, and even Kunle recognises that the haze has lifted from Remi's eyes.

'How are you feeling?' Kunle asks.

'Better,' Remi responds. 'Much better.'

Kunle nods. 'I can see that. I'm happy you had a good rest.'

Remi nods and instinctively checks the bedside table for his phones. They aren't there. 'What's the time?'

'Two thirty,' Kunle says, and picks Remi's phones off the carpet by the bed to hand to him. 'I put them on silent. Didn't want your sleep disturbed.'

'Thanks,' Remi says, and places the phones on the bedside table. 'I don't think I've had eight hours of sleep in a decade.'

'I'm sure,' Kunle says. 'I would let you sleep for the whole day, but . . . I have to leave now. They can't wait any longer.'

'They?'

'The EFCC. They are outside. Here to arrest me for not paying tax for the past thirty plus years. Dating to when I returned from London.'

'That's not true!'

'The truth is irrelevant, Remi. This is how the *heavyweights* have decided to attack us. Our money and our reputation. But I have it under control.'

'Dad, they are here to arrest you. How much control is that?'

Kunle accepts Remi's point with a nod. 'I was hoping you'd already be on your way to London by now, so you wouldn't have been aware of this. But it's nothing you need to worry about. It'll be sorted before you return.'

'Sorted in a month?'

Kunle nods. 'One way or the other.'

'One way or the other?' Remi asks with concern.

'These are high-stakes manoeuvres, Remi. There are always risks involved.'

Remi bites his tongue. Correctly reading that as a soft rebuke.

'But there is something more important for us to discuss before I leave,' Kunle says.

'Okay,' Remi says with expectation.

'We've found the person responsible for Kike's death.'

'Who?' Remi asks, straightening up.

'Malaki.'

'Malaki?' Remi questions, consumed with doubt – about the news, about his instincts. 'Are you sure? I spoke to him, and I didn't get that . . . I didn't . . . You understand.'

'It was him, Remi.'

'What? Did you speak to him? Did he confess?'

'He's dead.'

'Dead. How?'

'I don't care how, Remi,' Kunle says with a flash of anger. 'I only care that he's dead. They found the clothes she was wearing the day she died at his house. And he was also responsible for your ambush.'

Remi is stunned by the revelation and is suddenly filled with anger at himself for his foolhardy trust in his so-called instincts. 'I'm sorry . . .' he begins to say.

'No,' Kunle cuts in with finality. 'There is nothing for you to apologise for. I'm just glad you are okay. That you're safe.'

Remi nods, burying his anger at himself so his father has some peace.

'We have rescheduled your flight to tomorrow,' Kunle says. 'Go back to London. I'll see you in a month.'

'Okay, Dad.'

There is a quiet moment of affection before Kunle squeezes Remi's shoulder.

'Can I come down with you?'

'Come down?'

'To meet the EFCC with you.'

'Oh. They are not downstairs in the compound. They are outside the gates. But yes, please come with me. And no rush. They can wait a few more minutes for you to be ready. And I have a call to make. Meet me in the living room in ten minutes.'

'Sure, Dad.'

As Kunle walks out of the bedroom, Remi gets up to get ready, never doubting that Mrs Ibeh would've stocked the room with toiletries and a change of clothes.

Ten minutes later, Remi walks into the living room, freshly showered and dressed. Kunle isn't there yet, but Remi knows he soon will be, so he doesn't sit. Instead, he studies the art pieces in the room, curated by his sister.

Then, a headline on the muted TV catches his eye: THE BANKOLES' REVENGE. He focuses on the TV and sees drone footage of a large opulent house. Then he spots two people he recognises, even from the distance – Rasaq and Yinka, carrying a lifeless body that looks very much like Malaki out of the house. Then the video skips back a few minutes, and it's clearly being played on a loop.

Remi crosses the room, grabs the remote, and turns up the volume. He listens closely as the reporter recounts their version of the morning's events: the Bankoles taking the law into their own hands to avenge Kike's death. Four dead in the compound, including Malaki. Then, the police findings: large sums of cash in dollars, an arsenal of weapons, marijuana . . . and Kike's clothes, folded away in Malaki's closet.

Remi is so locked on the screen that he doesn't notice Kunle enter the room. Kunle had already told him most of what was in the news report. But the drone footage is different. Seeing its cold precision hits harder than words. And he's perplexed by how DBN already know this much. How did they get the drone footage so quickly? Why were there drones even recording the house at that time? His instincts were scratching at the edges. But then these same instincts missed . . .

'Remi,' Kunle calls.

Remi turns to Kunle. He wants to ask about the news, whether Rasaq, Yinka, or both killed Malaki in cold blood, and if it was on his orders. But he doesn't.

'Ready?' Kunle asks.

Remi nods, mutes the television, and places the remote on the coffee table before walking over.

Remi and Kunle walk side by side through the compound, the sun casting long shadows behind them. The weight of the moment is palpable, but you wouldn't know it from their relaxed, confident strides. However, with each step towards the gates, more of the household gathers behind them – loyal staff, silent but charged. Shina and Yinka appear first, then Mrs Ibeh, Kehinde, Nike, Ada, and many others – drivers, guards, aides. A quiet army forming behind the Bankoles.

Remi can feel their indignation crackling in the air. But Kunle's poise, his stillness, settles them.

They reach the gates, and the guards salute Kunle before slowly pulling them open. Outside, three EFCC vehicles wait beside a marked police convoy. The officers cluster near the entrance, visibly tense, and the nervousness only sharpens when they clock the silent force behind Kunle and Remi.

But Kunle steps forward alone, crossing the threshold without hesitation. He greets the lead EFCC officer with a firm handshake, his posture gracious but unyielding. Then he turns back to Remi and the loyal crowd gathered at the gate. His gaze passes across their faces before settling on his son. He offers a calm smile.

He turns to follow the EFCC officer to a gleaming Toyota Prado. A junior officer rushes ahead to open the door. Kunle nods politely, steps in, and the door shuts behind him.

The convoy pulls away a moment later. Without needing a signal, Shina and Yinka split from the group, climb into a Land Cruiser parked just outside, and follow close behind.

The gates draw shut with a deep metallic groan. The crowd begins to disperse. But Remi doesn't move.

'How are you feeling?' Rasaq asks from behind with deep concern.

Remi slowly turns to face him. There's so much he could say. So much he could ask. But no. Rasaq made a promise. He broke it. That's all there is.

'Better,' Remi says coldly. Then he turns and walks away, back towards the guest house.

Rasaq stays by the gates, watching him go. He knows something has broken between them, something that may never be put back together.

CHAPTER 33

The next morning, Remi walks down the guest house stairs on his way out of the house to head to the airport. He's dressed simply in a white linen shirt and tan flowing trousers, his travel bag already loaded into the Land Cruiser waiting outside.

He approaches the foot of the stairs and spots Kehinde, Bola and Ada waiting quietly by the door. There's sadness in their eyes, but also warmth and a flicker of pride. That particular pride is primarily due to the video of Remi and Rasaq's altercation at the studio, which went viral the day before. And not just across social media but also on the national news. DBN News, in particular, played it on a loop, slotting it into their breathless and increasingly sensational coverage of the *Bankole saga*.

The coverage began with 'THE BANKOLES' REVENGE', then shamelessly moved on to the 'THE BANKOLES' DOWNFALL?' hours later with their exclusive video of Kunle being led into the EFCC building as one of their reporters hounded him with questions about his tax evasion charges and the *true* source of his wealth. Kunle was composed throughout the long walk into the building, but Remi could see the surprise in his eyes. Things were not in control. Remi had switched it off then.

Remi approaches, and they all start bending at the knees to greet him traditionally.

'No,' Remi says, calm but firm. 'We're doing this my way.'

They glance at each other.

'Hugs,' Remi says. 'Come on.'

Remi hugs Bola first, then Ada, and finally Kehinde. There is no hesitation in each embrace.

'Safe journey, Oga Remi,' Bola says, with a slight bow.

'Thank you, Bola. I'll be back soon,' Remi says. 'If just to try some more of Ada's cooking.'

They laugh softly.

'Look forward to it, Remi,' Ada says. 'You haven't tried a lot of my specialities.'

Remi grins. 'Okay, Chef. Looking forward to those.'

Remi turns to Kehinde, and they exchange a fist bump.

'The house will be ready for you anytime,' Kehinde says.

Remi nods. 'Take care of yourselves.'

'You too, Remi,' they all respond in near unison.

Bola opens the door, and Remi steps outside.

Mrs Ibeh and Nike stand in the shade created by the overhanging roof, and Remi pauses at the sight of them, noting from their stillness that they had been waiting for him to step outside, not wanting to intrude on Remi's moment with his household staff.

Nike greets him first with a shy smile. 'Safe journey, Oga Remi.'

'Thank you, Nike,' he says, softly smiling back.

He turns to Mrs Ibeh, and she's her usual immovable self. But then she steps forward and opens her arms, catching Remi completely off guard.

She hugs him. Not a tight, emotional squeeze. But still a proper, full embrace. And she holds it for a moment longer than he expected before pulling back and straightening her wrapper like nothing happened.

Remi wants to respond. Thank her for the hug. For everything. But the words don't come. He just nods, then turns and walks to the waiting car.

The Land Cruiser is already running. Rasaq sits in the driver's seat, eyes seemingly fixed ahead, though he's acutely aware of Remi's approach. He hides it well, but his apprehension builds with every one of Remi's footsteps. Not because he fears confrontation but because he doesn't know how their fractured relationship will manifest on this ride. He hasn't spoken to Remi since yesterday's cold response at the gates and doesn't intend to push it this morning. Or ever.

He, too, has watched the clips, read the headlines, and scrolled through WhatsApp broadcasts spinning wild versions of yesterday's events. But after everything they've been through, if Remi truly believes he's the cold-blooded assassin these stories make him out to be, then all that time spent getting to know each other was wasted.

Remi opens the front passenger door and gets in without a word. And Rasaq exhales, not visibly, but deep inside. He's relieved Remi didn't take the back seat. It tells him that whatever Remi may be feeling – anger, disappointment, hurt, even betrayal – he hasn't let it shake his principles. He didn't sit in the back seat in their first drive together, and he won't now.

They greet each other quietly, almost like strangers, and Rasaq eases the car into motion.

The Land Cruiser rolls out of the driveway through the compound gates.

They don't speak as Ikoyi slides past their windows: bright vines spilling over high walls, morning joggers in high-end sportswear, house staff hosing down the pavements. Everything seems as orderly as Lagos allows.

They cross into the Mainland, and the atmosphere thickens. Markets are waking up, and traffic is beginning to pulse. People call out to Danfo drivers, and teenagers hawk bread through half-open car windows.

As they join the expressway in Ikeja, Remi spots an oddly shaped building that was once his marker that Aunty Aishat's turning was near.

'Turn left,' he says, gesturing at the road ahead.

Rasaq glances at Remi, almost about to object, to remind Remi of his flight time . . . almost. Then he makes the turn.

They drift into a slower part of town and through wide, cracked streets framed by tall old trees. The neighbourhood once had prestige, but now only traces remain – rusted wrought-iron gates, sagging tiled roofs, and peeling colonial-era façades. Yet pride lingers here and there.

Remi gives the next directions with extreme brevity – one word, two at most, punctuated by hand signals.

They pull up outside a large compound. It's old, clearly, but still proud. The paint has faded but not flaked. The hedges are trimmed. The brass nameplate beside the gate glints in the morning sun.

Rasaq kills the engine, and Remi steps out to approach the separate pedestrian gate connected to the main gate. He knocks on the pedestrian gate once, but then the main gate swings wide. Remi steps back instinctively, and a new silver Peugeot sedan rolls into view, its engine humming quietly. Behind the wheel, the young driver leans slightly forward, eyes wide to scan Remi.

Then the rear window rolls down. 'Ah! Remi!' Aishat says, and flings the car door open before it fully stops.

The driver instantly stops the car, and Aishat steps out in a long flowing boubou patterned with sunflowers.

'My dear Remi,' she says, and pulls him into a tender hug before he lowers himself to prostrate. 'It's so good to see you again.'

'It's good to see you too, Aunty,' he says, standing up. She smells the same, like she's used the same light floral perfume for decades.

'I saw the news,' she says, releasing the embrace to look him in the eye. She cups his face in her hands. 'Olúwa has judged, ọmọ mi. Not us. His justice may have taken time, but it was always coming for Malaki. Let your heart rest.'

The comment doesn't entirely sit well with Remi, especially because he doesn't think God had anything to do with it. But he appreciates the sentiment. He nods graciously.

'And it's not over for him, Remi,' she continues, fuelled with righteous fervour. 'That Malaki will burn in hell for eternity.'

Remi nods again, and she smiles lovingly at him, reading that he doesn't want to engage in that conversation. Not yet, at least.

'And that EFCC rubbish with Kunle,' she says, shifting the

conversation. 'Don't even worry yourself about that. You know your father. It will all be cleared up soon.'

'I hope so, Aunty.'

'It's money that they want . . . it's always money.'

'I hope so,' he repeats.

'You hope so?' she asks, softly smacking his shoulder as if chiding him for his seeming lack of faith. 'Are you praying, then?'

Remi cracks a smile, and she shakes her head, amused.

'I am on my way to Balogun Market,' she says. 'You would have missed me because I should've left ten minutes ago – Holy Spirit timing!' She turns to the driver. 'Switch off the engine small.'

The driver nods and switches the engine off.

She turns back to Remi. 'You're welcome to wait inside until I return. There's no light. NEPA has done their usual. But they'll put on the gen for you. Or –' she pauses, raising an eyebrow – 'you can come with me.'

Remi hesitates. He knows about Balogun Market. Everyone does. It's renowned for its labyrinth of stalls, the crush of bodies, the din of competing voices, and the spectre of sudden criminality. He also knows the video of the altercation with Suru Boi is looping nonstop on DBN and flooding WhatsApp chains, painting a target on his back for any Malaki loyalists.

'Nobody will recognise you,' Aishat says, reading his hesitation. 'And even if they do, they won't believe it's you. They would not expect you to be sweating with them in Balogun Market.' She leans in, grinning. 'Just don't talk too much. If they hear this your oyinbo accent, everything will double in price. And then you will be in deep wahala. With me.' She winks.

They both laugh.

'Okay,' Remi says, a quiet smile spreading across his face. 'I'm in. I'll go tell Rasaq.'

Remi walks back towards the Land Cruiser, parked by the kerb with its engine still running. Rasaq's hands are on the steering wheel, his eyes alert to their surroundings as he watches Remi approach.

Remi walks up to the front passenger side, and Rasaq lowers the window.

'I'm going with her to the market,' Remi says through the window, and offers no further information.

Rasaq's brow twitches, and it looks like he might say something, but he doesn't. In any event, Remi walks away without waiting and enters the back seat of the Peugeot with Aishat. The Peugeot eases into motion a moment later, and the Land Cruiser follows.

Balogun Market is a storm of colour and motion. Fabrics ripple like sails in the wind, traders shout prices in shrill harmonies, and the crowd of buyers vociferously haggle. The air is rich with spices, sweat, petrol and fried food. It's chaotic and exhilarating.

Aishat moves like a seasoned veteran, her steps confident, her tone direct but warm. Remi follows by her side, and she occasionally grabs his hand when the crowd thickens to check he's there and not overwhelmed.

'Akara,' she announces, pausing beside a woman frying golden balls of bean paste over a coal pot. She buys two portions wrapped in old newspaper and hands one to Remi. She glances around. 'Where's that your bodyguard?'

Remi also looks, but he can't spot Rasaq in the crowd. 'He's here somewhere,' he says, without an ounce of doubt. 'Giving us our space. Watching us from a distance.'

Aishat nods. 'He better be, oh. Because if anything happens to you in this my market, I'll first beat him before calling your father.'

They laugh softly, amused.

They make more stops. Buy more items. Aishat had initially planned to keep it quick and just buy the essentials when Remi agreed to come along. But seeing how comfortable he is, maybe even enjoying himself, she ventures deeper into the market, picking up things she hadn't even planned for. Especially now that she has a strong young man to carry her bags. She keeps handing things to Remi, and he accepts each one with quiet grace.

Then she decides to get Remi more involved at a grain stall. 'Oya, use that your lawyer mouth,' she tells him. 'Negotiate.'

Remi tries, stumbles, and mixes Yoruba with English. The trader bursts out laughing, then relents and lowers the price out of pity. Aishat laughs, delighted.

They walk away from the stall. 'What happened to your Yoruba?' she asks. 'How did it get that bad?'

'Kò sí nkan,' he says in smooth Yoruba, and smiles. 'Just trying to get the best price.'

'Jesu!' she exclaims, amused. 'You are dangerous!'

Roughly an hour later, they return to Aishat's home with a full boot. A house help closes the gate behind the Peugeot and the Land Cruiser and hurries to collect the shopping, but Remi politely waves her off and carries every bag into the house himself.

They settle in the airy kitchen, and Remi notes that it's one of the most beautifully maintained kitchens he's ever seen in Lagos.

But as Aishat immediately rolls up her sleeves to get to work enthusiastically preparing a meal, he quickly realises why the kitchen is so lovingly kept – this is where she spends most of her time. She loves it in here. And so does the house help, as they both work together seamlessly without any words.

'You remember this one?' Aishat asks, placing the moi moi leaves on the counter.

'Yes,' Remi says, smiling. 'Spicy moi moi with corned beef. Always looked forward to it when we were here.'

'Good,' she says. 'And you . . .' She points a wooden spoon at him. 'I heard you can cook, but not Nigerian food at all. You'll stay there and watch.' She looks up to the sky in prayer. 'God rest her beautiful soul . . . that's how your sister learned.'

Remi nods. 'That must've been recently,' he notes.

'Yes. She's stayed here a lot since she returned to Lagos. You know it's essentially just me in this house since your cousins have refused to move back. And I don't blame them, oh. Your uncle is off disgracing himself with young women that are you people's age.' She shakes her head, disappointed more than angry. She'd stopped letting her estranged husband's actions anger her years ago. 'Is this too much pepper?' she asks, gesturing to the chopped scotch bonnet chillies on the board.

'No,' he says. 'Go for it.'

'Okay, oh,' she says, and pours the chillies into the grinder before starting on the red onions. 'Anyway, your sister used to stay here when things got difficult with your mother. Which, unfortunately, was often. They were too alike but also too different.'

Remi instinctively nods. He had never heard it put like that, and he entirely agrees.

'When she wanted to decompress after those *Spotlight Nigeria* episodes,' she continues. 'You know she'd get so passionate about these videos when she was making them. She would be so exhausted when it was over.'

'I can imagine,' Remi says.

She nods. 'And when she wanted to stay away from the Island life. The "vanity loop", as she put it.' She smiles, remembering her special niece. 'She rarely stayed at that flat in Banana Island. A lot of her things are in her bedroom upstairs. I haven't touched them. Even the iPad she left for me to continue watching *The Crown*. I just put it back with her things.'

'Thank you for being there for her.'

'She was also being there for me, my dear Remi. More than I was for her. Much more.'

Aishat suddenly stops dicing the onions and takes a moment to focus on fighting back her tears. Remi walks to her, and they embrace.

Over Aishat's shoulder, he notices the house help shed a single tear and quickly wipe it away. He catches her eyes and nods gently.

CHAPTER 34

Remi and Aishat sit at the dining table in the living room, which looks pristine, as if no one spends any time here unless there are guests. Their plates are empty, save for a few flecks of moi moi, and it had tasted even better than Remi remembered. They're chatting now, drifting between his life in London and Remi and her sons' apparent refusal, or inability, to enter serious relationships, talk less of marriage. Remi does his best to stay engaged, but his thoughts drift upstairs. He feels a pull – a quiet, urgent need to see his sister's bedroom.

The current conversation winds to a natural close, and Remi seizes the moment before Aishat can start a new one.

'Can I take a look at Kike's room?' he asks.

'Of course, Remi,' she responds. 'It's Tutu's old room upstairs. You remember it, abi?'

Remi nods, then chuckles. 'I don't think he likes being called Tutu.'

'I don't care,' she says, with playful defiance. 'He's my son. I'll call him whatever I want.' She pauses, her smile turning cheeky. 'At least until he gets married.'

They laugh.

'I'll go and check if Rasaq wants more moi moi,' she says. 'Hopefully, he's not counting carbs like you.'

'I'm not doing that,' Remi protests, smiling. 'Just moderation, that's all.'

'Moderation?' she repeats, giving him a slow once-over. 'How are you feeding all this muscle you're carrying? It's not by moderation, oh.'

Remi laughs, then shrugs.

'Na you sabi,' she says, waving him off.

They rise and head out of the room in different directions.

Remi finds his way to the stairs easily, realising he still knows this place like the back of his hand. He also notices that none of the elegant décor has changed, and everything looks carefully maintained, with no speck of dust in sight.

He climbs the stairs and walks along the upstairs hallway, passing a couple of closed doors until he reaches the one that used to be Tutu's. He pauses for a moment, hand resting on the handle, then slowly pushes it open, as if half expecting to find Kike inside, fast asleep.

The bedroom is immaculate, but it bears the unmistakable imprint of his sister, not just as a guest but as someone who had made this space hers. A large-screen iPad and a stack of well-thumbed books sit neatly on a reading desk, and a beige silk scarf is draped over the back of the armchair set by the window. Her favourite perfume and skincare products are arranged on the dresser beside a framed photo of the two of them at his law school graduation.

The room feels lived in, not just visited. Everything about it feels deliberate, making the framed photo of him and Kike, the only photo in sight, land like a haymaker to the gut.

He steps further in, quietly closing the door behind him, and heads straight to the desk. He scans the books, and there are titles spanning investigative journalism, African feminist thought, and a battered copy of *Half of a Yellow Sun* that he recognises from years of her reading and rereading it. He sits on the chair, picks up the iPad, and is quietly pleased to see 40 percent of the battery left.

He enters the six-digit passcode Kike had used for decades – his, Zainab's and Kunle's months of birth in that order – but it's incorrect. He tries it backwards. Still wrong. He leans back, mildly surprised that she'd changed it after all these years. But he's not concerned because Aishat would know it. Then he reconsiders. If Kike meant for Aishat to use this iPad, she'd have made the passcode easy for her to remember. He types in Zainab's full date of birth. The screen unlocks.

As he suspected, no messages or emails are synced to this device. He taps open the Photos app. Only a handful of images. Nothing recent. All synced from another device. No surprises there; Kike preferred to be present. Her phone lived in her bag, not her hand. That's not to say she avoided taking pictures, but she let others take them, especially as she'd given up on social media long ago. Most of the images in the album were of art: sculptures, murals, paintings. All the pictures were close up and intimate as if she were considering them. And he recognises a few from their home.

The Notes app is empty, and that unsettles him more than he expects. In London, she used it constantly for restaurant and bar lists, television show recommendations, and thoughts on off-the-radar designers. She would've used it here, especially for her investigations. She was never one for pen and paper. So where were the notes, he thinks.

He swipes through the home screen, scanning for another app that might store her thoughts, but there is nothing. He takes a deep breath, fighting frustration, and then checks the iPad storage. That's when he sees it: a calculator app using over 30 GB of data. A smile creeps across his face, and he flips to the last home screen page to open it.

The app looks like any other calculator. It's clean and unassuming, but Remi knows better. It's a vault. He punches in the passcode he first tried on the iPad. Nothing. Just static digits waiting for a calculation. He tries variants – birthdates, reversed orders, day-before-month, month-before-day. Still nothing.

He stands and walks slowly around the room, letting his mind settle. Then, a date snaps into focus. He returns to the desk and doesn't sit before he enters the date of the last day he saw her, the morning he slapped her. The app opens instantly.

Five folders appear, stark against the dark screen: Stephen, the pastor, Malaki, Abe, and the most recent: Seun.

The sight of Seun's name hits Remi like a blow to the chest, and his throat tightens. Which Seun, though? His mind races. There were so many Seuns in their circle growing up. But deep down, he already knows exactly which one this is. Seun Daniels. Heir to the DBN media empire. And if this was the final folder she created before she died . . . He stops. He can't let dread or a thirst for vengeance cloud his judgement.

He taps to open the Seun folder, which has several subfolders labelled with first names. Some are unfamiliar, but a couple stand out immediately – Ngozi and Eki.

He clicks on *Ngozi*, the first folder. Inside, there is a list of audio recordings, each neatly dated. The oldest is from four months ago, titled 'Ope's Wedding'. Remi taps to play it, and crisp sound comes through, but it is slightly muffled by the echo from a tiled bathroom. He recognises Kike's voice instantly, low and urgent.

'Goz, what did you mean by that? About watching my drink?' Kike asks.

Ngozi's voice answers, tense and deflective. 'Ah ah, I was joking now. It's just Lagos men, you know . . .'

'No. Don't do that. Don't brush it off. You looked serious when you said it. And Eki didn't even flinch. What's going on?'

There's a pause. A shift in tone. Remi can almost hear Ngozi's internal battle through the silence.

'Kike, abeg. I shouldn't have said anything . . .'

'Goz.'

A long silence.

Then, quietly and reluctantly, Goz says, 'He did it to me. Seun. That bastard did it to me.'

Remi flinches, his hand tightening around the iPad.

'What? When?'

'A few years ago. We were working on that cooking TV pilot I was trying to develop. He got me drunk. I blacked out. Woke up and he was . . .' Ngozi doesn't finish the sentence. 'I never told anyone. Just tried to forget.'

Kike's breathing picks up on the recording. 'Jesus Christ,' she says.

'How are you this surprised?' Ngozi continues, bitter now. 'It's not new. You remember *Esther*?'

Remi hears Kike's sharp intake of breath. She does remember.

'She said he touched her,' Ngozi continues. 'Molested her in SS1. Her parents came to school and raised hell. Then silence. She left school. She moved to Canada with her mum. Her dad stayed behind. Suddenly, he got all this DBN work for his advertising company.'

'I didn't know that about her father. But I thought they said she lied. Even the teachers said she lied. That's why she had to leave. Oh my God!'

'Esther wasn't the only one, Kike. He tried it with me in school, too, in SS1 as well. Just a few months after the whole thing with Esther. He got so bold after that. But I had that boyfriend in SS3. So he backed off. He's a slimy coward.'

'Why didn't anyone ever tell me? Why didn't he try it with me? He was always trying to be around me.'

'He's a social climber. That's why he's still begging to be associated with you today. And he didn't try it with you because no one tried anything with you. You had Remi.'

Another pause. Kike's voice is now sharper. 'That's not fair. You think it was all because of *Remi*? I had agency. I handled myself. No one tried me even after Remi graduated.'

'I understand. Of course you did, and we all admired . . . admire it. But Lagos is Lagos. That protection? It helped.'

Silence again.

Then, a shift, Kike softening. 'What about Eki?' she asks.

'He started with her in school, SS2. And he's never stopped. That DBN job he gave her straight out of uni, the connections . . . all part of the trap. She can't leave. He humiliates her in public and abuses her in private. And everyone pretends they don't see it.'

Silence again.

'Goz . . . I need a list. Everyone you know he's done this to.'

'Why?'

'I'm going to destroy Seun.'

The recording ends.

Remi just sits there, the iPad resting on the desk. The room, the light, and the world outside all recede. Only Kike's voice remains. Clear. Certain. Filled with purpose. This was her final investigation. Her final cause.

He exhales slowly, steadying himself, before exiting the Ngozi folder and opening the Eki folder.

There are several audio clips inside. He chooses the first, titled 'The House'.

The audio begins mid conversation: soft clinking of cutlery in the background, muffled restaurant ambience, and then Eki's voice, tight and defensive.

'I don't know what you're talking about, Kike. Yes, things with Seun are . . . complicated. But abusive? No. That's a stretch.'

Kike's reply is immediate. Low. Unflinching. 'Eki, you're in a gilded cage. Don't—'

'I built my career from the ground up,' Eki cuts in. 'Don't reduce everything I've done to some—'

'I'm not reducing anything. You're the one lying to yourself. And worse, you're letting him keep you silent.'

'No one is keeping me silent. I just don't want to be part of some vendetta. You don't understand how things work in this industry.'

'I understand perfectly. You're afraid. Of losing your reputation and the career you've worked so hard to build, abi? But let me be very clear, Eki. If you don't tell the truth, I will tie you to Seun's abuse so tightly, you'll be buried right beside him.'

There's a long pause. The restaurant fades beneath the weight of the moment.

Then Eki speaks, her voice cracking at the edges. 'Why would you threaten me like this? After all these years? After everything we've been through?'

Kike doesn't raise her voice. 'Because your silence helps him hurt other women,' she says coldly. 'Every day you stay, every time you say nothing . . . you give him cover. You know what he does. You've known for years.'

Silence.

Then Kike again, her voice shifting – not warm, but gentler. 'You're worried about your career if you speak. Fine. Start your own thing. Like I did. No man will ever own your voice again. I'll help you.'

Another pause.

'But decide fast,' she adds, the scrape of a chair audible. 'And you pay the bill. Leave a very good tip. I have a reputation to protect.'

The clip ends, and Remi sets the iPad on the desk, exhaling slowly. Kike's voice – clear, composed, relentless – still hums in his ears. Since watching the *Spotlight Nigeria* episodes, he'd begun to see her not just as the sister he loved and lost but as someone who had grown far beyond him into something fierce and immovable. But here, in these recordings, her ferocity and determination are even more striking.

He looks at the screen again. Beneath 'The House' audio clip, there are more clips. Many more. Dates stretching forward. File names that hint at further intimate meetings. Eki had talked. Despite the fear. Despite the cost. At some point after that meeting, she had chosen to stand beside Kike, or at least not stand in her way.

Remi leans back in the chair, rubbing a hand over his face. He's not sure what he feels. There's admiration, grief and rage. But more than anything else, there is resolve.

He exits Eki's folder to open Seun's folder, and there are several audio clips titled with popular opulent locations around Lagos, from restaurants to polo clubs to art galleries. Evidence that she was softening him up, building trust, and preparing him for the final confrontation.

But the last two audio clips stand out. They are untitled. The older tape is five hours long, and the other is just three minutes, and both have timestamps minutes apart from each other around 1 a.m., just hours before Kike's body was found.

He taps the shorter, more recent clip. Listens. His body suddenly stills, then stiffens. Then he screams – raw and ragged – loud enough to rattle the windows.

CHAPTER 35

The night of the killing

Kike Bankole

The chic and exclusive rooftop bar on Victoria Island is mostly empty. A few tables flicker with candlelight, but the farthest corner – the one with the best view and the most privacy – is Seun Daniels's usual. He's reserved it again tonight, and Kike sits across from him, her back straight, legs crossed. The glass of red wine in front of her is untouched, but she's had an eye on it, the bottle and Seun from the moment it was placed on the table.

Her phone is in her mini bag beside her wine glass, recording as usual. But tonight's recording is set to be the most important so far.

They've been dancing around each other for a couple of months. But tonight is supposed to be the final push for the deal. A content partnership. DBN Plus will premiere each new episode of *Spotlight Nigeria* the day before it drops on YouTube. Greater visibility for *Spotlight Nigeria*, she'd be paid incredibly well and keep her production autonomy, and the network would win credibility. On paper, everyone benefits.

But the real reason she agreed to meet Seun tonight isn't the deal. It's to gently introduce the 'rumours' she's been hearing and have his response – dismissive denial and insults for his accusers, she is sure – recorded, so she can confront him with it alongside the testimonies she's been amassing from his victims during the final exposé interview, which will come next.

Seun listens and talks too smoothly while smiling too much. Bragging about DBN Plus's market share with young adults and DBN's international reach. About a new docuseries they're planning on DBN News that'll 'blow Al Jazeera out of the water'. And she spots him struggling to keep his eyes on her face. They keep drifting – lazy, entitled, and predatory – across her collarbone, neckline, and the bare skin of her arms.

She knows what he wants. He's always wanted it. Since secondary school. Since he used to follow her around, offering rides, pressing his hand to the small of her back for too long. She was always too sharp for him then, and she still is.

She feels a presence approach from behind her and instinctively glances over her shoulder to see a waitress with a tray of the Mediterranean tapas Seun ordered. The waitress places the tray between them, and Kike smiles graciously at the waitress. But Seun doesn't acknowledge her as he continues his bragging.

He continues bragging while eating. But then he likes the sound of his voice and talks about his father's achievements like they are his.

Kike offers him a warm practised smile to express some form

of engagement with the tired conversation and casually sips from her glass of wine. The wine burns bitter. Not quite the taste she expected, but she keeps her face neutral.

Seun says something – a compliment about her dress, she thinks. But the room is already shifting. Her vision softening at the edges. Her fingers suddenly lose their grip on the glass, and she places it on the table just before it falls out of her grasp. Her spine relaxes, slumping against her will. She knows what's happening. She's heard it described. And now it's happening to her. She fights it, but the fog is rising fast. Her limbs are heavy now, and she can't quite hold her gaze steady.

And then everything fades.

She wakes to cold. A hard, sterile kind of cold. Air conditioned. She feels her limbs and notes that she's on a firm bed. She sits up sharply, and pain pulses behind her eyes. She immediately knows it's not her room, but as she scans, she doesn't recognise anything that would give her a clue as to where she is. It looks like the standard guest bedroom in a lavish Lagos home. Then she spots the DBN brand signage on the clock on the wall. She's in Seun's home.

She hops off the bed to scan herself, and she's fully clothed, but something feels wrong.

She turns to her mini bag on the bedside table beside the lamp and quickly opens it to grab her phone. She thumbs through rapidly and finds what she hoped – the phone is still recording, nearly five hours long.

She stops the recording and drags the audio clip to the last thirty minutes. Her own voice comes through first – slurred, sluggish, resistant. Then Seun's – coaxing, gloating, pressing. Movement. Breathing. The creak of the mattress. But then her voice again. A groan of protest. A scuffle. A curse. Seun's breathing quickens, then falters. He mutters something – frustrated. Another curse. Departing footsteps. Then silence.

She stops it. Her breath catches, but she doesn't cry. She starts a new recording and walks out of the bedroom with focused ferocity.

Seun is in his bedroom. Shirtless and lounging on a fur bean bag sofa, scrolling through TikTok, when Kike strides in, phone in hand. She locks eyes with him, and he's startled by the burning rage.

She approaches him, and he scurries off the sofa.

'Hey, Kike, you're up . . .'

'You tried to rape me.'

He freezes.

'You spiked my drink last night. Just like you've done to so many women. And then you tried it. But I only had a few sips, didn't I? Because I *know* what you do, you coward.'

His mouth opens. Nothing comes out. He laughs nervously like it might dissolve the moment.

'That's ridiculous, Kike. You just had too much red wine.'

'I recorded it.'

That silences him.

She steps forward. Her fury focused.

'I've been investigating you. I know about the others. Maybe not all. Because you are a disgusting predator. But most. Even from secondary school. And I know about your parents paying people off, making deals, disappearing accusers, bribing witnesses. Enabling you. That all stops now.'

He lunges. But she's ready, and he's not half as quick as Remi or the others she trained Krav Maga and jiu-jitsu with for years. All that training comes back without thought, and she pivots, catches his arm, and throws him hard on to the floor. The breath is punched out of him.

She kneels on top of him, one hand pinning his hand, the other at his throat. Not choking. Just a warning. But then he's far more desperate than anyone she's ever trained with, so he spits in her face, and she instinctively lets go of his throat to wipe it away. He'd hoped she would release her hold on his arm or her pressure on his chest, even a little bit so that he could squeeze out from underneath her. But none of that happened. She was a good student. Instead, she rams the palm of her free hand into his chin, stunning him, and he genuinely sees stars for a moment.

She waits for his eyes to clear up. 'You're done, Seun,' she says. 'I'm going to destroy you.'

And that's when she hears the sound. A shift of air behind her. She turns. But it's too late.

Gloria Daniels

Seun's mother, Gloria Daniels, slips into his bedroom through a concealed door, wielding a sturdy ivory figurine like a weapon. Without hesitation, she hurries towards Kike and Seun from behind, her bare feet barely making a sound.

In stride, she swings the figurine on to the back of Kike's skull with sickening force. The sound of the impact is dull, wet, and final.

Kike's grip instantly loosens, and she slumps sideways. Seun, wild-eyed, scrambles from beneath Kike's body, wraps both hands around her throat, and strangles her, even as Kike twitches.

Gloria watches, silent, measuring. Then, when Kike's body finally goes still, she slaps Seun hard across the back of his head, stunning him, and pushes him off Kike's body with a strong kick. She doesn't acknowledge him or even look his way as she kneels to check for a pulse.

'Is she . . . ?' Seun asks, his voice suddenly thin and child-like.

Gloria turns to Seun with a hard slap across the face. He recoils, but she slaps him hard again. And then again. He's cowering now.

'You tried to rape a Bankole? You imbecile,' she says, scathing. 'And here? In our home? After we got you that apartment on VI for your filth?'

Seun is shaking and looking away from her, almost like a toddler being scolded.

Gloria looks away from him, searching for Kike's phone. She finds it a few steps away and hurries to pick it up. She instinctively bares her teeth with anger because the phone has already locked.

She closes her eyes for a moment to think. Then walks towards the intercom by Seun's bed. 'We need your father.'

Gloria watches her husband, Derin Daniels, hurriedly join them in the bedroom and flinch at the sight of Kike's lifeless body. She had told him the highlights when she called to wake him from sleep from their bedroom just a few doors down the long corridor. But it only became real for him now, seeing the body with his own eyes.

Gloria knows that it's not the shock of the body that made Derin flinch, but the amount of things they will have to do . . . bad things, evil things . . . to cover this one up. And not because the *victim* is dead – Gloria had already been preparing herself for that eventuality – but because it is Kike Bankole.

Derin turns to Seun, sitting against the wall, rocking, and he is filled with rage. But Gloria cuts in before it can surface. She steps into his eyeline to provide the details of the predicament coldly and efficiently.

'So, what do we do to take care of this,' she says to end her update.

Derin turns to her. 'If this gets out . . .'

'It won't. We will make sure it doesn't.'

Derin nods and takes a deep breath. 'I'll call Felix.'

Thirty minutes later, Felix, their loyal fixer, arrives. And unlike Derin, he doesn't flinch at the sight of the body – just simply acknowledges it.

Before he'd arrived, Gloria and Derin had come up with a plan to frame Malaki for the murder – they'd ask him to help them dispose of the body of a high-end ashewo who'd overdosed when partying with a foreign celebrity they were hosting. They know Malaki wouldn't get his hands dirty – his boys would take care of it – and none of them would recognise Kike. They'd tell Malaki to dump the body somewhere prominent for some vaguely plausible reason – but their real intention is for it to look like his brazen revenge. After that, they would arrange to plant her clothes in his house and use their media empire to lay an unquestioned trail straight to Malaki's door.

Felix listens to their plan and offers some suggestions to fine-tune it, mainly because he doesn't believe Malaki will dispose of a body for them, talk less a nameless body. Malaki is savvy and does not trust Islanders. Felix suggests they reach out instead to Suru Boi, who is desperate to keep his career afloat, engaging in increasingly ridiculous attention-grabbing exploits. They won't need to offer Suru Boi half as much as they would need to promise Malaki. Suru Boi is also far less savvy and would be easier to control. Derin and Gloria like the suggestion and give him the go-ahead to execute the plan.

Felix wraps Kike's body in a rug, and he and Seun drag it down to his car.

Seun returns to his bedroom and dumps himself on his bean bag sofa as Derin and Gloria proceed with the next stage of their plan.

Gloria hands Tari and Chizoba, two young housemaids who have been in her employ since they were teenagers, the keys to Kike's Banana Island flat and asks them to go to the flat and bring back every Apple device.

Tari and Chizoba return a couple of hours later with only a MacBook, and Gloria is gracious. Then she switches and orders them to strip off all their clothes in front of Seun and Derin.

They do, fighting back tears and embarrassment as Gloria inspects their clothes and underwear to ensure they didn't steal anything else from Kike's flat.

Satisfied, she smiles like nothing happened. The gracious matriarch returns, promising promotions, time off, and even holidays – luxuries she once called wasteful at the Bankole residence.

Tari then asks for money to visit her sick mother, and Gloria agrees without hesitation, offering a prayer for her.

As Tari and Chizoba leave the room, Derin calls in Bimo – a tech prodigy from the DBN cyber team.

Bimo arrives on a Bolt motorcycle half an hour later, surprised to be meeting the big boss, Madam and Seun, who doesn't even acknowledge him, in Seun's bedroom. But he acts normal.

'Wipe all the data from the last six months,' Derin says, handing Bimo the iPhone and MacBook.

'Sure, sir!'

Bimo unzips a battered case and lays out his kit – bespoke tools he's poured his earnings into, the only real assets he owns. He gets to work, running a select series of his tools. It takes longer than expected; the devices fight him. But he breaks in, finally, and begins to wipe the data. Then he hits an encrypted folder his tools can't open – the *problem*. He tries, and tries again . . . the tension in the room thickens. Gloria stands close, watching every move. Finally, he suggests a full system purge – local and cloud. Gloria agrees without hesitation and watches over his shoulder until both screens fade to black. The data is gone.

Derin promises Bimo quick promotions and, unlike the housemaids, an immediate bonus that will be credited to his account before the end of the day. Bimo leaves, elated but unnerved.

Minutes later, Gloria leans on the wall outside the house, watching Chizoba throw the devices into a fire pit behind the house. She watches until nothing remains, then walks back into the house.

She enters the palatial living room, where Seun and Derin sit several distances apart, watching DBN News for news of Kike's death. There is nothing.

'It's done,' she says, then turns to Seun. 'Now. Go out. Be seen. Smile. You have nothing to worry about.'

Seun nods and stands to get ready to leave. He glances at Derin, but Derin doesn't move his attention from the television.

Seun leaves the living room, and Gloria sits down where he had been sitting to watch the news.

By nightfall, Bimo disappears, never to be seen again. Tari and Chizoba vanish, too. So does Felix.

Derin Daniels

It's 6 a.m., almost exactly twenty-four hours since Kike's body was dumped, and Derin sits behind his broad walnut desk, the skyline outside still cloaked in a soft, early haze. The vast, lavish office, perched high above Victoria Island, is quiet but not still, as a large screen on one wall silently plays DBN's flagship morning show, and another, slightly smaller screen across the room quietly plays DBN News' 24-hour news coverage.

The vast room reflects Derin's taste and the confidence of a man who studied broadcast journalism in an elite US university before building one of West Africa's most influential media empires.

A weathered university pennant, framed in slim brass, hangs behind his desk. Just below it, an entire wall is dedicated to his career accolades: industry plaques, crystal awards, and framed letters from presidents and peers. Further along the room, a set of deep leather armchairs flanks a low table ready for more intimate conversations, and in the far corner, a turntable sits beside a curated stack of jazz vinyl.

On his desk, framed in dark oak, sits a single photo: Derin, Gloria and Seun – taken two decades ago on a safari holiday in Kenya, all three smiling in the sharp afternoon sun. Seun was twelve then, and the picture predates everything. Before that first accusation. Before the pattern and the cover-ups. Before he could no longer deny what his son had become. He keeps it here not out of sentiment but as a reminder of the last time he looked at his son without deep shame.

His phone rings, and he quickly picks it off the desk. He checks the caller ID, and it's a call from Governor Igwe, one of the heavyweights of the president's political party and the frontrunner to replace the president as leader when he succumbs to his illness.

'Chisom,' he says after answering the call, swiftly moving past any greetings. 'Is it happening? I heard all of you were called to Abuja.'

'Yes. But the president is very alive. I've confirmed it, so I don't know what this is about.'

Derin's chest tightens. When he'd heard the news, he had a faint worry that it had something to do with Kike's death. He knew Kunle was very rich and increasingly influential. But he didn't realise Kunle had the influence or power to pull a move like this.

'Maybe he has decided to move aside to focus on his health,' Derin says, more out of hope than belief.

'No. Not *Koye*,' he says, referring to the president by the shortened version of his first name. 'Too stubborn. He would rather die on the line. And my contact in his office says his health has not suddenly turned for the worse.'

'Okay. Update me when you know what this is about, and we will discuss what angle I have my people take with the news.'

'Thank you, Derin. But why, eh? Why the sudden interest in helping me?'

'Because you will be the next president, with or without my help, but I can make it easier for you. And you can make things easier for me.'

Chisom chuckles. 'True true,' he says. 'I will call you back.'

It's approaching noon when Chisom calls back. Derin is still behind his desk, and now the smaller screen shows his closest competitor's rolling news channel. He answers the phone immediately.

'What is happening, Chisom?'

'You will not believe it,' Chisom says. 'And it's not about the president's health.'

'Ah. But it must have been equally serious to gather all of you in Abuja on such short notice.'

Chisom offers a dry laugh. 'I will tell you because that is our arrangement. But you can't release anything because we have all been *warned* to keep this quiet . . . for now.'

'I will not. But you let me know, as I can get the story you want out there first.'

'I don't want any story with this. It's not that kind of thing.'

There is silence as Derin quietly waits for Chisom to confirm or ease his trepidation, and Derin notices for the first time that he has sweated through his shirt, even though the air conditioning is on maximum.

'Kunle Bankole's daughter is dead.'

Derin's chest tightens, and he pulls the phone away from his ear to try to calm himself quickly. He returns the phone to his ear. 'My condolences to Kunle and his family. But are you saying that all of you were called to Abuja because of her death?'

'Yes,' Chisom says. 'We all came to face the music. For Kunle to look into our eyes when he asked if we were responsible.'

'Kunle called this meeting?'

'No. Koye did. But at Kunle's request.'

'Hmm,' Derin mutters. 'Not much of a difference there.'

'Oh, but there is. Coming from the president, we could not refuse. No one did. People even flew in from overseas.'

'That is a big move from Kunle. He must have a serious influence on the president. I didn't know that.'

'Kunle likes to manoeuvre from the background.'

'If he's manoeuvring for the big office, it seems the president will back him. And maybe the voters, too. Important family. Clean reputation. Plenty plenty money. Very good chances from my perspective.'

'What are you trying to say, Derin?' Chisom challenges. 'Speak plainly. If you want to switch horses to Kunle, just say it. But you should know that you will forever be my enemy. I will make it my mission to demolish you and Kunle.'

Derin smiles, because that is the reaction he was hoping for.

'Watch who you are threatening, Chisom. And I never said I was switching horses. It's just that Kunle wasn't on the board when

I was considering the succession. I am fully behind you. But we will have to take a more direct approach with him now before it's too late.'

'What do you mean by that?'

'You know, Chisom. Give me what I need, and I will take care of it.'

'Hmm. Is this part of our arrangement?'

'No. He wasn't on the board when we discussed the arrangement.'

'This was less than twelve hours ago.'

'He wasn't on the board, Chisom. Abi, was he on yours?'

Chisom offers a wry chuckle. 'What do you want?'

'I don't know for now. But it will be commensurate with what I do for you.'

'I don't doubt it,' Chisom says sarcastically. 'We already have things in motion. So, I will update you when we are ready. Till then, nothing on Kunle.'

'That's fine. I will start some work on our end without mentioning him. This gathering, for one . . . we will push it hard. And when the time is right, we will use it to reveal Kunle's undue influence on the president.'

'Okay,' Chisom says, matter of fact. 'I will update you.'

Chisom ends the call, and Derin immediately leans across his desk to grab a handful of tissues from a tissue box. He wipes the sweat from his face, head and neck. Then he gets up from his chair – now covered in sweat patches to match the back of his shirt – to grab a bottle of cold water from the fridge by his desk. He downs most of the water and then pours the remaining on to his hands to rub on his head and neck.

He walks back to sit at his desk and calls Gloria. It's answered after just one ring.

'Are you watching the news?' he asks, without any pleasantries.

'Of course, I'm watching everything, waiting for news on Kike's death. But it's all about the president and this gathering in Abuja.'

'That was Kunle.'

'What do you mean?'

'It was Kunle that called the gathering. He thinks one of them is responsible for Kike's death.'

'We should use that, then,' Gloria says. 'Let's shift away from Malaki and lay the breadcrumbs that will lead to one of them.'

'No. That's too dangerous. We don't know why he thinks one of them is responsible. And we don't know if he suspects just one of them. If we are wrong, it will unravel.'

'That Kunle,' Gloria says, and Derin can hear that admiration he's always heard when Gloria speaks of him. 'He was like this in school. Always moving in . . .'

'I don't care. We need—'

'Don't interrupt me,' she cuts back in coldly.

There is silence before he continues. 'We need to send Seun to the Cape Town villa until this resolves.'

'No. There is a reason why Kunle is keeping it quiet. They are watching and waiting for someone to panic. Do something out of the ordinary. We will not. Seun will remain. And he will even go to that party tonight.'

'That's not a good idea.'

'Are you scared of Kunle?'

'Don't be foolish, Gloria. I'm not scared of anyone. But I do not trust Seun to keep his mouth shut.'

'I have spoken to him. He will listen.'

'Just like he listened when we told him to stop what he's doing? When you bought him a house in Lekki and told him not to bring any of that nonsense to our house?'

'That is different.'

'What? How?'

'It is different, Derin,' she says with finality. 'He will not talk about it.'

Derin shakes his head, frustrated, but doesn't push back. 'We need to end this relationship with Suru Boi before it becomes public. I don't trust him not to talk.'

'No, Derin. That is when Suru Boi will talk. Felix said he didn't even look at the body, so he doesn't know who she is.'

'For now. Once he hears the news, he'll put two and two together.'

'Yes. And then we'll make it clear to him that the two and two will add up to him and his mentor, Malaki, as the prime suspects.'

There is an uncomfortable pause.

'You will sort this for us, Derin,' Gloria says softly. 'I don't doubt it.'

Derin sniggers, remembering that Chisom used the exact words.

'What?' she demands with venom.

'I will deal with it,' he says, and ends the call.

CHAPTER 36

Two weeks later – loose ends

Derin Daniels

Derin is at his desk when he receives a rare call from Seun. Derin was finally allowing himself to believe he and his baby – the DBN empire – would avoid the storm, but he knows this call will shatter that belief. He answers.

'What happened?' he says.

'Remi just asked to meet with Malaki at Suru Boi's performance tonight,' Seun says, stricken with panic.

Before Derin can respond, Gloria cuts in – she's with Seun. 'And I said he should arrange it. It's good for us.'

Derin wraps his knuckles on his desk. 'How is this good for us?'

'He suspects Malaki. This is what we've been waiting for.'

'Are you sure?' Seun asks.

'Don't be stupid, Seun,' she chides dismissively. 'Why else would Remi want to meet Malaki?'

There is silence.

'I will have a word with Suru Boi to ensure things go *smoothly*,' she adds.

Derin knows Gloria is talking about her plans going smoothly. Not Suru Boi's performance or Remi's meeting with Malaki.

'Did you intend to be there tonight?' Derin asks Seun.

'No!' Seun immediately responds. 'I certainly—'

'Why?' Gloria cuts in. 'You will be there. It's your programme.'

'No. Seun is no longer going anywhere without protection. I will call the American and organise it. He will go everywhere with Seun. I don't care if you have to say he's your cousin or my illegitimate son from California . . .'

'Is he?' Gloria asks.

'Shut up, Gloria,' he responds, expressing some of his frustration.

'Relax, Derin,' she sneers. 'It was a joke.'

He bites his tongue to stop him from lashing out. 'Arrange the meeting between Remi and Malaki,' he says and ends the call.

It's approaching 4 a.m., and Derin sleeps on a comfortable and elegant long sofa in his office. He'd had it brought in, as he'd slept in the office since the day after Kike's death. His personal phone rings and wakes him, and he checks the caller ID. It's Gloria. He answers.

'What happened?'

'My plans didn't go *smoothly*. But we are on track to tie this up.'

'What happened?' he asks, sitting up.

'Remi didn't die.'

'What do you mean?'

'I arranged for a few of Malaki's more reckless men to kill him. But he survived. Two of them did not.'

'Are you crazy?' he demands, infuriated. 'Why would you do that?'

She doesn't respond for a beat. 'When will you come home?' she asks. 'Or do you want to sleep in the office forever?'

He has no response. He doesn't know.

'Anyway, the one that survived came to give us the news. We've taken care of him.'

'Kí ló ṣe ẹ?' Derin asks, concerned. 'What is happening to you?'

'I'm stepping up to protect the family. Since you're not doing anything.'

'What do you mean, Gloria? I've been working with Governor Igwe and the others. Everything is ready for Kunle's arrest later today. Then, all our platforms will push it. Bury them in the allegations and innuendo.'

'Good for you. But how is that protecting Seun? It will protect DBN by reducing Kunle's power and influence to destroy it. But what about Remi, who is just going around beating people up?'

'Beating people? What are you talking about?'

'Oh yes. There are videos. And these are not people he suspects of killing his sister. He's just an angry boy.'

'And does that surprise you?'

'Well . . . imagine what he will do to Seun. You think arresting his father for tax evasion and insinuating that he is corrupt will make Remi less angry?'

'I've hired the American to follow Seun.'

'Yes. He arrived at the house last night. But Seun is still scared.'

There is silence again, and Derin stands up to part the blinds and stares at a large, illuminated DBN monument sign just outside the building's gate.

'Let us finish this,' Gloria continues. 'Remi doesn't have to die. But Malaki will. The police officer survived but has already been detained. He will point the finger at Malaki soon, and Kunle's dogs will be on their way to arrest Malaki sharp. We can't let him talk.'

Derin considers. 'Okay. Do what you need to do. I will arrange for us to capture the arrest. We'll use night-vision drones. Then we'll push and push Malaki's guilt across all platforms.'

'That's good. Very good. But I need more than that from you.'

'What else?'

'I have already spoken to one of Malaki's house girls. She has planted Kike's clothes in Malaki's closet. But we need Suru Boi to kill Malaki. We already have the syringe with the laced heroin in the compound. Suru Boi is there. He just needs to pick it up and inject Malaki before Kunle's dogs get there.'

'Why would Suru Boi agree to do that to his mentor?'

'Because you will promise him the world.'

Derin sighs. 'It's almost 4 a.m. Why would he answer my call.'

'He wouldn't answer your call. He'll answer mine. He always does.'

Gloria dials, and after a beat, Suru Boi's slightly buzzed voice joins the call.

What follows is masterful: Derin takes over the call, like every other negotiation with difficult talent. He offers Suru Boi everything he's ever wanted – a DBN reality show, a film deal, 400 million naira. Then comes the ask – Malaki. Dead. Tonight. Suru Boi recoils, panicked, insisting he can't. But Derin presses, cool and relentless. He lays out the stakes – Kike's body, the CCTV footage of Suru Boi assisting Felix, Kunle's people already closing in. 'It's either you or Malaki,' Derin makes clear. Suru Boi hesitates, and Derin reframes it as ascension: King Suru will rise, but the current king must fall. And it'll be quiet, painless, and look just like an overdose – the syringe is waiting outside his door. That resonates with Suru Boi – he's tired of being *Boi*, he wants to be king. And just like that, the Faustian trap is sealed: Suru Boi agrees.

Gloria ends the call. 'You did very good,' she says. 'He will do it.'

Derin ends the call without responding.

CHAPTER 37

Present day

The audio clip ends, and Remi closes his eyes and unconsciously places a hand over his chest, trying to settle his heart, which is thudding against his ribs like a fist demanding to be let out. He opens his eyes, intent on listening to snippets of the five-hour clip to confirm what he knows happened and that there is proof of what Kike was intent on revealing. But something is wrong. The folders in the Calculator app are gone – every one of them. The screen is blank.

His breath catches, and his eyes flick upward. Aishat stands in the doorway, arms folded but eyes wide with concern. He forces a smile – not too much, not manic – something to reassure her, to disguise the panic threatening to overwhelm him.

'I'm okay, Aunty,' he says.

She nods slowly, not believing a word of it.

He looks down at the iPad and spots the Wi-Fi sign at the top of the screen, which shows a connection that wasn't there before.

He clicks into Settings and sees the iPad connected to Aishat's iPhone hotspot.

He freezes, immediately understanding what's happened. The moment Aishat climbed the steps, the iPad automatically connected to her iPhone's hotspot, and the iCloud contents synced with Kike's other devices. Someone had deleted the app's contents.

He checks the iPad storage, and the Calculator app's data is gone. Wiped clean. Then, he checks the iCloud settings to see that its storage is empty. Someone had deleted everything in there.

He stares at the screen, numb. Then looks up to Aishat. It isn't her fault. She doesn't even know what just happened. She just watches him closely from the doorway, unsure whether to approach or leave him to whatever grief he's processing. Rasaq is now behind her, too, watching with equal concern.

Remi takes a deep breath, and a thought triggers. He looks back to the iPad and opens the Find My app. Kike's phone is offline. But its last location pings with quiet certainty: a location in Ikoyi at 11:45 a.m., the morning after she died.

He zooms in to get the precise location, then pulls out his phone and selects Google Maps. He finds the location and switches to street view. It's a wide, leafy street with a solid, high gate. And there, etched in chrome lettering beneath a crest on the gate – THE DANIELSES.

He exhales through his nose. Calm. Terrifyingly so. He knows the killer. Seun Daniels.

He looks up again. Neither Aishat's nor Rasaq's gaze has shifted, still concerned. But Rasaq now steps forward a little, sensing something new in Remi's bearing.

Remi puts the iPad down and stands. He walks to Aishat and, without a word, pulls her into his arms. She holds him instinctively, though she doesn't understand. Then his shoulders shake, his breath breaks, and finally, without violence or rage, Remi cries.

CHAPTER 38

Remi stands in front of the full-length mirror in Kike/Tutu's room in Aishat's home. He's freshly showered, his skin still warm, and dressed in one of his dad's soft and elegant kaftans, which he'd packed to take with him back to London.

He walks closer to the mirror to check his eyes. They are red from what seemed like hours of crying, but steady. No more tears, just action.

Even while crying, a plan was developing in his head. He doesn't want revenge anymore; he just wants the truth from Seun. And he wants it out in the open, just like Kike would've wanted. Whatever happens after that, he's okay with.

First, he calls Balo.

'What's good, brother?' he says when Balo answers the call.

'Remz,' Balo says. 'I saw the news. That's wild. How you feeling.'

'Good. Just difficult all round, you know.'

'You should've told me you suspected Malaki. I would've made sure some boys were there at the studio.'

'I know. I wasn't sure. Just wanted to have a chat with him. And things spiralled, you know. I'm sorry for what happened at the studio.'

'Don't, bro. No need. I saw that video too. Na them wey start am. But na you wey finish am.'

'Fair. I still owe you a drink, though. Are you going to be at Yetunde's birthday party tomorrow?'

'Of course! Are you going?'

'Not sure yet. But I'm thinking about it. Is Seun going to be there? I need to apologise to him about what happened at the studio.'

'Ahn ahn. Stop this apologising nonsense.'

'I gave my word, Balo.'

'Okay, oh. Yes, he's coming. Talking about bringing some model. But I'm not sure because he's been chasing her for a bit, and she's not feeling him.'

'Fair enough.'

'If I tell him you're coming, he probably won't bring her. Everybody knows you are Mr Steal Your Girl.'

'Hey!' Remi said, and they laugh softly. 'That happened once. A decade ago. And she wasn't Kevin's girlfriend; he was just claiming her.'

'Exactly. That's what is happening here. Seun is claiming her. You will now come, do fresh guy, you and the model will now leave.'

'Nah. No need for Seun to worry about that. I'm looking elsewhere right now. Although, even that one sef.'

'Eki, abi?'

'Ahn ahn. Inspector Balogun, calm down.'

'No. I saw you two talking at Rose's party. She looked interested. Even Seun mentioned it.'

'Oh. Do I have to talk to him about that?'

Silence for a moment. 'Not sure what's going on there, really,' Balo says. 'Seun will be going around trying all the girls, but if someone shows interest in Eki, he will start misbehaving. I was there one night in Miliki when he told her he would fire her from DBN if she kept talking to some guy.'

'You think he'll do that with me?'

'No, Remi. Levels dey!' He chuckles. 'But I still won't recommend her to be your girlfriend or anything. Little something here when you are around, sure.'

'All right then, Tinder.'

Balo laughs. 'I'm just looking out for you, bro.'

'I know. Thanks. See you tomorrow. I'll buy you a drink from the free bar.'

They laugh soft again, and Remi ends the call.

Remi makes a few more calls, including to Yetunde's assistant to confirm his attendance at the party. Now, he's off to have dinner.

Several minutes later, Remi and Rasaq are stuck in the traffic along Third Mainland Bridge heading towards the Island, in the middle of a procession of red brake lights snaking into the twilight.

Inside the Land Cruiser, the air between Rasaq and Remi has shifted. It's not exactly thawed, but the silence between them is no longer uncomfortable. But that could be because Remi has barely looked away from his phone since they left Aishat's house. He's active on it: typing rapidly, switching between apps, and taking and making short calls, each with a perfectly judged tone. He's in his element, like in the hours before a billion-dollar acquisition closes. He's on top of every detail, pushing things with a firm hand.

Rasaq keeps his eyes on the road, hands relaxed on the wheel. But his attention drifts, glancing now and then at Remi, impressed by Remi's zeal.

At one point, Remi answers a call with a quick, 'Yeah. Go ahead.' His voice remains calm. But whatever is said on the other end isn't what Remi wants to hear because he responds, 'Not ideal. Thanks, though. I'll find a workaround.'

Remi ends the call and returns to typing rapidly.

'You want help with any of that?' Rasaq asks, glancing at Remi.

Remi doesn't look up. 'No, thank you,' he says gently. 'I don't need anyone dead for this one.'

Rasaq's jaw tightens, but he doesn't respond, keeping his eyes on the road.

Remi looks up and catches the shift in Rasaq's expression. He knows his words were sharper than necessary, regardless of his gentle tone, and considers softening the moment and reaching across the gap that's widened between them since Malaki. But instead, he turns back to his phone and lets the silence between them resettle for the rest of the journey.

The Land Cruiser approaches DBN's sleek headquarters in Victoria Island. Dusk light glints off the impressive glass tower, but Remi just glances at it for a moment before returning his attention to his phone, typing even quicker now.

Rasaq guides the car to the guest spot, and Remi continues to type for over a minute after Rasaq parks.

'I'll see you in a bit,' Remi says, turning to Rasaq.

Rasaq nods, and Remi steps out of the door.

*

The red light above the camera blinks off, and the DBN News studio falls into a hush. Eki turns to the two guests seated beside her on the sleek glass desk and offers a warm, gracious smile.

'Thank you both so much,' she says, unclipping her lapel mic. 'That was thoughtful and genuinely refreshing.'

The older guest, a retired Supreme Court justice, nods with grace. The younger, a firebrand lawyer turned activist, beams as she rises. Eki stands with them, exchanging a few pleasantries and promising to stay in touch before a studio coordinator ushers them out.

Just as Eki turns to debrief with the lead producer, who's already launching into feedback about camera angles and runtime, her assistant hurries in, tablet clutched to her chest like a shield.

'Sorry to interrupt, Eki,' the assistant says, a little breathless. 'But Remi Bankole is here to see you. He's waiting in guest reception.'

Eki's expression flickers – surprise, apprehension, maybe something else – but she recovers quickly. 'How long has he been waiting?'

'Not long. He just arrived.'

Eki glances at the producer. 'Give me twenty minutes on that debrief?' she asks.

The producer waves her off, and Eki disappears into the dressing room adjoining the studio floor. When she re-emerges a few minutes later, she's swapped her broadcast attire for a soft black tee and tailored navy trousers. Her heels are gone, replaced by low, sleek loafers. She is still camera-ready, but now she looks like herself.

She walks briskly down the corridor, swiping past security with her staff badge, and makes her way to guest reception, where Remi is waiting.

Remi smiles when he sees her, and she's relieved because she'd been running through all her segments on the Bankoles for the past few days, searching for any moment where she could've crossed the line. The directive from the top – Derin Daniels himself – was clear: no holds barred on the Bankole stories. Speculation, innuendo, and even outright misinformation were all fair game as long as each claim could be attributed to an external source – which, more often than not, meant anonymous tweets or bot accounts. She was somewhat shielded from the directive because her job wasn't to offer opinions but to coax them out of her guests. But she's pretty sure that, over the past few days, several of them have speculated openly about the speculations.

'That was excellent as always,' Remi says, gesturing at the screen in the room playing DBN News. 'I was watching.'

'Thank you.'

'And I must add, because I know you're sharp: I was watching before I came here. That's how I knew where you'd be.'

She chuckles. 'Thanks for letting me know, Joe Goldberg.'

'Wait,' Remi says, and raises a finger, smiling. 'I need to google Joe Goldberg.'

She laughs softly as he searches the internet for Joe Goldberg.

He looks up to her. 'Hey!' he mildly objects. 'I'm not stalking you.'

'Sure,' she says, and rolls her eyes.

'I'm returning to London in a couple of days and just wanted to grab dinner before then.'

'Oh,' she says, surprised. 'Now?'

He nods. 'I've made a reservation at NOK down the road. If we leave now, we'll be five minutes early.'

She smiles, drawn by the easy way he's taken the lead. 'Okay, Remi. My car is in the employee car park at the back, so I'll meet you there.'

Remi smiles back, partly because she agreed to the dinner but more because of how subtly she'd rebalanced control. 'See you there,' he says.

Minutes later, Remi and Eki are led to a prominent table beneath the soft glow of pendant lights, surrounded by sculptural furniture and bold artwork that give the restaurant its vibrant, curated elegance.

They order, eat, and drink – only one glass of alcohol each, red wine for her and gin and tonic for him – and enjoy their conversation, which is tinged with flirting and laughter. Over an hour in, after they've finished their mains and refused dessert – although it doesn't seem like either is ready to end the date – Remi shifts gear.

'So, what exactly is going on between you and Seun?'

The abruptness of the question catches her off guard, and she recovers quickly, but not quickly enough for Remi. He senses the dread in her.

'Nothing,' she says. 'Just, it's complicated. He's my ex, and I work for his dad's company in a role that can be judged . . . *indiscriminately* by those who make the decisions. So I have to tread carefully.'

'Seems like a tightrope to walk.'

She nods exaggeratedly. 'It is. But I've been doing it for a long time now.'

'Still. It must be very painful. Especially knowing what Seun is doing to you. To other women.'

There is a flash of realisation, fear, anger and betrayal that she can't cover up quickly this time. She glances around the room to see if any of the other diners who had been watching them all night noticed. Remi, for his part, just calmly observes her, waiting for her response.

'Is this why you brought me here? I thought . . .'

'I'm finishing what Kike started.'

'I don't know . . .'

'You do. I've listened to the recordings.'

She's stunned silent.

'Yours. And many others.'

She instinctively reaches for her empty wine glass and then drinks a gulp of the sparkling water in front of her. 'Remi,' she says with a low voice. 'If you listened to the recordings, you will know I was reluctant. Very reluctant. But Kike's natural approach – speak loudly and carry the biggest stick in the room over your head, ready to strike – convinced me. Because it is the only approach that could work to destroy them all. Not just Seun, but also his parents, and that entire network that has enabled him. But your natural approach is to speak very softly and cover the big stick with flowers, so people don't feel threatened by it. That will not work with this.'

Remi smiles, unsettling her. 'You're very perceptive . . . alongside being one of the most articulate people I've ever met.'

She doesn't acknowledge the compliments, which he expected.

'That is my approach,' he continues. 'Because I don't want anyone seeing the very big stick until it is too late. That way, I only need one precise strike. Because they never see it coming.'

CHAPTER 39

The sun hangs directly overhead, blinding, as the Lagos sky is cloudless. It's just after noon, and the marina is already abuzz with laughter, tinted sunglasses, and the shimmer of champagne flutes catching the light. Yetunde's birthday guests are gathered at the boarding point, mingling and posing for photos as they wait to step on to a sleek white boat that bobs beside the dock.

Rasaq pulls the Land Cruiser to a gentle stop beside the guests. Remi opens the passenger door, but before he steps out, Rasaq speaks.

'You want me to come with you?' he asks, trying to sound calm but with concern clear in his voice.

Remi turns to Rasaq. 'It'll just be Yetunde's security; the invite was clear,' he says, then softer, 'I'll be safe. Promise.'

There's a quiet pause before Remi reaches out for a fist bump. Rasaq holds his gaze for a beat, then bumps it. The gesture bridges more than just the moment.

'Don't do anything too wild while I'm across the water,' Remi teases.

Rasaq laughs, and it feels good. 'I'll have some more Mainland suya for you when you guys get back.'

'Nice!' Remi says, and salutes.

Remi steps out of the car, and his silky-relaxed kaftan flutters slightly in the breeze as he puts on his sunglasses and walks towards the other guests with quiet confidence. He ignores the eyes that follow him – curious, cautious, some even sympathetic. He spots Seun, dressed in all white with gold-framed sunglasses, standing with an unfamiliar companion. Remi looks away without acknowledging Seun and doesn't look back in Seun's direction again. Not even a glance.

Remi heads straight to Balo and greets him with a quick, close hug. Then shares nods and brief backslaps with a couple of other friends and acquaintances in the crowd, who look like they're eagerly waiting to ask questions but think better of it. Not here. Not yet, at least.

A pair of private security men in black polos and dark shades usher them towards the dock. At the boarding point, Yetunde's assistant stands with a tablet, ticking off names with practised ease.

When it's Seun's turn, the tall and unfamiliar mixed-race man beside him steps up as well.

Balo raises an eyebrow and grins. 'Ahn ahn. This isn't the plus-one you promised us, oh,' Balo says, and some others laugh.

Seun tries to laugh it off, shifting uncomfortably. 'Abeg, shut up. This Tokunbo. Toks for short. My cousin from the States.'

'What's up,' Toks greets in a distinctly Californian accent.

'I'm showing him the finer things of Lagos life,' Seun continues before anyone can even respond to Toks's greeting. 'And nothing is finer than a Yetunde island party.'

'Right,' Balo says, full of sarcasm. 'She no gree come, abi?'

Seun waves Balo off dismissively and strides on to the boat, closely followed by Toks.

The final guests, including Remi and Balo, are checked off and step on to the boat. Then the engines purr to life, and they pull away from the marina, slicing through the lagoon's glinting water.

The ride is smooth, and in minutes, the small beach island starts to grow in the distance. Soon, the guests spot the large stage beyond the coconut trees, the white canopies with gold decorations, and the white and gold fabric fluttering from cabanas that surround the beach and the pool. The shore itself glimmers with activity in preparation for the guests' arrival. Hostesses, photographers, videographers. The whole set-up hums with Yetunde's trademark mix of elite planning and deliberate excess. And it's all immaculate.

'Na wa, oh,' a guest says. 'She's just turning thirty-three. God help us when she turns forty. She will rent a whole country for her party.'

There's laughter.

Remi just watches. Calm, unreadable.

The party kicks off as soon as the guests are off the boat. Music, incredible food, endless drinks and merriment. Yetunde won't arrive for hours, but that doesn't surprise any of the guests, including Remi, who spends most of the day hanging with Balo and a few other close friends. As evening approaches, Seun and Toks drift into Remi's group, like Seun is being drawn by some magnetic force towards Remi. Still, Remi doesn't acknowledge him.

Eventually, someone in the group does what most, including Seun, have been waiting for. She brings up Malaki.

'Remz,' she calls, and he turns to her with a smile. 'You're really handling things admirably.' Remi nods graciously before she adds with venom, 'That Malaki is a bastard. He will rot in hell!'

The others in the group murmur or nod in agreement.

'He got what he deserved in life,' Remi says. 'Hopefully, he gets what he deserves in death, too.'

'He will, oh,' another guest adds. 'Hellfire does not quench!'

'Thanks, guys. Really appreciate your kind thoughts. But we're here for a party, and I don't want Yetunde to kill me because I dulled everyone's spirits.'

They laugh softly.

'No more talk of Malaki or death, okay?' Remi says, and turns to another person in the group. 'Apart from the dead python they wasted to make your slippers.'

Everyone laughs and returns to merriment.

It's nearing 9 p.m. when the sound cuts through the music – a resounding, rhythmic thump from above. At first, the guests think it's part of the playlist, some extended intro to the current Amapiano set. But then heads turn upward, and someone shouts, 'Helicopter!'

At the same time, the music switches, and a familiar beat breaks through the night – 'Fall' by Davido. Then, Davido appears on stage, lit by a rising column of golden light. He's wearing a white shirt unbuttoned just enough, gold chains resting on his chest, and a pair of statement sunglasses. He lifts the mic, and the crowd loses it, chanting along. Phones are up instantly. Guests rush towards the stage, some still holding cocktails, others ditching their heels in the sand to get closer. Joy and disbelief mingle in the humid air as Davido's performance takes over the stage and every single person on the island.

The helicopter, now closer, circles once and then begins its slow descent towards a landing pad just behind the stage.

Davido shifts to 'Unavailable', and the island explodes with even more joy and movement. No one, not even the more restrained guests like Remi, can help but vibe along.

Then, with perfect timing, as Davido launches into 'If', Yetunde emerges on the stage. She's radiant in a sweeping white and gold dress that gleams under the lights. Her braids are gathered into a high, regal crown, and her arms glitter with stacked gold bangles. Davido and Yetunde move together, not quite dancing, but in rhythm. She lifts a hand to the crowd, and they cheer louder. Davido sings to her, fluidly weaving her name into the lyrics. Cameras flash, and Yetunde soaks in the attention, owning every second.

As the final chorus fades, Davido walks with her to the back of the stage. They exchange a quick embrace, and then he disappears behind the stage as 'Funds' erupts through the speakers.

The helicopter lifts off moments later, its lights flashing as it rises back into the night sky and vanishes over the lagoon, taking Davido with it and leaving behind the chaos of a party now truly in full swing.

An hour passes before Remi settles with another group, but Seun is there as well. It's time.

Remi turns to Seun. 'We need to have a chat, don't we?' Remi says over the loud music, calm as you like.

There is a flash of fear on Seun's face before he buries it. 'Do we?' he says, trying to match Remi's calm but failing.

'Sorry?' Remi says, as if he couldn't hear.

'We do?' Seun raises his voice clearly over the music.

Remi nods. 'In private,' he says, and looks around. 'Not going to be shouting what we need to talk about.'

Seun nods, showing no fear.

Remi points to the beach villa just behind them. 'I'm sure it'll be quiet in there.'

Remi heads towards the villa without waiting for Seun to confirm or object, and Seun follows. But then Toks follows as well. Remi stops and turns to Toks, raising an amused eyebrow. Seun spins to Toks and whispers through clenched teeth into Toks's ears. Toks forces a smile and nods, then leaves Seun to catch up with Remi.

'Nosey cousin,' Remi remarks, and he and Seun walk together towards the villa.

'It's not that,' Seun says. 'He's just not comfortable with us, so he didn't want to be left alone.'

'That, I understand.'

The front door to the villa is open, and Remi tries to open the first door in the hallway, but it doesn't budge.

'Can you check that door?' Remi asks Seun, gesturing to the next door along the hallway.

Seun tries the door, and it opens. There are no lights switched on inside, but the space isn't dark because the lagoon outside catches the vibrant lights and colours of the party and reflects them through the floor-to-ceiling windows, casting ripples of movement across the floor and walls. It's an inviting sight.

Seun and Remi step into the room, and Remi closes the door

gently behind him, sealing out most of the loud music from the party, though faint notes still trickle in through a slightly open window across the room. The air inside is still, save for the light curtains swaying in the open breeze. The room smells faintly of salt and sandalwood, and a bottle of champagne sits untouched in a bucket of ice on a low table. Seun switches on the soft recessed lights and scans the room, intrigued by the set-up and the champagne.

'Whose room do you think this is?' Seun asks, a flicker of defensiveness in his tone. 'I didn't know anybody was staying over on the island. Thought the boat was coming back for everyone at 2 a.m.'

Remi doesn't respond. He crosses to the window, drawn by the view of the shimmering lagoon.

'This is beautiful,' Remi says, voice calm.

Seun lingers behind, watching him. Then he strolls over to the ice bucket and lifts the champagne bottle.

'Leave it,' Remi says, turning from the window. 'This isn't going to be a long chat.'

Seun defiantly pops the cork, and foam hisses over the lip of the bottle. He drinks straight from it, one eyebrow raised. 'Didn't think you were the jealous type,' he says, wiping his mouth. 'This about Eki, abi?'

Remi moves to the elegant writing desk opposite Seun and perches on the edge, arms resting on his thighs. His gaze is steady. 'It is.'

Seun chuckles. 'I've been there, bro. Over and over. She's sweet, oh. But there is no corner of her body I haven't tasted. I don tire.'

'Don't talk about her like that.'

Seun smirks, testing boundaries. 'Why? Are you going to beat me, too?'

Remi's reply is soft, almost indifferent. 'Yes.'

The word blooms in the air like a drop of blood in water. Seun stills slightly. Then he forces a laugh and paces a little. 'Relax, man. I'm just saying the truth. Is that not what you want to discuss?'

'Are you guys still an item?'

'No. We've been done as an *item* for a while. But we are still very *friendly* when the mood calls.' He drops on to the sofa. 'You know how it goes.'

Remi's expression doesn't change. 'That stops now. No more games. Give her some space. And don't use her job to threaten her again.'

Seun leans against the back of the sofa, cradling the champagne bottle. He grins, but the effort shows. 'Okay. I'll try, but . . . she's the one that keeps coming back. Girl like that, with those *tastes*? Not many options.'

Remi watches him for a long beat, then tilts his head. 'You don't know me much, do you?'

Seun's grin falters. 'What do you mean?'

'I mean, if you knew me well, you'd know I wouldn't have asked for this chat empty-handed.'

Something tightens in Seun's jaw. He puts the bottle down. 'What are you talking about?'

'I'm not trying to play you, Seun. I just want your word. That's it. Walk away from Eki and leave her job out of your mess.'

Seun shifts, agitated. 'What do you have, Remi?'

Remi offers a faint shrug. 'You know, Seun.'

Seun's face darkens. 'Those are lies, bro. Did Eki say anything as well?'

Remi straightens. 'As well? What does that mean?'

'No. No. I mean . . . some of these girls talking nonsense are Eki's friends. So she might've said something to you, that's all.'

Remi gives a slight shrug. 'It's not her. It's Kike. She was going to do a *Spotlight Nigeria* episode on your allegations. All of them.'

Seun laughs nervously. 'She told you that?'

'No. But I didn't need to hear it from her. I've seen the evidence.'

'Evidence? What evidence? That's all hearsay. Rumours. Jealous girls chasing clout.'

'Esther was a rumour? C'mon, I was in the same school. I remember all that stuff.'

Seun hesitates. Then, 'That was a lie, man.'

'Sure. And the next thirty? All lying too, abi?'

Seun takes a gulp of the champagne.

'Honestly, I don't care,' Remi continues. 'But now I'm starting to get worried that I can't just take your word.'

'Remi, these are all rumours and clout-chasers.'

Remi leans forward slightly. His voice is low but unwavering. 'Kike had recordings. Voices. Names. Timelines. This is what I mean by not being empty-handed.'

Seun is frozen now, eyes darting. But his defiance quickly resurfaces. 'These girls are lying. They are just following the same story. Sure! I probably slept with them all. But it was consensual. If you check these girls, you'll see that all of them were just trying to be on DBN. I might have used that . . . promised them a gig or audition. But it didn't work.'

'You're annoying me, Seun. And I just want to get back out there.'

'How am I annoying you?'

'Seun, there are videos. Some of these girls recorded you having sex with them when they were unconscious. At the George Hotel, Radisson Blu, Sheraton in Abuja.'

Seun is blindsided by the revelation and sinks on to the couch, his hands pressing against his thighs. Suddenly, he sits up, re-energised. 'Did you watch the videos?'

'I'm not watching that. Kike watched them and took notes.'

'It was a fetish.'

Remi instinctively raises an eyebrow. 'A fetish?'

Seun nods quickly. 'The girls wanted it. We recorded it together. It was consensual—'

'Seun!' Remi interrupts. 'You're saying they asked to be drugged? To be unconscious? You realise how that sounds?'

Seun flinches but keeps pushing. 'It was fantasy. That's why they recorded it. They even sent me the videos. I have them.' He lifts his phone and scrolls, his thumb trembling. 'We'd watch them together afterwards. It was part of the . . . connection. It got us excited.'

'That's not a connection, Seun. That's disgusting.'

'It was more their thing. They wanted it.'

Remi nods slowly. 'You have it on your phone, Seun. This is your thing.' He rises from the desk. 'I'm done.'

Seun lifts his phone again. 'Eki was into it, too. Want to see?'

Remi hesitates. He can't tell if this is some veiled form of blackmail or if Seun is trying to draw him into the perversion. He spots a grin breaking on Seun's face and turns away to walk towards the door.

'Wait,' Seun calls. 'You still want me to leave Eki alone?'

Remi stops, turns around, and slowly walks back to Seun. His voice is quieter now, more dangerous. 'Do you want to show me your fetish video of trying to rape my sister . . . before you killed her?'

Seun's breath catches in his throat. He slips off the sofa and scurries backwards.

'I've only heard the audio. But I'm sure you filmed that, too.'

Panic floods Seun's face, and he frantically searches for an exit. Remi is blocking his path to the door, so he glances over his shoulder at the open window.

'Sure, you should probably jump out the window. You've seen me in action, though. I'll catch you before you reach the party and drown you in the lagoon. You'll save me from having to carry your dead body through that same window to toss in the lagoon.'

'I didn't . . .'

'I heard the recording, Seun. The whole thing. You think wiping her iCloud means it's gone forever?'

Remi spots the recognition on Seun's frightened face and takes a step closer, giving Seun no more room to retreat.

'It was my mum. She's the one that killed Kike.'

Remi stills.

Seun rambles. 'Yes, I drugged her and, you know . . . I tried to have sex with her. I didn't know she was recording. But she was, and she found out, and she came to my room and attacked me. She was going to kill me, but my mum hit her on the head, and she fell. She died.'

Remi takes a step back, the weight of the confession sinking in. His fists clench, but he doesn't move.

Seun looks up, pleading now. 'Remi, please. I didn't mean . . .'

Remi doesn't hear the rest. The bedroom door bursts open, footsteps rush towards him from behind, and before he can turn around, there is a deafening gunshot.

CHAPTER 40

A few hours before

Rasaq

Rasaq watches as Remi strides towards the other party guests gathered at the marina, waiting to board the boat. Of all the days Rasaq has spent as Remi's personal guard, this is the one that unsettles him most. Not because of the guests – none of them, especially not Seun, would trouble Remi in a fight – but because he's heard enough of Remi's plans to know that Remi is determined to put himself in the eye of the storm.

Rasaq looks for Seun in the crowd and easily spots him, dressed flamboyantly as usual with a white silk scarf wrapped around his neck. Then Rasaq notices Tokunbo standing still beside Seun, and the hairs at the back of his neck rise. Tokunbo is dressed well enough to pass as a guest, but he still stands out distinctly from the others – not just because of his physique and posture, but because he's too still, too composed. He looks like a weapon, and that weapon, although wearing sunglasses to block his eyes, is tracking Remi, waiting for the signal to strike.

Rasaq considers stepping out to force himself on to the boat, but that will create a commotion that'll scupper Remi's plans. He pulls out his phone and calls Yinka.

Yinka answers just after one ring.

'Everything okay, Rasaq?' Yinka asks.

'I think we have a problem.'

Minutes later, Rasaq drives towards Chief Adeleke's lavish mansion in Ikoyi, where Rose's party had taken place. Once he had updated Yinka on the situation, Yinka had directed him to go straight there without any further explanation. Rasaq is somewhat tense as he approaches the mansion because he doesn't know what to expect. But as soon as he sees the heavily armed soldiers from his old army division guarding the large front gate, he settles, recognising each of them from the night of the party. He pulls up to the gate and lowers the window, and they all recognise him as well.

'Captain,' they call with fondness, and salute.

He returns the salute. 'Good to see you men again.'

'Likewise, sir,' the most senior soldier at the gate responds for them all. 'They are expecting you inside. Enter, park to the right and go straight to the front door. Mr Yinka is waiting there.'

Rasaq nods. The gate opens, and he guides the car into the grandiose compound.

Rasaq walks past a tall waterfall fountain towards the impressive front door, and a young soldier standing in front of it salutes before pulling the door open. Rasaq returns the salute and steps in.

Yinka is just beyond the door, waiting. They meet with a warm handshake.

'Follow me,' Yinka says.

Moments later, Yinka leads Rasaq into the main living room, moving with the ease of someone who knows the layout without needing to look. The space they step into is grand but hollow, like a showroom. High ceilings stretch above their heads, and wide-pane glass runs the length of the far wall, looking out on to a lush, sculpted garden that rolls gently into the lagoon beyond. Two armed guards pace the lawn in lazy formation, their rifles slung loose but visible. Inside, everything gleams – the tiled floors, the crystal fixtures, the lacquered surfaces of tables that look untouched. This isn't a home, he notes. It's a theatre set dressed for Lagos's highest society.

He's still taking it in when a side door opens, and Kunle – the man the headlines insist is in custody – steps in, mid conversation with Chief Adeleke. Their voices don't carry, but their body language does. It's warm, animated, and familiar. Rasaq's brow tightens. Last he heard, those two hadn't spoken in over a year. But Yinka stands with arms crossed, unbothered. That tells Rasaq everything. Still, he notes how Yinka's posture is sharp in a way it never is at the Bankole residence. Here, he's alert, contained. Not tense, but precise – because they all understand that the Chief is iron-fisted with his staff, proudly taking the polar opposite approach from Kunle. Not even a touch of friendliness. With the Chief, you do your job, and you do it well. You speak when you are spoken to. Or else.

Yinka and Rasaq lower themselves to prostrate as Kunle and the

Chief approach, and they remain in that position until Kunle and the Chief sit on one of the long leather sofas.

'Stand up!' the Chief orders.

Yinka and Rasaq stand, and Kunle greets both with a slight nod. The Chief does not greet.

'You're the Rasaq that has been keeping our Remi safe, abi?' the Chief says.

'Yes, sir,' Rasaq confirms.

'Good job,' the Chief says. 'But you should've made sure he got on his flight yesterday.'

'It's okay,' Kunle interjects softly. 'You know Remi. He was never leaving Lagos without his answers.'

The Chief nods.

'So, tell me about this problem,' Kunle says. 'Assume Yinka has not told me anything.'

Rasaq opens his mouth to speak, but Shina walks in through the same door as Kunle and the Chief. Kunle looks over his shoulder to Shina as if waiting for a signal, and Shina nods. Kunle nods back and turns back to Rasaq.

'Afternoon, Rasaq,' Shina says, and positions himself by the long sofa.

'Afternoon, Shina,' Rasaq responds.

Shina accepts the greeting with a nod and gestures for Rasaq to proceed.

Rasaq starts with Remi's ragged scream at Aishat's house, recounts the conversations he'd overhead Remi having over the phone with several women, some he'd known before, some he was just introduced to, convincing them to collaborate with him on an Instagram Live broadcast. Then, his date with Eki last night, followed by more calls this morning, and then an early morning trip to the island to set up for the broadcast.

'Why?' the Chief asks, tired of struggling to put the pieces together.

'Seun Daniels,' Kunle drops in, calm.

Rasaq nods.

'That one? Why?'

'He's involved. Derin, too,' Kunle says.

'In what?'

'Everything.'

The Chief leans forward instinctively. 'Kunzi,' he says, using Kunle's nickname. 'What are you talking about?'

'It fits with what I've been hearing from reliable sources and with what Shina has just confirmed,' Kunle says. 'You see my face on the news almost every hour, especially on DBN.'

'Eh, now. I mentioned it last night. Those ones are not resting. The other channels have listened. They are not even mentioning your name anymore. But that is Chisom and the others pulling the strings, no?'

'No. It's Derin.'

'Why?'

'Seun. He killed Kike.'

'Ehn!' the Chief exclaims. 'What about Malaki?'

'I'm not sure,' Kunle says, and turns to Shina. 'But it fits with what Shina just found.' He gestures for Shina to speak.

'Suru Boi . . . Malaki's protege,' Shina says. 'He has been going around Surulere, calling himself King Suru. Buying the loyalty of

Malaki's former followers with promises of appearances on his upcoming reality TV show and movie with DBN Plus. The ones who don't want to appear on camera are being promised vast sums of money. Even more than the amounts being promised by Malaki's nephews, who have taken over his marijuana distribution. Money that Suru Boi claims will be paid by DBN Plus.'

The others quietly take in the implications of Shina's words before the Chief speaks.

'The Danielses set Malaki up,' he says, voicing everyone's thoughts.

'Yes,' Kunle says. 'While making sure I was distracted.'

'Chisom arranged your arrest, so are they working together?'

'Not like that. Chisom has his motives, and we both know what those are. But Derin is using him for cover. Making this media storm look politically motivated, when it is personal.' Kunle takes a deep breath to bury the fury that is threatening to surface. 'Yinka is the one that first mentioned there might be a connection. Because those DBN drones were at Malaki's house too fast. Almost like they were waiting for us.'

Yinka nods.

Kunle turns to Yinka. 'You will go now to have a chat with Suru Boi.'

'Let me go, sir,' Shina says. 'I'm retiring soon, and I'd like to do this for Kike. Yinka can stay here with you. Start getting used to being in my shoes.'

Kunle nods.

'Thank you, sir.'

'Don't kill him.'

'Why?' the Chief demands.

'I want to hear him confirm it.'

'Then you kill him.'

'No,' Kunle says, and turns to Rasaq. 'It's not what Remi wants, right?'

Rasaq nods. 'Yes, sir.'

The Chief suddenly slaps the sofa. It's loud, like a gunshot. 'What are we going to do with the Danielses?'

'First, we are going to let Remi prove it.'

Kunle's calm confidence in Remi touches all of them.

'Then, we finish it.'

'I think it is going to be dangerous on the island, sir,' Rasaq says.

'You'll be there to watch over him.'

'No more boats are going to the island today, sir.'

'Leave that to me,' the Chief says.

Hours later, the helicopter skims low over the water, its rhythmic thump pressing against Rasaq's chest as he looks out across the island below. From this height, the party looks like something from a music video – lights shimmering against the ocean, bodies dancing around the stage, gold and white flashing everywhere. He keeps his expression neutral, but his grip on the harness strap is firm.

There are seven of them on board. The pilot, Rasaq, four of Yetunde's personal security officers, and Yetunde, who's excitedly peering out the window with pride and anticipation at her party below, where Davido performs to a roaring crowd.

The chopper begins its slow descent behind the stage. The vibrations grow more intense, and Rasaq braces slightly, alert but calm.

Once they land, it's smooth. He and the two other security officers are first out, stepping on to the helipad in a tight formation. The sound is deafening, but they are unfazed. Rasaq and another officer help Yetunde out of the helicopter. She looks utterly unbothered by the wind whipping at her dress. Regal as ever.

Rasaq remains by the helipad as the two security officers who had stepped out shadow Yetunde backstage. He scans the perimeter, and nothing feels off. Still, he stays sharp.

'Unavailable' comes on, and the crowd erupts again. From here, Rasaq can't see the crowd, but he can feel them.

By the time 'If' starts, Rasaq hears Yetunde's name being woven into the lyrics and knows she's stepped on to the stage. She'd been so particular about that, about timing her arrival with Davido's performance, and he's pleased to see it worked out as planned. He would've loved to see it live, but he knows this moment will be all over social media by morning.

Davido wraps his set, and within seconds, he's backstage, moving straight towards the helicopter with his guards. Rasaq doesn't speak; he just clears the path and opens the door. Davido hops in, fist-bumps the pilot, and Rasaq steps away from the helicopter as the rotors spin harder. Quickly, it lifts again, climbing fast into the night, taking Davido with it.

Rasaq watches it vanish above the lagoon, then walks towards the party.

Rasaq quickly spots Remi and then Seun and Tokunbo close by. He's close enough to see their faces, but to Seun and Remi, he's just another of the patrolling security officers in identical clothes. Not to Tokunbo, who notices him watching. They lock eyes, and Rasaq nods deferentially, like a security officer who is embarrassed to be caught idling instead of patrolling. Tokunbo looks away from him with disdain. In his mind, he's the elite when it comes to personal security; these security guards are minnows.

Rasaq walks over to a more distant position to watch. Then it happens – Remi engages Seun, and Seun seems keen to follow. Tokunbo attempts to join, and Rasaq is ready to act, but Seun makes him stay back.

Rasaq quickly considers who to keep an eye on – Tokunbo, or Remi and Seun. He stays with the danger. He keeps an eye on Tokunbo, who remains still, not interacting with anyone for minutes. Then, guests start to react to their phones. Nudging others to watch. Then it spreads like wildfire; everyone is on their phones, watching, listening over the loud music that continues to play. Initially, they watch with intrigue, then with a mix of horror and disgust. Remi steps closer to a guest to peek at their phone, and he sees Seun, unmistakable and in the centre of the screen, while Remi is just in the corner of the screen. It is Instagram Live, and Rasaq strains to see the number of people watching – 300,000.

Rasaq looks away from the screen and back towards Tokunbo, but he's gone. Rasaq panics, but he overrides that with action and runs. He knows exactly where Seun and Remi are.

Rasaq slides along the wall outside the villa towards the window of the room he knows Remi and Seun to be in. The music had stopped while he ran as the guests wanted to hear the broadcast clearly, so Rasaq moves as quietly as possible.

He peeks through the window and sees Remi, then Seun cowering and whimpering. Then suddenly, the room's door bursts open, and Tokunbo darts towards Remi, holding a large syringe over his head, ready to plunge into the back of Remi's neck. In a flash, Rasaq raises his rifle and shoots through the window.

Remi

The bullet whizzes past Remi's head before it pierces through Toks's eye and explodes out the back of his head. Toks crumbles to the floor, and Remi freezes, dazed.

Seun screams, then brushes past Remi and stomps on Toks's dead body as he scrambles out of the room and back towards the party.

'Remi,' Rasaq calls, and climbs through the window. 'Are you okay?'

Remi snaps out of his daze as Rasaq attempts to scan him for any injuries. But he grabs Rasaq and embraces him tightly. Rasaq lets go of his weapon and returns the embrace.

'He killed Kike,' Remi says. 'He confessed. He and his mother.'

'Everyone heard,' Rasaq says. 'Your plan. It worked. Everyone watched it.'

They release their embrace. 'Thanks for coming back for me.'

'Of course. You're my friend.'

Remi pats Rasaq on the shoulder. 'Yes. You're my friend . . . who has saved my life too many times.'

They laugh softly.

Rasaq glances at Toks's dead body and attempts to walk to it, but Remi stops him and gestures to the writing desk where the iPhone broadcasting on Instagram is surreptitiously hidden. Rasaq is just out of view of the camera. Rasaq nods, understanding.

Remi walks to the writing desk and picks up an iPhone from the hollow base of an exquisite desk lamp. He looks into the camera. 'Thank you all,' he says, and ends the video.

Remi and Rasaq walk out of the villa and immediately see Seun being held down by Balo and a couple of other guests as they pummel him with hands, feet and even python-skin slippers. Remi wants to say something. Ask them not to kill him. But then that's not what they do, right?

'Remi!' Yetunde calls.

Remi stops and turns to her, bracing for her deserved anger at destroying her party. But she rushes to him and hugs him tightly, affectionately. He hesitates for a beat, surprised, but then he returns her embrace, and she sobs.

But then she stops and looks up at him. 'You better be around for my birthday next year, because I don't know how I'm going to top this one.'

CHAPTER 41

Early morning, a week later

Remi and Kunle walk side by side across the polished floor of the quiet climate-controlled private terminal at Murtala Muhammed International Airport, their steps unhurried. Ahead, through the large windows, a private jet waits, engines quiet for now but stairs lowered, ready for Remi.

They don't speak, but the silence between them is more than comfortable. There is relief from an anxiety they were both trying very hard to ignore, and joy.

Shina, Yinka, and Rasaq follow a few paces behind, their eyes scanning out of habit, not concern. The danger has passed.

Derin, Gloria and Suru Boi are imprisoned. Seun is detained in a state hospital, recovering from the savage wounds inflicted on him by the guests at the party. Chisom and his other heavyweight allies in the president's party have been politically destroyed, tarnished by the exposure of their association with Derin and other disreputable acts in their quest for ultimate power. Leaving the Chief as the clear choice to replace the president when that time comes.

But all is not well. Zainab hasn't returned home. She hasn't called. Not after the ambush, not after the truth about Kike's death was revealed. Her absence lingers.

Remi and Kunle step out into the early morning light, and Remi pauses to admire the rising sun in the cloudless sky. This time, there'll be more than just the sunrise to look back on with feeling. They continue ahead towards the jet.

They approach the steps leading up to the aircraft, and Kunle finally breaks the silence. 'I love you, son,' he says with more warmth than Remi knew his father could exude.

Remi turns to Kunle. 'I love you too, Dad. Very much.'

Kunle nods, and they embrace. It's affectionate but restrained. Then suddenly, Kunle sobs. Then the dam breaks, and he weeps, tightening his embrace. Remi tightens his embrace and tries to hold back his tears, but he can't. They weep in each other's arms like nothing else matters. Just sharing that moment.

Soon, they release each other. 'I'll be back soon for Shina's retirement party,' Remi whispers, as it's supposed to be a surprise for Shina.

Kunle smiles, and they look over their shoulders at Shina, Yinka, and Rasaq, who are waiting a few steps away and watching. And it's clear Shina was also crying.

'One sec,' Remi says to his dad, and walks back to the others.

Remi embraces Shina. 'Thanks for everything,' he says.

Shina nods. 'Thank you for bringing that out of Kunle. It's been overdue.'

Remi nods, then shifts to hug Yinka. 'Take care of him, yeah?' he says, gesturing at Shina.

'Of course, Remi,' Yinka says. 'I've already bought his walking stick.'

They laugh.

Remi shifts to Rasaq, and they embrace each other like longtime friends. 'I'll check on you when I come back,' he says. 'Stay safe, yeah?'

'Always!' Rasaq responds. 'You be safe too, in London.'

'I can't promise anything,' Remi jokes. 'And abeg, keep updating your playlists.'

'For sure.'

They bump fists, and Remi walks back to Kunle.

'You'll tell Mum I love her very much, yeah.'

'She knows. But I will.'

Remi nods, climbs the steps, and disappears into the jet.

GLOSSARY

Abeg – Pidgin for 'please' or 'I beg you'.

Abi – Yoruba word meaning 'right?' or 'isn't it?'.

Agbada – Flowing, wide-sleeved robe worn by men on formal occasions.

Ahn ahn – Exclamation of surprise or mild disbelief.

Akara – Fried bean cakes, often eaten at breakfast.

Amala – Yam flour dough ('swallow') served with soups like ewedu.

Area boys – Street gangs or informal enforcers, often controlling territory in Lagos.

Ashewo – Yoruba word meaning sex worker or prostitute.

Baba – Term of respect for an older man, mentor, or leader.

Danfo – Yellow Lagos minibus used for public transport.

Dey – Pidgin for 'are/is/being' or 'to be' (e.g. *Na una dey run things* – 'You're the ones running things').

EFCC – Economic and Financial Crimes Commission, Nigeria's anti-corruption agency.

Ẹ̀fọ́ riro – Rich spinach stew cooked with peppers and spices.

Ewedu – Leafy soup made from jute leaves, often paired with amala.

Kaftan – Long tunic worn by men, common in West Africa.

Madam – Boss lady or female superior; term of respect.

Moi moi – Steamed bean pudding, often served as a side dish.

Na – Pidgin for 'is/it is' (e.g. *Na you start am* – 'You're the one who started it').

NEPA – Former national electricity company; still used to refer to power supply ('NEPA has taken light').

Oga – Boss or master; can also mean 'sir' in informal use.

Ọmọ – Yoruba for 'child' or 'offspring'; in slang, can mean 'person' or 'guy' depending on context.

Oya – Prompt to act quickly ('come on', 'let's go').

Oyinbo – Literally, a white person or foreigner. Can also refer to Westernised traits such as an English or American accent, style of dress, or mannerisms.

SS1 – First year of senior secondary school (equivalent to Year 10/ Grade 10).

Suya – Spicy grilled meat on skewers, sold at roadside stands.

Trad – Short for traditional clothing.

Wahala – Trouble or problem.

ACKNOWLEDGEMENTS

I'm deeply grateful to Lagos, the city that shaped my upbringing and continues to shape my imagination, my voice . . . everything I am today.

My thanks to Stef and the Quercus team for believing in this idea from the very beginning and guiding it with such care. To Antony, for his patience and faith as I balanced being an author with life as a lawyer and, most importantly, a father and husband. And to my wife, whose support has been the steady force behind every page I write. Nothing I do is possible without her.

RAISING READERS
Books Build Bright Futures

Dear Reader,

We'd love your attention for one more page to tell you about the crisis in children's reading, and what we can all do.

Studies have shown that reading for fun is the **single biggest predictor of a child's future life chances** – more than family circumstance, parents' educational background or income. It improves academic results, mental health, wealth, communication skills, ambition and happiness.[1]

The number of children reading for fun is in rapid decline. Young people have a lot of competition for their time. In 2024, 1 in 10 children and young people in the UK aged 5 to 18 did not own a single book at home.[2]

Hachette works extensively with schools, libraries and literacy charities, but here are some ways we can all raise more readers:

- Reading to children for just 10 minutes a day makes a difference
- Don't give up if children aren't regular readers – there will be books for them!
- Visit bookshops and libraries to get recommendations
- Encourage them to listen to audiobooks
- Support school libraries
- Give books as gifts

There's a lot more information about how to encourage children to read on our website: **www.RaisingReaders.co.uk**

Thank you for reading.

hachette UK

[1] OECD, '21st-Century Readers: Developing Literacy Skills in a Digital World', 2021, https://www.oecd.org/en/publications/21st-century-readers_a83d84cb-en.html

[2] National Literacy Trust, 'Book Ownership in 2024', November 2024, https://literacytrust.org.uk/research-services/research-reports/book-ownership-in-2024